Green Mountain Man

★————————————————————————

The Odyssey of
Ethan Allen

★————————————————————————

Green Mountain Man

★————————————————————

The Odyssey of
Ethan Allen

★————————————————————

Earl Faine

A TOM DOHERTY ASSOCIATES BOOK
NEW YORK

GREEN MOUNTAIN MAN: THE ODYSSEY
OF ETHAN ALLEN

A Forge Book
Published by Tom Doherty Associates, Inc.
175 Fifth Avenue
New York, NY 10010

Forge® is a registered trademark of Tom
Doherty Associates, Inc.

Library of Congress Cataloging-in-Publication
Data

Faine, Earl.
    Green mountain man : the odyssey of
  Ethan Allen / Earl Faine.—1st ed.
      p.   cm.
    ISBN 0-312-86078-1
    1. Allen, Ethan, 1738–1789—Fiction.
  2. Vermont—History—Revolution,
  1775–1783—Fiction.   3. Revolutionaries—
  Vermont—Fiction.   4. Soldiers—Vermont—
  Fiction.   I. Title.
  PS3556.A349G7   1997
  813'.54—dc21   96-54235
                                      CIP

First Edition: July 1997

Printed in the United States of America

0 9 8 7 6 5 4 3 2 1

This book is fondly dedicated to
James Ross Allen,
gentleman, fellow writer, friend,
lineal descendant of Ethan Allen

CONTENTS

Cast of Characters

At Fort Ticonderoga

Crocker—Benedict Arnold's valet
Colonel Benedict Arnold
Zadock Remington—tavern keeper
Colonel Ethan Allen
Lieutenant Colonel Seth Warner—Allen's cousin
Captain Remember Baker—Allen's and Warner's cousin
Noah Phelps
Jacob Wall   } —Green Mountain Boys
Elisha Cummings
Captain William Delaplace—British commandant
Lieutenant Jocelyn Feltham—Delaplace's second in
    command
Major General Philip Schuyler
Brigadier General Richard Montgomery
Major John Brown

In Bennington

Mary Brownson Allen—Ethan Allen's wife
Dr. Jonas Fay—Catamount Tavern's proprietor
Thomas Chittenden—president of the Republic of Vermont

In Philadelphia

John Hancock—president of the 2nd Continental Congress
Joseph Galloway—delegate from Pennsylvania

Robert Morris—delegate from Pennsylvania
Richard Henry Lee—delegate from Virginia

On the Richelieu River

Lieutenant Ira Allen—Ethan Allen's youngest brother
Crage Sentowanne—White Elk—Caughnawaga (Iroquois) scout
James Livingston—American patriot living in Canada
Lieutenant Colonel Rudolph Ritzema
Lieutenant Samuel Lockwood
Louis Kelly—militiaman
Lieutenant John André—British officer attached to Fort St. John's

In Montreal

Lieutenant Leland Covington—British field officer
Corporal Gravisand
General Richard Prescott—British commandant of the Montreal Garrison
Captain William McCloud
Sir Guy Carleton—British general and governor of Canada

Aboard the Gaspé

Captain Nicholas Royal
Dr. Ephraim Dace

Aboard the Adamant

Captain Brooks Watson—former lord-mayor of London
Pierre Cariou—French-Canadian volunteer in the American attempt to invade Canada

At Pendennis Castle

Private Aaron Heaslip
Captain William Hales

Colonel Boatwright—commandant of the garrison
Tom Coffin—Connecticut volunteer in the Continental
  Army
Wilkie O'Doul—Green Mountain Boy
General Fox—British Royal Secret Service director

In London

Lord Frederick North—prime minister
The Duke of York—member of the House of Lords
Edmund Burke—member of the House of Commons
King George III
Queen Charlotte Sophia

Aboard the Solebay

Captain Ezekial Symonds
Lieutenant Robert Bascomb
Lieutenant Douglass
Seamus Gilligan—able seaman

At Funchal in the Madeira Islands

Leo Shaugnessy—wine merchant

Aboard the Mercury

Captain James Montague
Dr. Wilson Ffolkes
John Crawley—secretary to Governor Arbuthnot

In Halifax

Governor Arbuthnot
James Lovell—Massachusetts congressman

Aboard the Lark

Captain Hosea Smith

In New York

Captain Given—acting warden of the provost jail
Matthew—jail guard
Chapman—attorney
Lieutenant Walter Dunbar
Captain Curtis Toombs
Major Conrad Worthy } parolees
Corporal Mason Weeks
Captain John Montresor—aide to General Howe
General Sir William Howe—British commander in chief in
  North America

On Long Island

Jan Van Wolk—Dutch farmer and Ethan Allen's landlord in
  New Lots

Aboard the Eloise

Captain Bellows
Elias Boudinot—representative of the American commissary
  of prisoners
Lieutenant Colonel Archibald Campbell—British prisoner

At Valley Forge

General George Washington
General Nathanael Greene
General Anthony Wayne
General Horatio Gates

Near Albany

General John Stark
Lieutenant Cox

The time is now near at hand which must probably determine whether Americans are to be freemen or slaves; whether they are to have any property they can call their own; whether their houses and farms are to be pillaged and destroyed, and themselves consigned to a state of wretchedness from which no human efforts will deliver them. The fate of unborn millions will now depend, under God, on the courage and conduct of this army. Our cruel and unrelenting enemy leaves us only the choice of brave resistance, or the most abject submission. We have, therefore, to resolve to conquer or die.

GEORGE WASHINGTON

Address to the Continental Army before the battle of Long Island, August 27, 1776

I

The King's Fortress

MAY 1775

1

★ **The** rain sheeted down on hats, hunched shoulders, and horses as the two riders sloughed through the quagmire that three days before had been the dusty Castleton road. The second man reined up sharply, pulling to the side, his horse narrowly avoiding the rain ditch channeling a torrent down the slight grade. The man in the lead halted his horse and swung about.

"What's the matter now, Crocker?"

"It's my saddle, sir, I think the strap's loose."

"It's called a girth, man. And call me by my rank."

"Yes, sir, Colonel Arnold."

The colonel got down. "Stay where you are." He tightened the girth by two holes and remounted his own horse, wiping his eyes and squinting through the thrashing curtain of water. "Not so much as a candle in a window. But it can't be too far."

"You said that twenty miles back."

"I know what I said. And it's 'Colonel,' 'Colonel!' "

He got out the map, wiped it, squinted, and found their approximate location relevant to Putnam Station, which they'd passed earlier. "A few miles more, that's all," he muttered. Refolding the map, he restored it to his inside pocket, maintaining his scowl.

"It's new," murmured Crocker, "it takes getting used to."

"What does?"

" 'Colonel.' "

Recently commissioned by the Massachusetts Committee of Safety, Benedict Arnold, accompanied by his valet, had left Boston for the lakes region of eastern New York State, specifically Lake Champlain, to join a company of volunteers. His mission was one dear to the colonel's heart and ambition, an expedition against Fort Ticonderoga and Crown Point, strategic strongholds lying midway on a line of fortified lakes and rivers that ran from New York City to Quebec. Built by the French to control traffic on Lake Champlain, the British had captured Fort Ticonderoga in 1759, sixteen years before. The star-shaped, reputedly impregnable installation was designed to accommodate a force of hundreds. Now, despite the loss of thousands of lives in wresting it from the French, and the Crown's expenditure of close to two million pounds, fewer than sixty redcoats manned the post. The prospect of delivering the fort into Patriot hands cheered Arnold. A cleverly planned surprise attack by night could take it easily. He could almost taste the glory awaiting his success. At the moment the first shot was fired he would step onstage into history.

They urged their horses on. Not a single light pricked the night. Arnold suppressed a shiver; the persisting chill had gotten into blood and bone, dampening his soul. It was early May, and the spring rains should have been over by now, but this was no late spring shower. It was all the fountains of the deep broken up, and the windows of heaven opened. He was Noah, arkless and struggling through the gloom, trailed by a servant with little heart for adventure, even less spleen, and no appreciation for the impending glory. It was as irritating as it was discouraging to be surrounded by fair-weather Patriots, so greatly outnumbering the few like himself who committed heart, soul, sword, and spirit to the fight for independence.

How many up and down the colonies had even taken sides yet? How many continued suffering the delusion that war was avoidable? What did it take to sway them?

They would come around. They would have to, or be left dangling between the two sides with allegiance to neither and no place to hide in the inevitable clash. And it was coming, as unstoppable as a juggernaut.

"Let's pick it up a bit, Crocker. We've got to be getting close."

"My horse is tuckered out. My arse too."

"Just do it!" Arnold heeled his mount. It failed to respond, continuing to proceed at a lope. "Move, you mangy beast!" Again he heeled it with the same result.

"There!" burst Crocker.

Arnold turned toward him. His valet's thin, dishearteningly homely face glowed as he pointed, shaking his finger. Ahead were windows, barely lighted; pale, saffron squares dimly seen.

"Zadock Remington's Tavern," announced Arnold. "It has to be."

Up to the hitching rail they plodded. The mud was six inches deep where they dismounted. Arnold had to lift each leg awkwardly to make his way to the door.

"Get the horses into the barn, wipe them down, and give them food and water. I'll be inside."

"Yes, Mister . . . Colonel."

Arnold shook his head and rolled his eyes at the storm as Crocker led both horses away. The door was locked. As he thumped it loudly he surveyed the area. A gloomier, more abandoned-looking landscape he'd never seen.

"Coming, coming . . ."

A short, impressively bellied man, his hairless head flushed pink by the firelight, his leather apron stained and grease-smeared, opened the door. Inside, Arnold could see the low, fog-quilted rafters and crude furniture scattered about the dirt floor. A plank set on two rum barrels served as a bar. Rancid liquor mingled its stench with the stink of rat droppings. The man turned aside to slip his wooden false teeth into his mouth before beaming a greeting.

"Come in, come in. Terrible night, awful!"

"My valet's tending to the horses. He'll be here with our things."

Arnold stood dripping, shaking off his hat. He set it on a table and divested himself of gloves and cloak, revealed his gold-braided scarlet uniform. The innkeeper took his cloak from him.

"You come up all the way from Albany in this?"

"From Boston."

"By Harry! It's been raining for three days."

"Has it really? You must be Zadock Remington. Colonel Benedict Arnold. I'm looking for an Ethan Allen. He's supposed to meet me here. I see I've gotten here ahead of him."

A thoroughly bedraggled Crocker came in yawning, setting down his bag and Arnold's portmanteau.

"Done with the horses?"

"Hold on . . . " said Remington, waving a hand to get Arnold's full attention.

"All taken care of, Colonel," said Crocker.

"Well, do you intend to root there? Move, get out of those damp things."

"Colonel," persisted Remington, "Colonel Allen's already come and gone."

Arnold, who had moved to stand with his back to the fire, reacted as if struck. "What?"

"He said Colonel Allen's already—" began Crocker.

"I heard what he said! Damnation! Gone on up to the fort, has he?"

"Yes. Him and his men, more'n two hundred of 'em. Rain don't stop them none. They come slogging in here early this afternoon, et and drank me down to crumbs and dregs, and left about two hours ago. What time you got, sir?"

Crocker took his place alongside Arnold at the fire, shoving his backside out ridiculously to warm it. He looked about to collapse.

"Bother the time," snapped Arnold. "Crocker, get your things back on. Go out and saddle our horses. We're leaving."

"But—"

"You heard what he said. We've got to catch up with them!"

Arnold sighed. Twenty miles ahead, where Lake George ended and Lake Champlain began, stood Fort Ticonderoga, site of his coming glory. Who was more entitled to capture it? Who put the project before the Committee of Safety and talked them into it? There it stood, bristling with cannon, undermanned, unprepared, ripe for plucking, waiting for him to conquer it. Now, suddenly, the bumpkin assigned only to assemble his men and wait for him to get there and take command was preparing to beat him to it. Arnold could smell it. He was never wrong about such things.

"No!" he barked. Both men flinched. "He can't do this to me!"

"Sir," said Remington, "you dasn't go back out in this . . . "

"*He* didn't hesitate to! Crocker . . . "

Crocker had yet to stir from the fire. Now a change came over him, the docile and submissive menial giving way to a stern-looking individual with improved posture and square shoulders, his outsize jaw set determinedly. "I'm not going anywhere, Colonel."

"Crocker . . . "

"I'm so tired I can hardly stand. My arse is sore as a boil. I need sleep. You need it, the horses need it. He's not going to attack the fort tonight. He won't make a move till you get there."

"How dare you refuse a direct order? This is gross insubordination!"

"Like hell. I'm no soldier. You don't command me. I just work for you, and I say we stay the night. At least I do. You can go on if you like. I'm not stirring two feet from this fire except to go to bed."

"He's right about one thing," said Remington, "nobody's going to attack nothing tonight. So why not just relax yourselves. I'll fetch you something to warm your innards, what's left, and prepare warm beds for you both." He had moved to the window. "It's letting up it looks like. Skies could clear by morning."

Arnold threw up his hands but not before glaring at Crocker.

"Bring me rum," growled the colonel. "Hot enough to melt a spoon in and no cloves!"

"I'll have the same," said Crocker, a bit too jauntily for Arnold's liking.

Ethan Allen and his Green Mountain Boys. He'd give him a piece of his mind when they caught up tomorrow, before sunrise. Ethan Allen. Typical backwoods, buckskin trash, he'd warrant!

2

★ **The** rain had let up just before dawn and the Green Mountain Boys had crawled out of their tents to be greeted by a glowering sky, the air still heavy and threatening. Ethan Allen emerged from his tent balanced on one foot, hauling on his second boot, breaking a nail on the finger-grip and purpling the crisp morning air with a curse. He stretched his solidly muscled six-foot-three-inch frame and yawned loudly. He had slept little, lying awake most of the night thinking about the impending action, recalling his words at the bar of Fay's Catamount Tavern in Bennington, on the New Hampshire Grants. "By God, I'd like to take that fort!"

A mile to the south, he could dimly see the majestic, rugged, star-shaped structure of earth, timber, and granite, perched on high ground close to the lake. How many men guarded its ramparts? At least two dozen cannons poked forth their muzzles, all doubtless loaded, ready to discharge lethal blasts of ball or grapeshot.

He ran a brawny hand over his two-day beard and considered his options. None came to mind. He'd announced his aspiration, and now here he was, prepared to fulfill it. Fort Ticonderoga, his for the taking. If he did not, and if others tried and failed to take it, the entire northern flank of the American colonies would find themselves at a serious military disadvantage. The fort secured communications to Canada. Its imposing presence threatened the scattered back settlements of the northern colonies.

Time was a critical factor. The fort had to be seized as soon as possible, before the British could install reinforcements and augment the artillery. Crown Point, less than ten miles down Lake Champlain, also had to be taken, but Fort Ticonderoga was the principal objective, the challenge, the prize. Allen stretched and looked about as men continued to come out of their tents, some not yet fully dressed. The rain resumed. Breakfast would be cold. One by one, the men began digging into their war bags for rations.

He could see only one problem with taking the fort. This wouldn't be like Concord, where four hundred Patriots stood their ground against and beat back seven hundred seasoned British troops bent on seizing the colonists' military stores. Ticonderoga was Crown property. To attack King George's fort was to attack His Majesty himself. It was flirting with treason. It *was* treason. It did give a man pause.

There was another aspect to the situation. The government of New York had officially and expressly forbid such an assault. Partisans on both sides still hoped for reconciliation with the Crown. But transcending Allen's qualms and reservations was a single, salient fact. If the British continued to control Lake Champlain, the cause of independence was doomed from the start. The Green Mountain Boys knew that; in his heart he knew it too. It came down to a case of taking John Bull by the horns.

Comparing this action with Lexington and Concord was comparing dogs to cats. Those two engagements had been a defense of private property; this would be deliberate offense. *Would* Lexington and Concord turn out to be more than merely a local fracas? Were they the first of many such clashes that would culminate in the revolution Ethan and others so craved? Taking Fort Ticonderoga had to help.

There was another good reason to seize it. The colonists would never drive the British out of Boston without artillery. Small arms would be ineffective against cannons. The Americans had to have cannons—Ticonderoga's.

Three men were approaching, two in buckskins, the other in a shabby forest-green jacket that gave no hint of his rank of lieutenant colonel. Seth Warner was six years younger than Ethan, an inch shorter at six-foot-two, and straight as a mast. With him was Remember Baker, Ethan's cousin as well as Warner's, and a longtime comrade in arms to both. Like Warner, Baker had grown up in Roxbury, Connecticut; also like him, he left home in his teens to fight in the French and Indian War. The third man, in buckskins like Baker, was Noah Phelps, who had left Bennington assigned by Ethan to spy on the fort. The colonel was eager to hear what he'd found out. Scattering mud in every direction, Allen ran up to Phelps.

"Hold the questions," said Noah. "I'll start from the beginning. Good news, Ethan. I got inside as easy as you'd swat a skeeter." Ethan's eyes glistened like a child's on Christmas morning, causing Phelps to laugh, as did Baker. Ethan's reaction even brought a smile to Warner's usually somber features. Phelps rubbed his hand over his clean-shaven chin. "I told the guard I was a woodsman and asked to be let in for a shave from the barber. I explained to the jackass that I'd lost my knapsack in the lake when a bear attacked me while I slept. I told him it grabbed the darned thing and threw it in the lake, and he believed me."

"I don't care about that, Noah, I want to know about inside."

"You've never seen so much artillery. Piles of cannon, iron, and brass, and storehouses crammed to bursting with ammunition."

"How many men?"

"About forty."

"Hell almighty!" Ethan grabbed him and kissed him loudly on the cheek.

Phelps nodded. "And only two officers. The commandant, Captain Delaplace, and a lieutenant. So says the barber."

"That's it?"

"That's it. Oh, reinforcements are on the way. If you're planning to pluck this particular star out of the Crown jewels you'd better get to it."

"That barber sure has a big mouth," said Remember Baker removing his tricorn and scratching his mop of sandy hair.

"What barber doesn't?" said Ethan.

"The place is a dump," said Phelps. "They're living in squalor in there. The commissary ceiling fell in a couple months ago, the barracks are in rotten condition, there's rats all over."

"It's still a fort," said Seth Warner. "Six defenders or six hundred, it won't be easy to take. And we can't swim over to it, not and keep our powder dry and do it so quietly the sentries won't hear."

"We'll need boats," said Ethan. "We knew that."

"There's more," said Phelps. "When we land over there we should make our approach under the grenadiers' battery—you can look over and see, it's on that slight bluff overlooking the lake—then pass under the ramparts . . . "

"To the east," said Baker.

"Right. Then turn to the right and make our way to the

south side of the fort. Look for a section of the wall that's broken down. They tried to repair it but only did a half-arse job. We can get inside through there."

"There'll be sentries we'll have to take out," said Ethan. "And quietly. Anybody shouts and they'll be up and on us in seconds."

"Let 'em," said Baker. "The sooner we get to it, the sooner it's over. And the sooner we bust out their rum and celebrate! I'm thirsty! Let's fight!"

"How far is it from the break in the wall to the gate and the inner quadrangle?" Warner asked.

"Half a stone's throw," said Phelps.

"It sounds as easy as falling down stairs," said Ethan.

"It's bound to be."

"What about this barber who told you all this?" Baker asked.

Phelps grinned. "I couldn't stop his tongue if I knotted it."

"You don't think he might have been leading you on?"

The Green Mountain Boys were crowding around leaning on muskets and rifles, listening.

Phelps shook his head. "Why would he? Do I look like a spy? They're not expecting a thing. The beauty of it was I didn't even have to pump him, it just poured out. He hates it there, he wants to get back to England. He can't stand Delaplace."

"Who?" Baker looked puzzled.

"The commandant. Captain Delaplace. Ethan, I didn't ask more than two questions, there's no way he could suspect me. If he did, would they have let me go?"

"They might," said Seth.

"They have no idea what's coming. I paid him a whole shilling for this shave and made sure he knew what he was getting before he even started stropping. There's nothing like money to loosen a tongue."

Ethan clapped a hand on his shoulder. "You did a grand job,

Noah. We'll do as you suggest, cross over and make straight for that hole in the wall."

"What'll we use for boats?" Baker asked.

"I took care of that before we broke up last night. Sam Herrick's taking thirty of the boys down to Skenesboro at the south end of Wood Creek to commandeer Major Skene's boats, and Asa Douglas will be taking off soon to get his family's boats at Crown Point. We'll have plenty of transportation."

"We've got over two hundred men," said Baker. "We'll need plenty. When do we attack, Ethan?" He showed his tongue. "Look at this thirst. It needs rum!"

"Tonight." A cheer went up. Ethan scanned the sky. "Let's hope this rain keeps up. It'll help drown out sound."

"Let's hope Skene's boats are in decent shape," muttered Seth Warner.

After they finished breakfast, the men sat about in their tents working on their weapons. Ethan walked around talking to small groups. Despite the weather, everyone was in an ebullient mood and eager to attack. Not a man he talked to seemed to harbor his own lingering concern over assaulting Crown property.

War was inevitable, there could be no hesitating now.

A shout went up. Four boys, sentries posted to the south, came marching up, surrounding two strangers on horseback. Both wore long cloaks and tricorns. Ethan could see scarlet between the halves of the shorter man's cloak.

"Look what we found, Colonel," said one of the Boys. "A redcoat spy."

"You're a fool, man," growled Arnold, dismounting. "Ethan Allen?" Out shot his hand. "Colonel Benedict Arnold. So I've caught up with you at last. And just in time, from the look of things."

"In time for what?"

"To take over command of the operation."

3

★ **From** a height of six inches above him, Ethan Allen stared down at the newcomer. Arnold stood with his legs slightly spread, his fists on his hips, chest out, exuding confidence. Then, removing a glove, he sent his hand inside his jacket and withdrew a sheaf of papers wrapped in oilskin.

"My commission from the Massachusetts Committee of Safety." Everyone crowded around the two men. Crocker's eyes darted about like a cornered ferret's. "I think you'll find everything in order."

"It appears to be," said Ethan. A collective groan followed by grumbling greeted this acknowledgment. "Take it easy, boys, and listen up. Colonel Arnold's commission is in order, and you could say it comes from an authority higher than our council in Bennington. My own has been conferred by you and your guns."

"Which be goddamn good enough for me!" shouted a man, raising his musket. Others shouted in agreement.

"Hold it," said Ethan. "I appreciate your loyalty, Jonas, I appreciate all your support. But right is right. Gentlemen, this gentleman, Colonel Benedict Arnold, will take over and lead the assault against Fort Ticonderoga."

A chorus of protests went up that were so loud and emphatic, Ethan thought he saw Arnold wince slightly. Seth Warner and Remember Baker were staring at each other, both gawking in disbelief.

"This is pure shit," said Noah Phelps stepping forward, glowering witheringly at Arnold.

Crocker stood by looking amused. Ethan thrust Arnold's papers into Phelps's hand. He started to read them, then tossed them away with a curse. The man next to him caught them deftly before they hit the muddy ground. He handed them back to Ethan, who returned them to Arnold, who stuck them back into the oilskin and inside his jacket.

"Take over, Colonel," said Ethan, his tone as hurt as he could make it sound. Without a murmur the men dispersed, walking to the edge of the clearing and stacking their guns. Arnold and Ethan watched wordlessly. The stacking completed, the men took their places in a line behind their weapons and stared at Ethan, Arnold, and the other officers.

"What do you think you're doing?" burst Arnold.

"What does it look like?" responded a man. "You can lead your arsehole against the fort, you sure as hell ain't leading us!"

"We're going home," said another.

Others agreed.

"Now, boys . . . " began Ethan.

"You're our colonel, Ethan. Only you!" snapped a raw-boned farmer who towered over those nearest him. "We're not following no spit-and-polish redcoat into this thing, nohow."

"Not now nor never!" shouted another.

Ethan sneaked a glance at Arnold. The colonel's cheeks were beginning to show a distinct pink glow. His fury was building fast. He looked about to draw his saber and run it through the next man who spoke up against him.

"This," he muttered, "is gross insubordination."

"These," said Ethan, "aren't soldiers, Colonel. They're not even militia. They're volunteers."

"They're soldiers in defense of liberty, whether they realize it or not!"

"Boys, quiet down the grumbling. You all heard me. The man's got the papers that give him the authority."

"He can shove his papers up his arse!" To a man, the Green Mountain Boys agreed.

Ethan scowled. "Now just shut up with the insults!"

"Colonel," said Arnold. "It would appear we're at a stand-off."

"No, no, Colonel, you're in charge fair and square. It's right there in your papers."

Arnold gritted his teeth. "Will you let me finish?"

"Please do. Boys, Colonel Arnold's got something he wants to say. Will you all just come back and gather around and listen like gentlemen? Come on . . . "

Reluctantly they returned, circling the two colonels.

"No more cursing, no mouthing off, just pay attention to what the man says," said Ethan. "Colonel . . . "

"Before you begin," said Seth Warner, the Green Mountain Boys' second in command, "let me just say that all of us, every man you see, agreed that we'd only follow the orders of our own elected officers."

"All well and good," said Arnold. "But my orders come from General Artemus Ward himself. By level of authority alone they take precedence."

"Who gives a shit?" bawled a man at the rear of the crowd.

"Quiet!" yelled Ethan. "Let him talk."

He was studying Arnold. The man may have looked a dandy, but there was nothing soft in his spine. He could see he was used to getting his way and stood on firm ground in this instance. He may have been slightly arrogant but not stupid; practical needs would encourage a diplomatic solution. Ethan's optimism stirred. He smelled an offer of compromise.

"Thank you, Colonel," said Arnold, clearing his throat and surveying the circle around him.

"But," said Ethan, "before you begin maybe you'd like to hear our plan. See if you think it's the most feasible way of taking the fort."

"I'd be delighted."

"Why don't we adjourn to my tent?"

Inside the tent Ethan outlined the plan of attack as dictated by Noah Phelps's intelligence report. Arnold listened politely, questioning only one aspect of it.

"In approaching, how will you cross the abatis?"

"Noah?" Ethan asked.

"All those logs stuck in with their ends sharpened are rotted away and they haven't bothered to replace them. We can clear a path easily just by kicking them down."

Joining them in Ethan's tent were Seth Warner and the redoubtable Remember Baker, along with Phelps. Phelps produced a crude map of the interior of the fort showing the site of the break in the south wall, the distance to the wicket gate, and other points of strategic importance. Arnold was visibly impressed. He raised his eyes from the map to Ethan.

"Colonel Allen, I'm sure we can come to a viable agreement on this."

"We can if you don't want to sashay into the fort all by your lonesome," said Remember Baker.

Ethan frowned at him. "Colonel Arnold," he said. "It would be my pleasure to invite you to accompany us in the attack."

Arnold looked long and hard at him, licked his lips, and nodded. "I accept."

"I'm honored."

Since Arnold had arrived armed only with his saber and a brace of pistols, Ethan presented him with a short blunderbuss, in token of their new friendship.

Together, Arnold told himself, they would lead the first American attack of the Revolutionary War. Oh well, half a loaf . . .

4

★ **By** nightfall the more than two hundred men, excepting the men despatched to obtain boats, had assembled at Hand's Cove on the eastern shore of Lake Champlain. There, in a grove of spruce, safely shielded from sight of any of the fort's sentries, they waited.

Time dragged on with no sign of boats from either direction. The two colonels discussed the situation.

"What do you think's going on?" Arnold asked. "They've both been gone for hours."

"I've no idea. Asa won't be bringing a fleet, only a couple of rowboats. He insisted on getting them so I let him go. Skene's people may be a problem."

"Is he with us or against us?"

"Oh, he's dead against us. A Loyalist to the core. He's a Scotsman, fought in the French and Indian War. He's been appointed as royal governor of Ticonderoga and Crown Point." Ethan leered and winked. "But as we speak he's on the high seas, on his way to raise a regiment of Loyalist troops to hold both forts. No, it's not old Philip Skene that Sam Herrick'll be bargaining with, but his people down there. Facing thirty armed men with their dander up should make them cooperate and give us all the boats we need."

"The question is when."

"Patience, Colonel." Ethan squinted at his timepiece in the darkness. "It's only just past ten-thirty. Plenty of time yet."

It resumed raining lightly. Ethan welcomed it with a broad grin. "The rain will cover the noise of our breaking down the pointed logs to make a path through the approach."

"You seem very confident, Colonel, I admire that."

"We outnumber them better than four to one, they'll have no chance to turn their artillery on us, and the place is a cheese box inside. Surprise is in our favor. We'll catch them dead to the world with their trousers off. It'll be easy as pie."

"Let's hope and pray."

The clouds ceased careening about the heavens, blending into a black blanket that seemed to lower by the minute. Fires had been forbidden, and the rain made certain none would be kindled. The men sat about conversing in low tones, an occasional laugh was audible, but as the hours crept by with still no sign of Samuel Herrick and his men or Asa Douglas, anticipation began turning into anxiety and the worry in Arnold's face grew progressively deeper.

By one-thirty, with just enough time left to ferry the men across before daylight, there was still no sign of any boats.

Seth Warner joined Ethan and Arnold. "It appears we'll have to swim for it, Ethan."

Ethan shook his head, his expression becoming increasingly grim. "Impossible. It's too choppy. We'd make too much noise, and it's too far. Besides, as you yourself said yesterday, we could never keep our powder dry."

By now Arnold had worked himself up into a state. He paced, flinging his hands, addressing Ethan and Warner, talking to himself, berating their luck to the glowering skies. But other than an occasional "damnation" he uttered no profanity.

"Marvelous! There it squats begging to be taken and we can't even get across the filthy water. Unbelievable!"

Noah Phelps joined them. He eyed Arnold. "Edgy son of a bitch, ain't he?"

"Shhhh," whispered Ethan.

Two o'clock came and went.

Two-fifteen.

"That's it!" bellowed Arnold. "We're calling it off."

"Give them a little longer," said Ethan.

"Why? They're obviously not coming. We'll have to postpone it till tomorrow night. This is great, just great!"

A man called from the water's edge on the far side of the trees. Everyone hurried toward him. Magically, as if sent by a friendly angel, a bateau, scow-rigged with a lugsail, was floating toward shore with nobody on board. Ethan could easily see why it had been abandoned. It was in dreadful shape; water sloshed around the oars lying in the bottom, and the tapered prow looked as if a good portion of it had been bitten off. It looked too rotted even for kindling wood.

"It's leaking," said Seth as men splashed into the water and pulled it ashore.

The sky in the east was losing its blackness. The rain fell sparingly. Ethan assembled the men and selected thirty-nine to be led by Noah Phelps. With their supplies and arms they so weighted down the vessel it threatened to sink. Ethan watched them row slowly, carefully across the choppy water.

"They'll never make it," said Arnold.

"With a little luck they will," said Ethan.

Warner nodded. "And maybe by this time their sentries will be nodding."

Spume-fringed water broke over the leeward gunwale soaking the men seated on that side. One cursed loudly. Ethan winced as it carried back to them and he held his breath. The bateau took ninety minutes to cross and return, a distance of one mile. Ethan, Arnold, Warner, Baker, and thirty-nine others made the second trip, leaving Crocker and more than a hundred volunteers unable to join the action. Arnold stood rigidly at the shattered bow defying the spume, his cloak wrapped tightly about him. Ethan, Baker, and Warner watched him from the stern.

"He's not exactly Green Mountain Boy material," murmured Warner. "But he's not short on gumption."

"He's got more than balls," said Baker. "He had brains enough to read the handwriting on the wall. Oh boy . . . "

"What?" Ethan asked.

"I'm starting to taste that rum over there."

"Hold off drinking till it's all over, cousin."

Baker studied the eastern sky. "You were right to limit us to two trips. It's getting light. It'd be suicide without the dark to cover us. How many men will we have?"

"Counting us, eighty-two," said Ethan. "It's not what I'd like, but it's still close to two to one."

They assembled about a quarter mile east of the fort and,

with Ethan and Arnold both leading the way, sabers drawn, started up the steep outer slope of fortifications, breaking a pathway through the rotted abatis. Past the unguarded redoubt they slipped, staying close to the northeast ramparts, clambering up the steep rise toward the main fort.

It was nearing six o'clock by the time the two colonels reached the main gate. It hung slightly loose from its top hinge, which prevented it from closing completely. Inside they could see a small wicket gate and sentry box. Arnold was surveying the main gate. He shook his head.

"Sheer idiocy. How can they let such a vital installation go to wrack and ruin?"

"Be grateful," murmured Ethan. "It has to be bad for morale. Makes the sentries indifferent, lax." He indicated. "See what I mean?"

The sentry in the box sat cradling his musket, dozing. They began slipping through the gate in single file. Arnold took the initiative, pushing ahead of Ethan, making for the sentry. Startled, he jerked awake, leveled his weapon, and pulled the trigger. Luckily for Arnold the prevailing dampness caused the gun to misfire. The sentry threw it down and started to run. Men chased him. All the raiders were now inside. A second sentry showed. Ethan was the first to get to him.

The man fired too high and charged with his bayonet. Ethan sidestepped and swung his saber at his head. It struck at an angle, staggering the sentry and dropping him in the mud. He was surrounded and pulled to his feet.

"That shot'll wake the whole fort!" burst Arnold, coming up.

"Take us to the commandant's quarters!" barked Ethan to the sentry.

Arnold pointed. "The main barracks are over there. Where the rifles are stacked out front. You . . . " He addressed four men standing apart. "Get others and get in there and take them in their beds." The men looked at Ethan. He nodded approval. Arnold continued. "While they're rousting them out we'll have more men move those weapons to the other side of the fort."

"Whatever you say," said Ethan, not taking his eyes off the trembling, wide-eyed sentry. "The commandant, son. Lead the way."

Arnold had gone off with the men, picking up others on the way to carry out his seizure of the barracks. Baker joined him and took over. Arnold, Ethan, and six men ran across the parade ground to the west wall, pushing the sentry ahead of them. They started up the stairs to the officers' quarters.

"No quarter! No quarter!" Ethan shouted.

At the top of the stairs, looking down a long hallway lit by a single wall taper, Ethan grabbed the sentry's belt, stopping him. Ahead, a half-dressed man had emerged from his room and was frantically pounding on the door opposite, calling loudly.

"Who's that?" whispered Ethan.

"Lieutenant Jocelyn Feltham, sir. That's Captain Delaplace's room."

"Stay where you are."

They waited, pressed against the wall, with a line trailing down the stairs. Ethan continuing to hang onto the man's belt, Arnold immediately behind him. Feltham turned from the door just as it opened. Captain Delaplace emerged in his robe, wearing his saber.

Feltham came out again, this time in a coat, his breeches in one hand, his saber in the other.

"We're being attacked, sir!"

"I can hear . . . "

Feltham raced down the hall, nearly running into the sentry and Ethan at the head of the darkened stairs.

"Stay where you are!" Feltham shouted. "By what authority dare you enter His Majesty's fort?"

Allen shoved the sentry to one side, stepped up to bring himself face-to-face with the lieutenant, and raised his saber between them, the blade a scant inch from Feltham's nose. Behind Ethan a clutch of men pushed ahead of Arnold and leveled their weapons at the lieutenant.

A smile set Ethan's face glowing. "In the name of the great Jehovah and the Continental Congress!"

5

★ **The** single shot fired by the sentry over Ethan Allen's head turned out to be the only shot in the taking of Fort Ticonderoga by the Green Mountain Boys. Samuel Herrick and Asa Douglas returned early the next morning. Herrick and his men failed to find Major Skene's schooner, which was cruising at the northern end of the lake. They had ended their search for other vessels when one of their number stumbled on a cellar that turned out to be the major's liquor storeroom. Asa Douglas brought three small boats back from Crown Point, and with the bateau, the remainder of the men were ferried to the fort.

Earlier, Captain Delaplace surrendered his saber and pistols and was permitted to dress, as was his wife. Both officers were placed under guard and the defenders lined up on the parade ground. The raiders found forty women and children and they too were collected. At that point the Green Mountain Boys were turned loose to loot. Arnold objected.

"It's vulgar and disgraceful," he complained to Allen.

"It's deserved. They've earned the right."

"It's wholly improper. It's His Majesty's property, private property."

"Ethan, Ethan, we found ninety gallons of rum in the wardroom cellar!" shouted a man.

"What are you waiting for? Start celebrating! And somebody find Remember . . . "

Within fifteen minutes all semblance of order and discipline had vanished. Allen ignored the goings-on around him, turning his attention to Delaplace and his lieutenant. Arnold fumed and ranted, protesting mainly to Seth Warner.

"I'll have to put all of this in my report to the Committee of Safety. You certainly don't approve . . . ?"

"Whether I do or don't doesn't matter, it's a part of war as old as war itself, Colonel. To the victor—"

"Anarchy's what it is! Colonel Allen!" He came over to Arnold. "Can't you at least order them to hold off their plundering long enough to finish the job? We've got to get these cannon and the gunpowder out of here and down to Boston."

"With what, a bateau? Try loading even a damned two-pounder. It'll bust through the bottom for sure. And Asa's boats are too small. Boston'll have to wait. Besides, see for yourself, the boys are busy."

"This is intolerable!"

By now, virtually every raider was roaring drunk. The redcoats, the women and children stood watching until one woman broke from the crowd and ran screaming to a raider who had found a sewing box. She tried to wrest it from him. Arnold rushed to assist her, infuriating Allen. He came striding over. "What do you think you're doing, Colonel?"

"What does it look like, Colonel?" Arnold had gotten the sewing box away from the looter. The woman was running back to the safety of the crowd of civilians, hugging it tightly. "I'm fed up with this barbarism!"

"I'm fed up with you and your puling! Jacob! Elisha!" He beckoned to two men reeling by, each clutching a sloshing cup of rum. "Hold your guns on him."

They dropped their cups and leveled their weapons at the startled and angered Arnold. Ethan reached into Arnold's inside pocket and got out his commission. The smaller man glared but made no move to stop him.

"I'm hereby relieving you of your command of the Massachusetts boys. You were invited along to watch and that's all.

You have no authority, no rank, no say. Henceforth you may consider yourself a civilian observer."

"You can't get away with this, Allen!"

"You're not paying attention."

Others around them stopped to watch. A drunken farmer raised his musket and fired. His wavering aim sent the bullet well over Arnold's head into the wall behind him. Women screamed. Disgust filled Captain Delaplace's heavy-jowled face.

"Get the hell out of here, Jabez!" barked Ethan.

Arnold threw up his hands and walked off. Ethan summoned Seth Warner.

"Fill Asa Douglas's small boats with men. Get up to Crown Point and take it."

"With pleasure, Ethan."

"And remember to count the cannon."

Over the course of the next three days an additional two hundred men arrived to nearly double the occupation force. Meanwhile, Seth Warner had returned from Crown Point with two prisoners, the only able-bodied men among the nine garrisoned there. He also brought back Sergeant Hawkins, who was in command. He reported that fifty usable cannons could be added to Fort Ticonderoga's.

Ethan spent the time relaxing, eating, drinking, and enjoying his victory. Arnold locked himself in a room and concentrated on writing up his version of events for the Massachusetts Committee of Safety. There was at least one point on which there could be no dispute between him and Allen—not one life had been lost in the action. The only wound was suffered by the redcoat whom Ethan struck in the head with his saber when he charged him with his bayonet.

For taking part in the capture of Fort Ticonderoga, the Green Mountain Boys and the Massachusetts militia each received payment of two dollars in silver.

And Captain Remember Baker imbibed so vast a quantity of rum he passed out and didn't wake for two days.

6

★ **Colonel** Benedict Arnold had diplomatically pocketed his commission and graciously accepted Ethan Allen's offer to accompany the raiders. He did not want history to remember him as the man who hindered the capture of Fort Ticonderoga. But now that the two colonels had fallen out, he made it a point to deal harshly with Ethan in his written report to the Massachusetts Committee of Safety, while maximizing his own role in the capture of the fort.

Ethan, like Remember Baker, got generously drunk. Magnaminity supplanted his irritation. He made peace with his rival, who set about taking inventory of the ordnance. Together, at Fort Ticonderoga and Fort Amherst, at Crown Point, there were two hundred and three usable or reparable mortars, howitzers, and cannons that, along with vast quantities of powder and ball, would be floated and sledged to Boston to assist the colonists in driving the British from the city.

The Green Mountain Boys' capture of the two installations proved considerably more valuable than the ordnance, ammunition, and supplies found there. It was by every standard a major military victory that promised to drastically change the balance of power in the northern colonies.

Captain Delaplace approached Ethan on the morning of the third day of the occupation wearing the sour look that seemed permanently fixed to his face.

"That rum your men stole was my personal property, fellow."

"Colonel, Captain."

Delaplace sneered. "And by what military authority have you been commissioned?"

"By the Continental Congress," lied Ethan.

"Humph."

"You're a little late, Captain, your rum is all drunk."

"I know that, I'm not blind."

"I'll give you a receipt for the value. Cross your fingers that you'll be able to cash it in at a later date."

"I'll warrant that's the best I can hope for."

"Really, how do you expect us to celebrate, with a prayer meeting?"

"What happens to us?"

"Lieutenant Colonel Warner brought prisoners down from Crown Point to join you. He says the fort up there is in even worse shape than here."

"There was a terrible fire there two years ago and little has been done in the way of repairs. About us . . . "

"Every uniform is a prisoner of war, including you and the lieutenant. All of you and your dependents will be treated with the utmost courtesy."

"I've seen little courtesy toward the women thus far."

"Men get drunk, they behave like arseholes."

"Where do we go from here?"

"I wouldn't know, I've nothing to do with it. A special contingent will be coming to take over."

Delaplace was eyeing him malevolently. Ethan responded with a grin.

"You're aware, Colonel, that you've committed most heinous treason against your king and country."

"Not my king, not my country."

"You're all British citizens, your allegiance is to His Majesty."

Ethan sighed. "Has all this somehow gone over your fucking head, Captain? Can't you see what's happened here? There's a war on. You may not have heard, but about three weeks ago, back on April eighteenth, British regulars fired on colonists at Lexington and Concord. Seven hundred lobster backs. At Concord, they were driven off and peppered all the way back to Boston." He leaned closer. "Your boys lost two hundred seventy-three dead."

"I don't believe you."

"You'll find out."

"How many Americans?"

"About ninety. It's war, Captain, and before fall it'll be busting out all over the map."

"Remains to be seen. By the by, your special contingent had better hurry so you and your rabble can get out of here. As we speak, reinforcements are on the way."

Arnold had come up. "He's right about that, Colonel."

"I'm shaking in my fucking boots. Which direction will they be coming from? It doesn't matter, we'll post sentries 'round the clock. They'll have to approach by water like we did. We'll blow them back to Canada with your cannons, Captain. If you're a praying man, you'd better pray we don't see red coming from any direction."

Ethan had no respect for Delaplace; the man was a confirmed snob and a poor choice to command any garrison. He'd been flagrantly derelict in his duty and ought to have had sense enough to recognize that Fort Ticonderoga would likely be the first target among the chain of forts stretching from New York City to the St. Lawrence. Its brief history underscored its importance to both the British and the French. The captain had to know that the fort's remaining in British hands would be disastrous to the revolutionary cause.

Arnold continued to fume at the rampant lack of discipline fostered by Ethan's indulgence of his followers. Despite being stripped of his command, Arnold persisted in trying to control the men, but they refused to obey his commands. One man threatened to blow his brisket out his back if he didn't stop bothering him. Failing to win over a single man, he again confronted Ethan.

"Colonel, I demand you return my commission and that we go back to holding joint command."

"Why the fuck should I?"

"Must you curse like a common field hand?"

"What's the matter with field hands? My father worked the fields, so did my brothers and me."

"I," Arnold corrected.

"You know what your trouble is, Benedict, you're all spit, polish, and regulations. And no goddamned heart."

"You're very perceptive."

"And you're very full of shit."

"You do have a way with words. Nevertheless, we had a deal. Back at Hand's Cove it was agreed that we would share command."

"No you don't. What I said was you could enter the fort by my side."

"The two of us sharing command. Joint command."

"Joint your arsehole. Look around, Colonel, you've got no men. The Massachusetts militia started out with me and my boys and they're still with us."

"I have my commission."

"It's not worth the goddamn paper it's written on. Tell that to your Committee of Safety when you get back. Tell 'em Colonel Ethan Allen politely refused to recognize it or you, but graciously let you tag along and share in the glory. Now if you'll excuse me, I've got letters to write to a lot of people telling what we did here."

He walked off. Arnold shook his head. The ignoramus's rapidly bloating ego was certainly playing hob with his small streak of decency.

"Arrogant, foul-mouthed hayseed . . . "

The tug of war over command, with the power firmly in Ethan's hands, threatened to become a standoff with the arrival of seventy more Massachusetts volunteers carrying orders assigning them to Arnold. Added to the fifty Massachusetts militia already at the fort, who had been somewhat cowed by the majority of Green Mountain Boys, the colonel now had more than a hundred well-armed, able-bodied men under his command.

He promptly, and without consulting Ethan, dispatched a party to Skenesboro, having heard from locals who had come to the fort to help in the looting, that Major Skene's schooner, which had been cruising in the northern waters of the lake, had returned home. The party found the *Katherine,* a fast, trim little schooner, at the boatyard across the neck of water east of the fort, at the base of Mount Independence.

Arnold hurried to Skenesboro and there set about converting the *Katherine* into a warship, fixing her with four carriage guns and six swivel guns. He then showed the men how to cut ports in the schooner's sides, and how to lash down the guns and run them with blocks and tackle.

Within one day the vessel was fully provisioned with food, rum, and ammunition out of Skene's stores. Arnold boarded her and renamed her *Liberty.* When Ethan got wind of his rival's audacious undertaking, he cheered and applauded, surprising Seth Warner, Remember Baker, and others.

"He sneaked off without your permission," said Baker.

"Which I probably wouldn't have given him. He knew that, that's why he didn't ask. Only don't you see, Remember? Boys? It's worked out in our favor. He steals Skene's boat and we're rid of the son of a bitch for good! Who's got some rum? This calls for a celebration!"

II

Bold Venture

7

★ **When** news of Ethan Allen and the Green Mountain Boys' capture of Fort Ticonderoga reached the colonies it was greeted joyfully. But when the first wave of jubilant reaction spent itself, it became manifest to intelligent men that a sticky situation had resulted, one of uncertain consequences and no little embarrassment.

Despite all rationalization to justify it, the capture of the fort was an act of rebellion. New York, where Ticonderoga stood, wanted nothing to do with its acquisition. Neighboring colonies did not rush to involve themselves in the situation. It was left to the Continental Congress to reluctantly agree to assume control over both Fort Ticonderoga and Fort Amherst, while announcing that their seizure had been a defensive action and that the king's property would be duly protected. Congress officially requested that the northern colonies join in removing the ordnance and other supplies to the south end of Lake George where they would be held until peace was restored between the two sides.

This infuriated Ethan. On May 29 he despatched a pithy letter to Congress protesting "official abandonment of the fort," pointing out that this would leave upper Lake Champlain, the people of the New Hampshire Grants, and nearby New York defenseless. Instead of being abandoned, Fort Ticonderoga should immediately be strengthened. The fort could then be depended upon to block any invasion from Canada.

He put forth every reason he could think of why Fort Ticonderoga should be utilized rather than left to rot, that the initiative taken should be pressed. He labeled faint-hearted Patriots who objected to seizing the day as being as inimical to the revolutionary cause as the Loyalists.

Twelve days later, his letter was read before Congress. Impressed with his audacity and courage, Patriots from Maine to Georgia agreed that the garrison should be brought up to fighting strength. Even Benedict Arnold so advised Congress, suggesting that only those cannons that could be spared should be removed to defend Boston.

Both men separately set about to enlist the colonies in the cause. Pressured by vulnerable northern colonies, Congress reversed itself, declaring that everything seized in the capture of Fort Ticonderoga should be considered spoils of war and as such employed in defense.

Early in June, his skirmish with Congress won, Ethan decided that Canada should be invaded before the British launched an invasion of the northern colonies and the Hudson Valley. To the Continental Congress and the northern colonies he began pleading for men and supplies to mount an offensive. News reached him that the time was ripe, that the Province of Quebec was all but completely defenseless. A well-planned and executed invasion could overrun southeastern Canada, secure control of the St. Lawrence, and eventually neutralize the entire territory.

"I will lay my life on it, that with fifteen hundred men, and a proper artillery, I will take Montreal!"

It was a bold scheme but one well worth considering. Since the Peace of Paris, February 10, 1763, which ended the Seven

Years' War, England's grip on Canada had been tenuous. A few British officers supported by a scattering of less than a thousand redcoats governed an area inhabited by a hundred thousand French. Since France's defeat, the habitants had displayed scant affection for their conquerors. Following implementation of the Quebec Act, on May Day eve in 1774 a crowd of French Canadians marched through the Place d'Armes in Montreal and assembled around the bust of King George III. It had been smeared with black paint, and a wooden cross and rosary of potatoes was draped around its neck. The gathering promptly urinated on His Majesty. It was this simmering hostility that Ethan hoped to turn to practical advantage.

But French Canadian cooperation in any invasion effort was far from a fait accompli. Although many habitants thought less than highly of the British, they held the Americans in even lower esteem, especially the New Englanders, who were militantly anti-French and anti-Catholic. In addition, French-Canadian priests favored the British, and their influence on their parishioners was considerable.

But as the summer warmed, and idleness became an itch that only action could scratch, Ethan persuaded himself that the Canadians so disliked and resented British rule, that given the chance, they would rise up and fight alongside American invaders.

Ethan wrote to Congress and received permission to lay his invasion plan before the legislators. On June 11, a radiant Sunday morning with not a cloud in sight and the sky a shimmering, brilliant blue, he set out from Ticonderoga on horseback for Philadelphia, accompanied by Seth Warner. Within the hour they gained the Castleton Road and headed east.

On the way, Ethan planned to stop off and visit his wife, Mary, and his family in Bennington, situated in the southwest corner of the Grants. Husband and wife had not seen each other for many months. Warner avoided discussing Mary with Ethan, for theirs was not a happy marriage.

Mary Brownson Allen was ill-equipped by nature, temperament, or intelligence to cope with a man as restless and ambitious as Ethan. Mediocrity was her lot in life and she was satisfied with it. Warner had never been able to understand what his friend saw in her. True, she'd brought him a generous dowry, and her father was considered wealthy, but she was acid-tongued, a bore, far from pretty, and six years older than Ethan.

He was, despite his lack of formal education, a scholar of sorts, reasonably well read and proud of his ability to compose his thoughts and ideas clearly in a letter, while Mary could not write her own name. For the second time, Ethan mentioned stopping, as if probing, testing to see if Warner would object.

"I hope you don't mind, Seth, but I should stop by."

Warner discreetly suppressed a groan and smiled. "Of course."

"It'll be less than a day out of our way. Mary's a good cook. She's sure to have something tasty in the pot. I just wish I had gifts to bring the youngsters. The girls don't expect anything, but little Joseph, his father returning from battle . . . "

"Tell them about Ticonderoga."

"Oh, Mary would love that. It'd scare the petticoat off her."

"Can I ask you something, Ethan? I've always been curious, do you cuss when she's around?"

"I try not to. I slip sometimes. Shit, she gives me a look that'll freeze me in my boots. All the same, it sure will be nice to see her again."

This last sounded lame to Warner, coming across leavened with self-consciousness and unmistakable guilt.

"I know what you want to ask me," said Ethan.

"Ask you?"

Ethan heeled his sorrel, moving up half a length until they rode side-by-side. The pungent fragrance of late spring filled the warm air. Delicate pink-and-white spring beauties tinted the roadsides, along with wild geraniums and thistles.

"How come I got married. At the time, I honestly thought I wanted a wife. You know, have sons, settle down on a farm and run a business to boot. I had no idea how restless the bug in me would get. It got bigger and bigger with all that's happening, with New York and the New Hampshire Grants and the Crown treating us all like we're indentured, with no more freedom than chickens in a yard.

"I got more restless. I've got to be doing, Seth, not sitting watching others. Mary understands. Hell almighty, she'd much rather me be away than home and underfoot anyhow, she's told me so. So we're both content. Sometimes I think we got us the perfect marriage."

8

★ **Faint** rays of sunlight angled down through the twin bull's-eyes of thick greenish glass at the top of the Dutch-style front door. The house was two stories and a half in front, with a peaked roof that sloped down nearly to the ground in the back over an ell covering the kitchen, added in the shape of a lintel. The three sat in round-back chairs in the fire-room at a fine walnut table that Ethan himself had designed. The room had a puncheon floor.

"So the children have all gone to Woodbury," he said. "Pity . . . "

"For the summer. My father and mother practically beseeched me to send them."

"But you're left alone."

"Praise God from whom all blessings flow."

Mary Allen sat broomstick-straight in her chair, her prominent chin thrust defiantly outward, her slightly large, somewhat raptorial nose aimed at her husband, her deep-set dark eyes, her most attractive feature, fixed on him, her graying hair pulled back severely in a bun.

They had finished a delicious pudding of Indian meal, molasses, and butter, and she had just finished setting out veal and bacon, a neck of mutton, and vegetables. Upon entering the house, Warner had noticed she shook Ethan's hand in greeting and almost, if not quite, surrendered a smile.

"How are your father and mother?" Ethan asked.

"Daddy's rheumatism bothers him. Mother's just got over the ague. Otherwise, both are fine. My brother Claude died last week."

"Oh. Sorry to hear it. And how have you been, my dear?"

"Healthy as a horse."

"Mary enjoys great good health."

"Praise God from whom all blessings flow. So you're on your way to Phil . . . "

"Philadelphia."

"And where might that be? Carrots, please."

"In Pennsylvania. About ninety miles south of New York City."

"What for?"

"To talk to the Continental Congress. My dear, war is about to begin. A revolution against the Crown."

"I haven't heard."

"Have you spoken to anyone in town recently?"

"I rarely go to town except to church. Why on earth do you want to start a war?"

"Nobody wants to," said Ethan. "It's simply inevitable."

"Why?"

"You know about the Boston Tea Party a year ago this past December. And what is being called the Intolerable Acts. To begin with, the British closed Boston Harbor until the colonists pay for the tea they dumped."

"And well they should."

"Bostonians don't agree. It's all quite complicated."

"Too complicated for me to understand."

"It's fairly boring," said Warner helpfully. "The short of it is the colonies have been pushed to the wall and rebellion is unavoidable."

"Well, I hope they don't shoot their guns around Bennington. Snap beans, please. What is this about you speaking to the Congress, Mr. Allen?"

"I've been summoned."

"It has to do with the war?"

"I intend to propose a plan for invading Canada."

Her jaw dropped, her dark eyes started, and she set down the beans. "Whatever for?"

"To prevent Canada from invading us," said Warner.

"Why, pray tell, would they want to do such a thing? It sounds to me, Mr. Allen, as if you're deliberately stirring up trouble."

"That, my dear, is my fondest hope."

She looked properly shocked. "I don't think I like this conversation. You go off and make your war. Try not to be killed. Only don't tell me anything else."

"How is your father's mill doing, my dear?"

"Well. He's working as hard as ever." She narrowed her eyes. "As ye sow so shall ye reap. I've tarts and gooseberry fools for dessert."

"I'm full," said Warner, wiping his mouth with his napkin. "Every bite was delicious. May I postpone a tart till bedtime?"

"As you wish, Mr. Warner, I'll keep them on the stove. Mr. Allen?"

He patted his lean stomach. "I'm full." He stretched and yawned. "Is there any more ale?"

"Only a nearly full hogshead."

He started up from the table. She snatched up his mug. "I'll draw it."

"I can."

"Sit, Mr. Allen, you're a guest."

"How are Loraine and the other children?"

"Healthy, happy. The boys ask about you."

"I know. I should get home more often."

"He's been home nine times in the past nine years," she said to Warner. "Once for each year. Invade Canada. It sounds as woolly-headed as your idea to attack Fort Ticonderoga."

"We captured it, my dear. And Crown Point."

"That's nice."

Ethan and Warner enjoyed a blueberry tart before retiring. Ethan put on his nightshirt and crawled into bed. Mary came upstairs, setting the candle on the nightstand and going into the next room to make her toilet, disrobe, and put on her nightgown. She got into bed beside him.

"Candle."

He blew it out, stretched, and relaxed.

"Is Mr. Warner going all the way to Philadelphia with you?"

"Yes."

"And to invade Canada?"

"Yes."

"When will the war start?"

"One could say it's started already."

"Not around here."

He told her about the clashes at Lexington and Concord. "You know that for the past two years things have been . . . touchy between us and the Mother Country. Ever since the Bostonians dumped the tea in the harbor."

"I seem to recall your telling me about that. Dressed up as Mohawks, weren't they? But what does a squabble in Boston have to do with Bennington? Or anyplace else for that matter?"

"It was a good deal more than a squabble, my dear. Now the pot's boiled over."

"You mean you helped tip it over."

"I'm proud to say."

He raised himself on his elbow, bringing his face close to hers. She set a hand against his chest.

"Please don't press your lips to mine, I have a canker sore."

"My manhood is getting hard, Mary."

He took hold of her hand to guide it to his penis. She pulled gently free.

"Please, Mr. Allen, I'd rather not."

"Not what?"

"I don't mean *that,* I mean touch your unmentionable. It's really not necessary."

"Then may I?"

"If you've a mind."

He mounted her, spreading her legs and placing the head of his member against her vulva. He could barely make out her features in the swath of moonlight that found the whitewashed wall above the headboard. She looked asleep.

"Are you awake, my dear?"

"About to fall asleep. You'd best begin if you're so inclined."

He entered her slowly and began pumping. She lay like a stone, her breathing barely audible. Faster and faster he drove. He was about to ejaculate when she began snoring.

9

JUNE 1775

★ **Filled** with a substantial breakfast of eggs, bacon, oatmeal, and johnny-cake, Ethan turned to writing letters to friends in Canada to alert them to the impending invasion and ask that they spread the word among people in sympathy with American independence. Warner was lukewarm toward a letter campaign.

"To begin with, we don't even know if Congress will authorize an invasion."

"Of course they will, Seth. They know better than most that the time is past for shilly-shallying. The die is cast. We have to go on the offensive."

"I bet you'll still have to talk them into it."

"And I shall. But look at it this way, they'd hardly invite us to appear before them if they weren't seriously considering invading. Nobody wrote me rejecting the idea."

Warner indicated the stationery spread about the table. "What makes you think some of those won't be intercepted by the British?"*

"I'm protecting against that. They'll be hand-carried by sympathizers. We'll ride into Bennington and I'll give them to Bailey Daulton and a couple other friends. They'll see that they get into the hands of travelers or scouts heading north and reach their proper destinations. It won't exactly smooth the way for us but it will alert those who favor invasion as to what we're up to."

"Not to mention the authorities. If even one falls into British hands, there goes the element of surprise."

"These letters say nothing about specifics: where we'll strike, when, how many men . . . "

"But it seems to me the longer we can delay tipping our hand . . . "

"My friend, you worry needlessly."

Mary came in with coffee, pouring it into china mugs, adding cream and white sugar.

"I left some money for you on the bureau, my dear," said Ethan. "And, hopefully, we'll be stopping by on our way back and I can give you more."

"I won't need it. I spend very little. I pride myself on my frugality."

"She is the most frugal wife in all the Grants, Seth. Mary, when this campaign is over I'll come home to stay for a long time, I promise."

---

* Two of Ethan's letters to Canadians were intercepted.

"Praise God from whom all blessings flow."

"Seriously."

"Drink your coffee while it's hot."

"If all goes as I expect we'll be back in three or four weeks to raise a regiment in town."

"Mmmmm."

"Your enthusiasm is most encouraging."

"*I* should be enthusiastic? I say let well enough alone. Rebellion and sedition are words as sour in my mouth as grapes from dead vines. For the life of me I can't fathom why you're determined to be the fly that bites the rump that sets the whole herd stampeding."

"Someone has to wake people up." He signed the last letter with a flourish, folded it neatly, and affixed the wax seal, closing it. "All done, my dear. We'll be on our way."

"I packed what's left of the mutton and some fools. Lord knows what you'll find to eat between here and Pennsylvania."

Ethan placed the letters in his pouch. "We're off to town then back on the road." He extended his hand. "Good-bye, my dear. Wish us luck."

"I wish you don't get a musket ball in the back or your horse doesn't throw you into a thorn bush." She shook each of their hands in turn, a single pump. "Good-bye, Mr. Warner, I'd say come again but you probably never will."

They rode off. Ethan turned once in time to catch Mary retreating from the window.

"I appreciate your indulgence, Seth. I really had to stop and see her. And it was nice getting home."

The second Continental Congress convened in the State House. Philadelphia was an odd choice of sites in which to sow the seeds of revolution. More Tories lived there than in all the colonies combined, including New York. The Quakers, Pennsylvania's dominant religious denomination, were much more interested in curbing radicalism in the colony than in opposing British tyranny.

Congress itself gave every indication of conservative leanings, its membership comprised as it was of America's wealthiest men. In John Adams's opinion the delegates were one
third Tory, one third Whig, and the remainder a collection of
all sorts of political or religious affiliations. With so many
Loyalists in the area, espionage was carried on openly. Despite
Congress's efforts to preserve secrecy, the British government
was apprised of all its proceedings.

The major obstacle to voting for independence was the minority of conservative delegates. At virtually every turn they
sought to block the liberal initiatives of Samuel Adams and his
fellow radicals, most of whom represented the New England
colonies.

But it was the Mother Country that ignited the flame that
was to blaze into independence, beginning with the Stamp Act
ten years before.

On June 16, George Washington of Virginia accepted Congress's appointment as commander in chief of the American
army. The wheels were beginning to turn even before Ethan
and Warner arrived in Philadelphia. Congress had launched
its own letter campaign to unite Canada with the continental
union.

Ethan and Warner dismounted, tied their horses, and surveyed the State House. Both took deep breaths before starting up the steps. Inside, John Hancock of Massachusetts sat
at a desk on a raised platform presiding over the assembly. At
a similar desk in front of him on a lower platform sat Benjamin
Franklin. To their left, three enormous windows admitted
spring air while overhead hung a magnificient girandole chandelier. Ethan had never seen so many perukes and so much
silk under one ceiling. His expression solemn, his tone appropriate to the gravity of the occasion, he introduced Seth
Warner and himself to President Hancock. Discussion of the
invasion of Canada began. Robert Morris of Pennsylvania set
the tone of the meeting, warning that once established in

Canada in force, a British army would "raise a nest of hornets on our backs that will sting us to the quick." Richard Henry Lee of Virginia pointed out that Canada and New York were "openings through which America may receive the worst wounds."

John Hancock nearly upset a wastebasket filled to overflowing with crumpled papers as he rose and spoke. "Colonel Allen, we've recently received a letter from Colonel Benedict Arnold enthusiastically endorsing an invasion of Canada. And he sent Lieutenant Eleazar Oswald with his plan of attack." Ethan struggled to keep resentment from altering his expression. "Now, sir, if my fellow delegates will quiet down we would like to hear your views on the subject."

"Mr. President, I'm as fully in favor of invasion as the colonel. My chief worry is that if we don't invade Canada, Canada will surely invade us, as Mr. Morris and Mr. Lee have so ably put it. I see the conquest of Canada as of vital importance because it will surely influence Parliament to throw out the tyrants presently ruling the country and open the way for reasonable men, men tolerant and understanding, to replace them.

"Gentlemen, is there a man in this assembly who does not recognize that war is inevitable? And the only way to independence is to slowly strip the Mother Country of her authority?"

"Too bold! Too bold!" exclaimed Joseph Galloway.

Others agreed.

"Boldness is a precious weapon," responded Ethan. "We cannot tiptoe into war. Not after Lexington and Concord."

The meeting lasted less than half an hour. Ethan and Warner came away with hearts high, despite the fact that no decision had been reached in respect to the invasion. They were requested to return the next day after a vote was taken. Outside, they paused to discuss matters.

"The vote'll be close," said Warner.

"Common sense will prevail, Seth. They'll vote to invade. Did you see Nathaniel Folsom's and John Sullivan's* eyes light up when I promised to raise a fresh regiment of Green Mountain Boys?"

"I sincerely hope that's a promise you'll be able to keep."

"Of course!" Ethan slapped him on the back. "If you're not the black bird of pessimism flying in the window. Cheer up, they'll vote to invade. We'll raise the troops. Jonathan Trumbull in Connecticut will send us six regiments. And six months from now we'll drop Canada into Ben Franklin's lap! I'm thirsty as a horse, let's go find a drink."

A decision was not reached the next day nor the day after. Meanwhile an official summary of the Patriots' victory at Bunker Hill on June 17 arrived in Philadelphia (June 23), the day after Ethan's and Warner's arrival. Ethan saw it as an "enormously" encouraging sign. The delegates wrangled for four days, setting Seth Warner pacing in his rented room.

After considerable squabbling, not a little name-calling, and more than a few delegates' courage called into question, Congress gave its approval to an invasion by the narrow margin of six colonies to five. Overcome with relief, Warner congratulated Ethan.

"If you hadn't shown up here when you did they'd never have done it."

"Do you know, you're right?"

The delegates attached two stipulations to the effort that had to be met. General Philip Schuyler, commander-designate of the Northern Department, had to agree that an invasion was practicable.

And it would have to be satisfactorily ascertained that it would not be "disagreeable to the Canadians."

Upon hearing the latter, Ethan laughed so loudly Warner worried that he might burst a blood vessel.

---

* *Delegates representing the New Hampshire Grants (part of which subsequently became Vermont).*

10

★ **Ethan** and Warner headed out of Philadelphia for New York City. Ethan carried a copy of the congressional resolution and a letter from John Hancock recommending him to the New York Provincial Assembly. Hancock was unaware that both Ethan and Warner had for years been officially listed by the Yorkers as felons with rewards on their heads.

But they had been ordered to make contact with General Philip Schuyler, and that could only be done through the Provincial Assembly. Crossing the Delaware River at Trenton, they got onto the Post Road through southern New Jersey heading northeast.

"We could walk into the assembly and in ten seconds be clapped in irons," muttered Warner.

"That could happen," agreed Ethan, drawing a shocked reaction from his companion. "Irons on, irons off when we show these papers and explain our mission."

A ball of starlings swirled over a bountiful chestnut tree off to their left. The day was sunny and very dry, and every step by their horses sent up dust.

"They need us," Ethan went on. "Our leadership, the Green Mountain Boys. All this back-stabbing, this sniping and provincialism now has to take a back bench to the common cause."

"Independence."

"It's real, it's upon us. They're not stupid, they see it as well as the delegates."

"*Most* of the delegates."

"I'll tell you something else, my friend. The old New York regime is out. All except our old friend Governor Tryon. That old fraud Cadwallader Colden is gone and the leftovers from the old guard will forgive and forget, you watch."

"I do wish I had your overwhelming confidence."

"So do I, Seth, so do I." With this, Ethan slapped him so hard on the back, Seth nearly tumbled from his saddle.

Arriving in New York, they got directions to the building where the Provincial Assembly met. Half an hour later, after introducing themselves, they sat in a gloomy, windowless anteroom while the delegates met in private to decide whether to speak with them or arrest them for past offenses against the province.

They were to be happily surprised. Seth Warner confessed to being flabbergasted when they were summoned inside. Ethan stated their mission and showed the copy of the congressional resolution and John Hancock's personal endorsement and recommendation that he be authorized to activate a regiment of Green Mountain Boys. Within twenty minutes, to Warner's astonishment, the assembly voted to sponsor a regiment of "not more than seven companies." Ethan and his men would receive back pay for capturing Fort Ticonderoga. The two Green Mountain Boys were wished Godspeed and ushered out.

The strength of the regiments of the army of the "United Colonies of America," as the assembly members called the Continental Army, had been determined only days before. Each company would comprise seventy-six privates, with officers, noncommissioned officers, fife, and drum. Officers' pay ranged from $50 a month for a colonel to $13.50 for an ensign. Privates would receive about $6.70 monthly, although out of this amount, uniforms that were furnished them had to be paid for at a rate of $1.70 per month.

Troops were to be armed with firelocks with eighteen-inch bayonets. Daily rations included one pound of beef or fish or twelve ounces of pork. They were also given one pound of bread or flour daily, a pint of milk, and a quart of spruce beer or cider. In addition, they were allotted beans, peas, or other vegetables, Indian meal or rice, and candles and soap.

On their way back to Bennington, Ethan and Warner stopped to visit Mary, still by herself while the couple's five children continued their summer visit with their grandparents in Woodbury, Connecticut. Mary stood in the doorway as Ethan and Warner dismounted.

"Kindly don't track your dust in here. I just finished sweeping."

With heather besom in hand she came out, ordered both to stand where they were, and proceeded to sweep them down.

"Was your Philadelphia a wild goose chase?" she asked, gesturing them to chairs and fixing Ethan with her well-practiced skeptical look.

"Far from it, my dear. It turned out all we could have wished for." He tapped the papers in his pocket. "I've been authorized to raise a full regiment."

"Do you think you'll raise any?"

"All we'll need in two days. I'll set up a recruiting table in Stephen Fay's Tavern. Once word gets around, the line'll be out the door and around the building. Most of the boys are home from Ticonderoga by now; they'll sign up again in droves. Is there any ale, my dear? We're both desperately thirsty."

She drew two tankards. "Will you be staying overnight again?" she said with little enthusiasm for the possibility.

"I did plan to. As I said, it may take two days to raise a regiment."

"It may take two months."

"Hardly. The Continental Congress has thrown down the gauntlet. They had to, after what happened at Bunker Hill."

" 'Bunker Hill'?"

"It's in Boston, my dear. The British were roundly defeated. Over a thousand men and officers shot."

"And the Americans?"

"Patriots, Patriots. Fewer than a hundred fifty killed."

"Appalling business . . . "

"The War for Independence is underway!"

"Are you still going on to Canada or is all that thrown out with the wash water?"

"Of course we're going. Why do you think I'm forming my regiment?"

"So you'll be gone all winter."

"We'll be home before Christmas."

"I doubt that."

Ethan's estimate of the time it would take to raise a new regiment missed the mark by twelve days. Like Seth Warner, he was now being paid by New York, and he had already drawn a month's advance, half of which he gave to Mary.

Their last night together was spent discussing Canada. Ethan talked about it and Mary politely pretended to listen. He noticed her yawning repeatedly as they lay in bed in darkness.

"This being your last night here for Lord knows how long, I expect you're thinking about your unmentionable."

"I wasn't, my dear. But I confess I'm ready when you are."

"I'm as ready as I'll ever be."

"Do you . . . ?"

"Do I what?"

There was no moon; neither could see the other's face. Ethan could tell by her tone that she was on the verge of falling asleep.

"Do you . . . enjoy it?" he went on.

"Enjoy what?"

"You know. Copulation."

"That, Mr. Allen, is a word unfit for polite company and a question unworthy of a response."

"Yes."

"Are you quite ready?"

"Yes."

"Then I'm ready."

He mounted her and began copulating. Unlike the night before and the night before that, as tired as she was she did not fall asleep.

"I'm finished, my dear."

"I gathered as much. Hand me the cloth."

He lay back eyeing the darkened rafters. "I'll miss you, Mary. Mary?"

She was asleep.

11

★ **Late** in the third week of July, Ethan and Warner set out for Fort Ticonderoga, where Major General Philip Schuyler had taken over command. They left behind more than five hundred recruits. All that remained to complete the new regiment of Green Mountain Boys was the election of its officers. Ethan and Warner had effectively paved the way, spreading the word in and around Bennington and getting signatures of intent. It had taken two weeks to enlist the required number of men and would have taken much longer had the two not been able to assure the men that their pay would be guaranteed by New York.

In all their years together, Seth Warner had never seen Ethan's enthusiasm higher, not even on the eve of the attack on Fort Ticonderoga. Heading up the Castleton road, they came within sight of Zadock Remington's Tavern. Their thirsts up, they decided to stop for a drink. Zadock was in the side yard at the chopping block decapitating a chicken. He lopped its head off; it continued to squirm in his grasp. He looked up.

"Colonel Allen! Colonel Warner! Welcome, welcome! On

your way to the fort are you? Got some old friends of yours inside—Captain Baker and a couple of your boys. In you go, surprise 'em . . . "

Remember Baker shot unsteadily to his feet, nearly upsetting his tankard. "Cousin Ethan! Cousin Seth! I'll be double-damned." He bear-hugged each of them in turn. His breath stung Ethan's eyes.

With him were Jacob Wall and Elisha Cummings, two of the original Bennington Mobb. The three were among the last of the Green Mountain Boys to leave the fort.

"I take it his nibs never came back," said Warner.

"Colonel 'Regulations' Arnold?" Baker laughed. "Naw. He's having too much fun sailing Major Skene's sloop around the lake."

"Having too much fun writing letters to the Continental Congress," said Ethan.

Zadock served ale all around. Two locals sat with their heads together at a corner table. Zadock's hound lay sleeping before the dead fire. Zadock brought in the dripping chicken and sat at a nearby table plucking it, his apron spattered with blood. The room boxed a mingling of animal and vegetable stenches. Ethan studied his tankard. Had it been washed out before being refilled? He thought about his last tankard of ale, served him by Mary, and pictured her sitting at the table sipping tea and looking at the pictures in her Bible. There were eight and she could sit by the hour staring at them. Was she praying for his safe return? Was she even thinking about him? He sighed, eliciting a questioning glance from Warner.

Remember Baker was rattling on. "General Philip Schuyler of Sar-a-to-gee, New Yawk, showed up day before yesterday."

"We know," said Warner. "He's why we came back." He explained their mission.

"So you see," said Ethan, "there's no point in you boys going home. We're all going to Canada for the summer."

"Canada?" asked Jacob Wall, a young giant and Bennington's best blacksmith. The word came out with disappointment in his tone and doubt in his eyes. He had been one of the first to sign up for the Ticonderoga expedition. His sole regret since was that he missed his hammer and anvil. He claimed his right arm was getting soft from inactivity.

"Canada," echoed Ethan. "Fifteen hundred men with backbones and bellies for the fight. Five hundred will be Green Mountain Boys. The heroes of Ticonderoga among them, including Jacob Wall, Elisha Cummings, and Remember Baker."

"Count me in," said Remember, slapping the table so loudly the two corner patrons looked up. "It's either that or go home to my wife."

Elisha Cummings shook his head. "Maw expects me home. I'm already six weeks late for the planting."

He was bigger and broader than Jacob, but far gentler. Other men chewed sprigs of grass, he chewed daisies—but no one ever teased him about it or about his deep devotion to his mother. There was a rumor around Bennington that Elisha had once come back from town to find his father beating his mother. At the time Cummings was only twelve. Two days later his father disappeared and was never seen again. A second rumor claimed he was still somewhere on the farm, possibly under the vegetable quarter-acre.

"So it's back to Bennington for you," Ethan said to him, tilting his head, appraising him from under his hooded lids. "Back to whittling and fishing and swapping stories about Ticonderoga and the glory days, brief as they were."

"Maw would be terribly disappointed."

Jacob sneered. "That you come home or that you don't?"

"You two listen," said Ethan. "Canada will make Ticonderoga look like a trip to the well. We're going up there to bring a hundred thousand frogs over to our side. What will that mean, cousin?"

Baker scratched his stubble. "It'll sure keep the redcoat bastards' hands full, keep 'em from invading the lake region and the Hudson Valley."

"Are you listening, boys?" Ethan lowered his head and his

voice. "The thing is, timing is critical. We can't invade six months from now, or even three. We can't give them time to build up their strength. Right now, they're weak as kits, too few and too widely scattered to mount a defense. Montreal is sitting there like the apple in the pig's mouth. But if we hold off . . . "

"Maw's expecting me," said Elisha. "Honest."

"Then you'd best get home. Drink up. You've done your bit. You go home and plow and plant and hold your mother's yarn for her and when we get back we'll tell you all about how we chased Jack Bull out of Canada."

Elisha licked his lips. Longing was creeping into his big, innocent eyes. Ethan could see Elisha's brain working, surrounding and picking at the invitation. Temptation was closing in on desire, and a decision was imminent. Ethan attacked, painting gaudy pictures of heroic exploits, guaranteed pay, plunder, and the incomparably sweet taste of victory over tyranny, even sweeter than what they had tasted at Ticonderoga. Baker nodded and nodded and nodded while Seth sat smiling cryptically, seemingly reluctant to inject his views.

"There's a job to be done, boys, and destiny and the Continental Congress have picked us to do it. Who else would they pick but the heroes of Ticonderoga? Even our old enemies, the Yorkers, are clamoring for us. They're willing to pay cash money to get us, equip us, and Godspeed us on our way. And since our glorious victory here, just about every man between sixteen and sixty back in Bennington who turned down the chance to join us before is flocking to our banner.

"But, Elisha, you go home. Please. You've earned the right to rest on your laurels. There's no shame attached to quit . . . dropping out."

"Look at his eyes," muttered Baker. "He's no more going home than Zadock's chicken there is going back to the henhouse."

"I have to think about it some," muttered Elisha.

"Careful you don't break anything," said Jacob.

"You're done thinking!" Baker laughed and clapped Elisha on the back. "You're with us. You, too, Jacob. Let's drink on it!"

Jacob smiled grimly and shook his head. "Oh, my Abby is going to be mad as a foaming hound. She's already picking the flowers for the wedding. I'll have to write her. What'll I say? I'll be home after the war? Keep ironing your wedding dress and keep picking the flowers?"

"When are the new recruits coming up?" Baker asked.

"As soon as the old bones back home pick the officers," said Ethan.

"All your old friends and admirers," said Jacob rolling his eyes at Ethan.

Baker laughed. Ethan snickered. He had next to no old friends among the patriarchs in Bennington or the west-side towns. Over the previous six years, applying himself to the task and making no effort to hide his true sentiments toward them, Ethan had managed to alienate all but about two selectmen. But they recognized his leadership abilities and applauded his taking of Ticonderoga. He had more on his mind than that fussy and predictable lot.

12

July 1775

★ **Major** General Philip Schuyler was one of the wealthiest landed proprietors in New York. He was forty-three, well-built, muscular, and commanding in appearance. He bore a faint resemblance to General Washington, although his nose was more prominent and his face unnaturally florid. His dark eyes were piercing, capable of riveting his listener, but this was offset by his high voice which, when he got excited, became shrill.

He was well-educated and intelligent, but as a military man he lacked the commander in chief's decisiveness in planning and execution. He had attained the rank of captain in the French and Indian War, but his experience in action had been limited and showed itself under fire. He had neither the stamina nor the ruggedness needed to cope with the harshness and difficulties of a wilderness campaign. Frustration came easily to him and he gave in to occasional outbursts of exasperation. He was a Patriot on a par with Ethan, unlike most of his class, wholly devoted to the cause of independence.

Brigadier General Richard Montgomery was his second in command. Montgomery had been promoted to captain in the British army at the age of twenty-six. In 1772 he resigned his commission to emigrate to America. Two years later he was commissioned a brigadier in the Continental Army. Unlike his superior, he was a complete soldier, cool under fire, conscientious toward his duties, decisive and forceful in command.

Both men returned Ethan's and Warner's salutes and were invited to sit. Schuyler had appropriated Captain Delaplace's office, disposing of the commandant's shabby furniture, replacing it with new chairs and an escritoire he sat behind. The fort itself looked little changed from when Ethan and Warner left it weeks earlier, except that it had been cleaned up and the serviceable ordnance had been removed along with the stores of powder and ball, leaving sufficient artillery to defend the fort should the British attempt to retake it.

Ethan was invited to lay out his plan for the invasion of Canada, as a courtesy. Neither general committed himself to approval, which Ethan took as a matter of course. Any decision on how to carry out the invasion at this point would have been premature. Schuyler's orderly came in with a tray bearing a decanter of sherry. The four men sipped and Schuyler offered cigars all around.

Generals and colonels were in sharp contrast, Schuyler and Montgomery resplendent in their bright blue jackets with buff trim, buff breeches, and white waistcoats. Like their fel-

low Green Mountain Boys, Ethan and Warner disdained uniforms in favor of civilian attire, even, occasionally, buckskins
with a sprig of evergreen worn in the cap providing all the insignia they needed.

Despite their social superiority, neither Yorker looked down
his patrician nose at the Bennington backwoodsmen. Pleasant banter gradually became serious conversation about
Canada. Schuyler held court.

"I've sent Major John Brown north to obtain information
about the post at St. Johns, the magazines in Montreal, and
to ascertain the sentiments of the Indians and Canadians toward a possible invasion."

"Good man," said Ethan. "Good choice."

"He left here last Monday with four companions, three
soldiers, and a Canadian. Since you and your men captured
this fort their journey cannot be made openly; Canada must
now be considered enemy territory. They should be back the
middle of next month."

Ethan frowned. "Are you saying, sir, that invasion will have
to be postponed until John gets back?"

"Yes."

"That's nearly a month," said Warner.

"Perhaps less."

"We can guess what conclusions they'll bring back," said
Ethan.

"Guess?" Montgomery fixed his gaze on Ethan question-
ingly.

"Easily. The French won't put up any resistance. The
Caughnawagas will be neutral, except that the British may succeed in persuading some to scout for them. That'll be a test
of how much influence the Jesuits still have over the tribes.
St. Johns will be brought up to full strength if it hasn't already
been.

"What we're mainly concerned with," said Schuyler, "is
enemy strength."

Ethan grunted. "They've no more than a few hundred men, scattered all over hell and beyond."

"How do you know that?" asked Montgomery.

"I questioned Captain Delaplace before he was marched out of here."

"How can you be sure he was telling the truth?" Schuyler asked.

Ethan smiled. "I can generally tell when someone is lying to me. The point is, gentlemen, if we wait until John gets back we'll just be frittering away valuable time. The British know we're planning to invade."

"How on earth could they?" Montgomery asked.

"The proceedings of the Congress in Philadelphia are an open secret. And you can bet your saber *somebody* John buttonholes up there will blab to the authorities."

"Good point," said Schuyler. "Your concern as to delay is duly noted, Colonel, but I'm afraid we can't do much to speed things up. The quartermaster has us at a disadvantage. We've no tents, no carriages for fieldpieces, no boats. Oh, everything's coming, we've been assured. Your Green Mountain Boys aren't here yet."

"They're on the way," said Warner. "Five hundred strong."

"We're awaiting reinforcements ourselves," said Montgomery.

"And when will they be here?"

Schuyler spread his hands helplessly. "They're also on the way, I've been led to believe."

Ethan glanced at Warner. "Gentlemen, I'll be brief and to the point. As I see it, any invasion of Canada must leave here no later than the first of August."

"That's only five days from now," said Montgomery.

"Impossible," said Schuyler. "Not that I personally wouldn't dearly desire to meet that date. It would unquestionably be to our advantage . . . "

"The Green Mountain Regiment will be here, outfitted and ready to march," Ethan went on. "Your men should be close behind. If necessary we could march out and your troops can catch up with us."

"Impossible," Schuyler repeated. "We can't rush things. We've just begun building boats to take us up the Richelieu River, to sail and portage our way to the St. Lawrence."

"The Richelieu is not in my plan," said Ethan.

"All the same, you'll agree that we'll need boats to get down Lake Champlain."

"Gentlemen, gentlemen," said Warner. "Isn't all this really no more than cigar talk? The troops aren't here, the boats aren't built, Major Brown has yet to return. Shouldn't we sleep on it until things begin coming together?"

"Capital suggestion," said Schuyler, looking straight at Ethan with an expression that asked his indulgence. The general smiled benignly. "With your permission, Colonel, my orderly will show you to your quarters. I trust you'll find them comfortable and that you won't mind sharing a room."

Ethan understood. Schuyler was politely appealing for patience. Clearly, impatience, in the form of threat and bluster, would do nothing, other than to alientate both Yorkers. That he could not do; they were being fair and candid. He would just have to wait. Seth appeared agreeable to doing so. Wasn't he always? As true to form as a dependable old clock.

Schuyler's orderly led them to Lieutenant Jocelyn Feltham's room, across the way from Captain Delaplace's, which was now, according to the orderly, occupied by General Schuyler. That night Ethan wrote a letter to his friend, Governor Jonathan Trumbull of Connecticut. It served to relieve his mounting impatience. Nevertheless, he was still tempted to greet the Green Mountain Boys at the gate when they arrived, turn them around, march them out and north to Montreal. The regiment would include upwards of two hundred of the force that had captured the fort. He was confident that their spirit would invest the greenhorns among them with the courage and daring to easily take Montreal. All that kept him from leaving as soon as they arrived, he told Trumbull, was

Congress's trust in him to adhere to his original instructions, the generosity and confidence shown him by the New York Assembly, and Schuyler's logistical problems.

At 4 a.m., unable to sleep, he woke Warner who, as he yawned and knuckled his eyes, good-naturedly agreed to discuss the situation. Ethan read him his letter to Trumbull.

Warner shook his head. "If all you want is to let off steam that certainly does it."

"I'm merely telling a friend and confidant what's going on before his delegates get back from Philadelphia."

They heard the watch sound the hour. It was as mournful as the hooting of an owl. It had started to rain, bringing back memories of the night of the raid. As the minutes slogged by Ethan began to consider the situation more realistically. It was one thing to attack a poorly defended, broken-down fort; it was another to journey through hundreds of miles of wilderness to engage a forewarned, well-equipped, and battle-hardened enemy. Numbers and equipment were needed, as were careful planning, money, and supplies, all of which took the time Schuyler insisted they take.

Warner was of the same mind. "We'll just have to wait till preparations are completed, Ethan. And that's out of our hands. The Yorkers and the general hold the reins. All we are are the workhorses in the shafts."

Ethan groaned. "Could you possibly find a more demeaning comparison?"

Seth laughed and slapped his knee, "Patience. It'll all work out splendidly."

"I'm sure it will. The question is *when*. We're sitting here squandering precious time. Just you watch, we won't get out of here until the first of September."

"If then . . . "

Again Warner laughed. Ethan swung playfully, Warner ducked the blow. They talked a few more minutes then went back to bed. Warner went right to sleep. Ethan didn't try. Out the window he watched the rain let up and stop altogether.

The stars emerged, then faded, and the sun came up over the distant Green Mountains. All the while, Ethan wondered when the boys would arrive to join Remember Baker, Jacob Wall, and Elisha Cummings.

13

★ **Ethan** fretted and groused to himself but diligently kept a smile on his face for Seth Warner and the two Yorker generals. Warner was right, it would all work out, and in the end he would lead his regiment of loyal Green Mountain Boys against Montreal. Again and again he envisioned himself sitting atop a powerful stallion, entering the city in triumph at the head of his troops. Again and again he examined the enemy's weaknesses. Canada's inhabitants fell into four distinct classifications. The basic population was made up of the descendants of the original settlers: French, Catholic, mainly tenant-farmers, roughly one hundred thousand of them spread along the rivers. The second group, the wealthy landowners, held the tenants' farms in a kind of feudal tenure. The wealthy were the seigneurs and aristocrats. Until the English victory and conquest they had been in firm control of the government. Now most of them, virtually all the military officers, had returned to France.

British civilians in Canada numbered no more than two thousand, and many of them were immigrants from the American colonies. The majority of these were in the fur trade in Montreal. They got along with practically nobody, not even their own military.

The fourth class was the Catholic priests, who had been all but stripped of their former power by the British, reduced to subsisting on the charity of the faithful, asking only that their presence and their work among the habitants be tolerated.

However, the people continued to hold them in high esteem and heeded their advice. The priests respected and obeyed the British minority, which, as General Schuyler saw it, did not bode well for any attempt to overthrow Crown rule.

As for Montreal itself, it was built along the riverfront and swept back over a series of terraces to Mount Royal. It rose nearly eight hundred feet above the St. Lawrence. Storming the city would take as much subterfuge as strength of arms. To Ethan, attacking Montreal's rear made the most sense. It had been fortified since its founding, originally against hostile Iroquois.

Ethan's knowledge of his objective was sketchy. Montgomery's knowledge, derived from the reports of scouts and spies, was, if not voluminous, sufficient in specifics to plan an attack. When Major Brown and his party returned, intelligence would improve.

As one idle day followed another, Ethan became increasingly suspicious that Schuyler and Montgomery intended to exercise full control over the campaign, leaving little for him and Warner to do but follow orders. Neither Yorker behaved condescendingly toward either New Englander; both were the soul of graciousness and civility, but it became clear that Ethan's value was his regiment and in the end he would have little to say as to strategy or in command.

He didn't raise the issue with either man, electing to bide his time until the expedition set out. Meanwhile everyone continued to await Brown's return.

A letter arrived. After leaving the fort with his four companions, eluding possible capture all the way north, Brown's men marched for three harrowing days through a wide-ranging swamp. They stayed overnight in one house only to awaken to discover themselves surrounded by a large party of the enemy. They fled out a back window. In all, they remained in Canada fourteen days, gathering information while protected by friendly inhabitants. They were now on their way back.

They arrived at the fort on Monday, August 14. Dirty and disheveled but with his spirits high, Brown was eager to divulge what they'd learned. Ethan held John Brown in the highest regard. He envied his Yale education and the fact that before enlisting in the Patriots' cause he had been a successful lawyer, having held the office of the king's attorney in New York Province. Bold and fearless, he hungered for action, which prompted him to leave his practice—removed to Pittsfield, Massachusetts—to join the fight for independence. During the previous February, the Massachusetts Provincial Congress had sent John Brown on a mission to Canada. The journey was made through deep snows, in intense cold. He had been frozen in for two days on the broken ice of Lake Champlain. It took him and his companion two arduous weeks to make it to Montreal where he spoke with a number of people, coming away persuaded that the Canadians would not join the colonists. However, he did succeed in establishing communication with a few inhabitants.

This time he returned with the same impression as on his first visit. He sat with Schuyler and Montgomery, Ethan and Warner in Schuyler's office sipping a reasonably good brandy, his handsome face still showing scratches from the long trek through the woods, dirt sticking to his ragged clothing.

"The French will not join us, but they won't fight us."

"You're sure?" Schuyler asked.

"I must have discussed it with forty different people from the border to the St. Lawrence. That was their opinion almost without exception."

"What about the Caughnawagas?" Ethan asked. "Will they scout for the British?"

"Nothing's changed there. No doubt some will, though they profess to neutrality."

"What of St. John's?" Montgomery asked.

"Sir Guy Carleton is fortifying it, which we expected. It's supported by the *Royal Savage,* with sixteen guns."

"What about troop strength?"

Brown yawned and swiped a grimy fist across his mouth. "We have all sorts of figures." He brought a piece of wrinkled paper out of his pocket to refer to. "The consensus is there are seven hundred British troops in all of Canada. Three hundred in St. John's, only fifty in Quebec, and the rest in Montreal, Chambly, and scattered around. Now I have a question. Where are our men? Where are the Green Mountain Boys?"

"Coming," murmured Ethan.

"When our own reinforcements come we'll have nearly two thousand men," said Schuyler.

Brown shook his head grimly. "I'd rather have half that right now. Now's the time we should be heading up there. We can take them easily. A month from now it'll be harder. Certainly bloodier."

"We can't leave here at least till the end of the month," said Montgomery.

Ethan studied his eyes. His patience was running out too. Only Schuyler seemed to be treating the delay with indifference. Discussion continued for hours, until Brown reached the verge of collapse. Schuyler took pity on him and sent him to wash up and sleep. The major had added little to his information. One troublesome fact did emerge: Schuyler offhandedly admitted that in the whole New York Department, no more than twenty-five hundred men were fit for duty, quickly adding that Congress did expect him to add the Green Mountain regiment.

On August 17, the general went to Albany to attend a council fire with the Iroquois, leaving Montgomery in command. The month before the Continental Congress had written "A Speech to the Six Confederate Nations," informing them about the Crown's oppression of the colonies and the impending hostilities. The letter stressed the Americans' wish that the Iroquois not take up the hatchet against the king's soldiers. The tribes were strongly advised to remain neutral.

Seven hundred Iroquois, mostly Mohawks and Oneidas, attended the council fire. The peace pipe was passed and the speech delivered. It took the Iroquois three days to mull it over. Then Little Abraham, a Mohawk sachem, replied. The Iroquois, at least the Mohawks and Oneidas, would remain neutral.

The same day word arrived of the Indians' decision, a courier came to the fort from Dorset in the New Hampshire Grants. He asked to speak privately with Ethan. Montgomery gave them Schuyler's office. Ethan didn't know the courier; he was not a Green Mountain Boy. He had come at the request of the area leaders who had met at Cephas Kent's Tavern in Dorset, little more than thirty miles north of Bennington. The man was short, chunky, and spoke with a distinct Irish brogue, though he said little beyond introducing himself. He handed Ethan a message. Beaming, he eagerly tore it open.

It was dated July 27. It was four short lines. Ethan read it and stiffened, read it a second time and swallowed. Twenty-three officers had been named for the Green Mountain Regiment. Among those chosen was Ethan's youngest brother Ira.

Absent from the list was the name Ethan Allen.

By a vote of forty-one to five, Ethan's neighbors had awarded command of the regiment to Seth Warner.

14

★ **Sober** reflection, after the courier left the office, persuaded Ethan that he should be neither surprised nor shocked. Independent of mind and of spirit as they were, the boys who had taken Fort Ticonderoga were not all that loyal to him. He was temperamental, he never sidestepped an argument, he ran a loose ship, and in his heart he acknowledged that he occasionally played favorites. He was possibly the most unmilitary military man in the colonies. He could be brash, insensitive, and insulting, and the elders in Dorset who had selected the regiment's officers had no tolerance for his deism. He did not attend church services and made no bones about his opposition to organized religion in general, ministers of the gospel in particular. No fewer than four ministers had been on the selection committee.

The men who rejected Ethan were not the rank and file but their fathers and older relatives. In four lines, on a piece of plain paper Ethan saw everything he'd worked for for the past six years taken from him. On the eve of the campaign of his lifetime, in spite of the endorsement of the Continental Congress and the New York Provincial Assembly, he was effectively stripped of his command—by his neighbors.

But he refused to be bitter, he would not sulk, he would not complain. He walked out of Schuyler's office straight to Seth Warner on the parade ground. He was talking to the courier. Ethan could see as he approached that the man had just informed him of the committee's decision, for Warner looked slightly nonplussed. His cheeks colored slightly as he greeted Ethan.

"Ethan, I had no idea . . . " he began.

Ethan laughed brittley. "Hell almighty, *I* don't think you put the stiff-necked, sanctimonious old bastards up to it. Never."

"I'll refuse it."

"Like hell you will. You're entitled to command. You've damned well earned it."

"What will you do now?"

"Give me time to think about that."

"You can't leave."

"Sneak off with my tail between my legs? Not on your life. When is Schuyler due back?"

"The council's over; he should be showing up anytime."

"I'll talk to him. I may not be good enough or popular enough to command but there must be something I'm fit for."

"What do *you* want to do?"

"I already told you I have to think about it. Will you be going back to Bennington?"

Warner glanced at the courier whose back was to them. He had walked off out of earshot when Ethan came up and was now pretending to inspect the wicket gate.

"They asked me to return with him. I suppose I should. Ethan . . . "

"Yes?"

"Did he mention . . . ?" Ethan's brow furrowed in puzzlement. "Your old friend Arnold is actually following through on that letter he sent to the Congress."

"No!"

"He's planning to march on Quebec with a thousand picked men."

"Sweet Jesus Christ! Is there no limit to the bastard's gall?"

"He does have a right, Ethan."

"He has to stick his goddamned oar into everything I do! What route is he taking?"

Warner nodded toward the courier. "He says he doesn't know, only that he'll be leaving shortly." Warner looked past Ethan. "Look who's coming."

Ethan turned. Schuyler was approaching them with his four-man escort, their horses dusty and weary-looking. As they neared, Ethan noticed that the general's normally florid complexion was displaced by a pasty look.

"Since I'm going back," said Warner, "would it be all right if I spoke to him first?"

"Go ahead. I'm in no rush. I suddenly find myself with nothing but time."

They greeted Schuyler. Montgomery came out. Warner asked to speak to both generals. Schuyler ushered them into his office, leaving Ethan staring at the courier's back, the accusation in his eyes hinting that he would dearly love to kill the messenger.

Schuyler slumped wearily into his chair, sending the flat of his hand to his forehead. "I'm running a fever, coming down with something. Everything turned out well, the Iroquois have promised to stay home. Anything happen while I was gone? Gregory!" His orderly appeared. "Brandy."

"Yes, sir, and welcome back, sir."

"The selection committee in Dorset picking the officers for the Green Mountain Regiment has picked me to lead it," said Warner, his eyes downcast.

"I thought Colonel Allen . . . "

"Colonel Allen thought Colonel Allen would," said Montgomery. Warner looked his way sharply. Montgomery cleared his throat. "Sorry, I don't mean to make light . . . "

"They want to leave the colonelcy open," Warner went on. "I'm to retain my L.C."

"My word," said Schuyler. "This is a surprise. He must have stepped on a great many toes."

The brandy came. Schuyler poured.

"He did expect to be named commander," said Warner. "He certainly earned it. I feel badly for him."

"How's he taking it?"

"Like the trooper he is. General, I want to speak on his behalf. Mind you, he hasn't asked me to. Sir, he doesn't want to leave, he wants to take part. In some capacity."

"I'm sure he does."

Schuyler studied his glass, turning it slowly. Then set it to one side. He looked quite ill. Warner sensed that this was becoming embarrassing for him. Watching the two of them together over the weeks, he knew that Schuyler was not at all antagonistic toward Ethan; he'd been courteous and friendly toward him since they arrived. But possibly, just possibly, the general saw this turn as his chance to get rid of him. Ethan wouldn't be commanding the regiment, he could hardly tag along as a common soldier. And for Schuyler to invest him with the rank of captain or major would have been an insult to the selection committee.

What would he do with him?

"What does Ethan want to do?" asked Montgomery.

Warner shook his head. "He hasn't said. I sense that he's still upset."

"I must be blunt, Colonel Warner," said Schuyler. "I know how close you two are, but at the risk of sounding heartless and, I assure you, I've no intention of being so, I have to say his reputation has . . . "

"Finally caught up with him," murmured Montgomery.

"Not that Richard and I aren't fond of him," Schuyler went on hurriedly. "We hold him in the highest regard. But he can be imprudent. He can be willful!"

"Pigheaded," said Montgomery.

"He's not one to bow his head and follow orders. And when he's crossed, he gets his back up."

"All true," said Warner. "But he's a hero. And a dyed-in-the-wool Patriot. He'd give his last drop of blood for independence. No man alive can question his courage or his commitment. This has been a terrible blow to him, and if on top of it you turn down his offer to help, in whatever capacity, it will crush him.

"Think of his record. He kept you Yorkers out of the New Hampshire Grants for six years. He led the assault on this fort. He raised the Green Mountain Regiment almost single-handedly. He had every right to expect to command. To be so overwhelmingly rejected, not even offered a lieutenancy, has to be shattering."

"You mention his five years holding off New York," said Schuyler. "Some in the Grants would say he stood in the way of a reasonable settlement."

"*I've* never seen it that way."

Schuyler went on. "Some say that since he took Ticonderoga he's become arrogant and overbearing."

"Have either of you seen him behave so? Not I."

Schuyler thought a moment, tapping his fingertips together in silent rhythm. Warner stared. Montgomery stared. The office had become sweltering.

"I'll tell you what I'll do," said the general. "He and I will talk."

"And you'll use him? Include him?"

"We shall see."

"I'll tell you something else about him," said Warner. "And you'll see for yourselves. Whatever his faults, real or imagined, he's not a sore loser. He's taking this in stride."

"What choice does he have?" asked Schuyler.

"The committee made a frightful blunder. Please, do what you can for him."

Schuyler nodded. To Warner, he was beginning to look bored. Warner got to his feet, saluted, spun about, and left.

"This is a surprise," said the general. "I took it for granted he'd be given command. I even advanced him money against his colonel's pay. What are you staring at, Richard?"

"You don't like him, do you?"

"Well, I . . . "

"You're delighted it turned out this way."

"Hardly."

"Delighted."

Schuyler eyed the closed door and lowered his voice. "It's not a question of liking or disliking. I've worked with many a man I'd never think of raising a glass with. I find Allen just too *impulsive,* too tactless, rough-hewn, for command. He doesn't campaign, he rampages. He's a wild man, and the way he carries on is bad for discipline."

Montgomery shrugged. "What you're saying is he's not a soldier. I'll admit he's undisciplined. But he's also capable, especially in this type of warfare. And I agree with Warner, he's courageous and deeply committed. See here, you won't turn him down . . . "

"I said I'd talk to him, Richard."

"I did start out treating this lightheartedly, but it's a serious business. The man's pride . . . You can't turn him down."

Schuyler sighed. Again, he felt his forehead. "I'm ill. I'm going to bed. Tell him to come to my quarters in half an hour."

15

★ **The** New York reinforcements began to arrive one company at a time. Ethan penned a note to Governor Trumbull in Connecticut informing him of his rejection in Dorset. He didn't complain, he merely explained what had happened, though adding that he failed to understand it. He gave the letter to Seth to post from Bennington. They said their good-byes outside the main gate. It was raining. Thunder rumbled over the lake; the surface became mussel-colored, rumpling and tearing.

"I hate leaving you like this, Ethan."

"I'm fine. Go. If you can, before you start back with the boys, stop by and see Mary."

"What do I tell her?"

"She knows by now I've been turned out. Tell her I'm well, that I'm on my way to Canada." Warner reacted slightly surprised. "As good as. Good-bye, Seth." Ethan pumped his hand. "It's been a great run."

"It's not over."

"Bet your arse it's not. We'll be back shoulder-to-shoulder in Montreal. When you get home stop by Fay's Tavern and raise a tankard for me. And my best regards to any members of the selection committee you might run into."

Warner and the courier wheeled about and rode off. Ethan turned to go to Schuyler's quarters. Blocking his way was Remember Baker, his massive fists bolting his hips, his expression as stormy as the sky.

"What's going on, cousin?" he asked.

"Great good news from Dorset."

"So I hear."

"What did Jacob and Elisha say?"

"Not the kind of language you want your kids to hear. Where's Seth off to?"

"He's gone to bring back the regiment. He can lead the boys, Remember." Baker scowled and spat. "Don't take this out on him."

"It's bullshit. We signed up to fight under you!"

"So now what, you go home? Let's get out of this rain."

They ran to the foot of the stairs leading up to the officers' quarters, where they had waited on the night they captured the fort. Nostalgia enveloped them both.

"What a night that was . . . " murmured Baker.

Ethan laid a hand on his shoulder, squeezing it fondly. "Don't run out on us now, Remember, we need you. Seth does. The boys." Baker grunted and again spat. "I have to go up and talk to Schuyler. I'll see you later."

"Don't expect him to do you any favors. Him and Montgomery are still sore as boils over that wrangling over the Grants. Every Yorker is."

"That's got nothing to do with this."

"It's got everything. He looks down his nose at everybody who's not from there. New Englanders to him are horseshit you walk around in the road."

Baker spat again. Ethan went up. General Schuyler was sitting up in bed swallowing small white powders and washing them down with tea. Ethan was surprised to see that he was as bald as the bedpost knob, matching the one his wig was sitting on. He looked worse than when he'd seen him earlier.

"I've a fever."

"Would you rather put this off till tomorrow?"

"I'll probably be worse. I'm burning, and my gout is flaring up. As far as this business goes, the good news is that you have two champions: your friend Warner and Richard."

"General Montgomery?"

"Don't look so surprised, Richard doesn't hold grudges. He respects you; and Warner's loyalty to you impressed him." He fixed his sick eyes on Ethan. "So what do we do with you, Mr. Allen?"

Loss of his rank in the question was an unnecessary barb, but Ethan ignored it.

"You're in command."

"Richard made a point—that your Green Mountain Regiment expected you to command. The men might resent it if you're dumped like an empty hogshead. It could hurt morale."

He dropped a pill. Ethan watched it roll and come to rest. He could pick it up, but Schuyler didn't ask him to. Not even with his eyes. He didn't offer. Instead, he moistened his lips and spoke.

"I've thought about it, General. I've decided I'd like to scout for you. A civilian scout. As well as sell the revolution to the Canadians."

Schuyler pursed his lips, crinkled his sweating brow, and thought this over. "You do know the wilderness up there."

"As good as Major Brown. Take me on and I'll give you my personal guarantee that the boys will follow Lieutenant Colonel Warner without any grumbling."

Schuyler finished his tea and lay back. He appeared to be having trouble breathing. "Very well."

"Thanks."

Schuyler nodded. He continued to stare without saying anything further. Ethan looked away and pretended to stifle a yawn to show confidence.

"Civilian scout," said Schuyler. "With absolutely no interference in military matters."

"None."

"Your word of honor as a gentleman . . . "

"Given."

"Done."

Ethan rubbed his hands together briskly. "Now, your men are starting to arrive. The boys will be here before the week's out. All they've been waiting on is their commander. It's nearly the end of August, we should get a move on."

Schuyler waggled a reproving finger. "Absolutely no inter-ference in military matters. I won't be rushed, Mr. Allen. Owwww!"

"What's the matter?"

"Blasted gout. It's exploding on me. I've got to stay off this foot. I may just go back home to Saratoga for a few days, get some decent care and rest."

Ethan suppressed a groan, but held comment, reluctant to get off on the wrong foot in his new job.

Schuyler set out for Saratoga, traveling the thirty-five miles to his estate by bateau up Lake George and overland by carriage. He left Brigadier General Montgomery in command. Three days later Seth Warner returned with the Green Mountain Regiment which, with the New York reinforcements, brought the number of men at Ticonderoga to twelve hundred.

Ethan noticed that the faces of the Green Mountain Boys all wore the same expression, at least those who had helped in the capture of the fort: pity combined with confusion. That he was still here? What for? What would he do? He took Warner aside.

"Did you stop by the house?"

"Yes. She . . . "

"What?"

"Wants you home. She was very insistent. She said there's nothing for you to do here."

"Schuyler's letting me tag along as a scout."

"Excellent."

"I would have even if he turned me down. Ahead of you, behind. Mary doesn't understand. Wives never do. They al-ways want to protect a man. Against himself. No matter how the old bastards voted I owe this campaign to me. I've fuck-ing earned it!"

"Mary knows that, Ethan."

"She blocks it out of mind, that and the fact that my pride's at stake. Pride to her is pigheadedness. And obligation is rashness. Women just don't want to know what drives a man."

"I think they know."

"You don't know, you're not married."

"Be fair, they just see things through different eyes. She sees you going off at half-cock."

"She hates this going to war. Most wives do. They don't want to understand why. I'll write her before we leave. With the children away she'll have to get Gladys Niles, the next farm over, to read it to her. I hate the idea of that old biddy knowing our private business, but what can you do?"

"News about your friend Arnold. He leaves in three weeks. Heading up the Kennebec River to try and take Quebec."

"He's a goddamned fool. The British can send shiploads of reinforcements up the river. Quebec's easy to get at, not like Montreal."

"At least he won't be stepping on our toes."

"Fuck him!"

Montgomery had resolved to act. During July and August no fewer than fifty bateaux had been built. Other craft had been acquired. By Monday evening, the colonial force was ready to set forth. Most of Colonel David Waterbury's Connecticut Regiment, four companies of Lieutenant Colonel Rudolphus Ritzema's 4th New York, the Green Mountain Regiment, and Samuel Mott's artillery, about twelve hundred men, set sail in the sloop *Enterprise,* a fleet of bateaux, birchbark canoes, dugouts, and row-galleys. The *Enterprise* boasted a twelve-pounder mounted in her bow.

Around ten p.m., it began raining heavily. They put ashore and bivouacked. The next day they passed Fort Amherst at Crown Point, drawing a friendly salute from a cannon. They headed down Lake Champlain.

Ethan's brother Ira, commissioned a lieutenant in the Green Mountain Regiment, had meanwhile been attached to Montgomery's staff as a scout-messenger.

A change in objectives was announced. Up ahead, the lake provided the headwaters of the Richelieu River, which flowed north to the St. Lawrence. On the west bank of the Richelieu stood St. John's fort, an inviting target, one which Montgomery decided was worth capturing before heading up to Montreal.

16

SEPTEMBER 1775

★ **The** expedition reached the Ile-aux-Noix in the Richelieu River situated ten miles up from its headwaters in Lake Champlain. They had passed innumerable islands en route, the largest being Ile-la-Motte, on which the French had built Fort St. Anne, only to abandon it more than a century ago. Ile-aux-Noix was a fraction of the size of Ile-la-Motte, but resembled it in miniature, with thick woods, tall grasses, wildlife; it was also home to a scattering of Caughnawagas. There as well, nearly seventy years earlier, the French began to build a fort to command the northern end of Lake Champlain, but the work had been halted for lack of funds. In time, nature regained possession of the site until now flourishing growth totally concealed the partially constructed walls.

Montgomery saw the island as an ideal base from which to attack St. John's, which had been Fort St. Jean until anglicized by the British. No sooner were the men settled in then the general summoned the Allen brothers to his tent. The three men sat by the small cookfire in front of the tent. Montgomery had laid out a number of maps on the ground.

"Ethan," he began, "I want you to take ten men and one of the interpreters, go into the woods, find Indians, and try and recruit them. We have to start somewhere; this is as good a place as any."

Ira, youngest of the six Allen brothers, who resembled Ethan not at all and was a head shorter than he, frowned. "These woods are thick with Caughnawagas, General. Might I suggest that instead of going at it piecemeal we detail a hundred men to sweep the isle from one end to the other?"

"No, Lieutenant. I don't want them thinking we've landed here to overwhelm them. The idea is to extend the hand of friendship and try to win them over."

"He's right," said Ethan, drawing a sour look from his brother.

"I'm not familiar with the Caughnawagas," Montgomery went on.

"They're nothing but transplanted Mohawks," said Ethan. "Their ancestors came from the castles along the Mohawk River. The Jesuits got to some of them, converted them, and they moved up here. It was a clean break. The Mohawks down below want nothing to do with the Caughnawagas and vice versa. But the Caughnawagas are loyal to the French, not the British."

"Most of them," added Ira.

"That's what we want," said Montgomery. "Recruit as many as you can. I'm sure the garrison at Fort St. John's is a thorn in their side."

"I don't know about that, General," said Ethan. "The ones on this island likely ignore it. There's fishing, good hunting, all they need without trading with the fort or even hanging around there."

"Whatever. You've a reputation among the tribes, let's try and capitalize on it. I won't presume to advise you as to how to approach them."

"Simple. I'll tell 'em we're the first wave coming to liberate all their people from the redcoats. They'll get back their hunting grounds and their freedom to move about. I'll tell them the truth, that the colonies mean to chase Jack Bull out of North America."

"Can you leave at dawn?"

"Before dawn. I'll pick my men when I get up."

"Ira, talk to one of the interpreters for him. What's funny, Ethan?"

"It's just that any Caughnawagas we run into who speak English are a dead giveaway. They learned by hobnobbing with the British, and they'll likely be the first to side with them." Ethan paused for a second. "Can I take Captain Baker?"

"I'll need him and Major Brown," said Montgomery. "I've a hundred questions for them." He stirred the dying fire with a stick. "I want to attack St. John's before the end of the week, so do what you can as fast as you can to win over as many Indians as possible. Dismissed."

Ethan almost saluted before remembering that he was now a civilian. Ira lingered with Montgomery, so Ethan repaired to his tent, rolled up in his blanket and went to sleep wondering if Mary had had his letter read to her yet.

An hour later a whale boat arrived with six men at the oars, a horse, and a single passenger—General Schuyler. The commotion attending his unexpected arrival woke the camp. Ethan staggered groggily from his tent, joining Ira, Remember Baker, and Seth Warner at the head of the little stone dock. Men crowded around as the general was assisted up onto the dock. Montgomery greeted him. Schuyler looked perilously ill to Ethan, as white as his shirt. But he retained sufficient energy to generate his temper. He glared at Montgomery, surveyed the gawking crowd, took Montgomery by the arm, and started up the dock.

"He's sick as a hound," said Ethan to his companions. "Look at that face. Look at the bandage on his gout, it's as big as a watermelon. He can barely drag one leg after the other."

"What in hell is he doing here?" asked Baker.

Ira snickered. "His ego sent him."

The crowd was ordered to disperse. The two generals did not get far before Schuyler exploded. His voice carried through the woods silencing the tree frogs and insects.

"How dare you, sir!"

"I did as I saw fit," said Montgomery. "I intend to launch a full-scale attack on St. John's."

"Nonsense! Montreal is the target."

"We'll get to Montreal, sir. St. John's is only twenty miles downriver. Major Brown has informed me that Major Preston's ship, the *Royal Savage,* lies at anchor there. We have to prevent it from entering the lake, possibly attacking Fort Ticonderoga."

"You don't even know how big a force he has!"

"Under five hundred!"

"It's too reckless, man. It's ridiculous! I forbid . . . "

Up rolled his eyes, down he fell.

"Montgomery should load him back in his boat," said Ethan. "Ship him back. Hell almighty, he won't come to till he's halfway up the lake."

Seth Warner assigned Remember Baker to take a squad downriver and scout the area surrounding the fort to determine the best positions for artillery emplacements and familiarize himself with the lay of the land. The party left in four canoes heading for the west bank of the river. Ethan happened to come out of his tent at that moment and saw them. Remember waved.

"See you, cousin!"

Ethan approached Warner. "Where's Remember going?"

"I sent him out to scout for three or four hours."

"Scout what?"

Warner told him. Ethan bristled.

"I thought I was chief scout . . . "

"I'm sorry, I didn't realize our scouts were ranked."

"Is that supposed to be humorous? What is this shit? Ever since you took over the regiment you hardly speak to me."

"That's nonsense. And I'm not playing favorites, if that's what you think."

"I don't know what the fuck you're playing."

"I've a meeting, Ethan, you'll have to excuse me."

"Oh, don't let me detain you, *sir.* Far be it for this civilian to interfere with important army business!"

Ethan waved him away and stomped off muttering. What the hell was going on? What was Warner doing sneaking Remember out of there behind his back? Hadn't he a right to know what was going on? With anything to do with scouting he did. The bastard could deny it till his tongue fell out, but Seth *had* changed toward him. It was like two different Warners. Looking down his nose at him, that's what Seth was doing! Pretending he was so goddamned busy. It was just to avoid him, that was plain enough.

"Jesus Christ, you give somebody authority and it goes right to their fucking ego. Sonovabitch!"

Remember and his men were supposed to return by sundown, according to Ira, but they failed to show. They still hadn't come back when the camp retired that night. Ethan was beginning to worry. Determinedly avoiding Seth Warner, he went directly to Montgomery. The general was already in bed but not yet asleep. Ethan practically barged into his tent.

Montgomery did not share his concern. "They'll probably be back within the hour."

Perceiving that there was nothing he could do about the situation and that he was probably the only one in camp who was worried, Ethan went to bed.

Schuyler's obstinacy won out over his common sense. He did not leave the next morning. Remember and his men had not returned.

Before learning of the latter, before sunrise, Ethan assembled the ten Green Mountain Boys he had picked the night before, among them Jacob Wall and Elisha Cummings. He took along Crage Sentowanne—"White Elk"—a middle-aged

Mohawk from the Schandisse Castle near the Mohawk River as well. A gloomy individual, White Elk's upper body was riddled with scars and liberally tattooed. Ethan instinctively sensed that he liked his drink. Before they even talked about the best way to approach the island's Caughnawagas, he handed White Elk a pint of *uiska*. The Mohawk's toothless grin of appreciation signaled friendship, and with it automatically, the loyalty Ethan hoped for.

It was White Elk's first visit to Ile-aux-Noix, but he knew his Caughnawaga cousins well, his own family having been divided by the Jesuits when his grandfather's brother took his squaw and four sons north, lured by the Cross and the Mother Church's charity and reverence for authority. Toward the "Praying Mohawks" White Elk held no personal antipathy, but he was wise enough to recognize that any he might encounter might not share his tolerance. He carried a Brown Bess with a razor-sharp bayonet.

As Ethan and his party left camp, with still no sign of Remember and his men, Montgomery assigned two hundred men to fell trees and build a log boom across the river to the north to prevent any British vessels from entering the lake and possibly threatening Fort Amherst at Crown Point and Fort Ticonderoga.

As to the immediate future, Montgomery's chief concern was not Major Preston, the commandant at St. John's, but Sir Guy Carleton, the governor of Canada and also a British general. It was he who controlled the colony's manpower. Carleton had come to Canada sixteen years before with James Wolfe, the hero of the French and Indian War. As matters stood at present, Carleton commanded only a handful of well-scattered troops, but he was a brilliant strategist, eminently capable, and he could anticipate the Americans' strategy and send reinforcements to St. John's within days, drawing volunteers from the large number of avowedly loyal French Canadians.

As to Benedict Arnold's projected assault on Quebec,

Montgomery was inclined to agree with Ethan's dim view of the idea. What neither General Washington nor Arnold seemed willing to consider was the critical point Ethan had raised to Warner back at the fort, that whoever commanded the sea could send fleets up the St. Lawrence to hold Quebec indefinitely, regardless of which side won on land.

Ethan led White Elk and his men through the dense woods until they sighted smoke.

"Jacob," said Ethan, "stay back with the men out of sight. If I yell, come running."

"I don't like it, Ethan," said Galen Truscott, a carpenter who had been in the first bateauload to leave Hand's Cove the night of the attack on Ticonderoga.

"Me, neither," said Jacob. "You could get knifed without so much as a gurgle. And I could get a hernia carrying your body back."

"Okay, okay. Climb that tree, Elisha, that maple thick with leaves. You can look down and watch what goes on. If there's trouble, yell your lungs out. Come along, White Elk."

Unlike their cousins to the south, the Caughnawagas lived in birch bark wigwams, and their canoes were constructed of birch bark instead of elm. But the clothing of the two branches of Mohawks was identical, both wearing breech-clouts, deer-skins, and even the same type of ornaments. However the Caughnawagas wore deerskin moccasins instead of the summer twined-corn-husk moccasins favored by all the Iroquois to the south. Entering a clearing, Ethan counted only fourteen people and only four men.

"Others are out hunting," whispered White Elk, indicating stacked beaver pelts, deerskins, and salted venison. A moose head with a splendid rack sat in the crotch of a tree. An elder, a wrinkled, wizened little man, with a face pointed like a rat's, appeared to be the leader. He wore a silver crucifix. He was squatting and relieving himself when Ethan and White Elk singled him out and approached.

"Tell him who we are," said Ethan. "That there's a war on

against the redcoats and that we know, *we know* the Caugh-nawagas will want to fight on our side. That we'll win and drive out the redcoats and give the people back their lands, their beaver, all their game, and all their freedoms. Tell him it will be like it was when their grandfathers' grandfathers ruled the woodlands. No palefaces except a few Canadians, who don't bother 'em, never have."

White Elk addressed the old man at length. Busy wiping himself with leaves and scuffing dirt and leaves over his movement in the manner of a cat, Ethan did not think he was paying attention, but when White Elk was done he showed that he had been.

"He knows you, E-than."

"I never saw the bastard before in my life."

"He knows your name. He says you are a friend of the people and welcomes you. He says he will speak to his hunters when they come in. If any are interested they will speak with you. He says to come back when the sun sits on the Tree-Eater Mountains."

"Damn. I guess we'll just have to make the rounds and come back the same route in reverse at sundown. They've all got to be out hunting."

When they left the immediate vicinity of the old man's bowel movement a different stench took over, that of rancid meat. The elder followed them limping badly.

"Ask him where his main camp is, Crage Sentowanne." The man pointed toward the north end of the isle. A narrow path led in that direction. "Ask him his name."

"Hodadenon," said White Elk.

"Which means . . . ?"

"Last One Left."

"Ask him how many braves here?"

"Oyere." White Elk held up all ten fingers.

"Hell almighty, I can see this is going to be piecemeal pickings after all."

They visited eight additional camps before the sun began

lowering, then revisited them in reverse order. Ethan strove
to be his most persuasive, citing every reason he could think
of to induce the braves to side with the Americans, but he still
managed to recruit only nineteen. And they were not the pick
of the crop; three, the most enthusiastic, were as old as Last
One Left.

He came away from Last One Left's camp with the impression that, strictly speaking, he was getting nowhere. The
problem was Ile-aux-Noix. Cut off from the mainland
through choice, isolated, what did any of the Indians, or for
that matter the Canadians living there, care about the war?
What difference did it make who won? He called his men
around him before heading back to camp. He tried to sound
optimistic.

"We're sure to have better luck tomorrow. I'll get the ones
we got already to talk to friends and relatives. I've got to
make 'em understand that when we win they'll have it lots better than now."

"They don't look to me like they got it so bad," muttered
Elisha, lying braced on his elbows and chewing a sprig of
grass. "For Injuns." Others nodded.

"You're a big help, Elisha."

"I'm just saying . . . "

"We heard."

They filed back to camp. Ethan was about to duck into his
tent when Ira came up.

"If you're going to ask how it went . . . " began Ethan.
"What's wrong? You look like you lost your best friend."

"As bad as that and worse. Come with me."

"What is it?"

Ira didn't answer. Instead he led him to Montgomery's
tent. A blanket had been spread on the ground in front.

"Jesus Christ!"

Eleven heads, among them Remember Baker's. Men stood
about gawking and conversing in low tones.

Ira spoke. "Seth finally sent out a search party."

"Where's their bodies?"

"Who knows? All they found were these, all stuck in the crotches of trees."

"Like that bull moose head!"

"What?"

"Nothing. Sons of bitches!"

Montgomery came up. "They were attacked by Indians."

"The hell they were," rasped Ethan. "Look and see for yourself." To both men's surprise and repugnance he bent and picked up Remember's head. "See that? That's a clean cut. That's no tomahawk, that's a saber. Lopped off clean. All are the same."

"Redcoats," murmured Ira. "Making it look like Indians did it."

Ethan continued holding the head and staring at it. "That search party couldn't find a single body?"

Both shook their heads.

"Put it down, Ethan," said Ira. "You're making me sick to my stomach."

"You're talking about Remember, little brother. What you should be is sick at heart." Again he looked at the dead man's face, holding the head six inches from him at eye level. Everyone, even Montgomery, watched him. "We'll get 'em, cousin. Every mother's son. Exterminate the sons of bitches!"

Montgomery cleared his throat. He gestured to a couple of enlisted men looking on.

"You boys pick up the corners and tie them together. Ethan . . . ?"

"No. I'm keeping him."

Ira took a step forward. "Ethan . . . "

"I'll bury him myself. What there is of him."

"Ethan, put it back in the blanket, please."

"It? It! This is our flesh and blood, you heartless jackass!"

"Put his head in the blanket," said Montgomery.

His tone, his expression, had the intended effect. Ethan complied. And with the others stood watching as the blanket was tied up.

"We'll bury them," said Montgomery.

"Cousin Remember separately."

"If you wish."

"I wish."

Ira touched Ethan's arm. "General Schuyler's been asking for you. Better go see what he wants."

"What? I'm not in the goddamned mood. Oh, hell."

Ethan found Schuyler lying on his cot raised on four pillows and in even poorer condition than the last time he'd seen him. Along with his fever and his gout he was now beset by rheumatic pains. Despite his condition, he'd managed to draft a letter to the Canadians. He gave it to Ethan to read. In it he stressed that Congress, through General Washington, had assigned him to expel the British troops from Canada. It went on to blow smoke with such phrases as "unchaining the people," "liberating them from the same slavery the Crown is determined to force upon your good neighbors to the south."

"I want you and Major Brown to take it to Chambly."

"Hey, would you mind not being in such a rush? I've just lost my favorite cousin."

"I heard. Damnable business."

"Yeah, damnable."

There was a weighty pause. Schuyler suddenly seemed to find it difficult to look Ethan in the eye.

"All right, all right," rasped Ethan. "It's not like it's your fault. Go on with what you were saying."

"Thank you. I must ask you to guard that letter with your life. Go through the woods well to the west of the river. Past St. John's, past Fort Thérèse to Fort Chambly. James Livingston lives in the village."

"Who's he?"

"One of the New York Livingstons. A merchant. He has his business in Chambly, he's on our side."

"You sure?"

Schuyler stared. "He's already raised four hundred men through a letter campaign."

"Oh."

"He and I have been corresponding for months. He'll see that copies are made of that and sent out to all the right people up and down the St. Lawrence. You should be able to make it up there before dark, if you start early enough."

"General, can't you get somebody else to be your messenger boy? I've got a funeral to go to shortly, and I've got to get back out bright and early tomorrow to try and line up Caughnawagas . . . "

"Attend his funeral, by all means. Only the Caughnawagas can wait. Better still, get somebody to take over that for you till you get back."

"Can't John Brown go by himself? He knows the woods."

"Mr. Allen, why, oh why, must you be so bloody obstinate?"

"Who's obstinate? Oh hell, if it'll make you happy."

"It'll make me delirious."

"No need to get sarcastic. I got some interesting news about the fort at St. John's from some Caughnawagas. For one thing, they're loaded with artillery. For another, the ship there . . . "

"The *Royal Savage*."

"She'll be ready to sail in three or four days."

"Downriver or upriver?"

"Up, of course. They want to get into Lake Champlain. You know what that means."

"I wouldn't worry. I've been informed that the log boom will be in place just to the north of us by sundown tomorrow."

"There's more. Major Preston's outfitting bateaux with artillery. And worst of all, don't count on any Canucks joining us, at least none along the river."

"Did you ask? Or did the Caughawagas volunteer that?"

"Volunteered."

"Take it with a grain of salt."

Ethan shrugged. "I'm just relaying what they said."

"Again, you and Major Brown must guard that letter with both your lives. You can go. Thank you."

The last two words were as cold as he could utter them. Ethan left snickering.

" 'Unchaining the people . . . ' Horse's arse."

His thoughts went back to Remember, setting his heart aching. What a way to die. What a way for a civilized enemy to act: no bullet, no bayonet. Lop off their heads like so many chickens.

"Bastard British are six times worse than Indians!"

Remember gone. His favorite cousin, the big bear who delighted in bear-hugging everybody. God, but he'd miss him! His chronic orneryness, his complaining, his uncontrollable eagerness to fight, his loyalty, his love.

"Remember, Remember, wherever you are, up or down, I'll avenge you! I swear!"

He thought too about Seth who, when they were gathered around the blanket with its grisly contents, stayed in the background, standing staring, his mind in the clouds. Ethan looked up. Think of the devil! Warner was coming toward him. He stopped a few feet away. Ethan felt a sudden compulsion to yell at him, upbraid him for sending Remember out, sending them all to such needless, painful deaths. Then he noticed the tears in Warner's eyes.

"Take it easy, Seth, it wasn't your fault. Crazy, isn't it? I got mad because you didn't send me out. But see here, you shouldn't take it to heart."

"Why not? He was my cousin, too. Are you still sore at me?"

"No. Besides, I wasn't sore, it was the green-eyed monster. We both know that."

Relief had spread over Warner's face. Ethan's understanding was important to Seth. In the time it took to fashion a friendly smile, the bitterness Ethan had felt ever since the day the courier showed up at Ticonderoga disappeared. He stuck out his hand. Warner shook it. They embraced.

Though neither had any way of knowing it, this was to be the last time they would see each other for years.

17

★ **The** stars burned with extraordinary intensity while the stone ball of the full moon was so sharply defined it looked ready to roll about, crushing the constellations in its path. It was nearing ten p.m.; most of the camp was asleep. Remember and the others had been buried with words said over them. Ethan sat drinking with John Brown.

" 'Unchaining the people.' You ever hear such bullshit in your life?"

"Flowery writing appeals to some, Ethan."

"To backwoods Canucks? Listen, I been thinking. How about you go on up to Chambly alone? If anybody asks, just pretend I went along. Meantime I'll get back to lining up Caughawagas."

"Not a good idea."

Down came the corners of Ethan's mouth. "Why not?"

"What if Schuyler found out?"

"How could he?"

"Livingston might inadvertently tell him in their correspondence that only one of us showed. You're not enviably high on Schuyler's list of favorites. Were it not for Montgomery and Seth . . . "

"I wouldn't be here, I know."

"I'm glad you are, old man. How would we fight this thing without you?"

"I keep telling myself the same thing only I got a sneaky

feeling that bald bastard is looking for any excuse to get rid of me."

"So why stick your neck out?"

"Waste two whole days, and Montgomery wants me to line up all the braves I can before Saturday. This is plain bullshit, John." He glowered, growled, and pounded his empty tankard on the ground.

Brown smirked. "Care for a detached, wholly objective opinion?"

"Not especially, but I'm going to get it."

"I think you're counting much too heavily on the Caughnawagas. If we get ten to come over and stick with us we'll be lucky. But once we take St. John's . . . "

"They'll come running."

"It could persuade more that we'll be the winners. It might influence the Canadians, too."

"Did you get so smart at Yale? Or did you bring it there with you? This bottle's dry; got any more?"

"No, and I don't want any. I'm turning in. As you should."

"I don't need sleep. Four hours and I'm fine."

"I'll wake you around five. It's more than thirty miles to Chambly."

"We should steal a canoe and paddle downriver right under Preston's goddamned guns."

"You do that. I prefer the relative safety of the woods. Have you the letter?" Ethan patted his pocket. "Don't lose it."

"I'd sure like to."

Ethan got up creaking, stretched, belched resoundedly, and walked off. Brown shook his head and grinned.

They started out before sunrise, taking a canoe to the east bank and following it downriver about fifteen miles before Brown suggested they might be pressing their luck to continue by water. Hiding the canoe on the opposite bank they started north through the woods. It was slow going. They couldn't locate a path, and shrubs and vines blocked their way at every step. Ethan got out his knife and began cutting his way forward. He ranted and cursed.

Brown laughed. "More reinforcements due in today," he said. "Colonel Benjamin Hinman's bringing three hundred from Connecticut."

"Fat slob," growled Ethan. "And a rotten soldier. He should stay home and send the men."

"Four hundred are coming from New York."

"Who's commanding them?"

"Goose Van Schaick."

"Never heard of him. Goose? Is that his real name, or does he just walk like one? Where does the army find these turkeys?"

"It doesn't; they find the army. More and more are buying their commands."

"At the expense of folks like us, the bastards."

"Not Van Schaick. I hear he's a good one. They're all Patriots, Ethan, even your friend Arnold. You have to give them that much."

A branch slapped Ethan across the mouth. He cursed. "I give 'em nothing in a busted barrel. I just wish they'd stay home and out of our war!" Brown laughed uproariously, frightening a quail, sending it scurrying. "I mean it, John!"

"I'm sure you do."

They passed St. John's fort about two hundred yards distant. Through the thick foliage they could see nothing, but Brown insisted it was there, east of them. To satisfy his curiosity, Ethan climbed a tree. Eighty feet in the air he could look down on the barracks, a few brick buildings, and a stone house. A redoubt about a hundred feet square surrounded the brick buildings; a second redoubt surrounded the stone house. There was a palisade with a deep ditch dug in front of it. It was partially fraised with pointed pickets in some places and abatised in the rest. It protected the fort on three sides while on the side facing the river a moat had been dug along the bank. Cannon were mounted on all the exterior redoubts. Ethan descended the tree.

"It's bristling with cannons. It's not going to be any lemonade picnic."

"It's certain to be a lot noisier than one-shot Ticonderoga."

"I hope the son of a bitch has got a plan."

"He has. Good man, Montgomery."

"You mean better than Schuyler? Who isn't?"

"Don't kick the man while he's down. If we don't get a move on we won't get past Fort Thérèse until dark."

"How in hell do you move in this? We need axes."

"The town is on the far side of Fort Chambly," said Brown. "Any idea where this Livingston's house is?"

"No, but we won't have any trouble finding it. Chambly's half the size of Bennington."

Chambly was only fourteen miles from the St. Lawrence, with Montreal situated on the opposite bank, Ethan knew. With the log boom securely in place to block any British ships from entering Lake Champlain, he could no longer see why Montgomery should bother taking Fort St. John's. Were he in command, he'd bypass it and go directly to Montreal. This was what Schuyler wanted originally, although in his present incapacitation he could hardly object to Montgomery's strategy, beyond telling him he disagreed with it.

Ethan made a mental note to remember to talk to Montgomery when they got back. Maybe he could talk him into bypassing the fort. He glanced back at Brown. Should he discuss it with him? No, his opinion would no doubt be contrary to his own. He didn't need contrary, wasn't in the mood. Better he save his ideas for Montgomery.

If only these people knew how lucky they were to have him around!

18

★ **They** stood before James Livingston's door. Brown nodded, and Ethan rapped the lion-head knocker. The house, a fine colonial painted white with black trim, was not in complete darkness. A solitary candle burned at an upstairs window. They stepped back and watched as it was taken from the sill. Someone descended the stairs and approached the door.

"Who's there?"

"Ethan Allen and Major John Brown," announced Ethan.

The door was opened. Despite the fact that it was just beginning to turn dark, Livingston was in his nightshirt. His blond hair was tousled. His eyes were a cornflower blue and Ethan perceived that, despite his attire, they hadn't awakened him. Brown explained why they'd come. Ethan produced Schuyler's letter.

"Come in, come in."

Livingston shook hands vigorously with Brown. "General Schuyler tells me you're doing a superb job, Major. And Ethan Allen . . . " He looked and sounded impressed. Ethan glowed. "A pleasure meeting you, sir. Your reputation has reached all the way to Montreal. Come into the living room. Excuse my attire. I was up all last night."

"We're sorry to—"

"It's all right. This is important, I'm sure. I imagine you're both famished. There's turkey and vegetables."

"What we really are is thirsty," said Ethan, eliciting a troubled look from Brown.

"Of course, what's the matter with me?"

It took less than a minute to persuade Ethan that he liked James Livingston. The former Yorker was about his own age, a gentleman without being a snob and without looking soft and pampered; wealthy, successful, and a Patriot, a class of American that men like him were grateful for, with so many among the upper class leaping into the ranks of the Loyalists.

He led them into the dining room to sit at his table while he got on a robe and brought in the turkey with squash and potatoes taken from the warmer. He winked.

"I always keep food warm for when I come down around three in the morning."

He poured whiskey and set a pot of coffee to heat. Ethan looked around. The dining room was green-paneled with a *kas* painted grisaille standing against an end wall. They sat in stuffed armchairs under a cut-glass chandelier sprouting twelve candles—which Livingston had lit—eating from delft plates in a blue-white pattern that matched the fireplace tiles.

Livingston had put on spectacles and was reading Schuyler's letter. Between helpings of turkey and vegetables separated by generous quaffs of the whiskey, Ethan cast glance after glance at their host, curious as to his reaction to Schuyler's appeal to the Canadians.

"This is all very sincere and well-intentioned, but among the three of us I don't know how much of an impression it'll make on them."

"Seeing as they don't exactly idolize us to begin with," said Brown.

"It's not so much that. I just think that a rousing victory over His Majesty's forces, either at Fort St. John's, or better yet Montreal, will be more apt to bring people over to our side than dire threats as to what's in store for them if the British win. My own guess is not much of anything different from right now."

Ethan slapped the table, jiggling the salt and pepper shakers and startling Brown. "My sentiments exactly, sir! I couldn't put it better. Tear that thing up."

Livingston grinned. "I couldn't do that to Philip. As I say, I don't know how effective it'll be, but it can't do any harm.

I'll see that copies are made and sent out; perhaps I'll enclose a note of my own." He folded Schuyler's letter, putting it to one side. "Now then, what's the news? When will Montgomery attack St. John's?"

"This coming Saturday," said Brown.

"How many men does he have?"

"As we speak, around seventeen hundred."

"Good, good. Excellent. And artillery?"

"Two-pounders, four-pounders, nine-pounders, mortars."

"Very good. What about Indians?" Ethan told him in brief about his assignment. "I'm not surprised. Oh, not that you're not giving the effort your all, I'm sure you are, but again it'll be a resounding victory that'll bring them over to our side."

Ethan nodded. "Not empty goddamned promises." He was rapidly warming up to James Livingston. They could have had the same mother so consistently did they agree. He couldn't place the name Livingston. Had he been in Albany during the years of wrangling over the Grants? If so, he hadn't been involved.

"Colonel Allen . . . ?"

"No longer a colonel, sir. Just plain citizen these days; volunteer scout. Lieutenant Colonel Seth Warner commands the Green Mountain Regiment."

"May I ask how that happened?"

"Politics, with a lot of jealousy thrown in. Long dull story."

"Never mind, it's no business of mine. Have you eaten your fill? If so, let's go into the drawing room for brandy and cigars. You'll be my guests tonight, and will have yourselves a hearty breakfast tomorrow."

In the drawing room, Livingston settled into a leather-seated Queen Anne corner chair and assumed a serious expression. "There's information I'd like you to take back to Philip and General Montgomery." They leaned forward. "At St. John's, Carleton's force of regulars is composed of men of the Seventh Regiment, and the Royal Fusiliers and infantry out of the Twenty-sixth Cameronians. Now it's just my instincts but I've a feeling he'd like to abandon St. John's and concentrate on defending Montreal."

"That's what I'd do," said Ethan.

"But he won't. Only because the Canadians and Indians might fault him for timidity, even fear. He can't risk such an impression, so depend upon it, he'll be making a strong stand at St. John's. He'll bring in reinforcements, if he hasn't already. He began scraping the bottom of the barrel last month. Drafted a midshipman and twelve sailors from the brigantine *Gaspé*. They're now in the garrison."

"Has he tried to enlist any Canadians?" Brown asked.

Livingston nodded. "With scant success. The habitants have sworn on the Cross never to fight the Americans, even if most won't join us. And the Caughnawagas, at least those around here, want no part of it."

"Nineteen do," said Ethan. "And that's only one day's recruiting."

Livingston smiled indulgently. "Cross your fingers they show up on Saturday."

"We shouldn't count on *any?*" Brown asked.

"They'll go where the whiskey is or stay home. You can't depend on their word, Ethan. They give it easily and let you down even more easily."

"We'll be satisfied if they stay home," said Brown.

Ethan frowned. "Not me."

"What's happening in Montreal?" Brown asked.

"All I get are rumors. But before we get to that, let's talk about the fort here at Chambly. Montgomery will want to capture it if only because of its location. It's smack on the corner where the road to Montreal starts near the river. It's wide open there, and it'll be hard for our boys to sneak by. The fort itself is stone, with sixteen-foot-high walls and bastions sitting even higher at the corners." Brown shook his head, discouraged. "Let me finish. The walls are stone but perilously thin and with only musket slits."

"How big a garrison?" Ethan asked.

"Under a hundred officers and men. Now listen closely. If Montgomery can spare fifty men and bring up a few nine-pounders, slip them by the guns at St. John's and land here, I'll reinforce him with at least three hundred Canadians. You have my word on it. It shouldn't take more than an hour to convince Major Stopford to surrender."

"That sounds great!" burst Ethan. "You got any more brandy?"

Brown examined the ceiling while Livingston smiled good-naturedly, got up, and went to the liquor cabinet.

"While you're up, I could use another cigar, too . . . "

Livingston poured another round and offered Ethan the box. Brown looked away when Ethan took five cigars, lighting one with his butt and settling back in his chair.

"Mind if I ask you something personal, James?"

"Ask away."

"Here you are a successful businessman, living in this big mansion, rich as hell. College education, from a fine family, all of 'em rich, I'm sure. You got the world by the tail. Whether we win or lose this war, none of it affects you. You'll just go right on being rich and successful. So how come you get yourself involved? How come you risk it all and bet on independence?"

"Why do you?"

"Because . . . because it's right."

Livingston raised his glass, "Colonel, Major, I can't think of a better reason than that." He grinned and winked. "Let's drink to it."

Ethan bolted his glass. "Whoosh! Sweet fire!"

"To what is right and to our free and independent nation," said Brown raising his glass.

"Hear, hear," said Livingston emulating him.

"Hey, boys," said Ethan. "Will you look here? I'm empty again."

19

★ **Shortly** after the sun rose on Saturday, September 16, Montgomery planned to send two row-galleys—each carrying a twelve-pounder, ten bateaux, the *Enterprise,* and three hundred fifty men downriver near the log boom to intercept the *Royal Savage* in the event it managed to break through. Were it to succeed in doing so, there would be nothing to stop it from reaching the lake.

The remainder of his force would embark in the rest of the boats for St. John's, leaving about thirty men on the island, among them the still incapacitated Schuyler. Two days earlier, Montgomery had dispatched Major Brown with a hundred men to return to Chambly. Ethan went along, at Brown's insistence, to take command of a group of Canadian volunteers. The day after the two friends split up, Ethan sent back a message informing Montgomery that he had moved on to St. Ours, twelve miles up from Sorel, and that he'd increased his force to two hundred fifty men. He boasted that by the time he returned to St. John's three days hence, he'd have double that number. He'd also brought along the ten Green Mountain Boys he had picked to accompany him on his recruiting mission among the Ile-aux-Noix Caughnawagas. At Longueil early Friday evening, hours before the projected attack on St. John's, he stood looking across the St. Lawrence at Montreal. Elisha Cummings and Jacob Wall came up to him; both were slightly tipsy.

"What's snaking around inside your head, Colonel?" Elisha asked.

"I'm thinking about a letter I sent to Governor Trumbull down in Connecticut last July."

He did not elaborate further but in the privacy of his thoughts saw once more his writing on the page. Had he been awarded command of the Green Mountain Regiment, he had informed Trumbull, he would have marched north and attacked Montreal, with or without Montgomery's or Schuyler's approval. Now there it sat, ascending from the river in a series of terraces to the foot of Mount Royal.

Livingston had said it was virtually defenseless. Ethan sucked in a breath. He could take it with his two hundred fifty men and win himself a feather for his cap ten times the size of Ticonderoga's. Cross the river and strike under cover of darkness, and it would be all over before dawn broke over Maine. He could taste the temptation, roll it around in his mouth like a piece of horehound. His heart quickened. Both boys were babbling on; as close as they stood to him he could barely hear them, so engrossed was he with the view, so overcome by the temptation. Storm it! Take it!

Only it would be so rash, so risky. If he failed, Montgomery would catch up with him, clap him in irons, and ship him home. He'd sit out the war in a cell in Bennington, the laughingstock of the area, the wild man who finally went overboard.

"The devil take Montgomery and Schuyler!"

"Devil take Montgomery and Schuyler?" Elisha repeated. "I'll drink to that." He raised his bottle and managed to get a swig down before Jacob snatched it away.

As strong as the temptation was, the next morning Ethan jettisoned all thoughts of attacking when he woke up to discover his Canadian volunteers beginning to drift away. By ten a.m., despite his every exhortation and appeal, only eighty remained of the original two hundred fifty. He held his temper, taking it philosophically, and set out upriver. In time he turned southeast, taking the road back to Chambly, a quagmire studded with rotted logs and riddled with holes.

He hated giving up on Montreal without even trying, but with fewer than a hundred men what chance would he have?

Boldness was one thing, rashness quite another.

"Look who's coming!" bawled Elisha, who was wearing a cloth strip around his head in an effort to ease his hangover. Ethan emerged from his thoughts and looked up.

Leading a large body of men came Major John Brown waving his arms and calling. They ran to each other.

"Where are you coming from?" Brown asked.

"Longueil, just downriver from Montreal."

"I knew you were up there chewing on it." He glanced past Ethan. "How many men have you?"

"Counting the boys, only about ninety, why?"

"Together we'd be almost three hundred."

"What are you getting at, John? What's going on in that cook pot you call a brain?"

Brown leered, narrowing his eyes, and took Ethan to the side of the road, lowering his voice to keep from being overheard by the men.

"What if I were to give you fifty of my men, Ethan? Divide the lot equally."

"What for? Say, you got any of those cigars left Livingston gave us?"

"Fresh out."

"Shit."

"Listen. What say we go back to Montreal? Attack it. Take it ourselves, you and me." Ethan licked his lips, his eyes widening. "Don't tell me you haven't thought about it? You're not dying to? Only—have you the guts?"

"Shhhhh."

"Well? Take it. Lock up the British, deliver the town to Montgomery tied with a blue ribbon."

"You're getting crazy in your middle age, John."

"Somebody has to do it. This is our chance, our one and only."

"You are slick. If I didn't know you I wouldn't trust you far as the end of my nose. Those two would hang us up by the heels for the crows to peck at."

"Pox on 'em both. Besides, what can they do after we take it? Take it from *us*? Ha!"

"I've never seen you like this. What have you been doing, drinking rotten cider? This is crazy talk."

"Were you crazy to try and take Ticonderoga? To stand up before the Congress and sell them on this? Schuyler didn't. Montgomery didn't. Ethan, Ethan, we'll take it and they'll pin medals on us. They'll have to, or look like fools to the Congress, to everybody!"

"You're forgetting you're still a major, three pegs down from Montgomery."

"How do we work it?" Brown pushed his face up too close.

Ethan sighed heavily and yielded to a grin. "First, spring it on the lads. See what they say . . . "

They *said* nothing. They cheered so loudly Brown was forced to clap his hands over his ears.

Ethan raised his hands. "Everybody quiet. Fall out, stand at ease, relax, smoke, drink. Major Brown and I need to talk a few minutes."

He steered Brown into the trees by his elbow. Ethan leaned against a paper birch.

"What if me and my bunch cross below the town, and you and yours up above? Move to the gates, yours at your end, us at ours."

"I'll fire a shot to let you know when we get there."

"Hell no! Caw like a crow. Then we bust in and overrun the place."

"It'll work, Ethan."

"When do you think?"

"Tomorrow before sunrise when everybody's in a deep sleep."

"Good, good, that'll give us time to smooth out our plans and maybe pick up some more Canadians."

"We'll need canoes to get across."

"Another good reason to hold off: Give ourselves time to steal 'em."

"This . . . is going to be fun, Ethan."

"Bigger and better than Ticonderoga! Let's form up and get on back there."

20

★ **Eight** hundred Americans, among them nearly two hundred Green Mountain Boys, set out from Ile-aux-Noix at about ten in the evening heading for a predetermined landing place about three quarters of a mile from their objective.

There, five hundred New Yorkers under Lieutenant Colonel Rudolphus Ritzema set out from the beach with the intention of circling the fort while Montgomery lay back with three hundred reserves. Ritzema sent out flankers who made their way away from the river northwest through pitch blackness. In time, although unaware of it, they gradually altered their direction and began edging back toward the river. Moving along, reluctant to spread out because it was so dark, envisioning an Indian behind every tree, imagining the *kak-kak-kak* of a goshawk to be a human voice signaling attack, blinded by the darkness, they returned to the open beach running into their own troops.

Panic erupted. Shots were fired and suddenly everyone began scrambling for the boats.

Hearing shouting and confusion, Montgomery rushed his reserves forward, quelling the uproar, calling the men to attention and forming them into ranks.

"Your nerves are getting the best of you!"

"We couldn't see shit in there, sir," complained one man.

"Quiet! Act like men, damnit! Obey your officers. Officers, obey your commander. All of you calm down. We'll take a few minutes to catch our breaths and start out again." A chorus of groans greeted this. "Quiet, I said! And pay attention. Why do you think we came all this way? To pick berries? We're taking that fort, and I expect every man to conduct himself properly, in disciplined fashion, with coolness and intelligence!" He had taken to pacing up and down the line. "If I see any man turning tail and running, I'll personally execute him on the spot. Is that clear?"

He moved to the head of the column, joining Ritzema, and they started out. They had gone about a quarter of a mile when a bateau anchored under the *Royal Savage*'s bowsprit began discharging grapeshot and two-pounders. They came whistling through the trees triggering panic. Half the company turned and ran back toward the boats. Montgomery bellowed, threatened, and swore volubly but did not fire his pistol. Saber in hand, he cast about looking for Ritzema, but in the confusion he had moved forward with about fifty of his men.

Exhorting them as they pressed on, Ritzema stopped abruptly and pointed his saber.

"Dot house dere. Dere could be munitions inside. Ve'll take it!"

He divided his men into three sections, dispatching two left and right and leading the third, fewer than twenty men, toward the house, less than forty yards distant. Shots came whizzing at them. They retaliated. Within seconds two defenders were killed. The Americans, relying on trees for cover, suffered no losses. At that point, as a sizable number of Ritzema's original force, having rallied, came up to rejoin him, he attacked in earnest. The skirmish ensued for nearly twenty minutes, but it was clear to the colonel that it was becoming a standoff. It was now closing on three a.m.

"Ve'll come back ven it's light und take dem. Fall back, boys!"

Curiously, by this time having experienced combat, his men's reluctance to fight vanished, displaced by eagerness to oust the defenders. Their disappointment was audible, but they retreated.

The next morning the men who had obeyed the command to stay clear of the boats were invited to join their officers in a council of war on the beach. Montgomery democratically put it to a vote and it was decided to try again then and there. Ritzema spoke with Montgomery. His eyes were filled with worry under their thick blond brows.

"I yust vorry, General, that some of dese may run out on us like last night ven the shooting gets heavy. It's dere artillery could do real damage to us."

Before Montgomery could comment Lieutenant Samuel Lockwood, who had left camp to scout downriver, appeared. He was dripping, as if he'd gone swimming fully clothed. Montgomery returned his salute.

"Sir, one of our galley twelve-pounders hit that bateau that was firing on us. Blew it to bits and either killed all on board or they drowned."

Montgomery clasped Lockwood's shoulder. "Good news for a change."

"Better than that, sir. I got a good look at the *Royal Savage*. It's almost fully equipped and getting ready to move out."

"How can you possibly know that, Samuel?"

"I overheard two deckhands talking. I was in the water hanging onto a hawser right under them." He paused. Montgomery instinctively looked behind him. Some of Ritzema's men and some of his own were edging toward the boats.

"Stay where you are!"

"Vot do you think you're doing?" snarled Ritzema.

The men shuffled back with sheepish expressions.

"Dis is useless, General," muttered Ritzema.

Montgomery shook his head discouragedly. "We seem to have collected every lily-liver in the army." He threw up his hands.

"Dis is disgusting . . . "

"The *Royal Savage* could come up here and destroy our whole fleet," said Lockwood. "Blow a hole in the log boom you could sail a six-master through."

Montgomery looked Ritzema's way. The German's eyes agreed.

"All right, all right," said Montgomery, his tone exasperated. "We'll give it up. Board the boats and head back to base."

They set forth rowing against the current, traveling about four miles south before Montgomery stood up in the bow of the *Enterprise* and called for attention.

"Pull ashore. Everybody!"

He indicated the west bank. There was no beach; the woods came down to within three feet of the water. One after another the vessels put ashore with only the *Enterprise* remaining in midstream.

At the general's command the officers assembled the men, and he addressed them.

"This is outrageous. Unthinkable! It sticks in my craw like a bone. We're running like rabbits. Is this what we came all this way for? If this is how we conduct ourselves against a piddling little installation in the woods, how will we ever take Montreal?"

He went on, no longer trying to shame them into fighting, instead appealing to their patriotism.

"The men at Concord stood their ground and fought like demons. And what of Boston? I ask you, are we men or spineless jackals!"

"Schooner coming!" yelled a man emerging from the woods downriver.

Like lemmings rushing to the edge of a cliff, the men headed en masse for the boats. Montgomery threw up his hands.

21

★ **Their** men staying back, concealing themselves in the trees, Ethan and John Brown knelt and peered through reeds at Mount Royal. Nestled in it, like a child in its mother's lap with her arms protecting it, was their target. That afternoon, along with stealing eighteen canoes, Ethan managed to induce thirty disaffected locals to join them. His own and Brown's men now totaled two hundred and twenty-three. As originally agreed, they would be evenly divided. Additional canoes were found, but when it came time to cross it was estimated that only about a third of the men could be transported at a time. The three trips were made without incident, half the canoes heading up-river, the rest downriver. Landings were made about four miles apart. It was now close to three a.m.

Establishing his base camp about two miles from the town, Ethan hunkered down to wait for one hour before daylight.

By now word had spread throughout town that the notorious Ethan Allen was preparing to attack. Unaware that he had lost the precious element of surprise, Ethan called his followers around and addressed them.

"We'll be starting out shortly, as will Major Brown from the other side at the same time. When we get to the gate the first crow you hear will be them. Once inside we'll head straight for the garrison and disarm them in their beds. There won't be more than two or three dozen of 'em. Once we get the upper hand, we'll disarm the civilians."

"You make it sound easier than falling outta bed," said a man.

"We'll make it easier than that. You surprise 'em with their britches off, that's key. When a man's drawers are down and his gun's out of reach he's more ready to give up than at any other time. Anybody's got any doubts about that I recommend they talk to Captain Delaplace, formerly commander at Fort Ti."

"Amen," murmured Elisha. "What a night."

"This'll be ten times as good," said Ethan. "It's like bowling pins. We knock Montreal down and one by one the other settlements topple. Hey, over there, put out that goddamned fire! There's civilians all around us!"

The fire was smothered.

"I'll tell you boys something else," Ethan went on. "Something that'll sit warm in your hearts, those of you who were with me at Ticonderoga. Mr. Colonel Benedict Arnold is on his way to Canada, this time to try and take Quebec. I predict he'll fall flat on his face. I further predict he'll be taken prisoner." Elisha applauded. "You heard it here first. They'll capture his arse and ship it back to England. Hang him on that movable gallows they got at Tyburn. While we, having cleaned up here, march home as heroes. Heroes!" Everybody cheered. "Shhhh. Hell almighty, keep it down. Taking this town will be easy as taking a pot at brag. Now everybody go over your weapons one last time. And when I give the signal we'll start out. Tonight we make history!"

In town, meanwhile, two hundred civilian volunteers had quit their beds in response to Governor Carleton's summons. Arming themselves, they turned out, joining thirty-five redcoats and a handful of Caughnawagas. And while Ethan's men were double-checking their weapons and relaxing before he gave the order to move out, the Canadians marched out the Quebec Gate toward his camp. Wisely, he had taken the precaution of posting sentries to the four points of the compass. He was about to give the order to start forth when two sentries came running into camp, wild-eyed and gesticulating.

"They're coming! They're coming!"

Ethan looked from one to the other. "Simmer down. Who? What?"

"Montrealers, redcoats, Injuns! Must be four, five hundred!" Ethan gaped. "Lemuel here spotted 'em and come running to my post. We come directly!"

"How far away are they?"

"Less than a mile," said the other. "And coming like the wind!"

"All right, men, you heard. Spread out. We'll ambush the bastards. Find cover. Double quick!"

The Montrealers arrived shortly, breaking ranks, finding their own cover and attacking so swiftly Ethan's men could barely get off first shots. He had sent his Canadian volunteers out to protect his flanks. It was the last he saw of them. Their desertion reduced his numbers by about a third. He was now outnumbered two to one. And as time went on and the fighting increased in intensity others fled.

He had ducked behind a tree and begun firing. The battle waxed noisily and spiritedly for about ten minutes, at which point he realized that the Montrealers, constantly shifting their positions, had surrounded the camp.

Back on the Ile-aux-Noix, morale was plumbing the depths. The troops returned to be greeted by catcalls and sarcastic sallies from the men who remained in camp. Added to their voices were some four hundred men who had arrived in Montgomery's absence. Among these were a hundred New Hampshire Rangers under Colonel Timothy Bedel, and a number of volunteers, including a handful of Dartmouth students. A company of New York artillery, led by Captain John Lamb, also arrived.

Montgomery met with Schuyler and recounted what had happened. Disgust clouded the older man's face.

"Arrant cowards! Shirking, deserting. They should be lined up like dogs and shot!"

"It wasn't easy down there, sir."

"Are you excusing their behavior, General?"

"Not at all, it was the most disgusting exhibition I've ever witnessed. It just snowballed. We sent out flankers who lost their way in the dark and ended up bumping into the main body. Somebody's gun went off, everybody panicked. It was more wholesale confusion than a planned desertion."

"Desertion is desertion, planned or not." Schuyler slammed his fist into his palm. "I knew we should have bypassed St. John's and gone straight to Montreal!"

Montgomery didn't understand the connection but made no comment. "I've an idea, sir."

"I wish I did. Hand me that water." Montgomery gave him the half-filled glass and Schuyler downed four pills. "Wretched things, they taste like bile! I'm listening."

"I think we should take a few days, settle down, regroup, and try to restore morale."

"Cowards are incapable of controlling their morale, Richard; they're too busy worrying about their skins!"

"Perhaps if you were to talk to them . . . "

This Schuyler dismissed with a sharp movement of his hand. "What would you have me do, have them crowd in here and listen to a speech? I look a leader to inspire courage, lift morale? In the midst of making a point I'd probably vomit. You're in command, you handle it. Just don't treat them with silk gloves!"

"We *will* be going back, sir."

"When?"

"When . . . the men are ready."

"Humph. You've got to at least give the impression of discipline, of command."

Montgomery stiffened. "I like to think I do, General."

"All right, all right, don't get your hackles up. Good God, hear that? We don't have troubles enough, now it's starting to rain. With our luck it'll keep up into October. So you intend to try again?"

"Definitely."

"The first thing will be to destroy the *Royal Savage*. Send down the *Enterprise* and some of the row-galleys. Picked men,

Richard, the veterans among us. And good strong rowers. Attack and board her."

"Blow her up."

"If you like. I'd rather she surrender. We could use her.
Look at what Colonel Arnold did with Skene's sloop. But of
course it's up to you, you're in command."

"You are, sir."

"Humph, I can't even command my bladder. Do as you see
fit. And bring back good news for a change. It just might get
me back on my feet for half an hour. Go, go, dismissed. No,
don't salute, I haven't the energy to return it."

The rain persisted all night and all the next day. Out of two
thousand men on the island, nearly a third had taken sick. Men
groused and sulked and openly disobeyed orders. In defiance
of Montgomery's posted order, groups wandered about stealing from the Caughnawagas and the few Canadians living on
the island, and from each other. Four rapists were killed by
Indians. Schuyler directed that the Caughnawagas responsible not be punished. Rumors of enemy attack so frightened
the men Montgomery gave up trying to elevate morale as well
as appeal to patriotic duty.

Then it stopped raining, and for a change there was good
news. The few Caughnawagas living at Fort St. John's deserted, further depleting Major Preston's already thin ranks.

On September 16 Montgomery organized his boats and
again sent men out to protect the log boom to prevent the
Royal Savage from reaching the lake. He then sent off the
main body of his troops and landed them without incident
near the fort.

Little did he realize, likely in his wildest dreams he wouldn't
have imagined, that the absent Ethan Allen was attempting on
his own to steal his thunder and seize Montreal.

And doing an uncommonly poor job of it.

22

★ **Enemy** fire became more intense, more concentrated. Ethan watched men fall on all sides. About ten yards in front of him an officer, holding his pistol upright, was approaching. He fired; the ball whizzed by Ethan's ear. He hurriedly returned fire from his musket and missed also. Again he glanced about. The Montrealers were slowly closing in. A massacre threatened.

"You there," he shouted at the officer who'd shot at him and was now down on one knee behind a stump reloading. "Give me your word that you'll treat us fairly and we'll surrender!"

"Order your men to throw down their arms and raise their hands and no one will be harmed," the man, a lieutenant, ordered him, rising and coming closer.

Ethan took a deep breath and took his hand down from his upper arm where, moments before, a ball had creased it.

"Do it, boys," he called and stepped out into the gray beginning dawn, setting his musket down and raising his hands. As the lieutenant came up, Ethan again looked about. At least three of his men had been killed and five had been wounded. The attackers came running, the Americans were speedily disarmed and marched into a tight group. A fiercely painted Indian came at Ethan, just as he handed his saber to the lieutenant. Ethan slipped behind him, setting him between himself and the Indian. Then a Canadian came running up brandishing his bayonet and driving off the would-be attacker.

"Colonel Ethan Allen?" the lieutenant asked. Ethan nodded. "Lieutenant Leland Covington. You are my prisoner, sir."

"That much I'd already gathered, Lieutenant."

"You're all our prisoners. Order your men to rank, sir; we're taking you in."

Learning that their prize captive was none other than the scourge of Ticonderoga, curious Montrealers quickly gathered around them. The prisoners were lined up in rows of four, and, with Ethan at their head, marched toward the Quebec Gate.

"This is not the capture we had in mind," Ethan muttered to Covington.

Jacob Wall stepped out of line and came up to Ethan.

"What the hell happened to the major?"

"He may already be inside."

"I bet they're back across the river and running for their lives."

"John wouldn't do that, Jacob. I know the man. We've been through too much together, he'd never desert us."

"If he did, he wouldn't have been able to get word to us."

Had he broken in the opposite gate? And would he be able to rescue them when they arrived? The possibility, as remote as it may have been, cheered Ethan the rest of the way to town.

"Your men will be incarcerated," said Covington. "You, sir, will accompany me to General Prescott."

Covington led the parade past a crowd of early risers, past the Place des Armes, passing King George's statue, long since cleansed of its black paint and relieved of its rosary of potatoes. They crossed a small parade ground to a brick building. Ethan saw no sign of Major Brown.

"Stand where you are, Colonel." Covington knocked at the door, got no response, knocked again. The door was opened by a sallow-looking enlisted man.

"Corporal Gravisand, I wish to see the general on a matter of great urgency."

"He's at breakfast, sir."

"Get him. Tell him I have a prisoner, Colonel Ethan Allen of the Green Mountain Men."

"Boys," Ethan corrected him.

Off went the corporal and into the office marched Covington with his prisoner, leaving Ethan standing by the stove as he sat.

"Mind if I sit?" Ethan asked. "I've been on my feet all day and all night." Covington gestured him to a chair. "Thank you, you're a gentleman, Lieutenant."

General Robert Prescott came in, a big man with a perfectly round paunch and pink pig eyes that struck Ethan as intended for a head half the size of the general's. He wore a neatly scissored mustache and reeked of scent. Passing the prisoner, he did not even look in Ethan's direction. He sat at his desk and spoke, still without looking.

"Dismissed, Leland."

"Yes, sir." Covington withdrew after an exchange of salutes.

"Name?"

"Ethan Allen."

"Would that be the same Allen who attacked Fort Ticonderoga?"

"The same Allen who took it."

Prescott slowly raised his face; with every elevated inch the redness seemed to deepen. He shot to his feet, jerking out his saber, waving it under Ethan's nose.

"Damnable rebel! Traitorous snake! You dare attempt to attack my town? Grimy bastard, I'll have you chained to a post in the Place des Armes for the whole populace to piss on!"

"Like they pissed on the king?" Ethan sneered. Prescott gawked. "Put that fucking thing down before you cut yourself and stop the shouting, General Arsehole!"

Prescott slowly lowered his blade. His little eyes bulged, his choler ascended his face like wine poured into a glass, and his lip began quivering. In seconds, he was trembling with rage. Ethan yawned.

"You touch me with that goddamned pig-sticker and I'll shove it down your throat! I'm a fucking prisoner of war and I'll be treated so. Or Carleton himself will hear of it!"

Attracted by the shouting, a captain barged in, stopping so quickly he nearly fell over. He moved behind the desk and whispered to the general. Whatever he said calmed him almost instantaneously. He glared at Ethan.

"I *won't* harm him. But you get out of here, Captain. Go round up the Canadians that were with him. See that they're lined up against the north wall and shot. At once!"

"Hold on!" burst Ethan. "I surrendered on Covington's promise that nobody'd be harmed. We'd be treated decently. You can't go killing them."

Prescott growled. "You're invited to watch, traitor. What are you waiting for, Captain McCloud?"

The captain started back around the desk. Ethan held up a hand. Then stepped forward and ripped open the top of his shirt, buttons flying.

"You don't kill them, General High-and-mighty. Kill me. Here! Now! Only before you do, I want your sworn promise you won't lay a finger on any of my men. They'll be treated honorably."

"General—" began the captain.

"Shut up." Prescott's little eyes flicked from one to the other. A sadistic leer crawled down his face. "Agreed," he said to Ethan. "They'll live. You die. Oh, not now. Not in Montreal. But as sure as God is in his heaven you shall wear a halter at Tyburn, goddamn your seditious soul! Captain McCloud, get this scum out of my sight and see that he's chained in the filthiest cage we've got. He's to be fed slops and water and held incommunicado till further notice."

"Fuck you and the Duchess of Marlborough's cat!"

Around came the saber. Ethan ducked, and the captain pulled him back and led him away.

Word that Ethan Allen had been taken by the British reached the camp in the woods near St. John's three days later. By that time Major John Brown had returned to join the attack on the fort. Ira confronted him moments after he walked into camp. It had stopped raining, but the woods dripped ceaselessly and leaden skies hinted at more rain.

"What happened up by the St. Lawrence, Major?"

Brown spread his hands innocently and assumed an anxious expression. They stood by a stack of hogsheads and crates of dry rations. Within the hour an attempt was to be made to board the *Royal Savage*. Montgomery planned to turn the vessel's guns on the fort while his men attacked the three sides protected by redoubts.

"I really don't know, Ira. I only wish I did."

"You were there." He searched Brown's eyes. "With Ethan."

"We started out from here together. But we split up."

"When did you last see him?"

"On the road between Chambly and the river. We were heading north, he was coming back."

"You spoke."

"Briefly."

"He said nothing about attacking Montreal?"

Brown had taken to studying the ground. A voice spoke behind Ira. "Tell him the truth, Major. Attacking Montreal wasn't your brother's idea, it was his. Mr. Allen just went along with it."

A man in stained and torn buckskins had come up behind Ira. He wore a saber and a tomahawk thrust into his belt. Ira turned. He did not recognize him.

"I know, I was there," he went on. He pointed to Brown. "With him."

"I don't know you. I don't know what you're talking about. I have to go, Ira."

He started off. Ira caught his arm, but he pulled free and went on.

"Tell me everything."

"We met on the road. Him, the major, talked your brother into trying to capture the town. He and his boys were to storm one gate and us the other at the opposite end, only when it come time to start out he, Brown, got cold feet and ordered us further upriver, so's we could cross back over without Mr. Allen and his boys seeing."

Ira growled. "Leaving Ethan high and dry."

"Brown got cold feet, like I say. Made me sick, but we had to follow orders. So we crossed back over."

"Without Ethan even suspecting . . . "

"How could he know? Being so far separated from us. And pitch dark and all."

"And he and everybody with him was captured. Now they'll hang him for a traitor."

The man gulped and sent grimy fingertips to his throat. "I'm sorry, Lieutenant."

"Not as sorry as Brown's going to be, the son of a bitch. What's your name?"

"Louis Kelly, attached to the Connecticut fifteenth. I volunteered when the major come around asking for me. I wish to hell I kept my hand down and my big mouth shut."

"You're not to blame for anything. Thanks, Louis. Now, if you'll excuse me, I want a further word with the major."

Ira found Brown talking to Montgomery outside the general's tent. The major's back was to Ira. Grabbing his shoulder, Ira swung him around and smashed him in the jaw. Down he went as if pole-axed.

"Lieutenant!"

"Sorry to interrupt you, General. This is personal between us; that was a small token of appreciation for his handing my brother over to the British."

Men had begun crowding around them. Ira explained briefly. Montgomery seemed incapable of closing his mouth. He finally spoke."

"You'd better throw some water on him."

"I'd rather a bucket of shit."

"Water, Lieutenant, plain water."

Schuyler was sitting on the edge of his cot in his nightshirt when Montgomery called to him from outside the tent flap.

"Come in, Richard. Yes, I've heard about your friend Allen. I hate to say I told you so." Schuyler rolled his eyes. "So erratic. As impulsive as a rattlesnake. He's certainly outdone himself this time. They've probably hanged him already. Carleton has to be ecstatic."

"Sir?"

"Don't you understand? I'll amend that. They haven't hanged him yet, he's far too valuable a prize. The hero of Ticonderoga languishing in a cell, to be paraded around town in shackles."

"Disgusting." Montgomery shook his head.

"You want to know what's disgusting? He's given them a lift when they least expected and most needed it. And if any Canadians were seriously considering coming over to our side, we can forget that. I'm writing a letter to General Washington, to apprise him of the dire consequences to our side, make sure he gets the facts. It's outrageous. He's a wild man. We should have shipped him home when we had the chance!"

"You wanted to, sir. Blame Lieutenant Colonel Warner and me."

"I'm not blaming anybody. It's a bit late and pointless for that. What burns me is that I've lived in fear *something* like this would happen all along. How can anybody control a man who writes his own rules, is as changeable as a weathervane, as reliable as a fox in a henhouse?"

"Ahh . . . "

"What?"

"One other thing, sir."

"More good news, no doubt."

"His brother just knocked Major Brown cold. It turns out Brown and Ethan made a pact. They planned to attack Montreal together. Only Brown changed his mind at the last minute and deserted him."

"You don't say?"

"He's evidently admitted it."

"John Brown. I thought those two were as close as brothers."

"They were."

"I don't like that, Richard. It's reprehensible. Granted, the idea was insane, a monumental blunder; lamentably poor judgment on both their parts, but when a man makes a pact he's honor-bound to stick to it."

"Brown should be disciplined. He might as well have shot him in the back."

"Agreed. But the horse is out of the barn. Let it go."

"His brother won't."

"He's on your staff; you talk to him. And keep them separated. We don't need another problem. And no duels."

"No, sir. Sir?"

"What?"

"Isn't there anything we can do for Ethan? How about a prisoner exchange?"

"Impossible. You're talking about the man who stole Ticonderoga. It's like picking His Majesty's pocket. I doubt Carleton would exchange him for John Hancock and half the Congress. Besides, any feelers we put out would take time, and there is no time. When they get bored with parading him around they'll hang him, which shouldn't be more than a few days."

Montgomery nodded. He wondered what Ira would do to John Brown when that grim news reached them.

23

★ **Montgomery** postponed the attack, delaying it until October to buy time to assess every possible strategy and increase his somewhat sketchy knowledge of the fort. While he waited, mindful of St. John's importance as the gateway to Montreal,

Governor Carleton sent Major Preston five hundred reinforcements.

Montgomery persisted in the belief that preserving the
Royal Savage intact as Schuyler had proposed would be of no
benefit. When he attacked the fort he would destroy the
schooner.

With Schuyler's permission he also resolved that before
throwing so much as a single canister of grapeshot against St.
John's he would capture Fort Chambly, an easier target in
many respects. When word of Chambly's fall reached St.
John's it would have a devastating effect on the garrison's
morale and possibly hasten Preston's surrender.

Intelligence from James Livingston established that Major
Stopford at Fort Chambly commanded eighty-eight officers
and men. Montgomery sent two bateaux carrying between
them four nine-pounders, slipping past St. John's artillery
and the *Royal Savage* during a drenching rain. Fifty Americans went along under the command of Colonel Timothy
Bedel and Major Brown. Livingston kept his promise and
contributed three hundred Canadians, much to Brown's astonishment.

Bedel set up batteries south and west of the fort and across
the river and opened fire. The thin masonry quickly became
riddled with holes, throwing the garrison into a panic. A chim-
ney was reduced to rubble. Within the hour Stopford surrendered. The Americans acquired three mortars, six tons of
gunpowder, a hundred fifty muskets, sixty-five hundred car-
tridges, three hundred swivel-shot, and a hundred thirty-eight
barrels of provisions.

Now St. John's was covered from above and below. Montgomery had one last task before attacking the fort: the *Royal
Savage*. Employing the two nine-pounder-mounted bateaux
sent downriver to Fort Chambly and adding four more, he
raked the *Royal Savage* and the bateau battery anchored near
it with a withering crossfire, sending both to the bottom.
This done he mounted a battery across the river, opposite the

unprotected side of the fort, there being no wall on the east side, the only protection afforded by a moat.

The east bank battery bombarded the interior, the first volley demolishing the stone house and wrecking the brick houses, detonating munitions stored in the largest in an ear-splitting explosion. But the garrison held on, courageously defending the walled sides against artillery and musket fire.

On the hill on the northwest side of the fort a battery had been set up, composed mainly of mortars and twelve-pounders. From dawn to noon the Americans concentrated their fire against the wall, the stockade fence demolished early on. But the wall was earthen and eight feet thick, and the artillery failed to breach it.

Montgomery met with Ritzema, Bedel, and Captain John Lamb, who provided the battery out of the Second Artillery.

"We're running low on cannon balls," said Bedel, a rugged little man, all sinew and spleen.

"Und can't dent that *verdamnt* vall," rasped Ritzema.

Montgomery scratched his chin. "We've got to change tactics." He sat on an empty powder keg, smoking a cigar. He began fingering the sweat from inside his collar. It had rained on and off all night and turned cold. He called to Lieutenant Allen. "Ira, bring us one of the prisoners. An officer."

"What's your plan?" Bedel asked.

"The obvious, Timothy," said Montgomery.

Ira returned with an officer in a somewhat bedraggled blue-and-white uniform. He looked barely out of his teens, his hair pulled back and tied in a bow, his eyes deep and black as an Indian's, his face soft, looking as if it had never felt a razor.

"Your name?"

"Lieutenant John André."

"Did you come down with the governor's reinforcements or were you in the garrison?"

"The garrison."

Ira explained. "He led a party out to try and circle the battery on the northwest corner. And got caught."

"Lieutenant," said Montgomery. "You will go back to the fort with four of our men under a flag of truce. Go directly to Major Preston. Tell him it's hopeless. Continuing the attack can only ensure additional unnecessary loss of life. He has one hour to decide. If in that time he declines to surrender, tell him we'll concentrate all our batteries on the interior from the east bank."

"Yes, sir."

"Ira, fetch Samuel Lockwood, pick four men, and escort this man inside with a white flag."

Ira swallowed lightly. André saw and suppressed a snicker.

Preston needed no urging. He surrendered, obliged to not just because of the enemy's superiority in numbers and firepower, but also because he had only three day's provisions remaining.

The shooting ceased. Four American drummers began beating in unison. Montgomery ordered his officers to line up the men in front of the main gate. Out of the fort marched a company of Royal Fusiliers in red coats trimmed with yellow. They were followed by Royal Artillery in dark blue coats, red trim and sashes, bucket-topped boots, and gold-laced cocked hats. Kilted Royal Highland Emigrants followed, with a throng of Canadians and civilian artisans bringing up the rear.

The victors' contrasting individualism showed in their uniforms. Lamb's artillery wore blue with buff facing. The Green Mountain Boys, no longer content with buckskins or civilian attire with a sprig of pine in their hatbands, wore green greatcoats with red trim. The men from Connecticut wore whatever pleased them, with no interest in brass buttons, blue coats, or cocked hats.

A representative detachment was selected from each colony. Captain Lamb led them past the smartly uniformed British and into the fort. Preston's men formally laid down their arms. It was all over.

III

In Durance

24

★ **Ethan** finished pacing his cell, determining that it was less than eight feet by about five and a half. No window. There was an iron bed with a badly stained straw tick less than two inches thick. It lay on slats. No pillow, neither sheet nor blanket. Bare walls, a bucket in which to relieve himself, nothing else. The slot in the iron door he judged to be about eight by four inches. No glass, no mesh, a bare opening.

He sat on the edge of the bed, his elbows propped on his knees, chin resting in his upraised palms. What had happened to John? Had he tried and found himself unable to cross the river? Impossible, *he'd* crossed without anything close to a mishap.

"He couldn't have lost his nerve. Not John. He wouldn't leave me in the lurch, not even to save his own skin. What the hell happened?"

Had his men talked him out of going through with it? He'd never have listened.

"Not John Brown."

Their combined forces could have easily taken the town. And all the glory would have been theirs.

"Colonel? Hell almighty, Washington would have made me a general!"

What truly galled him was that nearly two-thirds of his men had melted away.

"There sure is no duplicating the Green Mountain Boys, God bless 'em."

Familiar eyes appeared at the door slot. A key ring rattled. The door opened, in sauntered General Prescott.

"Well, well, well, Colonel Rebel. Living in the lap of luxury, I see."

"What do you want, General Short Fuse?"

"Please, spare me your bumpkin sarcasm. I came to tell you—"

"How about some paper and a pen? I'd like to write my wife and little ones. Don't you think they got a right to know what happened? I got other letters to write."

"Amazing, you can actually write? And read?"

"I'm entitled."

"They can wait until you're settled in your new quarters."

"How about taking off these shackles? What do I need with shackles when I'm locked up in here tighter than a tick?"

"You misunderstand. They're not to prevent your escaping, they're to teach you humility."

"Degrade me, you mean." I've heard of sore losers, but you're a lousy winner."

Steps sounded outside. The cell door stood ajar. A tall, urbane-looking man, wearing his own hair curled up around his ears, a high white collar with ruffle front, and an officer's jacket without epaulets filled the doorway. Prescott stiffened and began saluting in rapid motion. The newcomer gestured him to stop.

"Governor Carleton," said Ethan. "This is an honor."

"On your feet in His Excellency's presence!" snapped Prescott.

"Stay where you are," murmured Carleton. He set about adjusting his cuffs while he appraised the prisoner. "Colonel

Allen. The thorn in all our sides. I've news that should please you. Both St. John's and Chambly have fallen."

"They're on their way. Coming to see you, Governor."

"Coming to their deaths," growled Prescott.

"Richard . . . " Carleton looked Prescott's way, his expression bored.

"Yes, sir." Again Prescott launched into a series of rapid salutes. On the way out he paused to look back. "Sir . . . "

"It's all right," said Carleton.

"What am I going to do to him wearing all this hardware?" Ethan asked.

Carleton moved to close the door after the general. "I've a few questions, Colonel."

"I'm back to being a civilian, Governor. I was when your boys caught up with us." Carleton was staring at him. Admiringly? "What?"

"Amazing, you actually planned to capture Montreal?"

"Sure. And we will."

"Astounding. I scarcely know whether to commend you on your courage or reproach you for your recklessness. Now then, how many men does General Schuyler have?"

"I wouldn't know, I'm not privy to inside his head. Civilian, remember? Why don't you ask General Montgomery when he gets here?"

"How droll. That's what we've been missing around here, drollery. Again, how many men?"

"Come on, you know full well if I knew I wouldn't tell you. Anything. What are you going to do, torture me?"

"Hang you."

"You? Personally?"

"You'll be leaving here soon. But before that you're going on exhibition. The people are clamoring to see the Yankee wild man. We can't disappoint them, can we?"

"You disappoint me, Governor. That type of thing is more in Prescott's line. It's really beneath you."

"The people would never forgive me if they didn't get a look at you before you leave."

"Leave for where?"

"You'll see."

"When?"

"Day after tomorrow."

"England?"

"You sound in a rush to get to the gallows."

"Hey, can I get pen and paper so's I can write my wife?"

"I'll see to it."

"And can you get the bastards to take off these shackles? I mean, I'm locked up, with people on all sides who'd like nothing better than to slit my throat, what do I need with all this iron?"

"I'll inform General Prescott as to your request for writing materials. Good day, Mr. Allen."

And he was out the door. Ethan smiled. Carleton was such a sad man. One would imagine he was carrying Canada on his shoulders.

25

★ **Word** spread quickly throughout Canada and south of the St. Lawrence that the infamous Ethan Allen was to be taken to England to be hanged as a traitor. To his brother Ira this came as no surprise. His reaction was just as predictable. He went looking for John Brown. He found him relaxing in his tent. The major's chin was bruised and swollen. When Ira pushed inside, Brown got up quickly, as if afraid he would be assaulted again.

Ira glared at him. "Have you heard?"

"It's all over camp."

"It's probably already gotten back to Bennington. Mary will hear."

"What are you staring at?" The major sent his fingers to his bruise. "You could have broken it."

"I did try. Why did you desert him, John? You had to know it would turn out like this."

"Whatever I tell you, you won't believe me."

"Try the truth and we'll see. Louis Kelly says . . . "

"Louis Kelly is a liar. I . . . made the mistake of dressing him down in front of the others when he was caught sleeping on sentry duty. He fails to appreciate that I could have ordered him shot."

"Never mind him. Give me your version."

"It's nothing of the sort, Ira, it's the truth. I haven't told a soul what I'm about to tell you, only because it sounds *too* pat."

"What does?"

"Would you like a drink?"

"Not with you."

"Mind if I do?" He got a bottle out of a sack under his cot, uncorked it, swigged, and put it back. "We got across the river a good distance apart, well out of sight of each other. By 'we' I mean about forty men. Earlier, when we went looking for canoes I had three times that number. They melted away in the dark. Omar Luddington . . . you know Omar . . . "

"Just go on."

"From Connecticut. A cooper. Good man. I'd made him my second in command. He and I talked while the men pulled the canoes up and covered them with brush. He raised a good point. What if the same thing, all the deserting, had happened to Ethan downriver? That would leave us with under a hundred men between us. A hundred men to take Montreal? Of course, we didn't know if he'd lost any. The problem was, there was no way of contacting him. More than four miles separated us, with Montreal midway between."

"You could have sent a canoe downriver to check."

"To put ashore and look for them in the dark? Would that have made sense?"

"So then and there you just quit."

"Not exactly. It wasn't like that. Omar and I called everybody together and put it to them. I swear on my mother's head, Ira, I didn't paint it black, I didn't paint it white. I just set it out for them to discuss. We took a vote. Only four wanted to go on. About one out of ten."

"Of course you tried to talk them into it."

"Perhaps I should have. But I didn't. I honestly couldn't see the point in trying. Only four?"

"You got out, leaving Ethan. Oh, he might have put up a fight, but against such odds he'd either have to surrender or be massacred. You saw that coming, a six-year-old would."

"Yes."

"And still you left. Your friend, the bravest man you've ever fought alongside. You threw him away like a bucket of slops dumped over a ship's rail. And tied a noose around his neck."

"Yes. I did it. It's done. Now I have to live with it."

Ira's hands shot out, seizing his neck. "Die with it, bastard!"

Brown didn't struggle, didn't even move even though his face began reddening and he could not breathe.

"Goddamn your cowardly soul!"

He relaxed his grip, dropped his hands.

"What should I say? To you? To his wife, to anybody? What words can there possibly be? You hate the sight of me, Seth does, all the Green Mountain Boys do. Even Montgomery and Schuyler." He shook his head.

"You want me to believe that's how it was."

"That's exactly how it was. I've added nothing, left nothing out. Talk to Omar Luddington."

"I intend to."

He went out. Brown buried his face in his hands.

26

★ **About** ten yards from the statue of King George, a small platform about six feet high had been erected. Matching iron rings had been installed in the center. Twelve inches of chain were fastened to each ring, the opposite ends secured to manacles around the prisoner's wrists. So short were the chains that the prisoner had to kneel.

A crowd surrounded him. The platform was littered with broken eggs, squashed tomatoes, and other missiles. His face, his exposed chest, his whole torso were splattered with eggs. A drunk stood at the corner of the platform exhorting the crowd. Two redcoats stood below, their expressions impassive, their muskets at parade rest.

Ethan had been chained in place since midmorning. Now the sun was lowering over Mount Royal Lookout. Ethan had succeeded in escaping the discomfort and humiliation by fleeing into the sanctuary of his mind. Carleton disappointed him. He had allowed Prescott to indulge his malicious streak, let the citizens amuse themselves and vent their bitterness against the Yankee Satan in the basest way possible.

He did manage to write four letters before they came for him. The first was to Mary. Loraine, returned home from Woodbury with the other children by now, would read it to her.

Dear Mary,

A curious thing has happened, though nothing to worry about. In attempting to capture Montreal, we ourselves were surprised and captured. Just black bad luck. Fortunately, although they've put me in a cell, I'm in no danger of my life. They've told me I'm far too valuable a catch to waste on the gallows, so in that respect you can all put your minds at ease.

They are treating me well. My cell is clean and not uncomfortable. The food is tolerable, simple but nutritious. They've not harmed me nor any of my men. General Prescott has been a more gracious host than warden. We talk often, and it helps pass the time. As to what will happen, they'll probably keep us all here until our troops arrive in force and capture Montreal. At which point the governor can point to us as an example of how humanely they treat prisoners.

In the meantime I'm sending off letters to friends in high places and I'm certain that they will do everything in their considerable power to negotiate an exchange of prisoners whereby we'll all be freed even before the Americans get here. Once I'm out of here I will of course head directly home.

As I've said, they're treating us well. I'm in good health and mean to stay that way. I'll write regularly and keep you up on things. Take very good care of yourselves. You're all in my prayers, my dreams, and my thoughts. And I count the days until I can return to you.

Love to all,
E.

He ducked as a tomato came at him. A second one struck one of the guards, and an egg shattered against his shoulder. Ethan marveled, the man remained immobile. Ethan looked about the circle of faces; he'd never seen such hatred, it was as if he alone were responsible for rising up against the Mother Country. But the exhibition, the whole odious exercise, was beginning to bore, the crowd was slowly dispersing. He refused to duck as a piece of meat struck his forehead.

He also wrote to George Washington, Governor Trumbull, and John Hancock, emphasizing anew the importance of capturing Montreal and eventually ousting the British from all of

Canada. He knew that whoever posted the letters would read and censor them, but could not resist mentioning their intention.

He did not ask to be repatriated, electing instead to indulge his histrionic flair in unabashed appeal to their consciences. To all three he wrote:

"I don't ask to be exchanged. I know they will hang me as a traitor because they have already so informed me. I have not told my wife and family and trust that you will not. I look forward to the gallows knowing that I die as I have lived, a Patriot. Convinced that independence will ultimately be ours. It is the prize to which all free men are entitled. And my life and the lives of others are a small price to pay for it. I only hope that my country will remember me as a man who did his limited best to fight tyranny, help to establish the justice we so richly deserve, and bring precious liberty to these shores."

They released him at sundown, drenched him with a bucket of water, and escorted him dripping and shivering back to his cell.

27

★ **They** woke Ethan early, banging on the door with what sounded like a sledgehammer. He couldn't be certain of the time; with no window he was unable to tell whether it was light or dark out. He was fed a bran cake so dry it tasted like compressed sawdust. To wash it down he had the usual cup of tepid water with the strange, unidentifiable odor to it. He was given time to relieve himself and dispose of it in the hole dug for that purpose outside the front door. He was then marched to a small wagon drawn by a mule. Pieces of dried turnip and bits of straw littered the shallow bed. An armed guard shared the seat with the driver. Prescott did not appear to taunt him good-bye. He probably hadn't gotten out of bed yet.

"Where to?" he asked the guard, a man a foot shorter than the musket with fixed bayonet he carried, who hummed off-key to himself when he wasn't whispering to the driver.

"Down the river."

Thirty minutes later they creaked and jounced to a stop on a dock beside a derelict of a brigantine. Ethan read *Gaspé* on the stern. He was taken aboard and belowdecks, his shackles exchanged for a new set of irons twice as heavy as the old ones. He was pushed into a hold and his leg irons fastened by two chains to a bar bolted to a hanging knee on the hull.

Surrounded by fetid odors, lying in pitch darkness, he could hear rats scurrying at the far end. Ethan shuddered; he despised rats. He squinted, looking for beady red eyes, but could see none. He could hear bilgewater gently sloshing.

"Ah me, welcome aboard. On to England. London. Tyburn Hill. The gallows. Mary was right, bless her heart, I ought to have stayed home and tended to the planting."

Six weeks of this luxury crossing the Atlantic? By the time they let him out he'd be stone blind. He thought of the Book of Genesis and Joseph cast into prison. And the butcher and the baker of the king of Egypt, who had offended him. All the prisoners.

"At least Joseph had company."

Only didn't Pharaoh hang the chief baker?

What were they doing to his men, to Jacob and Elisha? Were all of them to be taken to England, or only the ringleader? He dozed until awakened when food was brought to him by a sailor. With him was an officer in a jacket with epaulets, some strands of which were unraveling. Light flooded down behind them through an open hatch cover, some of it reaching Ethan.

"Colonel Allen?"

The officer's companion set down a tin pot of stew and tea in a battered cup.

"He's not here," said Ethan. "He'll be back."

"Sense of humor."

"You want me to be serious?"

"Permit me to introduce myself. Captain Royal, master of this vessel."

"About these irons . . . "

"They're standard manacles, sir."

"It's not them, it's the shackles. They must weigh at least fifty pounds. And look, that bar they're attached to is only six-foot long."

"Eight. And here you have a chest you can sit on or that can serve as a bed. Get you off the floor."

"Not far enough so's the rats can't get at me."

"You're aboard ship, Colonel. Rats go with a ship like milk with tea."

"I don't mind the manacles, but I really don't need these leg irons. Can you get somebody down here and I'll gladly make him a present of them?"

"I'm sorry. The general specifically instructed me as to how and with what you were to be ironed."

"Pig-Eyes Prescott."

"General Prescott."

"My dear friend."

Royal was kneeling. He smelled of talcum; he was middle-aged, perhaps ten years older than Ethan. His face was pitted from the pox and one eye, his right, had a slight tendency to wander.

"I'm genuinely sorry, Colonel, but orders are orders."

"I swear, I don't know what that man has got against me."

"Possibly your treason."

"Carleton's at least a gentleman. But just as bad. Petty, sadistic . . . "

"Please, I'd rather we didn't discuss either."

"Done up like this I can only sleep on my back."

"So it would appear."

"I don't sleep on my back. I sleep either on my side or my stomach, but not my back. I can't."

"You'll learn to."

"Have it your way. When do we sail?"

"Sail?"

"For England?"

"Who told you that?"

"Aren't we?"

"Not this ship."

"Then what am I doing here?"

"This, Colonel, is your prison."

"For how long?"

"That I don't know. I know we're not going anywhere, not in the foreseeable future. We're not seaworthy, at least not to cross the ocean. We're awaiting repairs to the hull; we've been awaiting repairs since last winter."

"So you sit here, and now I sit here. I'll ask you again. And you think it over. These leg irons . . . "

"No."

Exerting all his strength, Ethan climbed onto the chest and lay on his back. "It won't work. They're too goddamned heavy. Look at the way that bar joining my ankles weighs down. The shackles cut into my insteps. Can't you at least get me a board or something to shove under the bar, to help keep the pressure off my flesh?"

Royal sighed, tilting his head and eyeing him. "I suppose."

"There you are, you're a human being after all."

"It's not me, Colonel."

"Pig-Eyes, I know."

"I've been ordered to treat you severely. I have no alternative but to do so. Try your food."

Ethan sampled the stew. "Not bad. A little salty, but it'll do."

"It's the best we have. It's what I, Lieutenant Bradley, and the other officers eat. And you'll be alloted a daily cup of grog. We're fresh out, but there's a delivery on the way."

"Thank you. Can I ask a question? What have you heard about my men? I mean are they staying in Montreal or coming here? Or going where? And are they unharmed?"

"I can't say. I don't know. General Prescott will be coming by."

"Oh, that I look forward to."

"Ask him."

"He wouldn't tell me shit, Captain, not if it put gold doubloons in his pocket."

"I'm sorry, I must go."

"Good-bye and thank you."

The door was closed, restoring the darkness. The rats kept up their scurrying.

"Get me out of here, General Washington, Jonathan, Hancock. Somebody. I don't deserve this, not me. I'm more than a hero, I'm a goddamned symbol! Hey, this is Ethan Allen talking. George, Jonathan, John, anybody out there listening?"

28

★ **Ethan's** prejudiced estimate of his importance to the cause was not without foundation. On the other hand, he'd never have imagined either the breadth or the intensity of the adverse reaction to his failed attempt to capture Montreal. Thousands shared General Schuyler's opinion. And more people expressed anger at Ethan than sympathy. His rashness was viewed as stupid and irresponsible. Even Seth Warner expressed strong disapproval, citing the fact that it couldn't have happened at a worse time, when the French Canadians were beginning to waver between loyalty to the Crown and siding with the Americans.

Montgomery was just as chagrined, just as disappointed. Impressed by Ethan's courage and daring, he had grown fond of him. But in the days following the fiasco, given time to mull

over the consequences, he became increasingly disenchanted
with the man he'd championed so ardently to Schuyler.
Among the Green Mountain Boys and the others who had
taken St. John's and Chambly, there was almost unanimous
disapproval of Ethan's actions. Schuyler put his sentiments
succinctly: "He's made us enemies and lost us friends."

Montgomery's hostility toward Ethan increased daily. He
denounced him as a selfish glory-seeker who cared only for
himself and his reputation, not the Revolution. The British
gloated that the action served to turn all the Canadians back
to them.

Among his countrymen in high places there was more than
resentment and dismay toward Ethan, there was relief that the
Army was rid of him. No one could deny that he had served
his country well in the early days, but now the war was taking a different turn, becoming a form of fighting with which
he had no experience. There was no place for an undisciplined
freelancer in carefully planned, strategically oriented warfare.
His special talents were no longer needed. He emerged as an
example of the harm a badly conceived attack can wreak.

Chained in the hold of the *Gaspé* and alone in darkness,
Ethan had no inkling of the reaction his rashness had stirred
up. He never suspected how much anger and how little sympathy he'd engendered. In his ego, the hero of Ticonderoga
had become a beacon to his countrymen, and his failure to
take Montreal would only spur them to greater effort to throw
off the shackles of tyranny.

While the shock waves rolled through the colonies and
through Schuyler's expeditionary force, one man held his
opinion, avoided discussing the incident, and kept to himself.
Major John Brown threw himself into his daily duties and
nightly wrestled with his conscience, and drank.

Captain Royal visited Ethan at least once a day. He was sympathetic to the prisoner's plight and frustrated by the severe
restrictions General Prescott had insisted be placed on Ethan.
Royal came to admire his prisoner's fortitude, which only in-

creased his disgust with the situation. Despite Prescott's orders to treat Ethan harshly, to deny him the smallest comfort, Royal saw to it that two small wooden blocks were provided him to slip under the crossbar connecting his ankle shackles, to prevent them from cutting into his flesh. Royal also gave him a candle, promising that it would be replaced when necessary.

"I appreciate it, Captain. 'They grope in the dark without light.' "

"Sounds like the Bible."

"Job. 'They grope in the dark without light, and he maketh them to stagger like a drunken man.' "

"You're a religious man."

"I know my Bible. But I'm not religious like you mean. I'm a deist. Me and Ben Franklin. I believe in God on the evidence of reason and nature only, no miracles, no supernatural stuff. None of that. Not the most popular religion."

"Don't tell General Prescott."

"Why not?"

"He's extremely devout. To him a deist is a heathen."

"He sure acts devout. I had thirteen Canadians with me, I wasn't in his office five minutes when he ordered 'em taken out and shot."

"He can be rigid."

"He's an arsehole. I made him back off that one. You should have seen him with the governor. He practically got down on the floor and kissed his feet."

"Yes, well, he'll be visiting you."

"No surprise there; he can't resist gloating."

"We must arrange a signal."

"What for?"

"That candle. If he knew I gave it to you he'd dress me down in front of my whole crew. And write a report. When he comes I'll knock at the door and call 'Allen.' That'll tell you he's with me and you must snuff the candle and hide it."

"All right. Captain, can you get somebody in here to empty

my excrement tub? It's getting so gamy my eyes are water-ing."

Royal leaned a little closer to him, sniffed, and smiled. "You are as well. Your food'll be here shortly. I'll see you tomor-row."

"Thanks for the candle and the visit." Royal shook his head and went out. "Man sympathizes, he really does."

Good. Don't play on it, don't encourage it in the least; like a seed, it would grow of its own accord. Wooden blocks to relieve the weight, a little light, next maybe get rid of some shackles, at least the ones on his ankles.

The candle aroused the rats' curiosity. They lined up at the far end and stared out of their ruby eyes. Ethan counted eleven, but there were more hiding in their nests. They looked identical. Three approached, leaving the others to watch them. They came within eight feet of him, positioning themselves on their bellies, their little feet together in front of them, studying him. He introduced himself.

" . . . hero of Ticonderoga."

He gave them names. General Prescott, Governor Carle-ton, His Majesty. King George was easy to identify, he bore a white patch on top of his head. And the governor was slightly larger than the other two.

Four days later a loud knocking startled Ethan out of his daydream.

"Allen!"

He snatched up the candle, snuffed it. Sitting up on his chest, he shoved the candle under his left thigh. The door opened. Light framed Captain Royal and a second man, a fa-miliar shape despite Ethan's inability to make out his face. Royal carried a lit candle, setting it on the floor. In strode Prescott, his saber swinging by his side.

"Look who's here!" he burst. "If it isn't Colonel Traitor!"

"Look who's here, General Nuisance. Hero of the Battle of the Desk Drawers!"

"Nicholas . . . " Captain Royal stepped forward. "Your handkerchief." Prescott gagged Ethan. Too tightly.

"I shall talk, you shall listen. Good Lord, Nicholas, he stinks to high heaven. Why isn't a bucket thrown on him daily?"

"I doubt if that would help, sir."

"He reeks of the sty!"

"He's been in here eleven days."

"Get a man in here to unlock him from that bar. I want him up on deck. Don't just stand there . . . "

What was this? A change of heart? Hardly. The venomous expression had if anything become more pronounced. Damn his black soul and his pig eyes!

Ethan was released from the bar, though his shackles were left intact. They brought him up on deck. Curious crewmen stopped their work to watch as he emerged into the sunlight. The sun struck his eyes, twin needles piercing. Prescott laughed.

Somebody fetch a rope. A good stout one. Traitor, you're going to take a bath. Much as that might conflict with your personal hygiene. Rags and all."

"But his manacles, his shackles," protested Royal.

"Leave them. If the rope breaks, so be it."

A hawser was brought, fastened around Ethan's waist and he was lowered over the starboard side, gag still in place. Into the river he was plunged over his head. It was freezing! He was pulled up, unable to sputter or gasp. He could hear Prescott laughing uproariously above. He was the only one. Looking up, Ethan could see Royal's men peering over the rail in a line. Not one looked even slightly amused. Nor did the captain.

"Again!" bawled Prescott. "And keep it up till we're rid of that frightful stench."

Down and up. Down and up. Ethan crinkled his nose trying to keep from drawing up water, closed his mind, and fueled his hatred. Each time he broke water he could hear Prescott laughing.

"You'll drown him," Royal protested. "He can't breathe through his nose."

"Can't talk, either. All right, that's enough. Haul him up."

He could hear men calling out "heave, heave" in unison. He stood on the deck struggling to fill his lungs. Prescott circled him slowly sniffing, holding his handkerchief to his nose.

"Ugh. Not much improvement."

"Sir, if we were to remove his irons," began Royal. "Give him a bit of soap, let him bathe himself in a tub."

"Give him rose water, call in a barber, dress him in silk and velvet. I don't think! His shackles stay on. Permanently!" He looked around. "Anybody here so much as loosens one, one!, he will earn himself fifty lashes. Yes, Colonel Traitor, they stay on until your flesh grows around them." Holding his handkerchief to his nose, he spoke through it, leaning too close. "You've no idea how fortunate you are. Were it up to me you wouldn't have survived this long. I'd have stretched your miserable neck the day they brought you in!"

"Is there any reason to keep his gag on?"

"Take it off."

It was removed. Ethan gasped and gasped.

"Well now, Colonel, what have you to say for yourself? Any more insults? Sarcasm? Or will wisdom prevail? Will you mind your mouth?"

"Fuck you and the Duchess of Marlborough's cat!"

Some in the crew laughed. Prescott bristled and set a hand at Ethan's throat.

"I could crack your windpipe like an egg, traitor. Should I?"

"General . . . " began Royal.

"Take him below. Make sure he's secured to that bar." Prescott slowly released his grip. "Next time you curse me I shall crack the egg."

"You wouldn't dare," muttered Ethan hoarsely. "We both know your orders are to keep me alive. If anything happens, if you cause anything, Carleton'll bust you down to shit-shoveler in the stables!"

"Restore his gag," ordered Prescott.

When Prescott left a half hour later. Ethan's gag was removed. Royal paced the hold, his expression glum, troubled.

"Must you talk to him so vilely?"

"Must he talk to me?"

"You don't seem to understand . . . "

"I'm the prisoner, I understand, I just don't like the son of a bitch."

"Would you talk that way to the governor?"

"Of course. I'd talk that way to the goddamn king, to God Almighty. Anybody snipes me I snipe back, that's the way it is."

"Incarceration must be affecting your mind." Royal set a hand against his forehead. "No fever. Listen to me, Ethan, he'll be back. I don't know when, but he will. Will you kindly, please restrain yourself?"

"Tell *him* to. What am I, his whipping boy?"

"You most certainly are."

"Like hell!"

"Lower your voice. What am I to do with you?"

"You could unlock me and turn your back. I wouldn't need more than sixty seconds."

Royal's smile creased his face. "Incorrigible."

"Tell me something, Nicholas, how much longer do I get to enjoy your hospitality? Until this tub's repaired?"

"I do wish I knew when that would be. I can't answer your question. I do know one thing, your fellow 'Patriots' will soon be moving against Montreal. That's the rumor in town."

"Montgomery. Not Schuyler, he'll be sick in bed the rest of his life. So where are they?"

"I can't say, but they're getting close and, they say, in force."

"How many men? Two thousand? Four? They'll take the

town as easy as pulling a cockleburr out of your grandfather's whiskers. And liberate my boys. Speaking of whom, they're still all right, aren't they? Prescott didn't execute 'em . . . "

"I . . . shouldn't say this but I doubt if he'd dare. For the same reason he's keeping you alive."

"Carleton's orders. *He's* afraid of what we'll do to him when he's taken prisoner. You can't go around executing living legends and get away with it."

"Aren't you getting a bit ahead of yourself?"

"Oh, he'll be taken prisoner, all right. Prescott too, the whole garrison. My friends'll come pouring in. It'll be a hundred to one. If Carleton doesn't want the town blasted back into the mountain by twelve-pounders and mortars, if he wants the civilians unharmed, he'll hang out a flag of truce the size of a bedsheet. Oh, this is good news! Great news! Thank you, Nicholas. Thank you, thank you. You can go now."

Royal stared, grinned, shook his head, and went out.

"Come ahead, Montgomery, come on, Seth, Ira. Bedel, Ritzema, John Brown!"

John Brown. Would he ever learn what had happened to him? Would he live long enough to? He'd turned it over in his mind a hundred times, examining it from every angle, but he still couldn't figure it out. The last words out of John's mouth before they headed in opposite directions to cross the river miles apart were "Good luck."

"John, John, what the hell happened?"

29

OCTOBER 1775

★ **Montgomery** started up the wide quagmire that passed for the much-traveled road from Chambly to the St. Lawrence on October 27. It snowed until midday, when the temperature rose and the accumulation turned to slush.

The men of the expeditionary force, around two thousand, were poorly clad with no gloves and worn-out shoes. Morale, which had risen in the wake of the victories at Chambly and St. John's, fell precipitously. Montgomery had treated the defeated British well. The enlisted men were given clothing out of the reserve store, the Canadians were allowed to return home. The army regulars were permitted to proceed to the nearest port to return to England. The officers were allowed to keep their sidearms and personal belongings. Looting by the victors was severely punished.

By this time Ethan had spent more than a month in the hold of the *Gaspé*. He continued writing letters to Washington, Hancock, and Governor Trumbull. He even wrote to General Schuyler. His letters to Mary were cheerful, optimistic, repetitive, filled with white lies regarding his condition, his treatment, the food and his "excellent chances for repatriation." He considered writing Prescott to appeal for more humane treatment. He did not, unwilling to lower himself to begging. He wrote three more letters to Sir Guy Carleton but got no response.

Indeed, no one answered him. Jonathan Trumbull and Mary—through Loraine—had to have written, but their letters were either lost or destroyed. For that matter, had any of his own been delivered?

Repairmen came to work on the hull. He could hear hammering and sawing all day as rotted planking was replaced and the vessel caulked and otherwise brought up to seaworthiness.

And when it was they'd leave, he was certain.

General Prescott had returned a second time, but that was more than two weeks ago and the last Ethan saw of him. He liked to believe his antagonist was too busy with preparations to defend the town to get away for a diverting afternoon of taunting and abuse. Captain Royal came daily. One afternoon he came in to tell him that he had a visitor.

"A Dr. Dace."

Ethan recognized the name. He had met the doctor years before during the wrangling over the New Hampshire Grants. Dace was in the New York delegation that met with the Grants delegation in Stephen Fay's Tavern in Bennington. He recalled the doctor's conduct in that meeting as strongly suggesting arch-conservative leanings. So it was no surprise that he was now a Loyalist, fled New York for Canada.

"What does he want with me?"

"He insists on seeing you. He's a powerful man, Ethan, I can't refuse him."

"You didn't answer the question. You don't have to. What he wants is to kick me while I'm down, obviously."

Dace came in all leers, a pigeon of a man in his fifties affecting a monocle which appeared permanently lodged between the top of his fat cheek and his brow. He was dressed expensively and looked even softer to Ethan than the last time they'd seen each another.

"Ahh, the prize traitor caught and caged! Delightful! Delightful!"

"Isn't it? You've put on twenty pounds."

"My, how the mighty have fallen!"

"All purely temporary, Ephraim. My friends are on their way to take Montreal, Quebec, and all points between. And send traitors like you running back to England to save their necks."

"Bold words but hollow. From one who himself will end up on Tyburn Hill."

"Too late for that now. Within hours what passes for the British army will be on the run. Montgomery's as good as got Montreal in his hip pocket. He'll free my men and march on to Quebec and join Colonel Benedict Arnold and . . . "

"Free your men? You're talking about the thirty-three prisoners? Brace yourself, they've already been removed to where nobody can free them."

"You're a liar!"

"You've intelligence to the contrary? Think about it, Allen, Sir Guy knows your friends are coming. Would he leave prisoners sitting about waiting to be released? Hardly. They're heading for England and Tyburn Hill with you. A mass hanging. His Majesty will declare a public holiday. All will turn out to watch the Yankee wild man and his cutthroats executed."

"You don't know what you're talking about."

"Oh, but you do."

"Royal. Royal! Get this fat turncoat out of here before I throttle him!"

Dace burst out laughing. "Look at you, with all those shackles you can't even reach me."

He bounced forward, pinched Ethan's thigh, and stepped quickly back out of reach.

"Get out!" Ethan screamed. Royal came running in. "Get him out. Get him up on deck and me out of these irons. Ten minutes is all I ask. Get us sabers. We're going to fight like men!"

"A duel? He wants to duel me? This is too rich!"

"You'd better leave, Doctor."

"Going, going. I just had to see you, Allen, chained up like a rabid dog. But still all mouth, empty threats, and vile language. By Tophet, I'd give my eyeteeth to be at your hanging. What a delightful spectacle!"

"Out!"

The door clanged behind them both. The candle sputtered; he estimated that the wick would last barely five more minutes. The rats named General Prescott and King George appeared.

"Did you hear? They've moved my men. God knows where. Where Montgomery won't be able to find 'em. This is great, this is grand!"

He threw back his head and emptied his lungs in a protracted howl. It sent the rats scampering off, it echoed through the bowels of the ship, it briefly stopped the hammering and sawing outside.

In Montreal, Governor Carleton took stock with General Prescott. They could assemble a hundred fifty regulars and a lesser number of militia. Carleton ordered them to remain at their posts, but as the days went by and scouts reported the Americans' arrival in La Prairie it became evident to all that Montreal could not be defended without inviting a massacre. The walls would crumble under the first artillery bombardment. Carleton ordered the most valuable military stores placed on board ships and the remainder destroyed.

Royal came to Ethan early one morning accompanied by a man carrying a tool box.

"Take them off."

Ethan gaped. "What?"

"You're leaving. You're to be taken by ship to Quebec and imprisoned there."

Ethan shook his head. "Carleton's not thinking. When Montreal goes down Quebec will be right after. It's all over."

"I shall remember to tell him."

They stood on deck. Ethan massaged his wrists. It was raining lightly. The repairs had been completed, the workers had left. Ethan had a question.

"Where's the *Gaspé* heading?" Royal grinned. "Military secret, I know."

A sloop had pulled alongside. A familiar figure attired in oilskins waved from the deck.

"Captain McCloud," said Ethan to Royal. "He saved my hide in Prescott's office. And you saved it here, Nicholas."

"Best of luck, Ethan."

"What could be worse luck than to sail off to Tyburn Hill?"

"Perhaps coming events will change that."

"You've a good heart, Nicholas, you're just not practical."

Royal offered his hand. Ethan shook it.

"Good-bye, Ethan."

"Good-bye and good luck to you."

He was tempted to bear-hug the captain, only one didn't behave so toward one's enemy. He started down the Jacob's ladder. McCloud and a crewman helped him onto the sloop.

"Colonel Allen . . . "

"Captain. This is a surprise, how did you get away from General Nuisance?"

"General Prescott has assigned me to escort you downriver to Quebec. I won't order you shackled or even manacled if you give me your word of honor that you won't attempt to escape."

"Given. You think I want to go swimming in this weather? It's freezing out."

"Let's get inside."

McCloud held the door for him. The cabin was tiny, befitting the size of the vessel. But it was out of the rain and the wind. Four bunks took up most of the room.

"How long will you keep me in Quebec?"

"You won't actually be in town. You're being transferred to a dispatch-carrier, the *Adamant*."

"What about my men?"

"They're already incarcerated elsewhere. In the vicinity. You'll all be together on the voyage to England."

"To Tyburn Hill. I look forward to it."

So Dace was right, Carleton had ordered the men moved. At least they were still alive.

30

★ On the eleventh of November, with the Americans closing in, and under fire from their shore batteries, Governor Sir Guy Carleton fled aboard the *Gaspé*. Just in time. After an initial bombardment, which destroyed a good portion of the south and west walls, Montgomery approached the town with a flag of truce and spoke to a delegation of citizens.

Two days later, Montreal surrendered. The fleeing Carleton, heading for Quebec, was fired on by a battery at Sorel. The *Gaspé* and the ships with it turned back. Major John Brown boarded her and informed Captain Royal that he had two thirty-two pounders in his battery at Sorel that had yet to be discharged. He further told him that if the *Gaspé* and the other vessels turned around and tried a second time to get by his batteries he would send them to the bottom.

The *Gaspé,* with its lone, very important passenger, two armed vessels, and eight smaller ships surrendered. Brown confiscated their cargoes and took their crews prisoner. Disarmed and taken prisoner as well were the regulars and militia from Montreal. General Prescott handed over his saber.

The *Adamant* was smaller than the *Gaspé* and had been pressed into service as a prison ship. Commanding was Brook Watson, a merchant and one-time Lord Mayor of London. Ethan knew the captain only by unsavory reputation. A few months before, Watson had tried and failed to capture his brother Ira, attempting to pass himself off as an American spy sent by Governor Trumbull to assist Major Thomas Hobby of the Fifth Connecticut. Watson told Ira that he needed help getting down the lakes. His suspicions aroused, Ira failed to show at a meeting Watson scheduled for that night. Sight of Ethan set the Tory beaming smugly.

"Colonel Allen! What an honor. Your reputation precedes you, sir."

"So does yours, Captain. What have you been up to since they kicked you out of the Lord Mayor's job?"

"For your information, I retired."

They stood on deck. Gulls wheeled in the bright sunlight, screaming petulantly. A galley hand tested the wind direction and threw slops over the larboard bow, drawing the birds close around him. Ethan appraised Watson. He resembled an undertaker, gaunt, with uncommonly dark eyes set in a pallid face. There was a vague similarity in his features to Carleton, suggesting that they might be related. Ethan disliked his eyes, they were too deep-set. He could see malice in them. Watson might not turn out as sadistic as Prescott, but he was definitely not to be trusted, no question about that after the business with Ira. Watson also displayed a painted-on smile, one, he was sure, that was only an inadequate mask for his dark intentions.

He found himself wondering if, when Watson showed his tongue, it would be forked. McCloud, meanwhile, had said his farewells and left, heading in the sloop toward town. Quebec was perched on a promontory between the St. Lawrence, which curved around it, and the St. Charles. The highest point of the promontory pointed northeast and featured Cape Diamond, a cliff ascending more than three-hundred feet above the river.

The town was defended at its south end by a blockhouse behind a stout double palisade, in the shadow of the cliff. The Upper Town spread along the high level of the promontory and was protected by a thirty-foot wall, from which six bastions projected, mounted with cannons.

Watson spoke, bringing Ethan's attention back to him. The captain's eyes twinkled icily. "Would you care to see your accommodations?"

"I'm in no hurry, I'm sure I'll see my fill of 'em by the time this tub gets to Bristol."

"Falmouth. In Cornwall."

"Wherever. Can I ask you something? Have you heard what's happened back at Montreal? I'm curious to know what's up with my old and dear friend Prescott."

"General Prescott was taken prisoner with his men at Sorel, en route here."

"They surrendered? Too bad, I was hoping they'd put up at least some kind of resistance and get blown into Hudson's Bay. But that is good news about Prescott. I can only hope he gets the same brand of treatment he's been giving me all these weeks. And he will."

"I doubt it will be as . . . rigorous."

"Rigorous. I like that word. Brutal is more like it. Tactical mistake, that. General Montgomery and I are close as brothers. He knows how hard Prescott was on me. Now it's tit-for tat-time."

"General Prescott is military, entitled to humane treatment as a prisoner of war."

"And what do you think I am, fresh off the boat from Ireland?"

"You're a civilian and have been for some time."

"That's how much you know. I'm a full colonel attached to the Green Mountain Regiment. Working as an advance scout for Generals Schuyler and Montgomery. You can ask Richard when you surrender to him."

"Spare me your delusions, fellow."

"That's Colonel Allen to you! Who took Ticonderoga? And helped take Montreal?"

Watson snickered. "Montreal took you. Why else would you be here now?"

"There was a slip-up, that's all. Where are my men?"

"They'll be coming shortly."

"And when do we leave?"

"Gracious. Questions, questions . . . "

"When?"

"When it pleases me to cast off."

"You mean when you get your orders from Carleton."

"Take him below and put him in irons!"

"Not again!"

The conversation was ended. Watson pivoted smartly and walked off as two sailors seized Ethan's arms.

"Stinking traitor!"

The taller one, with flaming red hair and a galaxy of freckles, spat in his face. His companion laughed. They marched him off.

31

★ **Time** sapped Ira Allen's bitterness toward John Brown. He could no longer, in conscience, blame him for Ethan's capture. And ironically, for all his anxiety over his brother's situation, his own commitment to the goal of the expedition became strengthened. But Ethan's misfortune did not have the same effect on Seth Warner and the Green Mountain Boys. As November moved toward the first day of winter, many of them lost interest in continuing the campaign and drifted away, heading home.

One who shared Ira's firm commitment was Richard Montgomery. He openly vowed to take Quebec. With its capitulation, the campaign to eradicate the British presence in Canada would be all but completed.

On board the *Adamant* Ethan was led to a narrow door less than five feet high that opened into a compartment that was to be his prison on the voyage to England. There was no bed, no chair, not even a stool; nothing except two tubs for prisoners' bowel movements. Knowing that once inside he would not be allowed out for perhaps as long as eight weeks, he balked.

"Not in there, not me!"

The two sailors accompanying him below pushed, but he set his manacled hands against the wall above the door and held his ground. When they pushed him a second time he swung his irons at them. They grabbed him, he struggled. The commotion brought Watson and four armed soldiers running.

"What's going on?"

"The prisoner refuses to enter, sir," said the red-haired man.

"It's a shithole, I wouldn't stick Prescott in there!"

Watson took up a stance at a safe distance, his feet spread, arms folded. His eyes gleamed maliciously. "It's good enough for a filthy traitor."

The sailors spun Ethan around to try again to push him inside. With Ethan's back to him, Watson smashed his fist into his kidneys. Ethan bellowed, bent backwards, his hands slipping from the overhead frame, and he was shoved inside. He sprawled, rolling over, agony twisting his face.

"Cowardly bastard!"

Watson bent over him as Ethan rose on his knees. "Let's get this voyage off on the right foot, Allen. Do as you're told, behave yourself, and you'll be treated decently. Never forget, I was Lord Mayor of London."

"I'll get you for this, you Tory slime!" He was up on his feet, teetering slightly, the pain flaring, a pinwheel of knives.

"I'm warning you . . . "

"I'm *warning you!* I'm a goddamned prisoner of war!"

"Goddamned rebel, you mean!" burst one of the soldiers.

He pushed close, a burly man with a scraggly beard. He stunk of rope tobacco, some of it lodged at the corner of his mouth. He sneered and growled and brought up his bayonet until the tip touched Ethan's Adam's apple. But when Ethan failed to show fear the other exploded.

"You shouldn't even be here, goddamned traitor! You shoulda' been hanged back when for your rebellion 'gainst us Yorkers!"

He spat in Ethan's eye. Ethan cursed, shoved him aside, and sprang on him, knocking him down. But he scrambled clear, and his three companions' bayonets prevented Ethan from getting at him. The Tory's sputum dripped down Ethan's reddening cheek. He was livid.

"You must be fucking proud of yourself, Watson, letting these sons of bitches spit at a helpless prisoner!" Ethan glared at the offender. "Get up and fight like a man." The soldier gulped and scooted backwards, getting clear before rising.

"Let's go," said Watson.

Out they trooped. The door clanged shut, the key turned, their steps faded, he was alone. Down the wall he slid to a sitting position, resting his manacle bar on his knees. A single barred window a foot square, too high up to see out, admitted light. So this was it. His men would arrive, they'd hear shouting outside as the sails went up, hawsers cast off, and the anchor raised. And off to Tyburn Hill.

He thought about Mary and the children and, as so often before, wondered if even one of his letters had reached them. News of his capture and rumors of what was happening to him would have to come in bits and snatches through the grapevine, at church, in Bennington, to Loraine when she went into town to shop. But not his carefully crafted, cheerfully optimistic version of events. And what, if anything, were Trumbull, Washington, and others doing to get him out of this?

Whatever anyone was trying, time was running out. Once at sea, pulling him back would be hard. Once they got to England, impossible.

He shivered against the cold. As the days wore on and winter set in, with no heat, probably not even a blanket, run down from lack of decent food, pneumonia would threaten. November. Ordinarily, he would be busy splitting firewood. Standing out at the block with the rising sun filtering through the apple orchard, bundled up, vapor issuing from his lungs, his ax as sharp as his razor. How he loved the familiar smells: the faint, sweet fragrance of chopped beech, the even sweeter scent of birch. That olive smell was butternut, and the same smell, only muskier, came from red oak.

And with plenty of wood and food and essentials they'd all settle in for winter. Let the cold and snow dominate through Christmas and into the new year. There was a comforting closeness about winter, families kept together; nobody wandered far from the hearth. Except to fight for independence.

Spring never came by the calendar. When the winter birds,

the chickadees, the nuthatches, and downy woodpeckers, and their bigger cousins, the jays and hairy woodpeckers, gave way to a whole new set of voices, the robins, the starlings, the sparrows, you knew that winter was over. You began hearing the ravens, the woodcocks and wood frogs in chorus.

And well before life returned to the earth his own life would end. The trap would drop, his feet would strain downward for the support that was no longer there, he would feel the soft snap as his neck parted.

"For what?"

For what, indeed. What did taking Ticonderoga and nearly taking Montreal mean now? Where was the glow that doubled the size of his heart when Delaplace handed over his saber? Why this hollow feeling instead, as if life had already deserted his body? In a way, he did not need the noose, he was already dead.

His conscience stirred, and he sucked a breath in slowly, quietly. What was he leaving Mary and the children? What had he left? A stack of letters, the memory of more time away from home than spent with them, his responsibilities as husband and father playing second fiddle to his dedication to the cause. Family neglected. He would not see his sons grow up. Because he chose not to, because he chose the excitement of the crusade over dull, daily routine.

"You're a selfish man, Ethan."

Mary had never said that; she didn't have to, it never left her eyes. For all their differences, their unsuitedness, she deserved better. All along, she'd been the deprived one. And the children.

"This could be the best thing I can do for all of them, to step up to the noose and be out of their lives."

He heard steps outside. They came closer. The key turned in the lock, the door swung wide. In they filed, all manacled, heads down, ragged, and filthy and grumbling. He slid back up the wall to his feet.

"Hell almighty, Watson, what is this? We can't *all* fit in here . . . "

Watson showed at the side of the door, leering. "Why would you have two excrement tubs? One for each of *your* bowels?"

"It's too small!"

"It's huge, twenty-two by twenty feet. Step it off." He laughed. "There are only thirty-four of you. Move it men, inside, inside."

32

★ **Fewer** than half of the new arrivals could lie down at the same time in such a confined space. Ethan lost no time in pointing this out to Watson.

"Those who ask to will be escorted topside to sleep on deck," said the captain.

"It's November, for Chrissakes!"

"It may get a trifle windy. You're their commander, I leave it to you to decide. And don't use that language with me. Remember, I was Lord Mayor of London."

The last man entered the cell, the door was shut and locked. Ethan spotted Jacob Wall and Elisha Cummings. Jacob hailed Ethan with a wave and a smile. Elisha frowned and looked away. Jacob took Elisha by the arm and squeezed through the crowd with him.

"Ethan!"

"Jacob, Elisha . . . "

"I got nothing to say to him, Jacob, after what he did," said Elisha. He pulled free of Jacob's hold to wedge back through the crowd.

Jacob stopped him. "Hold it. I keep telling him, Ethan, it was Major Brown who messed up."

"I don't muchly give a shit who it was. All I know is instead of going home to Maw here I am on the way to get hung." Elisha glared at Ethan. "You son of a bitch!"

A man a head taller than either younger man turned around. "Hey, by gar, don't blame Ethan. Pierre Cariou, Colonel, you remember me?" He offered Ethan a huge, hairy hand and beaming smile. Ethan shook his hand. The Canadian's beard was thick and black; his dark eyes twinkled merrily. He wore a red knit cap and red plaid jacket. "It's good to see you alive. All us Canadians made it too. Thirteen. Unlucky number, but by gar we didn't run away."

"Wish I did," groused Elisha. "Maw'll kill me for this."

"It's all right," said Jacob. "She won't have to bother."

"Let me put all your minds at rest," said Ethan. "Nobody's going to hang."

Hooting and snide remarks greeted this.

"Listen to the great Ethan Allen, boys," rasped Elisha. "He got us into this, now he's going to wave his magic wand and get us out."

"Shut up, Elisha," snapped Jacob. "Be a man, for Chrissakes!"

"I'm more a man than you'll ever be, Jacob Wall!" hollered Elisha. "And I see things a helluva lot clearer."

"You talk too much, Elisha," said Pierre, "you say nothing."

"You calling me a big mouth, Frenchy?"

"Just calm down," said Jacob to Elisha. "You were saying, Ethan?"

"I've written a stack of letters."

"He's written letters," echoed Elisha. "Hear that, boys? To who, King George? Parliament?"

"To General Washington and John Hancock, among others. You can breathe easier, I'm sure diplomatic negotiations are already underway to effect our release."

"You're full of wet horseshit, you know that, Allen?" Elisha glared. "You got no more pull with either of them than my crack-brained cousin Ned. You just talk and talk and talk and tell yourself everybody's paying you mind. They don't give cat shit about you or about us. You know what your mistake was? Surrendering to that Lieutenant What's-his-name. We shoulda' kept on fighting till they killed us all. It woulda been better; at least we wouldn't be stuck here like apples in a barrel and dying inch by inch. I could fucking kill you, you big-mouthed, know-it-all bastard!"

He lunged, but Jacob and Pierre Cariou both intervened. Jacob pulled Elisha back.

"Lemme go!"

"Will everybody kindly quiet down?" Ethan asked. "I'd like to try and explain something here. Forget about our people for a minute, put them to one side. Think, if you will, about the English. There happen to be a lot of people in England who don't want this war. The Whigs in Parliament don't. They believe a war against us is impossible. Edmund Burke is just one. Lord North's administration is going down and could easily be out by the time this ship gets to Falmouth."

"He's dreaming again," muttered Elisha. "Everything's always so rosy with you. That's how you dragged me into this, dragged us all. I never wanted to come, you twisted my arm behind my back!"

"He did like hell," said Jacob. "I was there. You wanted to go on home, he said go ahead. You changed your mind on account we wanted to go back to Ti: him, me, Captain Baker. Don't go blaming him, you talked yourself into it." He laughed. "You should know by now not to listen to yourself."

Ethan remembered. That was exactly how it was, only being reminded of it did little to mitigate his bitterness.

Still, Elisha had every right to be bitter. He was barely into his twenties, and a noose was waiting for him, all because he'd stopped to quench his thirst at Zadock Remington's tavern instead of keeping on to Bennington and his mother. Only doesn't everybody's bad luck hinge on such quirks and mistimings?

Even so, the resentment in Elisha's eyes pricked Ethan's

conscience. He could see it in others' eyes. Not in Pierre Cariou's, though, and not in Jacob's. He managed to get close enough to the Canadian to talk with some degree of privacy. Pierre read his thoughts.

"Do not mind the boy, Ethan. It is his fear talking."

"No. He's bitter. And he has a right."

"Mais non, I disagree. He made his bed. So it turned out full of snakes. Go forward. We are all men here, all with minds of our own, *n'est-ce pas?* No man worth his salt shows his fear of death, no matter how it gnaws inside. It gnaws me, I can tell you." His eyes grew larger. "But tell me, do you really think they might not hang us?"

"I really do. Cross my heart."

"What makes you certain?"

"Little things. As I said, a lot of Englishmen don't want this war. Killing and maiming their own flesh and blood? Don't like the big bully picking on the little member of the family just because he wants to go out on his own. They think the laws Parliament passed for us are unfair. Then there's France."

"What about France?"

"She lost the French and Indian War. Paris is still bitter. I predict France will come in on our side."

"Mais non."

"Mais oui. You watch, they've already begun supplying the Patriots with arms. French volunteers are coming to serve in the army."

"You win. France gets even. We get back Canada."

"That could happen. And a lot of Englishmen realize it. Another reason why they don't want this war."

"You make sense."

"Of course. Always do. I'll tell you something else, we would have taken Montreal as easy as you pick up your fork at the dinner table. Bad luck beat us, not the British. Think about it. They marched out to capture us, meantime John Brown marches in the other gate and overruns 'em. With all the defenders out after us, he would have taken it in fifteen minutes."

"They march back with us, and he ambushes them."

"Exactly. And then and there it's all over. We win."

"Only he runs away like a *lapin*, we lose."

"Like I say, bad luck. When did they move you downriver to here?"

"A week ago. We came by bateaux. The prison in Quebec was even filthier than at the garrison."

"Did they treat you badly?"

"Better than in Montreal."

"Prescott's in Montreal. He *was*. He surrendered when General Montgomery captured it."

The Canadian's eyes lit up. "Will they hang him?"

"I wish. I wish they'd draw and quarter him. But they won't. He'll be exchanged."

"You should be."

Ethan shook his head and fingered the fringe of his buckskins. "No uniform. No military standing."

"Where did they take you?"

Ethan told about his time in the hold of the *Gaspé*, his brief reunion with Captain McCloud and arrival on the *Adamant*.

"You say McCloud took off your irons coming here? By gar, you could have gotten away."

"I gave him my word of honor I wouldn't try."

Cariou grunted. "A shame. He wasn't like that *cochon* Prescott, he was a gentleman, he wouldn't have cared."

"Maybe not, but Prescott would have. And would have set fire to his arse if he . . . "

"You are right, *mon ami*. Listen . . . "

"Sails going up. And that's the anchor chain."

"Good-bye, Canada."

Ethan looked around. Every face held the identical expression of apprehension. They could hear the sails flapping, the terns and the seagulls. A sharp whistle sounded. Now practically every expression was reproving him, mutely proclaiming this is your fault. You got us into this, get us out.

Governor Sir Guy Carleton had seventy men of the Seventh Regiment of British regulars and a handful of artillery left him after the defeats at Chambly, St. John's, and Quebec. Added to these were eighty Royal Highland Emigrants, veterans of the French and Indian War. Hector Cramahé, Quebec's governor, raised five hundred British and French militia. Also available to Carleton were four hundred marines and sailors.

Montgomery arrived with three hundred men to join Colonel Benedict Arnold, bringing artillery, ammunition, clothing, and badly needed provisions. With winter coming, the clothing captured at Montreal would be indispensable. British uniforms were made up of heavy overcoats with hoods and padded underjackets with corduroy sleeves, and heavy cloth leggins strapped over sealskin moccasins and reached to the waist.

The siege of Quebec got underway. From the outset it threatened to be long and drawn out. The temperature dropped lower with each passing day. Trenches could not be dug in the frozen ground, and hunkering down, hoping to starve out the defenders, called for more provisions than either Montgomery or Arnold had. Also, if the town was not captured before the ice broke British reinforcements would arrive shortly thereafter.

Montgomery addressed a note to Carleton, but the woman who carried it inside was made to stand and watch as the governor ordered the paper thrust into the fireplace. Back she went to Montgomery to relay Carleton's message: The governor of Canada does not read communications from rebels.

Ten days later Montgomery tried again, this time curtly advising Carleton that "if he persisted in an unwarrantable defense," the consequences would be on his head. Carleton ignored him. Then, in a final effort to bring the governor to his senses, arrows, each one carrying a copy of the letter, were shot over the walls.

There was no reply from within.

Arnold advanced to about two hundred yards from the walls and set up five mortars. Seven hundred yards away, in the midst of a heavy snowstorm, the colonials set up a battery walled in by blocks of ice. Five six- and twelve-pounders and a howitzer were placed. Heavy fire was poured into the town. Carleton replied with thirteen-inch shells and thirty-two-pound balls, shattering the ice battery and killing several men. The guns that escaped damage were removed.

While the battle for Quebec continued in fits and starts, the *Adamant* reached the mouth of the St. Lawrence some three hundred miles away and set out into the Atlantic. It was so cold it was impossible for even the hardiest prisoners to escape temporarily the sweaty, stinking, intolerably cramped cell for the relative freedom of the deck. In a space approximately four hundred feet square, thirty-four men attempted to sleep nights. Few managed it, and even those for no more than an hour or so. They ate, relieved themselves in the two tubs, quarreled, and worried. Conditions became so bad Ethan got everyone to shout at the same time and beat upon the walls, bringing Watson and his four soldiers running. The door was opened. He stood back two paces. His men at his sides pointed their muskets.

"What's all the noise, Allen? Can't you control them?"

"We got you down here to tell you we can't keep on like this. It's inhuman. We're squeezed in here worse than pigs in a crate. There's got to be quarters you can move at least half of us into."

"There are."

"Good!"

"Unfortunately, they're in use. We're carrying a full cargo of West Indian rum and it's packed in every available space. There's barely room for the rats in the hold. Even if there were space for you, there are so many you'd be bitten to death."

"How about the space from here to the companionway?" asked Jacob.

"Of course. What a jolly idea! I'd be apt to let you roam about belowdecks."

"So shackle us," said a man.

"We haven't more than three full sets of shackles on board. Only manacles like those you're wearing."

"Well, we can't all of us stay in here," said Ethan. "It's becoming sheer torture."

"Is anyone ill?"

"I'm getting sick," said a man. "Nobody wants to sit with their back against the tubs inhaling that stink every waking minute. The whole place smells like a shit pile. It's getting so I can't eat nothing. And last night Benjamin Dick throwed up."

"Son of a bitch got it on my trouser leg," said another.

"I did like hell, you liar!"

"Did too!"

"Didn't!"

"All right, all right," said Watson. "I'll acknowledge you do have a problem, Allen."

"It's getting worse by the hour."

A chorus sounded agreement.

"But as I say, considering how cramped we are for space, there's nothing I can do about it. Unless, as I suggested before, some of you want to volunteer to stay up on deck. We've plenty of blankets."

"They'll still fucking freeze to death and you know it!" burst Ethan.

"It's up to you, men."

"Brook, you've got to do something. You can't just turn around and walk away from us. Or else when we get to Falmouth . . . "

Watson started, his carefree expression giving way to a

frown. "Are you threatening me? Me, the former Lord Mayor of London?"

"I'm asking you to stick some of us in different quarters."

"You did threaten me. I don't like that. Here I am racking my brain trying to figure out something for you, and this is the thanks I get? You threaten me? Arlis . . . "

"Sir?"

"Close it up."

The door was slammed and locked and off they marched. Ethan turned slowly around to a mass of angry and hurt faces.

"What in hell did you do that for?" bawled Elisha.

"Shut up your mouth," said Pierre. "Were you not listening? That sadistic weasel *did* it. What you got to make trouble for all the time? What for? To cover up your fear? Your jelly guts?"

"Watch it, Frenchy, or we'll see who's got the jelly guts!"

"Enough!" Ethan could not keep the weariness from his tone. "Pierre is right, Elisha. He's got another room somewhere. He just enjoys making this situation even more miserable than it is. He likes pulling wings off flies. But when we get to Falmouth, when I get to talk to somebody with authority he'll get an earful."

"By gar, Ethan, I got better idea for him. Next time he comes and stands outside like that I will stand close alongside you, reach out, and pull him in here. Zip, zip, quick like a knife and he's our hostage." He strangled the air. "You order his men to drop their guns or I squeeze his neck till it pops."

"And we take over the ship!" exclaimed a man.

"I . . . don't think so," said Ethan.

"Me neither," said Jacob. "Up comes a bayonet against your throat, Pierre, and zip, zip through to the back of your neck before you can squeeze or even blink."

"Let's just all get a grip on our edginess and our imaginations," said Ethan. "But taking over the ship's not a bad idea. It's how. Let's talk, maybe we can come up with something.

Take over, turn her around, and sail for Portsmouth or
Boston.

"Okay, who's got the first bright idea?"

33

DECEMBER 1775

★ **Montgomery** waited patiently for the first stormy night to
attack Quebec in force. The Lower Town had the weakest defenses, so he singled it out as his primary objective. About
seven hundred men would feint, seizing the Cape Diamond
bastion, using ladders to scale the walls. Another seven hundred would concentrate on the Lower Town. On November
27, snow fell heavily and the operation was about to begin
when the weather suddenly cleared and the moon came out.

A deserter joined Carleton and informed him of Montgomery's plan. Carleton knew the Lower Town's defenses
were weak and now expected to be attacked there. He took
bold steps to strengthen its protection. Houses that could
shelter the attackers as they made their way into town were
demolished, others were sealed with planks. The Sault au
Matelot was barricaded and covered with guns. Within two
days, the weakest entryway into the town became the most
strongly fortified. Unfortunately for the Americans, it remained the only feasible way in. Again they waited for bad
weather. Saturday, December 1, was fair up until noon, then
the sky clouded over, the wind rose, and snow fell. By sundown, darkness thickened by black clouds, settled over the
area. As night came on the snowfall increased, driven by powerful winds.

It was time.

* * *

The North Atlantic in December was treacherous going, even in the fairest weather. In foul weather, the sea heaved and rolled, tossing ships about like wood chips flung into a rushing, stone-strewn stream. Progress eastward defied control as the *Adamant* hurtled down into a trough, then was lifted high on a surging mountain, twisted about like a top on the crest and plunged down to repeat the sequence.

In the cell, all thoughts of taking over the ship vanished. Its motion, turbulent and wholly unpredictable, roiled the prisoners' stomachs, and virtually no one could keep food down. Most of the men sat with their arms wrapped about their drawn-up knees, heads down, praying that their stomachs would not rebel, that the sea would settle, that calm would prevail and level passage would return. Only Nature was not to be so considerate.

The skies, unseen by any of them, blackened: A squall struck. With nothing to hang onto the prisoners were tossed about like wheat in a winnow, banging bodily into one another, hurting and injuring themselves, cursing, pushing at each other to regain their precious space. Fights broke out and were quelled. This went on all day and all night, until the sun rose and the surface finally settled.

Pierre wedged his way between bodies, crawling up beside Ethan, who sat with his back to an excrement tub whose contents, like the one beside it, had sloshed about so violently during the squall it was feared they would spill all over the cell.

"I wonder how far out we are, *mon ami?*"

"Not an eighth of the way. There's nothing slows the fastest vessel like heavy seas. And these have been heavy since Cape Rave. Worst time of year to cross."

"The men can't take much more. Look at them."

Ethan didn't have to; he need only close his eyes to see the ashen faces, the sunken cheeks and hangdog looks, the terror in everyone's eyes. Underscoring their abject helplessness was their lack of control over their fates, not knowing how well or poorly the ship was handled, how experienced the man at the helm. They were locked in a box, the box was in the heart of the vessel, the vessel at the mercy of wind and wave.

"You know something, Ethan? If there was one small knife among us all, one, about now it would be passed around."

"You think they'd kill themselves?"

"To escape all this? Yes."

"Not one would. Not these boys. If they didn't have hearts as big as their heads they wouldn't be here. They've proven, every man jack, that they can take what ordinary men shrink from. Besides that, they're angry. With Watson. They hate him, they wouldn't give him the satisfaction of taking the coward's way out. I wouldn't. You wouldn't. What makes you think any of them would? Look at their faces. They may be pale as sheets, sick, at the end of their ropes, but they'll never let go. They're too bitter, too angry. If there's one thing I've found in all the fighting, all the danger, the close shaves, it's how to separate the men from the mouths."

"And these are men."

"Even Cummings?"

"Especially Elisha. He's devoted to his mother. Worships her. His fear is that he'll never see her again. But he's not afraid to die."

Cariou bunched his chin and nodded slowly. "In a way he's lucky. At least he has someone to live for, like you. Your whole family."

"Seven of us." Ethan chuckled hollowly. "One good thing, I don't worry about how Mary will get along without me. She mastered that a long time ago. She needs me like a dog needs fleas."

"Ah, but you need her, *n'est-ce pas?*"

Ethan thought a moment. "Indeed I do. She's much more than my wife and the mother of my children, she's the steady hand on my tiller. Not that she controls me. Hell almighty, I can't even control myself. But she exists, the biggest element in my life. And she's back there in Bennington, set in her ways, steady, reliable. No surprises with my Mary, but no disappointments, no calamities."

"Your *rocher*. Rock."

"Married to me, a milkweed floss in the breeze. What a preposterous combination."

Jacob was coming toward them. Ethan sighed. He looked deathly ill.

"You look terrible, son."

"It's this air. It's so thick with sickness you could saw it. If that goddamned cabbage stew doesn't turn your stomach, the air stink will."

Pierre nodded. "There is no, how do you say it, *ventilation.*"

"If that window was lower we could take turns standing at it," said Jacob. He brightened. "I got an idea. Let's set up a clamor. Watson'll come down with his bayonets and at least open the door."

"Everybody," called Ethan. "Listen up, Jacob's got a good idea."

At four a.m., signal rockets were discharged, and the attack began. The storm had become a blizzard. The wind drove snow and hail like needles into the faces of the Americans as they stumbled through drifts.

The rockets lit their way, but they also aroused the sleeping town. The cathedral bells were joined by the bells of the Jesuit College, the Hôtel Dieu, the Recollet monastery. Fireballs flew over the walls to illuminate the advance outside. American mortars responded, throwing shells into the town. Troops came up in ever-increasing numbers, mounds of snow heaped upon existing drifts, ladders were placed and men poured over the walls, only to be met by withering fire from the barricaded houses.

The battle became bloodier by the minute. Sixty men followed Montgomery inside and began advancing on the blockhouse. No defending fire greeted them. They drew closer and were within a few yards of their target when a flurry of grapeshot and bullets came at them. A dozen men fell. Montgomery was shot through the head.

Ethan argued all the old problems with Watson: lack of space, lack of air, the food, the stench. And managed to keep the door open for about three minutes before the captain's patience deserted him and he ordered it shut. Unfortunately, the air in the corridor leading to the companionway was virtually as close as that in the cell, although lacking the foul stench. Still, opening the door had helped to improve the air within.

The sea stayed reasonably calm for three days, then the wind rose coming from the northeast and resumed building waves. The *Adamant* lifted and plunged and twisted and careened about as before. The midday meal was brought in a single barrel: cabbage stew again. Elisha Cummings took the first taste, scowled, and spat.

"It's rotten!"

Men pressed forward to taste the dipper before pouring it into their bowls. He was right. Watson or somebody had cut up a rotten cabbage to add to the ingredients, spoiling the whole barrel. A few attempted to pick out the offending chunks and sip the liquid. It was useless.

"It ain't bad enough they spit in it," complained one man. "Now the bastards throw in a rotten cabbage."

Ethan pondered. The stew was usually difficult to get down because the ham in it was so salty. Even the gill of rum allotted them daily was unable to slake their thirst. But maybe, just maybe, this insult added to injury could be made to work to their advantage.

"I've got an idea, boys. Trying to take over the ship may be too wild, too dangerous, as most of you agree. Especially in these seas. But what's to prevent us from going on a hunger strike?"

"What the hell does Watson care if we don't eat?" asked Elisha. "If we die o' starvation?"

"Oh, he'd care all right," said Ethan. "How would he explain delivering twenty-five or thirty corpses instead of thirty-
four breathing prisoners? Or only nine or ten of us, with the
rest slid overboard off a plank?"

"Listen to the colonel," said Pierre. "He is on to something.
They want us to put on a show for them . . . "

"Tyburn Hill," said Jacob. "Line up for tickets here."

"If we do not make it to there somebody's head will roll,
n'est-ce pas?"

"Meaning Watson's," said Ethan. "Think about it. We can't
eat this slop. They'll come and take it away. Tomorrow they'll
bring another barrel. Whether it's rotten or edible we don't
touch it. Are you with me?"

Some were all for the idea. About half. The remainder were
either lukewarm or dead against it. Those against it included
Elisha and the handful that shared his resentment toward
Ethan.

"You will have to talk them into it, Ethan," whispered
Pierre. "You can do it."

"The question is should I?"

"What do you mean?"

"I don't know, it's just that the longer we're stuck here the
more I feel I shouldn't be in charge. I've had my day. It's
reached a point where it's every man for himself. Don't you
think?"

"Mais non. Not at all. If anything, we need you to run
things more than ever. Watson takes it for granted that you
are our leader. Now suddenly you do not want to be?"

"It's not that."

"Then what?"

"I don't know. I've never felt like this before."

"You are tired, you are weak, your morale is down in the
hole."

"It's not that either. It's just . . . the fire is dying." He set a hand against his stomach. "I can feel it. I'm getting past caring. It happens. It happened at the camp when we were getting ready to start out for Montreal. They showed up, surrounded us, outnumbering us five and six to one, then and there all the can-do, all the courage in the world wasn't going to get us out of it. There was nothing for it but to surrender. It's the same now."

Cariou's face had darkened. "That is lousy talk. Coming from you, it stinks. If your guts fell down into your bowels and came out your arse and are floating around in the tub that is a shame. *Tout à coup,* you are not the man I have thought all along that you were. You disappoint me, Ethan."

"Not as much as I do myself. Maybe if I get four hours sleep tonight instead of the usual one or two I'll wake up feeling different. It'll stir the old fire. Bear with me, *mon ami,* give me a little time."

Pierre grinned, showing two gaps in the gleaming rows where teeth had been knocked out. His hand found Ethan's shoulder. "I give you until tomorrow morning, until Watson shows up at the door again. That's all you need. His face, that sneer, the way he struts and poses like a turkey, that will stir your fire."

Neither realized it, but Jacob had been listening.

"Then you really do think they plan to hang us all when we get there? Be honest, Ethan."

"Be honest?"

Others crowded around, their eyes asking.

"I'll answer your question with a question, Jacob." He cleared his throat. "Who knows, son, who knows?"

IV

Pawns in the Game

34

★ **Montgomery** was dead. But the siege of Quebec went on and would continue throughout the winter. On board the *Adamant,* on Christmas Day, Captain Brook Watson's heart opened unexpectedly and he charitably authorized an extra gill of rum for the prisoners, to go along with a meal of too-salty ham and vegetables. There had been no hunger strike; it was decided that such a rash tactic, even if successful, would not significantly help conditions. What could Watson offer them to "meet their terms," better food? He had no better, not in quantity, not for prisoners. Additional quarters to relieve the congestion? He insisted that he had none. Better ventilation? More frequent emptying of the excrement tub? Were such improvements worth jeopardizing the meager nourishment they were already receiving?

Watson did "find" a cache of army blankets. Only by now the men were so run down, afflicted with so many minor illnesses, his largess proved to be too little, too late. The ship had now been at sea nearly two months. The prisoners had no way of knowing how far they'd come. Pressed by the others, Ethan resolved to pin Watson down. He came on Christmas Day, his spirits high, elevated by a feast and three kinds of liquor.

"Happy Christmas, happy, happy Christmas to all!"

"If this is happy I'd hate to see miserable," said Ethan.

"Everybody enjoy their dinner? Everybody reasonably comfortable?"

"Living in the lap of luxury, as you can see. I've a question, Brook, where are we exactly?"

"The North Atlantic, I thought you knew that."

"How far from port?"

"I really can't say."

"You mean you won't. What is it, a military secret? Who are we going to tell?"

"How far?" Pierre asked.

Watson made a sly face and rocked his head back and forth. "Brace yourselves. Here comes your Christmas gift. We'll be within sight of the Scillys before nightfall. And around Lizard Head and the Manacles . . . "

"Speaking of manacles, if we're that close, isn't it time you took off ours?"

"You interrupted me. Around Lizard Head and the Manacles and up into Falmouth Bay sometime tomorrow. What? No huzzahs? I'd think you'd be ecstatic to finally set foot on dry land."

"Getting out of this box is welcome," muttered Jacob.

"Where to from Falmouth?" asked Ethan.

"To a true lap of luxury, Pendennis Castle."

"What luxury? Will the cells be bigger?"

"Dungeon. Bigger? I believe so."

"How long will we be staying there?"

"Questions, questions. I've answered enough for one day. It's time for my nap. We'll be parting company on the dock, Mr. Allen."

"Colonel."

"It's been an experience. Note, I'm not saying pleasure."

"Oh, it's been a great pleasure, Brook. Be honest, you haven't enjoyed yourself this much in ages. Can I ask, are you a married man?"

"I am. With two fine boys."

"And does your wife love you?"

"Isn't that a trifle personal?"

"Just curious. If she does she must be unusual. She's got to be as sadistic as you are."

Watson's face fell. He stepped back. "Arlis, lock up."

"Yes, sir."

Laughter followed the captain through the door to the foot of the companionway. Only Elisha didn't think it funny.

"You trying to get us into more hot water? Is that what you want?"

"Elisha, Elisha, what can he do he hasn't done already? Cheer up, we beat him. All of us. We took everything he threw at us and swallowed it or threw it back. He wanted to break us so bad it got his stomach all knotted up. For sure, he wanted to break me. I didn't think it possible, but he turned out an even bigger bastard than Prescott."

"I think Prescott was worse," said a man.

Others nodded.

"Really?" Ethan lofted both hands. "Let's put it to a vote. Who turned out worse, Watson or Prescott? All for the Lord Mayor, raise their hands."

Prescott won by two votes.

"Another vote, another vote. Which is the biggest arsehole?"

Watson emerged the near-unanimous winner.

"We're all forgetting something here," said Ethan when everyone had quieted down. "It's Christmas. Where's our Christmas spirit?" This was roundly jeered and scoffed at. "I'm being serious."

Jacob snorted. "If we're standing on the gallows next Christmas Day, what are we supposed to do, sing carols?"

No one laughed.

"Listen to the man," said Ethan. "That's an idea, let's all sing carols."

He had to talk them into it but within a few minutes, after three or four started, all the others joined in. They sang lustily: "The Cherry-Tree Carol," "Joseph Was an Old Man," Pierre and the other Canadians sang carols from *Noei Borguignon de Gui Barôzai*. The singing became more and more spirited, louder, and more heartfelt. It also, unfortunately, had the reverse effect of what Ethan had hoped for. When the last notes of the last carol faded away he surveyed the tear-stained cheeks and tried hard to smile.

"I know we don't have much to be thankful for this Christmas Day, but at least we're alive, nobody's so sick they're in danger of dying, and there's still hope. So merry Christmas, boys, and a happier New Year than we expect this one coming up to be."

That night he sat with his back to the wall under the high window surrounded by snoring. One man—in the dark he couldn't make out who—whimpered like a child. A few of the Canadians prayed softly. He sent his thoughts back over the previous six months, recalling each event in sequence up to the present. So many things had gone wrong that could easily have gone in their favor.

How long would they hold them at Pendennis Castle? However long, from there they'd be moved to London, to Tyburn Hill. In all this time that had elapsed what were Trumbull, Washington, Hancock, what was *anybody* doing to, if not repatriate them, at least halt the execution? The question loomed larger and larger, a big, black hook standing in his mind: Did anybody care enough to make an effort? Or had the lot of them already been entered in the bloody ledger as casualties of war?

Who would they contact? Not Lord North. He was too loyal to the king, and the one Englishman above all others de-

termined to defeat and humiliate the upstart Americans was
George III.

Still, there *were* men in high places who sympathized with
the colonies. Edmund Burke saw the wisdom of calling off
hostilities and granting independence. From the first, William
Pitt had no stomach for war, and his words carried great
weight in Parliament, despite the fact that he no longer held
office, being so old and infirm. People continued to idolize
him and listen to him, and he had favored conciliation all
along. There were others. Trumbull, Washington, and Hancock must know who they were.

He was not afraid to die on the gallows. He'd taken his
stand and would stick by it to the end. Never would he re-
nounce his principles. But to be forced to watch the others
executed would be intolerable. It was he who had rallied
them, who'd brought them to Montreal, and he'd surrendered. The situation was his doing, the guilt all his.

35

★ **A** pushcart heaped with chains designed to attach to the
prisoners' manacles and, at the lower end, to ankle shackles,
was brought up, and two men in smiths' aprons began fastening them in place. It was raining lightly. Uniformed guards
aimed their muskets as one man after another was shackled.
A crowd had gathered on the dock even before the *Adamant*
put in.

Ethan studied the faces of the curious. He saw no hatred,
nothing to match the expressions of the men on board the
ship. In the women's faces was pity, in the children's, curiosity, in the men's, for the most part, puzzlement. Here were
people of the same blood appraising each other. Did Fal-

mouth wonder why the war? Why fight to hold onto a wilderness three thousand miles away? Too distant to properly govern. Witness! Too variagated in population: English, French, German, Swedish, Dutch, a dozen nationalities, along with red Indians. A horde of farmers, merchants, and frontiersmen. Why keep a wild dog chained? Give it its freedom. Let it run and fend for itself.

A captain stepped forward under an umbrella held for him by his orderly. He was old, too old for his rank. He fingered his mustaches and gazed disdainfully. A large, floppy-eared hound scampered playfully around him.

"Here you are, true-born Englishmen returned to your native land."

Ethan spat. "Who you calling English? I'm American, born in Litchfield, Connecticut. Except for the Canadians, we're all Americans."

"English colonials to the core."

"Like hell."

"I am a bloody cockney," announced Pierre, drawing laughter from the crowd with his preposterous accent.

The captain stiffened. "No one is addressing you. Now then, pay attention. Once you are safely shackled, you will be marched through town to the east road to Pendennis Castle." He indicated a round, black shape on a distant promontory. "There you are to be confined for the present. You are, one and all, enemies of the Crown. Any attempt at escape will be dealt with harshly. Captain Watson, have you any last words for the prisoners?"

"I do, Captain Hales. Good riddance to bad rubbish."

"I couldn't put it better myself, Brook," said Ethan, and spat at his feet.

Men tittered. Captain Hales scowled and came over to Ethan.

"Don't be so free with your ingratitude. Show a little appreciation for the good treatment you received." He came closer, fished spectacles from his pocket, and set them astride his nose. "You must be the arch-traitor Allen."

"That's me."

Hales slapped him with his gloves. Ethan started for him, but a guard holding up his musket stepped between them. Hales curled his lip.

"That was a warning. To mind your tongue. No more back talk. Any subsequent misconduct, any insults or sarcasm will earn you ten lashes. Do you understand?"

"Understand this, tin soldier. If you slap me again, if you harm me or any one of us you'll answer in a court of law to a charge of cruelty to prisoners of war. Do *you* understand?"

"He's all mouth, Captain," said Watson. "But he can be amusing."

"Insubordination is never amusing, Captain Watson."

"Leave him alone, Willie," called someone from the crowd.

"Let's see you slap him with his hands free," said another.

A few people began jeering Hales. He colored behind spectacles and mustaches and fixed Ethan resentfully with his moist eyes.

"Just behave, rebel."

The shackling was completed. Hales mounted his horse and took his place at the head of the line. Behind him a drummer boy readied his sticks. Ten guards took their places, five on either side of the line. Hales raised his saber.

"Forward!" He brought it down. "March."

Unlike their manacles, the prisoners' shackles were not joined by a bar. They were able to stride properly. Marching to the drum, they maintained a good pace into town despite their weariness and weakness. Past the town hall and past the market-house, and past other municipal buildings and homes they marched. Women and boys ran up to the line with jugs of water. Many shouted "God bless you," and "Keep the faith." Hales paid no attention to the displays of compassion. The parade passed through town. Ahead, Ethan could see two

castles, one on either side of the estuary. To the east Pendennis Castle rose, while on the opposite side the picturesque inlet
of Porthcuel River opened between Castle Point to the north,
with St. Mawe's Castle, and St. Anthony Head and Zoze
Point to the south. And the captain's hound, whom he called
Sheba, ran in and out of the line.

As they neared their destination along the east road Ethan
studied the castle. The grounds lay on the promontory like
an enormous rectangular cake, with the castle at one end facing the sprawling fort at the other. Arriving at a point level
with both structures he saw that Pendennis's round tower was
enclosed by a chemise with a wide gun emplacement. The
tower was two stories above the chemise, and Pendennis itself stood higher than St. Mawes on the other side of the estuary.

A guard walking beside Ethan noticed his interest in Pendennis.

"It's got some history, Mr. Allen. Back when the Spanish
Armada attacked us it bristled with guns. But not a one was
fired. There's stories and stories."

"Anybody living there now?"

"Not at the castle itself. We live in the fort at the opposite
end."

"I bet it's freezing inside."

"It gets cold nights. Don't all castles?"

"What's the dungeon like?"

"You won't be staying there. You'll be in the great hall.
They bolted rings into the wall."

"So we'll still be shackled."

"Afraid so. I overheard the captain of your ship talking to
Captain Hales. Captain Hales asked if he thought you should
be chained up and he . . . "

"Watson?"

"Said yes, sure. To be on the safe side."

"To be on the safe side. Look at this bunch, have you ever
in your life seen a weaker, more bedraggled lot? Every man's

lost at least forty pounds since we were captured. How we crossed the Atlantic with nobody dying was a miracle. Does Captain Mustaches honestly think we're going to cook up a plan of escape? In the dead of winter? To where, Lizard Head? Listen, has anybody said how long we're supposed to be here?"

"I haven't heard."

"But you heard they're going to hang us."

"I guess so."

"No idea when?"

"No."

"How far to London?"

"Over three hundred miles."

"Watch, they'll march us all the way. Who's Hales's superior?"

"Colonel Boatwright."

"Where's he hiding?"

"He's at the castle now, but most of the time he's at the fort."

"Not a very gracious host, he could have at least been at the dock with a bouquet." Ethan turned to look back. Falmouth spread below to the west. The *Adamant* had docked in the inner harbor and had not moved. Would Watson be delivering his rum here or up the coast? What did that matter? At least he'd seen the last of him. In his place they now had Captain Hales. Why did they all take their Toryism so seriously, except for Captain Royal? Why work so hard generating hatred for the Patriot opposition? Why take the breach so personally? It was, after all, only a difference of political opinion. Whether the colonies were Crown or became independent didn't affect any of them personally.

Still, the Revolution was a slap in His Majesty's face. So suddenly every Tory on both sides of the water was his defender and champion.

The crowd petered out as they neared Pendennis. They ascended to the grounds, were drummed to the castle, and inside to the great hall. A pleasant thought crossed Ethan's mind for a change. Gone forever were the stinking excrement tubs, replaced by garderobe and cesspit.

The guard who had accompanied him now joined the other guards at the opposite end of the hall, summoned by the captain. He talked to them in low tones. The prisoners milled about waiting at the other end. Banners hung on high. Torches flickered in sconces along the walls. Two huge tables with benches were set up.

"Look at the wall rings," said Pierre. "They are at least three feet apart, by gar; at last, space to breathe."

"On the way over did you get to talk with any guards?"

"*Mais non,* but Jacob Wall did. I saw him."

Ethan gestured Jacob to join them. "Did you find out anything?"

"If you mean how long we'll be here, no."

"I think all winter," said Pierre. "The day they hang us will be a holiday, *n'est-ce pas?* They'll want a nice day, reasonably warm, sunshine. Winter is too risky. They could pick a day, people come for miles around and it turns out a blizzard."

Ethan sucked a tooth and considered this. "You could be right. They're sure to be putting up stands and hanging banners and bunting and suchlike. And when we get to London I doubt they'll want to lock us up. Just march us through town to Tyburn, up the hill, and up the steps."

Pierre studied him solemnly. "Ever since Quebec you have been saying it will never come to that. Changed your mind? Given up?"

"Just babbling."

"Just telling the truth," said Jacob. "Oh Abby, Abby, farewell my heart."

Elisha and others crowded around them.

"When do they hang us?" Elisha stared at Ethan.

"Are you in a hurry?"

"It's a big joke to you, isn't it? All of us have to die because of you and you think it's funny."

"Do not start, Elisha," said Pierre. "It is not a good time."

Hales was approaching, his heels clicking against the stone floor. Self-importance puffed his chest. He led two guards up to them. Sheba cavorted playfully.

"Allen, you'll come with me. Colonel Boatwright wishes a word with you."

"I'd like a word with him."

Boatwright's office was small, but behind his chair was a lovely recessed window with an iron grill that could be closed off with wooden shutters. The window looked out on the sea. It had stopped raining. The sun was out gloriously. A table served as the colonel's desk. Papers were stacked neatly, and a quill and inkwell set separated two groups of books held upright by bronze lion-head bookends.

There were two chairs. Hales indicated that Ethan sit.

"Wait here. Don't move from that chair. He'll be back shortly, I'm sure."

He started toward the door.

"Wait. Can we talk a little before you go?"

"About what?" Hales stared. He seemed to be trying his utmost to be as cold as humanly possible.

"About that. Why do you take all this so personal?"

"Personal?"

"Like I'm to blame for the whole, entire Revolution. Me, all by myself. I cooked it up in the kitchen or something."

"Frankly, since you ask, my chief problem is that I cannot abide your sort."

"What sort would that be?"

"You're not a military man, you're not even a civilian playing soldier. What you are is a pirate. As barbaric as Kidd or Teach. An arrogant, undisciplined wretch who wouldn't last two days in His Majesty's service. You, sir, are unfit to polish a drummer boy's boots!"

"A pirate. Where'd you get that?"

"Your deportment at Fort Ticonderoga was deplorable. Yes, a pirate, a swashbuckling lout without the slightest inkling as to how the simplest military exercise should be carried out."

"We won, didn't we?"

"Disgusting! And yet typical of you and your treasonous ilk!"

"Don't go getting all worked up. You're getting red all over."

"Wait here, traitor. Colonel Boatwright will . . . "

The door, which had been ajar, opened fully revealing a benign-looking man in his sixties wearing a wig with too much powder on it and spectacles set so far down near the tip of his nose they threatened to drop off. Lowering his head, he looked over his spectacles at Ethan.

"Colonel Allen . . . "

Instantly, Ethan liked him. As he had instantaneously disliked Hales.

"Sit. Sit. William?"

"Just going, sir. I must see that my orders to chain the prisoners to the wall are being properly carried out."

The colonel returned his salute. Ethan looked out the door as Hales vanished. The colonel shut it.

"Been browbeating you, has he?"

"I'm used to it."

"Actually, he's not as harsh as he sounds."

"He hates my guts. Which is one thing people on your side all seem to have in common."

Boatwright got out his snuff box, offered some to Ethan who declined it, sniffed a pinch himself and sneezed resoundedly.

"He resents you. For obvious reasons." Ethan stared. "You mean he didn't tell you? Captain William Delaplace is his brother-in-law."

"Do tell? Well. I don't know what he's mad at. Delaplace and I got along all right."

"Since Ticonderoga he's been repatriated. He's now back in England."

"Lucky for Mrs. Delaplace. Sir, how long are we here for?"

"Until you're asked for in London."

"To be hanged."

"I can't say. I don't know."

"What do you think?" Boatwright hesitated and lowered his eyes. "That's good enough."

"We'll try to make your stay here as comfortable as possible, keeping in mind that you are still prisoners of the Crown. To be restricted and under guard at all times."

"You've got fireplaces in that hall big enough to stand in. Can they be lit? Tonight it'll be freezing."

"You'll be pleasantly surprised. Even in the dead of winter it doesn't get that cold around here. Geraniums, hydrangeas, and camellias bloom all winter long. Ahem, be that as it may, I'll see to it that the fireplaces are lit."

"Thank you. How's the food?"

"I trust you'll find it both edible and nourishing. Bread is baked fresh daily."

"Can we have blankets for tonight?"

"Of course."

"Everybody's pretty run down after the trip. Sir . . . ?"

"Yes?"

"Do we have to be chained to the wall?"

"I'm afraid so." He leafed through papers. "The order's here somewhere. It specifically states . . . "

"All right, all right."

A knock sounded.

"That'll be your escort back. Come in. As I say, Colonel, we'll endeavor to make your stay as comfortable as possible. I instructed Willie . . . ah, Captain Hales, that you and your men are not to be harrassed or insulted. I'd appreciate it if you so instruct your men in that regard."

"I will."

Two guards escorted Ethan back to the great hall. In his absence the others' leg shackles had been removed and their manacles chained to individual wall rings. Ethan was fastened to his ring between Tom Coffin, a farmer from Salisbury, Connecticut, and Wilkie O'Doul, an apprentice shipwright from Portsmouth in the Grants. Tom was bright and a good soldier, but Ethan personally found him a bit strange. Of all the men under his command, Tom worried the least about the possibility that all would be hanged. He worried not at all. He claimed that his guardian angel—he called him Azaran— would protect him from such a fate, even if it meant strangling the hangman to prevent his slipping on the noose. He didn't show off Azaran, talking only privately to him. Frequently, Ethan had seen him mumbling while those around him stared. Tom didn't resent others kidding him about Azaran, he merely ignored their sallies, and now nobody commented or inquired about his angel.

But Ethan kept an eye on him, telling himself that he wouldn't be at all surprised to be awakened one night by Tom's howling as Azaran or some otherworldly force pulled him around the bend.

Wilkie O'Doul had no such familiar spirits. He was a typical seventeen-year-old: insecure, naïve, and easily awed. But despite his strength and well-developed physique, his health was poor. Had Ethan any idea how poor he would never have permitted him to enlist. Wilkie had nearly died of pneumonia when he was six and had never completely recovered. He coughed constantly, his nose was always running, he looked as sick as Schuyler back on the Ile-aux-Noix. And their surroundings since only aggravated his condition. Ethan found himself wondering if Wilkie would survive to climb the gallows stairs.

Tom and Arazan took care of him as best they could under the circumstances. But Wilkie never seemed to improve, nor have any desire to, confirming an old suspicion of Ethan's, that some people are practically born into martyrdom.

Pierre Cariou was chained on the other side of Wilkie, and Jacob and Elisha were farther down the line. Hales stood with four guards and a beefy-faced sergeant. Another guard had just finished distributing pots.

"You all have your piss pots," bawled the sergeant, his voice echoing. "If you got to move your bowels call out and you'll be escorted to the hole."

"How about lighting the fireplaces?" someone asked.

"They will be. You'll be fed before dark. Also, blankets will be passed out. Any questions?"

"Yeah," snapped Jacob. "How come you stick us in this barn?"

"How come?" asked Elisha.

"If you prefer the dungeon, it can be arranged," said Hales. That was all. They trooped out.

36

★ As Hales and the guards walked off, Ethan indicated a balcony that stretched the length of the great hall and featured a wall about ten feet long at the center. No one was on the balcony, but there was a small recessed hole at eye level in the wall.

"They're spying on us," he said to Wilkie. "That's the reason they're keeping us here instead of in the dungeon. This way they can watch us day and night."

Tom Coffin pointed at the tables and benches. "Don't they eat their meals here?"

"No. The garrison's in the fort at the other end of the parade ground. They eat and sleep there. They just keep a few men on duty here for us."

"You talked to the colonel," said Tom.

Curiosity widened his dark blue eyes. Others edged as close to Ethan as their chains permitted.

"He's decent, not like the Lord Mayor of London. Hales is the one we should keep our eye on. And no, Boatwright doesn't know how long we'll be here."

Wilkie's fingertips went to his throat and he swallowed lightly. Despite his sickliness and sunken chest he was big, with hands half the size of hay forks.

"That rope is all I think about morning, noon, and night. The little bristles scraping, the trap dropping from under my feet. Will it be fast, Colonel? God willing, it'll be fast. Will it?"

"You don't really want to talk about it."

"What else is there to talk about?" Elisha spat. "What else is in everybody's mind? I've got a knot in my gut that won't go away."

"It won't happen," said Tom.

"Because your guardian angel says so?" Jacob asked. "What is he going to do, steal the gallows?"

Ethan watched as Tom gave Jacob an "oh-ye-of-little-faith" look. "Boys, let's give it a rest."

He glanced down the line to his right. Elisha was seated six men from him. He felt Ethan's eyes, looked his way, and assumed the requisite disapproving expression. Ethan sighed. Elisha and those who agreed with him would go to their graves faulting him.

Twilight darkened the windows high up, brightening the flickering wall torches. Blankets and the meal were brought. It wasn't as good as Colonel Boatwright had led him to believe, but it was an improvement over the food on board the *Adamant*. Only there was no rum, just tepid water.

One by one, the men began snoring.

Wrapped snugly in his blanket, Elisha lay on his side, his eyes misting. He closed them and saw his mother feeding the chickens, her striking blond hair hanging loose and trapping sunlight, her cheeks glowing. She was pregnant with his sister Susannah, her ninth child, all girls except him and six-year-old Walker. He was the oldest, and when Ethan issued the call for volunteers for the Bennington Mobb he'd been first in line to sign up. No hesitation, no second thoughts. Join and fight because he must. Ethan had stood on a box in front of Fay's Tavern and delivered a fiery speech, a clarion call to the Patriots in the crowd. Freedom! Independence! Throw off the chains of the monarchy!

He shifted his hands, rattling his manacles lightly.

He was twenty-three. He would die before he'd even begun to live. Never fallen in love, only walked out with a girl twice, and that was Emily Slavin, who didn't count because she was such a tomboy. Only a friend. She hadn't made his heart flutter or his cheeks warm. He'd never come close to kissing her. No girl. Oh, he'd admired Lydia Frame, but only from a safe distance. She was beautiful and unapproachable, all he could do was look.

He'd only spoken to her twice, at church. She didn't know he was alive. Besides, she already had a steady beau. No one to love, no prospects, no wife, nothing. It all ended here even before it could get started. It wasn't fair, and it was Ethan's fault. Big mouth. Big horse's arse! Dead before his twenty-fourth birthday. And the worst was Maw and the kids would never even get to see his grave. How could they mourn him properly with his corpse so far away? And it would be months before they'd even know he'd been hanged. What a rotten life!

Jacob rolled over and came awake choking, sweating furiously. *The* nightmare yet again. The noose tightening, cutting off his wind. It was as hideous as it was frightening: The crowd looking up, leering, cheering on the hangman. His knees were so wobbly they had to help him up the steps. They'd stood him on the drop, slipped the noose around his neck. His heart thundered, his knees were water and shook uncontrollably.

One of the boys had told him two nights before that the hangman would adjust the noose so that when the trap dropped your weight snapped your spinal cord and death was instantaneous. He'd not feel a thing. Wrists tied, steps, noose, knot, hood, trap door, and dance. But what if the drop didn't kill him? What if he died slowly dancing? Oh Abby, Abby, Abby . . .

Who would pump the bellows and hammer the anvil now? Old Chapman? So old he could barely life a six-pound hammer. And he drank so, his hands shook so, his eye wandered so he made a mess of the simplest job. No, Jacob Wall was Bennington's blacksmith. The best in all the Grants. Everybody said so. Only off he went to war, to Ticonderoga, to St. John's and Montreal. Dear God, if only the river had been up that night and they couldn't get across. And the next night, and the next. Ethan would have had to give it up, they would have turned around and marched back to the Richelieu to rejoin Montgomery.

No! He wouldn't need any help getting up the gallows stairs. He wouldn't shudder and balk and cry out. He'd ascend under his own power, square his shoulders, fill his chest, die like a man! Oh dear, sweet Abby love.

Pierre studied the ceiling. The torch flames left blackened tongues on the wall opposite. The balcony was deserted. Was anyone watching them through the hole? Why would they bother at this hour?

So here you are, *mon ami,* last stop before the gibbet. The foolishness of it did gall, though. What was he doing here with all these Yankees? It was their war, not Pierre Cariou's. What did he care if the British ruled Canada? He'd been under French rule, now he was under British, and couldn't see any difference, not to him personally. He bought and sold beaver pelfry; some otter, some other creatures, but mainly beaver. The price hadn't changed since Montcalm went down to defeat on the Plains of Abraham. He'd fought in that one with other loyal French Canadians, but France's defeat had turned out no loss for him. No changes whatsoever, good or bad. So why had he volunteered for this *mission toquée?* This *idiotie?*

Only it hadn't impressed him as idiotic when Ethan described it. It was his chance to help chase the British out of power, and more importantly, avenge Montcalm, whom he had always greatly admired. Restore the habitants to the government, take Montreal to start. He knew it was a gamble when he shook Ethan's outstretched hand and agreed to join him. Knew if they failed to take Montreal they could all end up swinging. Had it been worth the risk? With a little luck it would have been.

"C'est la vie, mon ami."

Ethan's frustration over their situation surfaced to compete with his apprehension. Had Jonathan Trumbull, Washington, or Hancock written *anyone?* Bothered to? One new tiny glow penetrated the gloom, an aspect of the situation he had failed to consider previously.

The people. In the crowd at the dock he hadn't seen a single face that showed anything like the malignity on Hales's face, and Watson's, and Prescott's. The English, at least here in Falmouth, pitied the New Englanders, possibly even sympathized with their desires for independence. Was it that way throughout the country? If public opinion was against the war it would definitely be against executing them in the spectacle surely being planned. The king's advisors must be aware of the public opinion, must realize that sanctioning such harsh punishment would hang the tyrant's mantle from His Majesty's shoulders, strengthening opposition to continuing the war.

Or was all this wishful thinking?

What troubled him more than anything the past few days was realizing that the moment he handed his saber to Covington he relinquished all control. It was lost, evidently for good. In his heart he didn't consider himself any great leader of men, but he did pride himself on maintaining a firm hold

on the tiller, whatever the situation, however bad or dangerous. Not now. He'd given it up, and with it, the iron in his
spine. How can one possibly maintain strength and resolve
when one's no longer in control?

That was what troubled him most.

37

★ **Mounted** on black stalks of varying heights and shapes, a
sea of cauliflowers engaged the eye. Lord Frederick North, the
second earl of Guilford, prime minister of England, called for
silence. Participants in knots of conversation ignored him.
Heat was in the air, the line had been drawn: members in favor
of and those against the fighting in the colonies. The Duke
of York rose, asking to be heard.

"My lords, I have received a letter from an American gentleman, Jonathan Trumbull, governor of the Connecticut
Colony." Catcalls greeted this disclosure, presumably directed
at the duke's use of the word gentleman. Lord North patiently
restored order.

"With his lordship's permission, I will read a portion
thereof."

Spirited objection erupted.

The duke directed an appealing look at the prime minister.
Lord North was staunchly loyal to His Majesty, but privately
he had little enthusiasm for the effort to subdue the colonies.
No one could accuse him of causing the war, but one of his
first actions upon taking office was to retain the duty on
tea, and it was he who introduced the notorious Boston Port
Bill of 1771 that closed the port to all commerce and block-
aded it.

However, when war erupted he urged the king to make immediate peace. His Majesty refused to listen, and, not want-

ing to leave his sovereign at the mercy of the anti-war Whigs, against his better judgment he devoted his energies to promoting the hostilities.

"Proceed," he virtually shouted over the persisting clamor.

The duke hurriedly read the letter to himself. "Here we are, your lordship. 'Colonel Ethan Allen and his Green Mountain Boys captured Fort Ticonderoga and greatly assisted in paving the way for the eventual capture of Montreal. Prior to General Montgomery's success there, Allen and thirty-three of his men were taken prisoner in an ill-advised attempt to themselves invest and capture the town.

" 'Since then the prisoners have been transported to England, where they are to be hanged as traitors. I strongly urge your lordship to consider most earnestly the wisdom of exchanging these prisoners for British officers held by the Americans, among whom is General Richard Prescott, commander of the garrison at Montreal.' "

Shouting went up, making it impossible for the duke to continue. From his expression, however, the reaction was not unexpected. But he was not alone in agreeing with Trumbull's point of view. Still, there would be no further reading; louder voices took over, and the prime minister did not try to still them.

"Your lordship, your lordship, your lordship," bellowed one leather-lunged member with a face the color of a pomegranate. "We cannot, we must not succumb to this brazen petition! Ethan Allen's vile reputation precedes him to our shores. The man and the men who follow him are undisciplined rabble, renegades who acted out of their own nefarious impulses. They cannot even be considered prisoners of war, for they have no connection to the rebels' military. They are two-legged jackals, and they should be hanged without trial, as an example to others of their stripe.

"I would remind your lordship, I would remind you all of His Majesty's feelings toward this so-called Revolution. They are a warning beacon which we ignore at our peril. If the

Americans should succeed in this uprising England will surely face revolt in other colonies. With the end result that we could lose them one and all, and eventually be confined to this island."

"Hear, hear! Hear, hear! Hear, hear!"

The Duke of York shrugged, crumpled Trumbull's letter, and sat.

The prisoners of Pendennis Castle had unexpected visitors. A crowd of gentlemen and ladies dressed in their finest came from town the next morning. They stood in a loose line opposite and stared at Ethan and the others, and commented in low tones behind fans and gloved hands.

"By gar," said Pierre. "I feel like an animal in a zoo."

Ethan grinned and waved. The woman he waved to, young, pretty, and expensively dressed, tittered and turned away. "We're the biggest thing to hit Falmouth in years. What a spectacle, the raggedy rebels, filthy, sick, and half-starved."

A man in his twenties, a sallow-looking individual resplendent in silk and lace and bear-fur collar overcoat, came striding up to Ethan.

"You're Ethan Allen, aren't you?"

The man's boldness encouraged others to venture nearer.

"No, I'm George Washington."

"You are not, you insolent dog. You're the arch-traitor. Gerald, Hubert, this is the one who attacked Fort Ticonderoga."

"Captured it."

"Look at him, chaps. He's filthy as a Turk. Look at the animal skins he's got on." He whipped a handkerchief from his sleeve and held it to his nose. "And he reeks. Tell me, fellow, don't you Americans bathe?"

"Piss off," rasped Elisha and shooting to his feet stretched the length of his chain pretending to go for the dandy's throat. He gasped and stepped hurriedly back.

"Don't you dare touch me, you filthy rascal. Oh chaps, if

these are the best the Americans can send to war, our lads will make short work of them. Beasts of the wilderness is what you are, not men."

"Go home and play with yourself, arsehole," snapped Jacob.

The others laughed and smiles flicked on and off some of the visitors' faces.

"Mind your tongue, boy, there are ladies present."

Jacob stared straight at him. "So I see."

The laughter increased. The dandy's hand went to the hilt of his short sword. One of the guards, the man who had walked alongside Ethan coming from the dock, stepped quickly forward. His name was Heaslip and on their way to the castle he and Ethan had gotten as friendly as circumstances permitted.

"Please stay back, sir," said Heaslip.

"You think he might bite me? He thinks he'll bite me, chaps. How deliciously waggish. Ugh, the stench really is intolerable. I can't stand it."

"We can't either," said Ethan. "Why don't you get back over the other side?"

Colonel Boatwright appeared. Ethan studied him. The visitors surprised him. Maintaining his aplomb, however, he graciously invited the crowd to accompany him outside to see the grounds. They trooped after him. Heaslip came up to Ethan.

"The bigwigs in town have been clamoring to see you. Captain Hales relented."

"What you mean is he jumped at the idea. Only forgot to tell the colonel. Tell me something, Aaron, whatever happened to Willie's cousin, Captain Delaplace?"

"Oh, he retired."

"Hear that, boys? The Green Mountain Boys were too much for him. Aaron, do me a favor and get me some paper and ink. I'm getting behind in my letter writing."

"I'll have to get the captain's permission."

"If he won't give it, ask him to speak to me. Better yet, never mind him, go ask the colonel."

Heaslip blanched and sucked air in sharply. "I really daren't."

"Aaron, just get him the paper and ink," said Jacob. "It's not like he's asking for the Crown Jewels."

Heaslip nodded and went off.

"Who will you write to, Ethan?" asked Pierre.

"Lord North."

"Oooooh," said Elisha, leering.

"Maybe even the king. This nonsense has gone far enough. Hey, you, guard!"

A tall, dark-skinned corporal looked Ethan's way, furrowing his high forehead and pointing to himself.

"Yes, you. Go tell Colonel Boatwright that Colonel Allen wants to see him."

"Go fuck yourself."

Off went the corporal. Ethan made a wry face.

"Oh well, no harm in asking, sonovabitch."

Tom sighed. "I'm so sick of all this foul language."

"It relieves the pressure," said Jacob.

"I've never uttered a curse word in my life."

"I bow to your superiority. You know, I've been wondering. I wonder when we get to Tyburn Hill will they have a special gallows for your guardian angel?"

"You're not funny."

"I mean if you're going, he goes with you, doesn't he?"

"Cut it out, Jacob," said Ethan. "Let's all quit sniping at each other. All you're doing is entertaining the guards. Look at the bright side, we're off that stinking tub, we can at least get a decent night's sleep now even if it's on stone, the food's not bad, this chain's got some play, and Boatwright is trying to do right by us."

"Here comes your *bon ami* Willie," said Pierre. "He is the one you had best keep an eye on. Him and his dumb *chien.*"

38

★ **Edmund** Burke was by nature nervous and excitable. He was also as tenacious as a tiger, having been so described by his friend Charles James Fox. He was an eloquent, if not extraordinarily persuasive orator. Ten years before he had been elected to the House of Commons from the borough of Wendover. He now represented the city of Bristol. He began his career defending policies unpopular with the people, the Ministry, and the king. He played no favorites, declared Fox, his road was not mapped to popularity nor to preferment.

He was brilliant, he was an encyclopedia. He advocated freedom of trade, he attacked the slave trade. He attempted with some success to soften the severity of the penal code and the rigorous regulations of a soldier's life. He stood up for Ireland and India. He stood up for America. He stood by his principles against his king, the tiger protecting his cubs.

Prior to Ethan Allen's capture, Burke had warned his countrymen that any effort to force America to accept and obey British laws would lead to disaster. As William Pitt, the Earl of Chatham, cautioned the House of Lords, Burke warned the Commons that to deny America independence would redound to England's discredit, and risk eventual economic ruin for the nation. He dedicated himself to dissuading the House of Commons and the Ministry from waging war against the colonies. In this he failed, but he refused to surrender. When war broke out he altered his goal, pleading for conciliation, reminding his fellow members that trade with America had increased tenfold in the first half of the century. Appealing to reason and practicality he asked why England should deliberately sacrifice such successful commerce to a war the country could not possibly win on a battlefield so distant.

"How will we arm and provision troops in the numbers needed on the other side of the ocean?"

Like the Duke of York, Burke's sentiments on the subject were well known. He, too, had received letters from Trumbull, Washington, and Hancock. General Schuyler wrote sixteen pages of arguments against executing Ethan Allen and his men, summing up the advantages of leniency to the Crown.

Burke sought allies among his fellow representatives. He acquired too few, but he was not discouraged.

"Mr. Speaker, I raise today the issue of the prisoners recently brought to our shores. His Majesty and Lord North, in their infinite wisdom, are determined to execute these men. His Majesty continues to be incensed by Colonel Ethan Allen's temerity in boldly seizing Crown property and dispossessing and imprisoning officers and men of his army. I come before you today to plead for leniency for these men. Not for forgiveness, not for condonation, and not in their interests or America's. In, gentlemen, our own interests."

"Here we go again," bawled the member from Nottingham.

A furor arose, those in disagreement with Burke, the few favoring his position, shouting at each other. Order was restored. He resumed.

"To hang these prisoners would be a vindictive act unworthy of this king and this country. Unworthy of every one of us. I ask you to consider it from the Americans' point of view. We may drain the exchequer dry, we may buy soldiers from every petty German prince willing to sell and rent his subjects, but the effort only serves to deepen and increase the pain of American resentment. Buying and renting the manpower to bring the colonists to their knees is a tactic that can only firm their resolve in their quest for liberty, for independence. Were I an American, while a single foreign soldier was active against me in my country, I would never lay down my arms. Never!"

"They'll lay down like dogs when we overwhelm them!" bellowed the member from Suffolk. "Might makes right."

"I respectfully disagree," said Burke. "But I'm digressing. I mean to restrict my words to this situation with the prisoners."

"Hang them!" shouted a member.

The chorus was taken up; it took the Speaker fully five minutes to quiet the chamber.

"Hang your father? Your brother? Your cousin? Hang our own? British subjects? Brave men who seek only their freedom? Not dethrone our king, not alter our laws, nor affect or afflict our lives in the least."

"He attacked Fort Ticonderoga by night, in foul weather, putting at risk the lives of loyal soldiers!" shouted the member from Chelsea.

"No one was injured," responded Burke. "Not a single even superficial wound."

"The filthy beggar slapped His Majesty in the face!" exclaimed the member from Leeds.

"The filthy beggar seized Forts Ticonderoga and Amherst to prevent their protecting an invasion of the colonies from Canada."

"A treasonous act!" shouted the member from Rockingham.

"Defensive strategy, well conceived and boldly executed. And for this he should hang?"

"For Montreal! For Montreal!" shouted the member from Taunton.

Burke sighed. "I respectfully ask the honorable Speaker to put it to a preliminary vote."

" 'Preliminary'," repeated the member from Taunton. "He's testing the waters. Careful you don't fall in over your head, Burke. You're doomed and you know it."

"Shall we or shall we not recommend to the House of Lords, to the Ministry and to His Majesty that the American prisoners presently being held in Pendennis Castle be spared the gallows? Nays agree that the executions shall go forth."

The vote took only a few minutes to tally. Burke lost handily—two hundred eighty-two to sixty-six. He expected to lose, indeed he was surprised by the sixty-five aye votes added to his own.

It was a start.

Only how much time was left him before the noose was knotted?

39

★ **The** onset of winter and the heavy snows that prevailed in the north failed to discourage the Americans in their plan to capture Quebec and thereby—with the earlier fall of Montreal—secure the St. Lawrence against incursions by the British navy. Montgomery was dead. He had planned to meet Arnold and his force at the foot of Mountain Hill, ascend it together, and find the main gate opened by Patriots who had gotten inside the night before. James Livingston, meanwhile, would lead his volunteers across the Heights of Abraham and join both men in accepting Carleton's surrender. Quebec was the last British foothold in Canada, and its symbolic importance, particularly after the loss of Montreal, was not lost on the governor. He assigned fifty well-armed veterans to defend the Près-de-Ville barricade. It was their musketfire that killed Montgomery, his two aides, and ten other colonials, as well as wounding others who had come up to support them.

The stiff resistance in the confined area between the cliff and the river thwarted the Americans and it was immediately decided that it would be impossible to flank the barricade. A general retreat was ordered.

Colonel Arnold, meanwhile, had come around the opposite base of the cliff, with the intention of smashing the Sautau-Matelot barricade. Conditions—the freezing temperature, a ferocious wind, and heavy snows on the ground—conspired against him. His single howitzer stuck in a drift and he was badly wounded by a shot from the top of the wall. A battalion of British sailors fired down on the Americans a hundred feet below. Colonel Daniel Morgan returned fire with deadly results. A desperate fight ensued, but just as it appeared that the Americans were gaining the edge, reinforcements joined the sailors, Morgan was attacked from the rear, and four hundred of his men were forced to surrender.

The attack on Quebec ended in failure. Two days later, Arnold left for Montreal to recuperate from his wounds. With him he brought the dead, including Montgomery.

Three thousand miles away only vague and fleeting thoughts of what was happening at Quebec crossed Ethan's mind. Something much more immediate and more personal commanded his attention. In his conscience, guilt rooted and flourished. It affected his appetite, it affected his disposition. Sarcasm degenerated into surliness, and he spared no one. His hitherto philosophical outlook degenerated into bitterness, his frustration mounted, matters reached a point where he could no longer speak to anyone without barking, without criticizing. Even the easygoing, supremely patient Pierre complained.

"You are behaving like a pig, Ethan."

"Then why bother talking to me? Would it be too much trouble to leave me alone?"

"It would be my pleasure."

Ethan crossed swords with Captain Hales, a trivial incident, one which was neither's fault, setting them shouting at each other. Hales's dog, Sheba, was allowed to run free. Ethan had yet to see her leashed. She was big, clumsy, and salivated constantly. Hales appeared during the prisoners' evening meal, Sheba scampering in after him. Running about near her master, she ventured too close to Ethan's bowl of stew, nearly upsetting it.

"Get the hell away, you mangy cur!"

Hales, engaged in conversation with two prisoners down the line, paid no attention. Then Sheba again came too close, skidded to a stop too close to the bowl, and drooled into it.

"Goddamn son of a bitch! Get that damned mongrel out of here, Hales!"

The captain came running. "Mind your mouth, Allen!"

"It drooled in my stew!"

"If she did, it was an accident. And lower your voice, you don't address a British officer in such a tone."

"You're lucky I'm chained up. I'd fucking address you with both fists!"

"I said lower your voice! Here, Sheba, good dog, keep back, dear . . . "

"It's a little late. Well, are you going to stand there or get me a fresh bowl? Clean. Don't go refilling this one. Here . . . !"

Ethan flipped over the bowl, clamping it to the floor and splattering its contents in all directions. A glob of fish landed on the captain's instep. His eyes blazed.

"Look what you've done. Deliberately!"

"What, you think I was aiming at your goddamn boot? Are you crazy?"

"Deliberate! Guard . . . guard!"

Two men came running. Hales glowered, pointing at Ethan, his hand shaking. "Unlock this one and bring him along. You've been begging for this, filthy traitor!"

40

★ A guard led the way through a maze of narrow corridors, the walls dripping, the occasional scratching of rats audible. The torch flame painted eerie shadow figures that seemed to materialize solely to watch them pass. Ethan walked two paces behind the guard. Hales followed him with Sheba, and the second guard brought up the rear. Hales had said nothing since they started down the stairs from the great hall. Now he called to the man ahead of Ethan.

"Halt." He indicated a door to the left. "Open it."

The guard produced a key ring and began trying one key after another.

"Give me that . . . "

Hales snatched the ring from him, fit a key into the lock, and opened the door. The guard behind Ethan pushed him up to the doorway, prodding him with his musket. The room was a torture chamber. In the center stood a flogging post. Against the opposite wall stood a rack, beside it a scavenger's daughter that compressed the victim into a ball. There was an iron maiden, a cuck-stool beside a huge vat for ducking, and sundry other devices. Whips hung on one wall: cat-o'-nine-tails, knouts, even one with lead imbedded in the tips of the lashes.

"Impressive, wouldn't you say?" Hales leered.

"You wouldn't dare. Colonel Boatwright would bust you down to private."

Torture had been outlawed in England for centuries, but not flogging. In the army and navy, a taste of the lash was standard punishment. Ethan eyed the flogging post, imagining he heard distant screaming.

"He might, indeed," said Hales. "Providing he learned of it."

Hales handed back the key ring. They moved outside.

"Lock it."

They kept on, coming to and ascending stairs, Sheba running ahead, prancing back, her tongue lolling, drooling. Once she ran near enough to Ethan so that he could easily have brained her with a well-aimed kick. He was tempted, but if he injured her he might never see daylight again. They arrived at a door about two-thirds the size of the door to the torture chamber. The guard unlocked it. Holding the torch high, he entered. The chamber was a cell no more than eight or nine foot square, with a low ceiling, no windows, no opening of any kind other than a small hole in the ceiling permitting ventilation. No bed, no straw, not even a pot.

"Your private quarters, Colonel!" Hales chuckled. "I do hope you find them comfortable."

"You can't do this. Not for turning a goddamn stew bowl over and accidentally—"

"Silence! This is your new home. Until further notice. Until you satisfy me that you've learned your lesson and will never again address me or any member of my command in such a manner. You may be here two days, you may be here two months. I've yet to decide."

"You going to starve me too?"

"Hardly. You'll receive your meals regularly."

"You going to leave the torch?"

"No."

"How about at least a candle?"

"No. You'll get used to the dark. Use it, it'll block out distraction, clear your thinking. You'll be able to concentrate more acutely. Reflect, Allen. Consider the errors of your ways and what you can do to improve. Make peace with God and with yourself. I can assure you when you're eventually released you'll be a better man for your time spent here."

"You are so full of shit. Sir."

Hales smirked. They left. Sheba was the last one out. She paused in the doorway to look back at him. By the light of the torch outside, she actually looked sympathetic.

"Beat it . . . "

The door clanged shut. He listened until the last faint sound of steps faded and was lost in silence. He stood in the center; now he sat down. The floor was slightly moist and very cold. There was a sound directly overhead and down plopped a rat, striking his shoulder, squealing, falling onto the floor, righting itself, and scrambling into a corner.

"Who are you? General Pig-Eyes? Sir Guy? Your Majesty?"

Though Ethan had no possible way of knowing it, the Earl of Chatham continued pressing his fellow peers to reprieve the prisoners. Edmund Burke did the same in the House of Commons. Letters pleading for amnesty and reprieve continued to arrive in London. Ethan's daughter Loraine wrote to Queen Charlotte Sophia, a letter dictated by her mother. If Her Majesty received it, or if it fell into sympathetic hands and was read to her and she, in turn, read it to His Majesty, it failed to change his thinking. The executions would go forward.

Sitting in the dark, in his solitary confinement, Ethan compared it with sitting inside a lump of coal, so black was it. Some years earlier he had read about Tyburn Hill. Its long history was as colorful as it was fascinating: the infamous Middlesex gallows, Tyburn Tree.

"Deadly Never Green, Captain Hales . . . "

He cupped an ear listening for his new companion. He heard no sound. Was Captain Rat even there? Was there a hole in a corner where he got in and out?

Tyburn had been a place of execution for five hundred years. Open galleries surrounded the gibbet. These choice seats commanded high prices and had to be reserved weeks in advance of a hanging. Reserved by the wealthy and influential, not even the condemned's immediate family were permitted to occupy them. England's version of the Colosseum in ancient Rome.

The original gallows was replaced by a portable gallows in 1759, in effect allowing the noose to search out its victims. The roster of unfortunates committed to both gallows was impressive: John Felton, murderer of Villiers, Duke of Buckingham. The notorious and colorful Jack Sheppard. Nobles and commoners without preference, traitors, deserters, political foes of the Crown. The skeletons of Cromwell, Ireton, and other regicides were hung there.

It occurred to Ethan that he and his men would be the first North Americans to test the Tyburn Tippet.

Though hardly the last, with George III on the throne.

41

★ **"Now,"** growled Pierre, "now is the time to go on a hunger strike."

A guard stood within earshot but, from his expression, he didn't hear. Or pretended not to. To a man, the guards treated the prisoners humanely and fairly; only Hales acted the martinet. Now he'd taken Ethan away and buried him somewhere in the bowels of the castle. For engaging in ten seconds of heated disagreement. Cariou, for one, disapproved.

Tom Coffin spoke. "Hales kept saying it was deliberate, slopping stew on his boot. But it wasn't. Ethan was just mad, and it happened. You don't hole a man up in the dark for that."

"You don't," said Wilkie O'Doul.

"Pass the word down the line both ways. When they bring supper we tell them take it back, by gar!"

"You," said Elisha Cummings. "Not me."

"Me, neither," said the man beside him, and a third man nodded.

It took little time to confirm that they were the only prisoners who refused to join the strike.

"He asked for it," Elisha went on. "Why should we have to go without just because he can't keep a rein on his mouth? Shit, we wouldn't even be here if it wasn't for him."

"You keep saying that, Elisha," said Pierre. "Only it is *un mensonge,* and in your heart you know it."

"He's calling you a liar," said the man beside Elisha.

"Which is what you are," said Wilkie. "Either that or stupid."

Neither man could possibly reach the other but it didn't prevent them from flushing angrily. It encouraged it.

"It's no good if those three don't come in with us," whispered Tom to Pierre. "It's got to be all."

Pierre nodded. "Elisha . . . ?"

"What now?"

"You cannot scab on us."

"When they bring the food I'm eating, I don't care about him. He didn't ask us if he could mouth off to Hales, we don't have to ask him if we can eat our goddamn meals. That's all there is to it. Now shut up and leave me alone."

"He means it," muttered Wilkie.

"What now?" Tom asked Pierre.

"We, the rest of us, are on strike!" boomed Pierre.

An hour later the two carts were trundled in and the bowls, bread, and water distributed. One after another the prisoners refused their meals. Only Elisha and his two allies accepted theirs. All eyes were on Elisha as he picked up his spoon. Before dipping it he paused and glanced up and down the line.

"It's his fault, goddamnit! It's got nothing to do with us . . . "

"Eat," said Pierre, "before it gets cold."

Elisha dipped his spoon bringing the contents slowly up to his mouth and blowing on it. Again, he paused.

"It's stupid!"

"Eat," said Tom Coffin. "Eat, eat, eat." The chant was taken up by the others. The four guards, including the two who had rolled in the carts, glanced nervously at one another. The single-word chant echoed from the ceiling.

"Eat, eat, eat, eat, eat!"

Elisha threw down his spoon. The other two men set theirs down.

"All right, all right, but this is bullshit!"

The strikers cheered. The guards gripped their muskets nervously.

"It is all right," Pierre assured them. "Nothing is going to happen. Just take away the food. All of it."

The three meals were restored to one of the carts.

"Now take them out of here," said Tom.

Aaron Heaslip stepped forward. "What do we tell the captain?"

"That we are on a hunger strike, by gar. Have you not been paying attention? Until Ethan is let out and brought back here we eat nothing."

"Willie . . . Captain Hales is not going to like this," muttered Heaslip.

"Just get it out of here."

It had become routine for the two prisoners at each end of the line to be released to bring in wood for the two fireplaces. Both fires were crackling and roaring and the four men had been restored to their wall rings when Captain Hales came striding in.

"Here comes Willie," said Tom.

"Attention, prisoners. I've been informed that you are on a hunger strike. Not a wise tactic, I'm afraid. In five hours your supper will be brought in, if you refuse to eat *it,* so be it. But it will be the last food you'll see, and from then on we'll watch you slowly starve to death."

"That is the last thing you want, *Capitaine,*" said Pierre.

Hales came scowling over. "Are you their spokesman, Frenchman?"

"*Mais oui,* you could say that. Think about it, what would the colonel say? What would the general, if they come to take us to London and find only corpses? How do they explain that to your king?" He waved a reproving finger. "But first comes Colonel Boatwright . . . "

"*I* am in command here. Colonel Boatwright commands the garrison."

"You want to protect your arse, don't you?" Wilkie asked. "Maybe you better talk to him."

This wisdom was not lost on the captain. He propped an elbow on one cupped hand, tweaked his mustache, and narrowed his eyes in thought.

"As I said, your supper will be brought to you. When it arrives you will eat it and this stupidity will end then and there."

"You can bring it in," said Tom, "but nobody's going to eat it."

A chorus of agreement pulled Hales's head up sharply.

"You will eat it! All of you! Or you'll be punished, as your friend Allen is being punished."

Wilkie laughed. "Now that'd solve everything."

"Mind your mouth, traitor!"

"He makes sense, *Capitaine,*" said Pierre. "He is warning you that it is no solution. You keep pushing this snowball and it will roll faster and get bigger and more dangerous. For you."

Hales licked his lips and stared stonily. The cause of it all came scampering in, careening to a stop, and wagging her tail. He bent to pet her. She wagged furiously. He said nothing further, turning about and striding off, Sheba following.

Ethan sat in the middle of the floor, his hand upright in front of him fanning and closing his fingers. They were no more than a foot away and could have been in focus had he been able to see them. He moved his hand toward him then back. He could see nothing. It was as black as inside the hangman's hood would be.

"If he leaves me here ten days I'll walk out stone blind."

Steps. The key turned in the lock. The door opened. Torchlight filled the frame. Into it Hales intruded.

"On your feet." Ethan got up. "Out of Christian charity I've decided to rescind this punishment. You're no longer to be confined."

"Thank you, Willie."

Hales glared. "Don't you dare! Don't you ever call me that again!"

"William?"

"Nor that. I'm Captain Hales to you, traitor. Come along."

Ethan glowed. He'd won! And he appreciated the torch-light, getting used to it would make it easier to get used to daylight, at least the interior light of the great hall. The guard with the torch led the way, Hales followed, he followed Hales, two other guards brought up the rear, one of them Aaron Heaslip, who had managed a wan smile of greeting behind Hales's back.

"Halt! Unlock!"

The guard in the lead handed the torch to the captain who handed it to one of the other guards. Ethan paid no attention, focusing on the door to the torture chamber.

"What are we stopping here for? I've already seen—"

Up came the captain's hand stopping him. "What did I say back in your cell?"

"You rescinded my punishment. It's over."

"Not exactly. What I said was, I've decided to rescind *this* punishment, confining you. After what you did you're not getting off without some type of punishment."

"You're going to torture me, you son of a bitch?"

"Keep it up. Heaslip . . . "

"Sir?"

"Hold your bayonet under his chin, the point at the soft flesh. Hold it steadily. If he makes one move to resist, one, thrust!"

Heaslip swallowed. "Yes, sir."

"What in hell do you think you're doing, Hales?"

"Sssssh. Cooperate and it'll go far easier. Benedict . . . "

"Sir?"

"Remove the prisoner's shirt."

"You're not flogging me . . . " Ethan glared. The tip of the bayonet fixed motionless half an inch from his flesh.

"Heaslip! Be ready."

Ethan read the boy's eyes. He hated this. It looked as if it was making him sick. Hales's eyes showed that he was reveling in it. He moved closer, bringing his face to within two inches of Ethan's.

"Think back. Do you remember when we were introduced back on the dock the day you arrived? I slapped you with my gloves. What did I say? I'll refresh your memory. 'Any misconduct, any insults or sarcasm will earn you ten lashes! You, Allen, have earned ten lashes ten times over. Now you're going to get them. One word, one. Or so much as a hint of resistance and the number will double.

"Now look up on the wall. Which one will it be? I think the conventional cat-o'-nine-tails. Very popular with the navy. Do you approve? I asked you a question!"

"Whatever you want, Wil . . . Captain."

"The cat it is."

Stripped to the waist, Ethan was tied to the whipping post. He craned his neck but could not see behind him.

"You've selected a longtime favorite among lashes. Noted for its pain, though I'm told it's not nearly as painful as the Russian knout. *Its* thongs are dried and hardened and interwoven with wire. Sometimes the wires are hooked and sharpened so that they dig in and tear."

"Can we get it over with? I don't want to be late for my appointment with the colonel."

"Tsk tsk, Colonel Boatwright's not around, I'm afraid. He hasn't been over in days. He's stuck at the fort with a visiting general."

"What are you waiting for?"

"He's in a hurry. Extraordinary. Let me warn you before we begin, try not to tense. Tensing the muscles actually increases the pain." Ethan felt Hales's hand brush his upper back. "Oh my, you're tense already."

The first stroke was like a dagger pulled diagonally down his back almost to the waist. The second crossed it. His back caught fire, flame seared the flesh, consuming it, liquifying it. He imagined he could feel it dropping off in blobs. Seven, eight. Now he was fighting to keep from passing out. Nine . . .

"Still with us, Allen?" He grunted softly. "One more . . . "

He waited. He could hear Hales breathing heavily from his exertions. He himself could barely breathe; it was excruciatingly painful, however slightly he moved his upper body. Down came the lash, slicing through him.

"Ten! Untie him."

V

A Royal Dilemma

42

★ **Seven** liveried retainers, bewigged and white-stockinged, stood in a row at the far end of the salon. At a table in the center, an eighth carefully poured tea for their majesties while a ninth added the preferred amounts of milk to each cup, no sugar.

Queen Charlotte, resplendent in a white satin gown trimmed with pearls and lace in festooned fabalus edged with silver gimp, touched her liberally powdered upswept hair and grasped the handle of her cup. She was not pretty, but her eyes were attractive and her trim, slender figure a triumph, considering that she had already given birth to ten children. She had a somewhat flat nose and a dishearteningly wide mouth.

Her husband smiled, his striking blue eyes sparkling. He had the thick lips and prominent nose of the earlier Georges, but he was tall and well-built with fair skin, healthy coloring, and reddish-brown hair. He was a pleasant man and gracious: toward his wife, to whom he was devoted, toward everyone, regardless of station, even his adversaries in Parliament. At the moment, however, stirring his tea, his mood was far from gracious. He was uncomfortably close to furious.

"Do calm down, *Liebchen,* drink your tea," the queen said. "It will soothe—"

"Walpole!"

"Horace is one of your greatest admirers. I remember he wrote glowingly of you just after your coronation. What was it he said? That you were graceful and genteel and . . . "

"Flattery! Just to curry favor. He's turned on me. That rapscallion John Wilkes is trumpeting it in that scurrilous rag of his, the *North Briton.* Walpole, my 'dear friend and admirer' is now supporting the American colonies against me. Pitt keeps beating the same drum in the House of Lords; Burke, in Commons . . . "

"I've read the *North Briton,* it's not a scurrilous rag, *Liebchen.*"

"It's a scandal sheet! You forget what Wilkes did when I was a boy. That business about Lord Bute and my mother. The scoundrel printed the most vicious rumors. I should have closed him down years ago. I wanted to charge him with treason back then, but there was no way to prove he was the actual author. Oh, he wrote all those lies, no question. Printed them! Peddled them! Damn his black soul!"

"Georgie, Georgie . . . "

"Now he's publishing all sorts of pro-independence drivel and lies, and important men, men whose support I've counted on for years, are beginning to cock an ear. It's disgraceful! Independence! I'll show those ungrateful rascals independence!"

He snatched up a scone, started it toward his mouth, changed his mind, and flung it to the floor. The eighth retainer picked up the pieces in a napkin.

Unperturbed, Charlotte calmly sipped then set down her cup. "Maybe this isn't a good time."

"For what?"

"You've dribbled down your chin, *Liebchen.* Here . . . " She leaned across and wiped his chin with her napkin.

"Good time for what?"

"To talk about the Americans."

"What about them?"

"Guess who's received a letter from there."

"Who do you know in America?"

She withdrew an opened envelope from her skirt pocket. "A Mrs. Mary Brownson Allen. She wrote pleading for her husband's life."

"Husband?"

"Ethan Allen."

"Never heard of him."

"He's your prisoner. He and others were captured and shipped here."

"Oh, oh, oh, the wild man who attacked Fort Whatever-they-call-it."

She skimmed the letter. "Fort Ti-con-der . . . "

"Oga, oga, oga. Yes, yes, yes, they're to be hanged. And nobody more deserving, impudent dogs!"

"Her letter asks, *begs* you to reconsider. Shall I read it?"

"Tear it up."

"It's very touching. You read it and you can see where tears have fallen and dried."

"Pity. I feel sorry for the woman."

"And their five children?"

"Charlotte, her husband is guilty of a serious criminal act. Against his king. He seized Crown property. He helped to seize Fort St. John's and Fort Something-or-other nearby. He tried to take Montreal, which turned out a fiasco for him."

"But must he be hanged, Georgie?"

"My beloved, we've a pact, you and I, remember? You're not to clutter your brain with politics, and I'm not to interfere with your bringing up the children."

"How many prisoners?"

"How should I know that? Fifty, sixty?"

"And this Ethan Allen is their leader."

"Ringleader. Despicable brigands, no better than a Liverpool street gang. They're not soldiers, they're not even mercenaries, so they can't be prisoners of war and treated as such. Exchanged, whatever."

"They must hang?"

"They're untrained, undisciplined, they have no reason to exist. But they were caught; now, yes, they'll hang. To set an example."

"To whom, *Liebchen?*"

"Isn't that obvious? He and his rabble have become a symbol of defiance and . . . ingratitude. They oppose everything we try to do for them. Oppose our laws, which are only in force for their protection. Oppose taxation. Oppose their king. Were I to knuckle under to their demands and grant them independence, the whole empire would begin crumbling. Canada would be next to go. Then Ireland, then India. Once it starts there'll be no stopping it. I've made the only decision that makes sense."

"No independence."

"No independence. I can't back down. My subjects expect me to be firm, decisive. I make up my mind, I stick to it."

"Unwavering."

"Unwavering."

"Unswerving."

"A rock."

"Only I don't think that's it, *Liebchen.*"

"What?"

"That you worry about losing other colonies. That you worry what the public will think if you back down. I think you're *gebeleidigt.*"

"Offended? What are you talking about?"

"Offended that they don't want you for their king."

"I *am* their king!"

"But they want to be free. Of you, of Parliament, of England. And that rubs you the wrong way."

"You see? There's a perfect example."

"Of what?"

"Why you shouldn't clutter your brain with politics. You don't understand politics. You're missing the point entirely."

"Am I? Oh dear . . . "

"It's all right, all right." He patted her hand, then touched his temple. "It's all clear as a bell to me. Here, try one of these scones, they're scrumptious."

43

★ **Private** Aaron Heaslip smuggled in a piece of muslin liberally saturated with vinegar for Ethan. Pierre set it gently against his badly lacerated back.

"Ooooo, it feels good."

"I am sorry, Ethan."

"What have you to be sorry for?"

"The hunger strike. It was not supposed to work out like this."

"It could be worse, I could have gotten fifty lashes. How does it look back there?"

"Like a bear spent an hour clawing you. And it is swelling . . . "

"You won't be able to lie on your back for six months," said Jacob.

"I heal fast. Elisha?"

"What?"

"I heard what you did, joined the strike. I know you still blame me for all this, and you have every right to. But sitting in the dark I thought about it long and carefully. I must say this: I'm no hero, I'm no leader. Montreal proved that. I only got into this because I believed in it so strongly. We're entitled to liberty, to be a free and independent nation. To live under the king's thumb is wrong."

"Hear, hear," said somebody.

"I've made bad mistakes, I've brought us to this. I've no excuse. Whatever happens, you're right, I'm to blame. I can't change that now, and I can't ask your forgiveness. I wouldn't. I'm telling you this so that you'll know that *I* know what I am. And why I got you into this."

Wilkie O'Doul had restored Ethan's shirt over the vinegar-soaked rag.

"I want to say something now," said Pierre. "What you just said, Ethan, is in all our hearts. We got in because we believe in this thing. And a man has to have real faith in something or he is just a shell, empty, with no purpose. I cannot speak for anyone else, but I have no regrets. I am proud to be here."

Elisha was staring at Ethan. "Me too." Elisha grinned. "It's not me complaining, it's just my mouth."

Not a man among them had the least doubt that the day was not distant when they'd be transported to London and hanged. They were unaware of the rising tide in Parliament, among the public, and in Queen Charlotte's heart, favoring reprieve.

What to do with the rabble in arms that had threatened Montreal inspired considerable soul-searching among all classes of Britons? Everywhere people gathered it was discussed. To classify them as prisoners of war would permit them to escape the noose. But doing so would legitimize the Revolution. Nevertheless, it could scarcely be disputed that they had fought as soldiers. To treat them now as civilian criminals would be to ignore the obvious and invite the criticism of other European nations.

It would also ensnare British forces in the colonies in a dilemma. The Americans had seized General Prescott and other British officers, and they had been imprisoned with common criminals in retaliation for the Crown's treatment of Ethan and his men. Were the Americans to be hanged, the British prisoners could expect the same fate.

Colonel Boatwright, an infrequent visitor to the castle, came to see the prisoners. He and Ethan were not thirty seconds into conversation when it became apparent to Ethan that Hales had not informed his superior of either the confinement or the flogging. This was within the captain's right, since he *was* in command of the prisoners. But he had a moral obligation to apprise Boatwright; it would have been procedure, it would have been correct. At which point Pierre interrupted them and informed the colonel as to what had happened in graphic terms.

Boatwright appeared taken aback. "How are you feeling now, Colonel Allen?"

"Never better, sir."

"Seriously, *are* you all right?"

"I'll live."

"Can I get you anything? Perhaps something from the doctor for the discomfort?"

"The vinegar's doing fine. How's Captain Hales?" Boatwright stared. "Is he satisfied? Are we all square?"

Boatwright looked uneasy. Ethan dropped it.

"Release this man," said Colonel Boatwright to one of the guards. "Colonel, I'm taking you across the way to the garrison. Do you feel up to the walk?"

"Sure. What's all this about?"

"General Sims wishes a word with you."

"Who's he?"

"Head of the Royal Secret Service."

"What does he want with me?"

"He'll tell you."

Ethan was released and with the colonel escorted across the long field separating Pendennis Castle and the fort. Soldiers hanging about the main gate stared curiously as Ethan was escorted inside and into Boatwright's office. It was twice the size of the small room he utilized in the castle for his office, furnished with an escritoire, comfortable chairs, an Isfahan carpet, and other impressive appointments. General Sims stood at the small window, his back to them. He was barely three or four inches over five feet tall. His neck was deeply seamed and his shoulders wide, but when he turned his face surprised Ethan. It did not go with his frame. It was the face, the complexion, the softness and pallor of a poet, not a military man. He was clean-shaven. Boatwright introduced them and made as if to leave.

"Stay, Colonel. I'll want you to hear this. Perhaps you can contribute. Mr. Allen . . . "

"Colonel, General."

"As you wish." The general produced a letter. "This is from the king's solicitor-general. With His Highness's full approval he proposes that you be released."

"And my men?"

"All of you."

"On what terms?"

Sims smiled. "Perceptive man."

"Just practical."

Sims cleared his throat. "I'll put it in a nutshell for you. His Highness is generously willing to let bygones be bygones, if you return to the colonies and perform certain services for the Crown."

"Services?"

"Which is vastly better than going back a prisoner of war. Let's consider your situation. As a result of your heroic exploits at Ticonderoga your own people rejected you for command. Your property in the New Hampshire Grants is still, as it were, in limbo; you may never be able to claim title to it. On the other hand, if you accept this offer you'll be granted a full pardon. You'll be commissioned a captain and given command of a company of rangers. Your lands will become yours free and clear and . . . " He winked. " . . . I can't say how much, there'll be extra remuneration in it over and above your captain's pay."

"That's very generous of you, General."

"Very generous of your king and the solicitor-general."

"I'm overwhelmed."

"Then I take it you accept?"

"I said overwhelmed, not tempted."

"Then you refuse."

"It should be stronger than that. Give me time to think of the words."

"This is a serious proposal, Allen."

"Oh, I'm serious, General. Keep it. And tell the solicitor-general to tell His Majesty he can't buy me like he buys everybody else."

"Careful, fellow, that's not an attitude that will endear you to His Highness."

"I'm not looking to endear myself to any foreign king. You know what this is? It's an official insult. You ought to be ashamed. Colonel, take me back."

"I wouldn't be in such a rush," said Sims. "You owe it to your men to at least lay the offer before them."

"You do it. Tell them how impressed I was, see what they say."

"You're impertinent, fellow."

"And you're naïve."

"Gentlemen, gentlemen, please," said Boatwright. "Colonel Allen, we'll take you back. The general's right, they are entitled to hear the proposal."

"Sure. In . . . in an hour."

Sims' eyes narrowed. "Of course. You want time to talk them out of it."

"Perceptive man."

Ethan explained. "Remember, it's like the colonel said bringing me back here. If you agree you'll get to fight on the winning side. Get to shoot at your friends and neighbors. It's the chance of a lifetime, being paid every month to be a traitor. Forget Ticonderoga, St. John's, Chambly. Forget Lexington and Concord and Bunker Hill. That'll all be forgiven. All you do is sign up and put on a red coat."

Captain Hales, Colonel Boatwright, and General Sims were coming in. Sheba was nowhere in sight. Seeing the captain triggered pain in various places on Ethan's back. He returned his scowl in kind. He'd get him; by hook or by crook he'd pay.

Boatwright introduced the general.

"Has your commander detailed the offer?" Sims asked.

"Yes, sir," said Pierre. "And a very attractive offer it is."

"Tempting," said Tom Coffin.

Others nodded and murmured agreement.

"This is an official offer put forth by His Royal Highness, one which you would do well to consider with the utmost seriousness."

"Are you saying if we don't accept it you'll hang us?" Ethan asked.

"The consequences of refusing should be self-evident."

"That's what he means," said Wilkie. "They'll hang us."

Sims shrugged.

"Don't believe it," said Ethan. "They're desperate. The last thing they want is for Prescott and the others *we* captured to be hanged. You know that's what'll happen, General. Every day that goes by it's getting worse. Parliament, the people, they just don't have the stomach to go through with it."

"This is useless," said Sims to Boatwright. "For the last time, are there any, any of you, who might consider—"

A chorus of no's greeted this. Sims turned about and strode off, with Boatwright hurrying to catch up with him. Hales lingered.

"You're making a big mistake, men, listening to this one. He got you into this, now he's keeping you from getting out."

"Beat it, Captain Dog Fucker."

"Who said that!" He began running up and down the line, his face reddening, his hand going to his hilt. "Speak up!"

"I did," said a man.

Hales ran to him. Another up the other end spoke.

"He's wrong, I did."

Hales started for him, but a voice spun him about.

"They're both lying. I did," said a third.

"I did, I did" rose in raucous unison. Hales glared and pounded off. Not until the door slammed in his wake did all four guards burst out laughing.

44

★ **Debates** over the captives' fate continued in Parliament and in the press. No two people in all of England could get together without discussing the situation. The king fumed; he took the prisoners' rejection of his magnanimous offer as an outright insult. He sat on the edge of the bed in nightshift and cap, staring into the crackling fire, softly thumping the counterpane, hurt supplanting his anger at the Americans.

"Their devilish impertinence. I'm to blame, partially. I'm *too* good-hearted, *too* generous. It was my father's fault and his father's before him. The people mistake it for softness. And they refuse to take seriously what's happening over there. Parliament doesn't. Neither house understands. They don't understand their king."

"I understand you, *Liebchen.*"

Charlotte crawled across the bed on her knees to embrace him from behind and snuggle against his neck. He sighed a trifle too melodramatically.

"You're the only one. Except for Freddie North. And lately, I'm not too sure about him. It's a rotten job, being king. But I know one thing, this empire was not built with the sweat and blood of our great men for me to stand by now and watch it taken apart, piece by piece. Not on my watch, by God!"

"You're getting yourself all worked up, you won't be able to sleep."

"Who can sleep?"

Up on her knees she began massaging his shoulders. "What happens to the prisoners now, Georgie?"

"I know what I'd like to happen. That we pack a picnic basket and take the coach to Edgeware Road, join the crowd, and watch them hang!"

"You won't hang them."

"Only because the situation in America has deteriorated so it no longer makes sense to."

Charlotte lay atop the counterpane, her hands folded across her midriff. She eyed him sympathetically and reaching out began rubbing his upper back. Incense burning on a nearby chiffonier filled the room with the scent of lavender.

"It's now a full-scale war over there. I go to sleep, they're criminal rebels, I wake up, they're prisoners of war. The colonial secretary says they are. So does the solicitor-general."

Perhaps to atone for Hales's unwarranted cruelty toward Ethan, perhaps because of the national "shift in the wind" toward the prisoners, perhaps because he was fed up with seeing them chained in the great hall to be ogled three times weekly by visitors, Colonel Boatwright ranked Captain Hales and ordered them released.

"Immediately. For as long as you remain in custody here," he added when the cheering subsided. "Henceforth you'll have the run of the place and the grounds. You will keep your distance from my men. Speak only with your guards, and only when necessary. You may walk about the grounds, you may explore to your heart's content. You'll eat your meals here at the tables from now on. You will not take advantage and try to leave. Anyone who tries risks being shot on sight. The garrison has been so informed, as have the townspeople. We shall play fair with each other. Do I have your word that you'll abide by these rules, Colonel?"

Ethan glanced up and down the line. All eyes agreed.

"You have my word."

*   *   *

Their shackles were removed.

"Refusing to change sides was a smart move, Ethan," said Pierre.

"It was the only move." Ethan massaged his wrists. "Let's go out, I'd like to see the sun. It's been too long."

The day was mild. Cornwall's winters were generally mild compared with winters elsewhere in England. Hales was standing in the rose garden talking to a sergeant, Sheba by the captain's side. Ethan, with Pierre, Wilkie, Jacob, and others, stopped to survey Ethan's antagonist. At sight of them the captain's expression became sour. Ethan smiled inside. Boatwright had likely dressed him down for his cruelty.

"So you've free run of the place, have you?" Hales came over, Sheba trotting at his heels. "See that you don't abuse the colonel's generosity."

"We wouldn't dream of it, Willie."

Hales bristled and curled his lip. Ethan looked down at Sheba as she bounded up asking to be petted. He obliged her.

"She likes you," said Hales. "A good dog, but no taste in people."

Ethan rubbed her behind her ears. "Good girl." He indicated Hales. "Good Sheba. Sic him. Sic him!"

She started, confused, turning back toward the captain, back to Ethan. He laughed, his friends laughed. The sergeant to whom Hales had been talking grinned. The captain looked as if he were tasting something bitter.

"Come here, girl." She bounded back to him. "Enjoy your newfound freedom, Allen, gentlemen. As I say, see that you don't abuse it. And you, Colonel, don't even dream of attempting to avenge your punishment."

"Oh? Does that worry you?"

"On the contrary, I only wish you'd try something." He patted the hilt of his saber. "They'd have to bury you in two parts."

Ethan's friends "ooh"ed derisively.

"Let me give *you* some friendly advice, Willie. Take very good care of your dog. Come along, boys."

They walked off toward the fort. The sun blazed spectacularly, although the air held a mild chill, fetched by the wind from Dartmoor Forest to the east.

"You wouldn't harm his dog," said Tom Coffin.

"Hardly. Just slipping a little worm of worry into his hairy ear."

Elisha spoke. "If you try to get even with him he'll take it out on all of us."

Ethan stopped, stopping him. "You think I don't know that?"

"All the same, *mon ami,* you can't let him get away with it," said Pierre.

"I'd rather not. Let's sit back and see what happens. Who knows, maybe a bad, maybe even fatal accident is, like they say, just around the corner."

Two days later Aaron Heaslip smuggled a newspaper to Ethan, a week-old copy of the *Exeter Mercury.* On the front page was an article devoted to what had come to be called the "Prisoner Problem."

Ethan read it aloud to the others. They were finishing dinner at the tables in the great hall. " 'The thinking at the Ministry regarding the prisoners has changed in the past week. This correspondent has it on reliable authority that they will be shipped back to America as prisoners of war.' "

Everyone cheered.

"Wait, wait, there's more. 'The man-of-war *Solebay,* commanded by Captain Ezekial Symonds, will transport the rebels.' "

Another cheer.

"Everybody quiet down!"

"What is the matter?" Pierre asked, lowering his cup and returning Ethan's worried expression.

"I wonder . . . "

"What?" asked Tom Coffin. The group around Ethan moved in closer.

"It could be a trick. They get us back on the high seas and halfway home hang us from a yardarm."

"They wouldn't," said Jacob.

"Wouldn't they? Think about it. It wouldn't be like Tyburn Hill, with the king and a crowd and all the hoop-la. It'd be halfway to Boston, with nobody watching but this Symonds and the crew."

"Then they dump our bodies overboard," said Elisha. "And nobody on either side of the ocean the wiser."

"Gone and forgotten." Ethan snapped his fingers. "Like that. The news would be weeks getting back here. If it ever did. Parliament, the press, the people, would all take it for granted we just sailed home. Back home they wouldn't even know we sailed. I'm not trying to scare you, I'm trying to figure it practically. Look at what they've done to us up to now— treated us like dogs until Boatwright released us. You've all got to understand something, His Majesty hates us like the plague, what we're trying to do to his precious empire, what we symbolize. Out of pure contempt and vengeance he'd love to lose us at sea."

Jacob's eyes widened. "They could even be planning to change the name of the ship in mid-ocean. Pretend this *Solebay* went down with all hands lost. And turn about and sail back here with another name."

"Nobody's stretching this neck," growled Wilkie O'Doul, "sure not on the way home."

"Ethan's right about one thing," said Pierre. "They could keep it secret. The Americans and our people could never find out what really happened, so they couldn't take revenge on Prescott and their other prisoners. How could they?"

"All I'm saying," said Ethan, "is let's be on our guard. I don't trust 'em, any of 'em, not even Boatwright, who's played fair and square up to now. Not like I trust my instincts." He tapped the side of his nose.

"We'll just have to play along, wait and see," said Tom. "What else can we do?"

"One thing," muttered Ethan. "Nobody leaves here for the dock without bringing his dinner knife to sneak on board."

45

JANUARY 1776

★ **Three** lines near the end of the news report in the *Exeter Mercury* contained the key to the king's unexpected turnabout regarding the prisoners. Reports from America had it that in retaliation for the harsh treatment of Ethan Allen and his men, particularly en route to England, General Prescott and his officers were also shackled, confined, and made to suffer similar deprivations. From all appearances the prisoners were being made scapegoats in the conflict.

Captain Symonds, commander of the *Solebay*, was a stiff-necked, humorless, no-nonsense veteran from a long line of navy men. He bridled at the onerous duty given him: fetching rebel prisoners back to America. Not an assignment calculated to enhance any master's reputation. But the Admiralty's orders were not to be questioned, although as he informed his first officer after reading them: "I'll be cursed if I'll go out of my way to make the voyage comfortable for the traitorous scum, especially that renegade Allen!"

For the first time in forty-one years snow fell on Falmouth and the surrounding countryside. It happened late in January while the town slept. It was still snowing lightly when the Americans were assembled in front of the castle and marched down the east road to the dock. The public's curiosity having long since worn off, few townspeople gathered to watch the departure. Captain Hales rode his charger and was accompanied by Colonel Boatwright astride his horse. At the dock, the

Solebay's three masts poked the whitened sky. Her full canvas was up. She strained at her hawsers. The snowfall had settled on ratlines, sheets, spars, and yardarms, creating a frosted ship out of a fairy tale. On her foredeck was a white-clad battery, a light battery was on her spardeck.

Captain Symonds, a huge man, appeared frozen to the railing, his face a pink mask. Crewmen busied themselves about the deck. Boatwright dismounted and faced the line of prisoners. Hales called attention.

"I trust you will all have a comfortable voyage home," said Boatwright. "Once arrived, expect to be incarcerated, for you are still and will continue to be prisoners of war. For the duration or until you are exchanged. For the most part you've conducted yourselves well in custody. It's a damnable pity, this rebellion, pitting blood against blood as it does. It is in all respects a family squabble blown all out of proportion. I can't say I wish you luck, but I do earnestly hope that you all survive the uncertain future to eventually return to your towns and farms and build happy lives for yourselves and your loved ones. After your leaders come to their senses and surrender."

Loud hooting greeted this. He managed a good-natured grin. Hales frowned. Boatwright glanced his way.

"Relax, William, they're entitled to their opinion."

Ethan had taken to watching Sheba slip in and out of Hales's horse's legs. Then he raised his eyes to the captain's face. Hales's mustaches looked like horizontal icicles. Ethan clucked regretfully; unless he whipped his stolen knife out of his sleeve and hurled it at Hales's heart, accounts between them would never be properly settled. He'd sail away, they'd never see each other again, not unless the captain was shipped over to fight. And was revenge as sweet as they claimed? Was it even required? Ruminating on this, he felt no discomfort down his back. By now he had healed almost completely, although he'd be scarred for life. What did that amount to? What actually was it but a badge of sorts commemorating the risks assumed in the fight for independence? His son Joseph would be impressed, if not Mary. Hales had dismounted. He came over to him.

"Good-bye, Allen."

"Good-bye."

"No hard feelings, I trust. All's fair in war or something like that."

"Something like that." Sheba came up. Ethan bent to pet her. She wagged appreciatively. "I used to think this clumsy mutt wasn't worth kicking, but she sure does grow on you, she's so friendly. Aren't you friendly, little girl? Yes you are. How much do you want for her?"

"She's not for sale."

"Sheba? What do you say, girl? Want to come to America with me?"

Her tail whipped furiously. Ethan laughed. Boatwright looking on grinned. The gangplank was laid, the prisoners began filing up it, Ethan taking his place at the end of the line, the shepherd trailing his flock. He was done petting Sheba. He shook the colonel's hand and flipped a wave at Hales.

"Goodbye, Aaron," he called to Heaslip. "Good luck." He started up the gangplank. Sheba trailed after.

"Sheba!" called Hales. "Come back, girl!"

A poor choice of tones, too stern, authoritative, ill-calculated to induce her to obey. Ethan said no more to her, nor did he turn to look back. He could hear her nails clicking against the gangplank. The ship above him looked so dazzlingly white it hurt his eyes.

"Sheba! Sheba!" shouted Hales. Ethan was now two-thirds of the way to the deck, and still she followed. "Allen!" Ethan stopped and turned. "Send her back, would you?"

"Sheba, go back to him. Go."

Everyone watching was grinning.

"Sheba, come back here!"

Ethan knelt and rubbed her head. "Go to him, little girl. Good girl. I can't take you, no pets allowed. And don't go jumping in and swimming out after us . . . "

Hales called again and again. Ethan turned her about and patted her rear, urging her back down. At the foot of the gangplank Hales produced her leash, fastening it to her collar. She tugged, yapping frantically. Ethan waved one last time and stepped on board.

The *Solebay*'s hawsers were loosed, losing their snow mantels. The yards creaked, the vessel groaned and eased away from the dock, heading south down the bay, with Lizard Head looming through the mist and persisting snowfall to starboard. Captain Symonds summoned prisoners and crew on deck.

"I am Captain Ezekial Symonds, commander of the *Solebay*. It is my duty under Admiralty law to read you the Articles of Command. Pay close attention and do not interrupt."

He got out a well-worn pamphlet and launched into a monotonous recitation of the articles. Ethan could feel his upper lids growing weighty. He surrendered to a yawn. Engrossed in his task, Symonds failed to see but a lieutenant, standing beside him displaying watery eyes and an impressive crop of pimples, noticed and flung a look so absurdly menacing it was all Ethan could do to keep from laughing out loud. On and on droned Symonds until, after what seemed like an hour, he closed his pamphlet.

"Any questions? None. Good. One last thing, you prisoners. You *are* prisoners, my prisoners, and from here to port I don't want to see a single one of you on deck. That particularly means you, Colonel Allen. My deck is a place reserved for gentlemen to walk, not scurvy rebels. Bascomb . . . " The pimply lieutenant stepped smartly forward, executing a quarter turn toward his captain and saluting so sharply he risked dislocating his shoulder. "Escort Colonel Allen to his quarters."

"Follow me, Colonel Allen."

Again Ethan had trouble holding back a laugh as, from what he could see, did most of his men. The lieutenant seemed determined to imitate his captain, and was doing a poor job of it. Leading the way, he marched down to the hold, stopping before an iron door. Flinging it wide, he stepped in.

"Your quarters. Remember the captain's order, you are not to walk the deck."

He left. Inside was about the size of the dark chamber in the bowels of Pendennis Castle, with no light, unless he left the door open. There was a double bunk, a small toilet, and a three-legged stool.

The castle's eternal dampness had taken its toll. Ethan had come down with a cold that became severe the day before. He undressed down to his underwear and slipped under the blanket. It provided little warmth, so he added the blanket from the bunk overhead. He was exhausted, despite the early hour. Ordinarily he would have fallen asleep the moment his head touched the mattress, but worry set his mind whirling. Worry about his men, their welfare, their survival. After all the threats of Tyburn Hill they'd gotten out from under the noose and out of the country so easily. Too easily? The suspicion that they would be conveniently "lost at sea" while captain and crew were miraculously saved came back. *Was* that the Admiralty's plan? Would they ever see America?

He felt under the mattress for the knife he'd slipped there when he'd removed his clothes. Smuggling the knives aboard was risky. All Symonds had to do was find one and he'd search and find more and jump to the obvious conclusion.

What would he do to them? Punishment of some kind, something short of keel-hauling. Like Prescott, Watson, and Hales before him, he was consumed with hatred for the "traitors," although all four betrayed their prejudices in different ways. Prescott was an out and out sadist. Watson was cruel, actually more harsh, but stayed within bounds, wise enough to realize that he had to deliver his cargo intact. As for Hales, all he did was take out on them his frustration with the army that should have promoted him to colonel by his age. But this one . . .

For all his bluster and all his efforts at intimidation, it well could be that he feared them. Not of their taking over the ship, nothing that extreme. It was that he had to know them, him especially, by reputation. Know that the king himself was sufficiently impressed to change his mind about hanging them. That would have meant a death sentence for Prescott. Symonds knew about Ticonderoga, about their exploits after that. He'd probably never seen any action himself beyond the monthly rat extermination rounds every ship's master leads his crew on.

"He needs testing, that's what he needs."

46

★ **Suspicion** of the Admiralty's intentions troubled Ethan for the next two days. Being hanged was bad enough, but the deaths of his men on his conscience would be far worse. He didn't believe in heaven or hell, but punishment of some kind had to be the lot of anyone responsible for such a massacre. And what bothered him most was meeting some of the men's eyes since they set sail. His worry was too obviously their own.

Surviving hinged on getting back to America. Once they set foot on the dock in America, this tormenting guilt, this overblown consciousness of responsibility, would lift from his shoulders. Not that it would then be every man for himself, but being home did alter the situation. No one blamed him for the debacle at Montreal, not even Elisha Cummings and his friends, not at this stage. Perhaps it was that reality that whetted his guilt. Now all, even Elisha, appeared to share Pierre's opinion that each was a grown man responsible for his own decisions, his own actions. So why did he continue to feel guilty?

On the morning of the third day at sea, with the Scilly Isles well astern and a stiff wind bellying the canvas, Ethan arose, sponge-bathed himself, and went up on deck. He spotted Captain Symonds standing in the wind, his blue overcoat falling well below his knees. He looked Ethan's way.

"You were ordered never to set foot on this deck!"

"I believe what you said was that it's a place reserved for gentlemen to walk. I'm Colonel Ethan Allen of the Green Mountain Regiment, I don't think we've been properly introduced."

Symonds waved away his outstretched hand. "Damn your traitorous hide! Take care you don't walk on the same side of the deck as I do!"

The man was afraid of him. No question. It filled his eyes, and he couldn't hide it.

Unlike their captain, many of the crew were neither resentful nor aloof. They were friendly, outgoing, and talked to both Americans and Canadians, to Symonds's displeasure. Ethan fell into conversation with the ship's master at arms. Seamus Gilligan had a brogue so heavy he flirted with unintelligibility. He was a back-slapper with a laugh that boomed down the deck like a barrel on the loose. He was fond of grabbing Ethan by the lapel, pulling him close and conversing like two spies. They stood leaning on the taffrail watching the terns fight over the cook's garbage. Gilligan pulled him close, though no one else was within twenty yards of them.

"You must have made some impression on His Majesty, the way he changed his mind about stringing you lads up."

"You could say he and a lot of others finally came to their senses."

"And now you're heading home."

"Heading is good. I wonder. Will we make it?"

"Oh, never fear, this ship's as seaworthy as they come."

"It's not the ship I worry about, it's Jack Bull. It'd be so easy to slit our throats and dump us overboard in mid-ocean."

"Never happen at all, at all."

"Who knows?"

"Never. They hang you lads and the Americans'll kill every prisoner they've taken so far. Fifty for one. Think o' the uproar that'd cause."

He had a point. Conveniently losing prisoners at sea, as against hanging them publicly at Tyburn Hill, would not go down well with the other nations of Europe. It was the devious tactic of buccaneers, not responsible English Admiralty members.

"Where'd little Bobby Bascomb stick you, Ethan?"

"In a room the size of your hat down in the bilge water."

"I think I know the one. See here, bucko, why not come up and share with me? It's small, between decks, and there's only a piece o' sailcloth for a wall separating it from the crew's quarters, but you can fit another bed in."

"I'd like that, Seamus; anything'd be better than that rathole."

In the afternoon black clouds gathered, and a winter storm struck, testing the *Solebay*'s rigging and the crew's skills and spleen. Ordered below, the prisoners clutched anything at hand to keep from being tossed about. It wasn't nearly as violent a storm as the one that had struck the *Adamant* coming over, nor did it last as long, but it did set Ethan to worrying. Traveling the North Atlantic at the worst time of year would not have been his choice.

The next morning, with the waves depleted of their fury, the *Solebay*, having suffered no appreciable damage, deserted the open water and put in at Cork, winding between the headlands past Roche's Point and Ram's Head into Cork Harbor. From there, Symonds guided her along the coast of the Great Island, through Lough Mahan to the River Lee and the city. Gilligan delighted in pointing out the sights to Ethan and the others, for Cork was his hometown. Symonds had personal business there, accounting for the stopover. Tom Coffin, Wilkie O'Doul, Jacob Wall, and Elisha Cummings joined Pierre, Ethan, and Gilligan.

"The captain'll be tied up all day. We'll go ashore," announced Gilligan.

"Will they let us?" asked Jacob.

"Lieutenant Douglass won't care, and Lieutenant Bascomb hasn't the guts to stop us. Come, you'll be me guests. I'll introduce you all around town, I will."

Their first stop was a woolen merchant's in St. Finbar's Street: Donnelly & Sons. Gerald Donnelly was ancient, weighed close to three hundred pounds, relied on the stoutest cane Ethan had ever seen, and made the sign of the cross every time he swore, which was about every other sentence. He ushered them across the street to Houlihan's Ale House and bought drinks all around.

During the day Gilligan introduced them to dozens of other Corkers, all of whom received them graciously. Loyal Irishmen all, they resented Parliament's high-handedness, as well as the king's threat to hang them as traitors. Many of the businessmen they met had economic reasons for their disapproval. They wanted the war to end soon so that trade with America could be restored, and put all the blame for what one called "The Great Quarrel" on king and Parliament.

Gilligan's friends offered them new clothing in place of their ragged buckskins and homespun. Each was given an overcoat, a suit and two shirts, and additional outfits to take back to their fellow prisoners. Ethan started back to the ship late in the afternoon, his arms piled with eight shirts, neckcloths, enough broadcloth to make two suits, two pair of shoes, wool and silk hose, and two beaver hats. Geneva gin was sent on board, whiskey and wines, roast turkeys, ham, and other stores. One particularly free-handed banker talked Ethan into accepting a gift of fifty guineas.

Everything was delivered on board while Symonds was absent. When he returned early that evening he exploded. He ordered everyone assembled on deck, prisoners and crew.

"You damnable rebels will not be treated like kings by

damned Irish rebels! All wines and liquors are hereby confiscated!"

A prolonged groan greeted this.

"Silence!"

Lieutenant Douglass stepped forward. Although Ethan had yet to make his acquaintance, Gilligan had pointed him out, and it was he who'd given him permission to take Ethan and the others ashore. Gilligan had praised the lieutenant as a good officer, intelligent, and fair-minded. He was an admiral's son.

"Sir," said Douglass to Symonds, "with all due respect, I'm the one you should be angry with. It was I who gave permission and accepted everything on board."

"In either, you had no right, sir!"

"It seemed harmless enough, Captain."

"These men are prisoners. Enemies of the Crown. And you choose to treat them like royalty?"

"Sir—"

"Silence! I'm speaking. Attention, prisoners, not only will your wines and liquors be taken from you, but all food as well."

Another groan. Douglass shook his head. Ethan watched Lieutenant Bascomb leer sneeringly at him.

"You disagree, Lieutenant Douglass?" Symonds snapped.

"I do, sir."

"Go to your quarters, sir, and wait for me. Everyone dismissed!" He called to four deckhands. "You men, go through their quarters, confiscate all comestibles, all drink. Bring everything to my cabin. Hop to it."

The incident set Ethan to wondering. Was it pure meanness that prompted Symonds's action? Or fear? Could he be afraid of a mutiny? Did he see tightening the screws as the way to discourage it? Some such thoughts must have come to his mind, because two hours later he again called everyone out on deck. Even Lieutenant Douglass reappeared. Ethan couldn't believe Symonds had disciplined him beyond a reprimand, not the son of an admiral.

"Colonel Allen, you will pay particular attention to this. Before we resume our voyage your group will be split up."

"What for?"

"Because I so order it. As I speak a number of vessels are assembling in Cork Harbor. Five men-of-war and forty transports, a fleet carrying an invasion force to the Carolinas. We will be joining it. Your group will be divided into three equal groups, I leave it to you to select who is to be transferred."

"This is bullshit."

"Sir?"

"We prefer to stick together."

"I'm not interested in what you prefer. My order is clear. You will obey it."

"Shove your order up your arse!" bawled a man.

"Who said that? Speak up! At once!"

Elisha Cummings raised his hand. Furious, Symonds strode up to him. Pierre, at the other end of the line, raised his hand. Other hands raised between the two until nearly everyone's was up. Ethan was the last to raise his.

"Lower your hands! Immediately! Allen, divide them up."

Ethan held off doing so merely to spite the captain. Instead, he retired to his and Gilligan's quarters to examine and taste one of the two gallons of whiskey he'd managed to hide before the captain's search party struck. His stomach glowing, relaxed for the first time in days, at reasonable peace with himself, he sat down and wrote a gracious thank-you note to Gerald Donnelly, Esquire, thanking him for their day in Cork and requesting he thank all the merchants for their generosity.

Every one of his men wanted to stick with him. There was nothing for it but to draw lots. Jacob, Elisha, Pierre, and eight others remained. At sundown the other twenty-two prisoners were taken off the ship and evenly divided between two other men-of-war.

"There's one good thing to come out of this, *mon ami*," murmured Pierre standing beside Ethan with the others as they waved away their friends. "They must plan to take us all the way."

"So it seems."

"The sharks will be disappointed. Why are you so down? As long as everybody survives . . . "

"It's just that we've been through so much together." He interlaced his fingers. "Thick and thin. It's made us like a special confraternity. Now comes this nonsense, all because Symonds has jelly for a spine. And he commands a man-of-war. With many more like him our boys'll sweep the British navy off the seas from Quebec to Charlestown."*

Ten minutes later Ethan and the others were still leaning on the rail when Symonds emerged in his dress uniform and descended the Jacob's ladder to a waiting dory.

"He's going over to one o' the other men-o'-war to chin with a friend o' his," explained Gilligan coming up.

"The son of a bitch," muttered Jacob. "He stole all our drink, all that good food."

"It's all sitting down in his cabin," said Ethan. "Why don't we go down aft and take stock? Maybe lose all self-control and risk a sip and a taste."

"Ahhhhh." Pierre beamed.

"I didn't hear a thing," said Gilligan pulling away from the railing. "I'll be seeing you boys."

Ethan and his chosen eleven huddled.

"Elisha, can you open a cabin door without busting it?"

"I can pick the lock with a nail, easy as pie."

"Good. Here's how we'll work it. We'll scatter, you get your knives and sneak after one at a time so's not to arouse Bascomb's or anybody else's suspicions."

Charleston, South Carolina, was called Charlestown until 1783.

"What do we need with our knives?" Jacob asked.

"Not to defend ourselves. Not anymore. No, I'm thinking of the turkey and the ham."

"I don't care about either," said Elisha. "I just want to get my hands on that bottle of French brandy old Donnelly gave me. It has to be worth twenty dollars and just the thought of Symonds drinking it makes the hairs on my neck stand up stiff."

"We'll get your brandy for you."

Ten minutes later they gathered in Symonds's cabin.

"Close the door, Pierre."

The cabin was richly furnished, mainly in teak, with a capacious canopy bed. Pierre flopped on it, his hands behind his head, moaning contentedly. The windows were draped, Savonerie carpet dominated the floor, there were three fine matching gilt chairs and a round table with carved lion heads at the bases of the legs. On it was piled the loot, including not one but four roast turkeys. They set about feasting.

"When he walks back in here he'll go wilder than a wet hen," said Jacob.

Ethan smirked. "Hopefully, only he won't know who did it."

"He'll have a good idea."

"Only how can he prove it?"

"How long do you think he'll be gone?" Elisha asked.

"Seamus Gilligan said he's visiting an old friend. They'll likely get to drinking and reminiscing. He probably won't be back till dawn. We'll be snug in our bunks long before that. Eat, try some of this white meat."

They gorged themselves, they drank into darkness, they resisted making merry too loudly, not wanting to bring Lieutenant Bascomb or some other curious officer to the door. They finished three of the four turkeys and the ham down to the gleaming bone, and downed the best of the wines and liquor. They finished off Elisha's brandy in multiple toasts to Gerald Donnelly, Esquire.

47

★ **The** seven retainers stood stiffly in line at the far end of the salon. In the center at a marble table trimmed in gold sat Their Majesties playing chess.

Queen Charlotte was an excellent player, cautious, shrewd, and perceptive. The king was her match, but he was easy prey to distraction, and lack of concentration in chess can be the downfall of even the most gifted player.

"Charles will arrive and overwhelm Washington's forces."

"I thought you didn't like Lord Cornwallis. You said he opposes your policies in North America."

"He is still my best general, and he's loyal to a fault. We talked before he left."

"*Liebchen,* are we playing chess or discussing affairs of state? Are you sure you want to move that knight?"

"Of course I'm sure."

"But not there, certainly. Look at my bishop . . . "

"Oh."

"If you must move it, move it on the diagonal. There you are . . . "

No sooner had he moved then out flew her hand moving her own knight and capturing his. He gasped.

"You! You deliberately misled me. For shame, that's devilishly unfair!"

"How can it be unfair? *You* insisted on moving him. You had two moves. Either one, I take you."

"You might at least have warned me."

"I'm playing to win, *Liebchen.*"

"Devilishly unfair! Still, despite his lukewarm sentiments toward the war, I've great faith in Cornwallis, tremendous faith.

It's vitally important at this time that he strike and strike hard. Set Washington reeling, scatter his ragtag troops, discourage them, break the back of their so-called Revolution before he can build up his army."

"Watch my queen . . . "

"Before he can drum his men into shape, impart discipline."

"I'm queening."

"What we don't want is another Seven Years War. Nip this one in the bud, I say."

They played on. On he prattled, extolling Cornwallis, deprecating Washington and his army.

"Check," said Charlotte. "No, check*mate*. I win."

"How did you do that?"

"I keep telling you, Georgie, you've got to keep your mind on the game. Full concentration, else you'll lose every time."

He smiled good-naturedly. "But I shouldn't, I'm the king."

"Ah, *Liebchen,* on this board not the king but the queen is the most powerful piece."

"I still wonder how you did it."

"You don't really want to know. You know it'll only depress you. It always does. Shall we go again?"

Ethan was awakened from a sound sleep by a frightened-looking and trembling Bascomb in his nightshirt.

"The captain wants to see you in his quarters at once!"

"Go away. You busted up a beautiful dream."

Gilligan came awake. "What's he doing here?"

"On your feet, Colonel. He's mad as hell. Purple. I've never seen him so. You'd best get over there fast as your legs can carry you!"

Symonds was indeed purple. His eyes bulged their sockets, he hissed like a snake when he spoke. "You . . . you did this, you and your filthy rabble!"

"I beg your pardon."

"Don't play cozy with me, traitor. Look what you've done to my beautiful table. Destroyed it! Animal!"

The table had been cleared of all food and drink and the empty brandy bottle sat in the center. Twelve knives stood on their points in a circle around it.

"Twelve! Count them. Eleven traitors still on board and you, the arch-traitor."

"Are you implying these are *our* knives? Hell almighty, have you been drinking? Where would we get knives?"

"Smuggled aboard in Cork, of course. Do I look dim-witted to you?"

"You sure are acting it. We didn't bring any knives aboard. There were clothes, food—"

"Silence! You'll pay for this, Allen. Not your men but you personally."

"What are you going to do, hang me?"

Symonds brought his trembling face too close. "I'd love to hang you. I'd give a year's wages to see you swinging from a yardarm."

"Only you can't do it. You don't dare. They'd cashier you. Or bust you down to able-seaman."

"Silence. What do you intend to do about this?"

"You're not listening. I didn't do it. Did. Not. Do. It. None of us did."

"Oh yes you did!"

"Prove it, Ezekial."

"Don't you dare call me by my Christian name! You did it as sure as God's in his heaven."

"Can I ask something?" Symonds only glared. "Since, as I say, we didn't do it. And since you roused me out of a sound sleep just so I could come here and tell you so, don't you think you owe me?"

"What!"

"Seriously. The least you could do is offer me a drumstick off that turkey and a whiskey."

"Get out. Out!"

* * *

On February 12 the convoy sailed out of Cork Harbor. The ships moved steadily down to the Bay of Biscay and there ran into a storm that sent waves crashing over the decks. Spume was flung to the tops of masts. The storm lasted a day and a night and one ship, the *Thunderbomb,* sprang a leak and had to put about and make for Southampton.

The fierceness of the storm had an unexpected effect on Captain Symonds. Before it struck he was still fuming over his ruined table and decrying the audacity of the Americans in stealing *his* food, *his* wine and liquor. But when the storm passed on and the ocean settled, an unaccountable change came over the man. Ethan couldn't understand it, nor could Seamus Gilligan.

Ethan scratched his head, his expression puzzled. "He spoke pleasantly to me this morning. Like we were old school chums. He even kept me company walking beside me on the foredeck."

Gilligan nodded. "And he sure doesn't glare when he sees you, like before."

"Is he religious?"

"Oh yes. He reads his Bible every night. He's always running off to his quarters to pray."

They stood near the foredeck battery. Ethan pondered.

"The storm must have scared him. He likely had visions of Jonah cast into the deep. He saw himself swallowed up by the fish. 'For thou has cast me into the deep, in the midst of the seas; and the floods compassed me about.' "

"Are you a religious man?"

"In my own way. But that has to be it. He got scared. All his sins came home to him, the way he's been treating us, me. He was all prepared to meet his maker, only God gave him a reprieve."

"Speak o' the divil."

Symonds was approaching. "Seamus, Colonel Allen. Lovely day."

Seamus touched the bill of his cap. "It is that, Captain." He started off.

"Don't go. I don't want to interrupt. Colonel, I just wanted to say . . . that broadcloth you got in Cork, I suggested to the ship's tailor that he make you a suit."

"That'd be great. I'd pay him of course."

He showed Symonds the fifty guineas given him by the banker.

"Gracious, they did treat you handsomely. At any rate, give Mr. Hines your cloth, he'll take your measurements and make you a fine suit. He's very talented."

"Thank you, Captain, you're very kind."

Off strolled Symonds. Ethan looked after him shaking his head.

Gilligan gaped. "What in the world has gotten into him?"

"It's got to be the storm. Fear can give people a whole different slant on things."

"Not that different."

The convoy headed south for the Bay of Biscay and around Cape Finisterre down to Madeira, fleeing the winter's gales in favor of balmy breezes and calm seas. The *Solebay* dropped anchor in Funchal Bay. Ethan and the others asked permission to go ashore. To everyone's surprise, Symonds readily consented.

Funchal looked beautiful from the water, with its whitewashed houses set in gardens resplendent with tropical plants. Palm trees were everywhere. The town was built along the curving shore of the bay, and spread up the lower slopes of an amphitheater of mountains. Country houses, with terraced gardens, vineyards, and sugarcane plantations occupied the surrounding heights, which ascended to nearly four thousand feet.

When the dories put in, the Americans split up into twos and threes. Ethan went off by himself, coming at last to a sidewalk cafe. A man sat engrossed in a newspaper, the *Dublin Intelligencer*, his broad back to the sun, his hat on the table near a cup of espresso as black as a pocket. Venturing closer as he passed, Ethan was struck by his appearance. He did not look Portuguese, he looked Irish, pale complexion, sandy hair, and green eyes that seemed riveted to the item he was reading. He was well dressed, and on the little finger of his left hand was a gold ring with a large diamond. As Ethan passed he lowered his newspaper.

"Top of the morning to you."

"Hello."

Few people were about. Dogs dozed in the shade, a cat strolled up and down a window box filled with hibiscus at a window on the second floor of the cafe.

"Won't you join me?"

He stood up as Ethan approached. He was at least six-feet-six-inches tall, not powerfully built but not slender, although his shoulders were quite narrow. His name was Leo Shaughnessey.

"Originally from Kinsale."

"Isn't that down the coast from Cork?"

"It is." He called over the waiter. "Bring us stout. Will stout do?"

"Whatever," said Ethan.

Shaughnessy closed one emerald eye, cocked his head, and pointed. "Your accent, you're not English. American?"

The stout came immediately, as if the glasses had been sitting on their tray just inside the door.

"American. A prisoner." He laughed. "On shore leave." He explained how the *Solebay* happened to be there, telling about the fleet and the projected invasion. "And what are you doing here?"

"I live here. Have for twelve years. My business is here. I export wine, the best Madeira in the world."

Ethan shaded his eyes looking toward the sea. "How do you manage that? There's no docks."

"All ships anchor out in the roadstead. Everything's rowed

in and out. It works fine. The bay's sheltered from every wind except the south. You say you're on your way back to America? Where?"

"Captain Symonds is keeping it secret. Wherever we put in give us an hour and that's the last they'll see of us."

Shaughnessy pushed his folded *Intelligencer* aside and propping himself on his forearms leaned closer.

"You're jumping ship?"

"Have to. There's a war on." He told about their capture at Montreal as Shaughnessy signaled the waiter for a second round. "Lord Cornwallis is bringing over an invasion force. Twenty or thirty thousand crack troops. General Washington'll be ready."

"Does he have spies in England?"

"There's no shortage of sympathizers."

"It says here in the paper Corwallis plans to land in the Carolinas."

"Let me see."

"Here, bottom of page one."

Ethan read. The invasion seemed to be no great military secret. Evidently, the only reason Symonds had kept the information from them was out of spite. Nevertheless, Ethan was mildly surprised that the Admiralty held the Americans in such low esteem as adversaries as to disclose their plan in a penny newspaper.

"What can Washington do against such overwhelming odds? I mean, militia against trained regular troops? Is he capable? Experienced?"

"He's a better man than Cornwallis. And you watch, that'll be the downfall of their regulars and their knockwurst mercenaries. They're used to fighting well-planned battles, standing in ranks out in the open. Not hit-and-run skirmishes, not defending against ambushes along country roads. They're in for some surprise."

"Does Washington have a master plan?"

"You bet."

"Tell me about him."

Ethan lauded the Virginian, summarizing his experience before the Revolution.

"And you and your men plan to link up with him?"

"Over the railing and swim for it, every man Jack."

Shaughnessy deluged him with questions. Washington, in particular, appeared to intrigue him.

"How big an army can he raise? I mean, aren't there as many Loyalists and Patriots in the colonies?"

"Thousands have not yet committed themselves. A couple more victories like Bunker Hill and they'll be flocking to our banner."

They talked for nearly two hours, Shaughnessy ordering omelettes and other food to ward off intoxication.

"I should be going," said Ethan at last. "Round up my men, make sure nobody's strayed."

"You're returning to the *Solebay?*"

"Yes."

"Why?"

"Why?"

"The captain let you come ashore, why not cut for the mountains? Hide out till the ship sails. Wouldn't that be less dangerous than jumping ship when it reaches port?"

"And what would any of us do here? What would I do with this fire in my belly? Sit out the war with my feet up, sipping wine, basking in the sun?"

"You could sign on the next western-bound ship."

"No thanks, we've wasted enough time already."

"You keep saying we. I'm talking about you."

"Are you suggesting I desert my men who've stood with me since Ticonderoga? They've taken everything I have and are just as determined as I am to get back into it."

"You're prisoners. Isn't it every man for himself?"

"I've got to go. Thanks for the food and drink, Leo, it's been a pleasure."

They shook hands.

"You did say the *Solebay*?" Shaughnessy asked.

Ethan indicated the ship out in the bay. "That warship."

"Let me send over a cask of my finest Madeira. I'll have a boy row it out before you up anchor. Good-bye, Ethan, good luck, and if you should change your mind I've a cottage up near the top of the mountain where you can hide out. Just follow the path to the top and partway down the other side. You can't beat the climate."

Ethan waved and walked off around the corner heading toward a plaza. In the center a lovely fountain sparkled in the sun. Flowers in abundance blended their fragrances in the warm air. Jacob and the others came stumbling out of a cantina hailing him. Turning the corner after leaving the cafe, now out of sight of it, he did not see Shaughnessy get up, shove his folded newspaper into his pocket, and start inside the cafe, only to stop when he heard his name called. A man came up, and they went inside together.

Around midafternoon, when Ethan and the others returned to the *Solebay*, Symonds stood at the top of the Jacob's ladder counting them. They discovered that while they were ashore he had jettisoned his newly found benevolent persona, restoring his characteristic scowl.

"About time you got here. That's the root of the problem, Allen, I magnanimously give you an inch and you take a mile."

He walked off. He ordered the ship underway before Shaughnessy's Madeira could be delivered. Ethan stood with the others at the railing looking ruefully back at whitewashed Funchal.

"A shame, *mon ami*," said Pierre. "Missing out on your cask."

Ethan shrugged. "I wonder."

"What?"

"If Shaughnessy really intended to send it over. He was a bag of wind. Questions, questions, questions. All he did long as we sat there was pump me: about our plans, about Washington's, about the general himself, politics back home, all sorts of things. But all connected to the war. I looked into those pretty green eyes and there was something missing. Something you saw in every eye in Cork, whatever the color. I didn't altogether trust Mr. Leo Shaughnessy from the first pint. He was much too nosy."

"You think he might have been a spy for the British?" Elisha asked.

"He's sure not spying for the Portugees."

The storm and the frightening reminder of Symonds's mortality were now past and forgotten. He reverted to character with the speed of an anvil dropping. Ethan asked his permission to purchase some necessities from the ship's stores. The captain turned him down.

The extreme change in the weather brought back Ethan's cold. He asked to buy cough medicine. The purser, a small man with a large mouth who shared Symonds's disdain for Americans, refused him.

"How come?"

"Captain's orders."

"How could he even know I've got a cold?"

"His orders are not to sell you anything."

"I'm talking about medicine."

"Nothing. Go away."

"I'll go away and bust you in the eye for good-bye!"

"Don't threaten me, Yankee. If not giving you medicine means you get really sick and die, that'd be my pleasure."

Ethan went looking for the captain. He found him lying down in his cabin. The knives had been removed from the table and the place tidied. Ethan stood by the table aimlessly walking his finger from one knife dig to the next.

"Hands off the table."

"Sorry. I came to ask permission to buy cough medicine from the purser."

"You've a cold?"

"Look at my eyes, listen to my voice." He snuffled wetly. "My throat's raw from coughing. It's keeping me awake. I need some kind of cough syrup. Don't worry, I'll pay."

"I can't help you."

"What do you mean you can't help me? It's not coming out of your pocket."

"You should take better care of yourself."

"I'm a goddamned prisoner of war. With skimpy, half-putrid rations, one skinny blanket in the dead of winter, I'm all run down. Let me ask you this. If England doesn't treat me like a criminal, what right have you to? If I get pneumonia and die, it'll be on your head. But if I live, I can be swapped for one of your officers, maybe even General Prescott."

"Don't flatter yourself. You're not worth a foot private."

"That's your opinion."

"And you're stuck with it." Symonds's lip curled in a sneer. "Frankly, you're not worth a wooden shilling to me. All you are is extra cargo that occasionally spills out on deck and that I have to feed."

"This stinks. Americans treat British prisoners like human beings. I know, Gerald Donnelly in Cork showed us a newspaper."

"And why do you think that is?"

"Because we're humane."

"*Afraid* is what you are. You Americans expect to be defeated and hope that treating British prisoners leniently will bring you the same consideration. You'll see, we'll win this war. Absolute mobs of Loyalists are preparing to join our ranks. We'll win, we'll hang your Congress, hang you and your ilk and restore peace and good order to America. As for you, my advice is behave yourself, keep that big mouth shut, take what you're given and be grateful for it. Grateful I don't give you what Captain Hales did back at Pendennis Castle."

"You know something, Ezekial? That's exactly the attitude

that's going to lose you this war. You Tories are all so damned cocksure of yourselves. You hold your noses up so high you can't see the dogshit in your path. Watch and see what Lord Snob Cornwallis steps into over there. When he surrenders, I'll get hold of his saber and send it to you. Souvenir of a war England should never have gotten into. Because you can never, never win!"

48

★ **After** two days at sea the order was signaled to separate the fleet. Some of the ships headed north. The *Solebay* and the *Sphynx* stayed on course to escort fourteen of the troop transports. As it happened, eleven of the twenty-two Americans sent to the other two men-of-war had been removed to the *Sphynx,* so now two-thirds of Ethan's men were still together, although it remained to be seen if they would reach the Carolinas without being separated.

Thinking ahead to the day when all his men, even the eleven sailing north on the *Lennox,* would return to the fighting, Ethan found himself reflecting on his boast to Symonds. Could the Americans mount a strong enough army to defeat the invader? Would General Washington prevail? Most of what he knew about the commander in chief he had picked up during his and Seth Warner's stay in Philadelphia when they appeared before the Congress. He sat in the bow picking at his pork and beans, talking to Jacob and Elisha. Both were curious about the Virginian. He had been summoned from his plantation in Mount Vernon County from a life of ease and luxury. Would he be up to the rigors of command?

"Has he ever been under fire?" Elisha asked. "I mean, before Boston?"

"Some. He was in his early twenties during the French and

Indian War when they sent him out with two companies to the Ohio. He won his first battle, he whipped a force of French and Hurons at Great Meadows."

"Then where?"

"If I remember, Fort Necessity. Someplace in Pennsylvania. That one he lost, he was forced to surrender. He was with General Braddock in Virginia."

"They took a terrific beating," said Jacob. "On the Monongahela. Everybody knows about that one. Wasn't Braddock killed?"

"He died after. But Washington got his own men out in good order. For the next two years he defended a frontier three hundred fifty miles long with only seven hundred men. That was his best experience, what really made him."

"How so?" Elisha asked."

"His troops weren't really troops, more a collection of renegades, criminals, ticket-of-leave men. They had about as much discipline as six cats in a sack. But he maintained order and carried out the assignment. After that he commanded the advance guard of an expedition under General John Forbes. They occupied Fort Duquesne and renamed it Fort Pitt."

"That was it until Congress appointed him commander in chief, seventeen years later."

"That's some leave," said Jacob.

Ethan went on. "John Hancock wanted to be picked. They say he was mad as a hornet when Congress passed him over for Washington. But it makes sense to me. If anybody can win this, it's George. The British think so."

"How do you know?" Elisha asked.

"You should have heard Shaughnessy in Funchal. They don't know beans about him and they're curious as hell. Once Shaughnessy got onto Washington he couldn't get off. Questions, questions." He cleared his throat and leaned close. "Something else I've been thinking about: the difference between us and them."

Jacob snickered. "They're rich, we're poor."

"You could say that. We've got the holes in our britches, but that won't stop us from winning. That right there is incentive to try harder. Also, this fight is in our yard, right? Our wilderness, a battleground they don't know, they've got mostly no maps of. And their supply lines—they stretch across the ocean! It takes months for them to get anything from a howitzer down to a bullet mold. And they're relying on knockwursts to do their fighting for them. Germans, English, whoever they draft, they're not *defending* England. Ask yourself, can they get all worked up against us like if they *were?* Like they would against the Spanish or the French?

"It's the difference between fighting to win and fighting to keep from getting killed. We're fighting for the most precious thing any country can have: our liberty. Our freedom. Independence. Look at us, that's what's kept us going since Ticonderoga."

"Look at his eyes," said Jacob. "He looks like some kind of Bible-beater."

"Hey, I'm serious. The big difference between them and us is what Symonds doesn't understand. I don't think Cornwallis does. Or either of the Howes. Or Carleton, or Clinton. Gage is probably the only one who does. He looked into American eyes at Bunker Hill. He *knows* how committed we are, how dedicated, knows we'll fight to the last ball, the last pinch of powder."

"I just want to get back into it," said Jacob. "I want to so bad it makes my teeth ache just thinking about it."

Both looked Elisha's way. He lowered his eyes to his half-eaten food. "I'd like to. I guess."

Jacob stared amused. "You think you might decide before somebody hands you a musket and it's back to work?"

"I'd first like to get home to Bennington. See Maw. Make sure she's all right. I worry so. And I'd like to explain everything to her."

Ethan patted his back. "There's nothing you can tell her the neighbors haven't already."

"Lord in heaven but I miss her. Miss the farm, the chores, the sweet smell of hay, the crops shooting up, even the birds. I can't stand these squawking seagulls. I'm talking about bobwhites and bluebirds and pretty singing robins. My whole world's back in Bennington."

"Ours too," said Ethan. "And that, Elisha, is what we're fighting for—to keep it. What we've sweated for, what we've built, what's ours. Buck up, you'll see your mother. Knowing her, she'll give you her blessing."

"Mmmmmm. You must miss your wife and youngsters."

The breeze dipped over the gunwale, snatching at Ethan's plate. He grabbed it before it flipped over. Then he lifted his eyes to the horizon, suddenly plunged into reminiscence.

"I do. Only with me it's different. I've been away so long and home for such short stays my family hardly knows me anymore. You make your choices and the months go by. And the years. And you suddenly stop and look back and say to yourself I started something back there and just walked away from it. It's no good, it's wrong. Sometimes it sits on my conscience like a cold, wet rock, pressing, chilling, and regret just seeps through me into every part. And every time I do get home I tell Mary I have to leave, but I'll be back before she knows it. Only I've never been able to keep my word. Boys, you are looking at one god-awful husband and worse father."

"She understands," says Jacob.

"Whether she does or not, what's the difference? That's the way it is, and we're both stuck with it. No, not the way it is, the way I've made it. I haven't written to her since the day before we left the castle. When you write steadily, then the letters stop, what's a body to think but that you've been killed? By God, the first thing I do when we land and get away is head home."

Jacob stared. "What about us? Are we all supposed to scatter and run home and tell our kin 'here we are back, all safe and sound, only we've got to leave, got to get back to the war?' Not me, I figure it's better to write, tell the truth, and when it's over go home and stay there."

"If I go home to Maw now, I'll sure enough stay there," said Elisha.

"I suppose," said Ethan. "Goddamn King George III, may he fall down a hole in the backyard of Buckingham Palace and bust his fool neck!"

Lieutenant Bascomb came up. "Captain Symonds wants to see you, Colonel Allen."

"So tell him you found me and send him over."

"In his quarters."

"What's up?"

"I think it's something about two gallons of drink that should have been confiscated."

"You mean somebody's been searching me and Gilligan's cabin? You sneaky bastards!"

Ethan rose, dusted off his seat, and followed the lieutenant down the rolling deck.

"There goes the one man on God's green earth I'd follow into hell," said Jacob. "More fool me. He sure is one of a kind. What in hell drives him? Here we've been with him since before Ticonderoga, and damned if I can figure it. Whatever it is, he's got no more control over it than a man with no legs over a wild horse."

"He's out to prove *something* to himself."

"What? How brave he is? How loyal an American? How much he despises British rule? I've seen men catch fire but only for a time, not blaze up and stay that way. You know what I think, Elisha? That he'd like nothing better than for all of us to go home and leave him by himself to stand up to the whole British empire. Him and the king in a fistfight or a wrestling match, winner take all."

"He sure never takes a step back, not even with chains on and his back flogged raw."

"Ethan Allen. The wild man of Bennington. On your guard, War, he's coming back!"

The voyage to the Carolinas took nearly three months. It was a Friday, the third of May, when the fleet anchored in the harbor at Cape Fear, North Carolina.

VI

The Warrior Waits

49

May 1776

★ **Cape** Fear, North Carolina, was situated across from the easternmost reach of South Carolina, at the southern extreme of Onslow Bay. There, on a Wednesday morning in the first week of May, with the sun brilliant and already warm at the beginning of its ascent, with an equally warm offshore breeze flapping the canvas, the convoy anchored and the troops were disembarked, without opposition from the few Americans roaming the swampland and forest areas. But before the first dory set off for the mainland, Captain Symonds received his orders from the convoy commander. The *Solebay*'s prisoners were assembled on deck, seated, and held under guard by six men with muskets.

"This is ridiculous," complained Ethan. "What do you think we'll do, jump overboard and swim for it?"

Symonds leered. "An acquaintance of yours, a Mr. Shaughnessy, is certain of it."

Jacob, Elisha, and Pierre looked Ethan's way. All shared the same expression of reproval.

"I was just leading him on," growled Ethan.

Symonds laughed. It was the first time Ethan had seen him

laugh. He seemed to have difficulty working up to a smile. He walked off, his hands joined under his coattail, his stride jaunty. Ethan called after him.

"Hey, come back. There's something I want to ask you."

Symonds pretended he didn't hear. It was almost as if then and there his assignment to care for the prisoners ended.

"That stout and the breakfast that Irishman gave you in Funchal was not free after all," said Pierre.

Jacob nodded. "It turns out you paid. Us too."

"Aw, cut it out. Hey, even if we never put in there, if I never met that nosy bastard, you think Symonds wouldn't pull this? Guard us this close once we drop anchor?"

Pierre shrugged. They sat on deck all day, taking their meal there and watching group after group of redcoats ferried to shore. Lieutenant Douglass appeared in the middle of the afternoon. Ethan got his attention.

"Lieutenant, what happens to us now? Symonds won't tell us a thing."

Douglass looked both ways and lowered his voice. "You're to be transferred to the frigate *Mercury.*"

"All of us? Even the boys on the *Sphynx* and the *Intrepid?*" Douglass nodded. "Where will they take us?"

"I don't know. I can tell you this much, you won't find life any easier with James Montague."

"Who?"

"The captain of the *Mercury.*"

Symonds was returning; Douglass hurried off. Later that afternoon, before the last few hundred troops were debarked, Ethan heard from Seamus Gilligan that a detachment had been sent up the Brunswick River to clear the route that Cornwallis planned to take inland of any rebels who might be roaming about. The redcoats returned the next day in a foul mood, having lost thirty-one killed. When Symonds told the crew and the prisoners this, Ethan brazenly led his men in three loud cheers.

Late in the morning of the third day at anchor the frigate *Mercury* appeared.

The twenty-one prisoners on the other two men-of-war and Ethan and his men were collected on board her. Once reunited with Tom Coffin, Ethan learned that Wilkie O'Doul had dived overboard and escaped in a hail of bullets.

"He made it?"

"He did, praise the Lord."

"Praise some rotten shooting eyes."

Captain Montague addressed the prisoners. It took less than thirty seconds for Ethan to conclude that Lieutenant Douglass had not exaggerated. Ezekial Symonds was turning out as kindly and considerate as Colonel Boatwright compared to the master of the *Mercury.* Symonds at least made some effort to contain his animus.

"Attention all," began Montague. "First off, it may surprise you to learn that we have no vermin on board." He laughed, slapping his thigh. "You're the first. You filthy traitors are now in our charge. We are heading for Halifax, Nova Scotia. There it will be our pleasure to see one and all of you hanged for treason. And may God have mercy on your souls."

The men groaned as one. Ethan broke from the line, turning and facing it. "Pay no attention boys, he's lying in his wooden teeth."

Up strode Montague. He was short but powerfully built, with a face that vaguely reminded Ethan of Captain Hales's Sheba. Montague wore one glove and the hand it concealed looked solid, as if it were made of wood or metal.

"You must be Allen." He leered, drawing his thin lips back over his ill-fitting teeth. "We've been waiting for you."

"Well, here I am."

"All ours at last. Insolent scoundrel, how dare you accuse me of lying?"

"The feeblest mind here knows you are. If they intended to hang us, why bring us all the way back? King George was practically bleeding to march us to Tyburn Hill. But he changed his mind. The whole country changed it for him. And nothing's happened since to change it back. Am I right or wrong, Captain?"

"Hold your insolent tongue. From now on you will speak only when spoken to!"

"What are you going to do, gag me?"

"Mr. Billings!" The boatswain's mate stepped forward. "Bind this one's wrists behind his back and gag him."

"You miserable son of a bitch!"

"Stick him below where we won't have to see his ugly face."

"Where I won't have to see yours. That I'll appreciate! You! Are! Ugly!"

The prisoners looking on uttered a collective sigh. Ethan was bound and gagged.

"He's off to his usual good start," murmured Jacob to Pierre. "Man's got a special talent for making friends. He should have been a diplomat."

Pierre laughed. "I think, *mon ami,* he is trying to make a point. The same one he makes with all of them. That no man can ride roughshod over him. He refuses to back down. Do not worry, we will get him back up here before we sail, I bet."

"How do we do that?" Elisha asked.

"By living up to our reputation. Behaving like disorganized rabble. Like an unruly mob that has no leader, *n'est-ce pas?*"

The *Mercury* was a prison ship. Ethan was locked in a cell, his wrists still tied, gag in place. He protested as best he could, to no avail. The gag was only removed when his food was brought, and restored immediately after he ate. The same held for his wrist bindings. This went on for two days. Meanwhile Pierre's protest strategy was implemented. The prisoners took to wandering about pretending interest in ropes and gear on deck, getting into things in the manner of annoying six-year-olds. They had mock arguments and two mock fights. Montague was besieged by complaints from his men. But instead of releasing Ethan he solved the problem by ordering the rest of the prisoners incarcerated, an alternative Pierre should have perceived but did not.

Montague came to visit Ethan. He removed his gag.

"What's with all the door slamming?" Ethan asked.

"Thanks to you we have been obliged to lock up all your men."

"Funny, I didn't understand why you didn't do that when we came on board. What, are you hoping some will try to escape overboard? Give your men a little target practice?"

"Shut that incessant mouth of yours and listen. We'll begin with a question. Think before you answer. Are you ready to behave yourself? Mind, we can leave you here bound and gagged all the way to Halifax and for as long as you stay on board. Which could conceivably be two years."

"All right, all right, I'll cooperate."

"We thought you might."

"If you let my men out. You have my solemn word nobody will cause any trouble."

"Done."

"Good."

"We will release four a day for all day. They'll be free to walk about the ship—"

"Wait, wait, what do you mean four a day? That's nine days locked up to one day free!"

"Ten days locked up."

"Why you . . . !"

Up came the gloved hand. "Don't. One more insult out of that mouth, just one, and we'll order you ironed and put on bread and water until we reach port."

"All right, all right. Are we going to just sit here attracting barnacles or are we going to Halifax? What?"

"There's been a slight delay. One of the prisoners on the *Sphynx* jumped overboard. They're searching for his body. It shouldn't take more than four days for it to rise to the surface."

"It was Wilkie O'Doul, and don't bother waiting because he got clean away."

"Impossible."

"Listen, Captain, man to man, we've been shackled and locked up for months, treated like dogs in the manger, ill-fed, ill-clothed, allowed to run down like a bunch of cheap clocks. How about giving us a break? Can't we spend at least part of each day on deck? I mean all of us? It's healthier than being buried down here. You do want us to get to Halifax healthy, don't you?"

"We don't particularly care if we slide one of you at a time down a plank into the sea until you're all gone. Only while you persist in surviving, your treatment will be as harsh as we can make it."

"That's good news. Why?"

"Because, Allen, you're traitors. The lowest form of life on earth. Seditious scum who dare to defy your sovereign and your country. Tell us, are you a married man?"

The abrupt change of subject surprised Ethan. "I am. With five youngsters, One son, Joseph, after my father. My pride and joy."

"Don't you miss your family?"

"What do you think?"

"We would if we were you, knowing it could be years before you see them again. And probably never. It must be hard lying in bed nights thinking of your wife. Her sleeping by herself . . . "

"Captain . . . "

"Or is she? Is she attractive? Is there a friend or neighbor who might be interested? Would she be interested in companionship to help while away the lonely nights? It must be devilishly hard for a woman, being deprived of her husband for so long. How long has it been?"

"Would you just leave?"

"You haven't said. Is Mrs. Allen attractive?"

"Are you married?"

"Is she easily aroused? Some women are, they can't

get enough. And aren't choosy who from. And depriving them—"

"Out!"

Montague laughed uproariously. "We must talk again about your wife. A pity she's being made to suffer so. Being innocent and all. Congratulations, traitor."

"For what?"

"For putting us in an uncommonly generous mood. Brace yourself, we will grant your request. You and your men will be given the freedom of the deck from one hour after sunrise till dusk. But take heed, the first evidence of insubordination will be severely dealt with. And the privilege summarily withdrawn. You'll be returned to your cells to remain indefinitely. Are we clear on that?"

"Yes, Captain."

"Good. Ellsworth. Ellsworth!" The guard came in. "Round up three or four men and release the prisoners."

"All of them, sir?"

"All. See that they're assembled on deck. We wish to speak to them. This one too."

Montague left.

"Hard man, the captain," muttered the guard who looked to Ethan to be somewhat confused. "This is very unlike him, being this good-hearted. What in the world did you say to him?"

"Nothing. And he's not being good-hearted. He's just giving so's he can take away if one of us so much as blinks."

50

★ **Poor** treatment over such a long time was beginning to take a serious toll on the prisoners. The three-month voyage from Falmouth had eroded their spirits as well as their constitutions.

Their rations had been edible, but there were never enough. Deprived of medical care by Symonds, men afflicted with various illnesses remained sick for prolonged periods, with only the stronger among them able to recover. Everyone fell prey to what appeared to be incurable exhaustion. They slept badly, they were unable to maintain even minimum standards of hygiene, but worst of all was the pervading and growing impression that few of them would survive to eventually be freed or exchanged.

Seeing how rapidly their health was deteriorating, Ethan suspected that the Crown had decided to let them die slowly, one by one dropping out of life into oblivion.

They had been without fresh provisions since Cork. Scurvy broke out. It came on gradually. The initial symptom was a general weakening. One after another men began having trouble breathing. They took on a sallow look, their eyes sank in their sockets and they felt pain in their muscles and limbs. Once the illness took firm hold the patient went rapidly downhill. They began to look haggard, their teeth loosened and dropped out, and many lay down and did not move for days.

Some began to bleed from mucous membranes in their noses, eyes, and respiratory tracts, steadily coughing up blood. Others broke out in ulcers. Diarrhea became prevalent. Ethan fell ill, although not as seriously as some. He confronted Montague. The captain heard him out and scowled.

"You're asking us for medicine from stores to treat this rabble? These treasonous dogs? Are you mad?"

"Some are already so sick they can't stir from their bunks."

"So let them stay in their bunks."

"They can't keep food down."

Montague beamed. "Our hearts go out to them."

"This is serious, Captain."

"You've asked, we've answered, end of discussion. Dismissed."

Ethan accosted the ship's surgeon only to be similarly rebuffed. But two midshipmen, who looked to Ethan like father and son, took pity on the Americans and risked reprimand or worse by smuggling a quantity of citrus fruit to Ethan who doled it out to the sickest prisoners.

On the morning of June 3, a Monday, the *Mercury* dropped anchor off Sandy Hook, New York. They would be laying over for three days to take on provisions. On the afternoon of the second day two visitors boarded, both old acquaintances of Ethan. Old enemies: Governor William Tryon and his lackey, Attorney General Kempe. Ethan had never met Tryon, but it was the governor who nearly six years before had put a price on his and Seth Warner's heads during the wrangling between the representatives of the New Hampshire Grants and those from New York Province. Ethan had met Kempe just once, recalling that he had eyes and lips resembling those of a snake.

The two walked with Montague on the windward side of the deck. Ethan walked the leeward side by himself. Passing Ethan, the captain and Kempe kept their eyes straight ahead. Tryon looked squarely at him, all the bitterness accrued over their years of contention lodged in his glare. Ethan returned it with equal degree. Neither man came near him during their brief stay on board, but after they left Ethan watched Montague call his men together and speak with them. He couldn't hear what was said, but from the next morning on the treatment of the prisoners became noticably harsher. The midshipmen who'd befriended Ethan stayed clear of him.

By the time the *Mercury* reached Halifax—about the middle of June—the scurvy was rampant. The afflicted among the crew were taken ashore. The sick prisoners, confined below and denied fresh fruit, vegetables, and medicine, continued to suffer, all but ignored by their captors. Their number rose to twenty-six, including both Jacob and Ethan. Conditions got so bad, to protect his crew, Montague ordered the stricken Americans removed to a sloop anchored near McNab's Island at the mouth of the harbor. There they were watched by a single guard.

Four canoes carrying Micmac Indians ventured into the

harbor to sell strawberries to the men on the ships. One prisoner spent every cent he had and was cured virtually overnight. But the Indians never came back, and the others on board the sloop continued to suffer and decline.

Ethan asked to speak with Montague. The captain refused to see him. Ethan sent letters decrying the plight of his men, they were ignored. Then one of the midshipmen who had earlier befriended him smuggled a vial of ascorbic acid aboard the sloop. It was doled out to the sickest men.

Ethan gave up appealing to Montague. The same midshipman who had sneaked the ascorbic acid out of the infirmary smuggled a letter to Governor Arbuthnot in Halifax. Within hours a boat brought a doctor, a civilian, a fussy little man who appeared to be wearing his bigger brother's clothing. Montague stood at the rail.

"Dr. Wilson Ffolkes, Captain. I've been sent by the governor to treat the prisoners."

"They don't need treating, Doctor. You can turn around and go back."

"The governor has expressly instructed me to board the sloop." With Dr. Ffolkes was a man who introduced himself as John Crawley. "The governor's private secretary. You'd best follow orders, sir, or be prepared to suffer the consequences."

"The sloop's over near McNab's Island."

"We know where it is," said Crawley. "We're merely informing you of our mission as a matter of courtesy."

Dr. Ffolkes treated every man, leaving them medication and fresh fruit. Two days later all thirty-three Americans, those not yet stricken and still on board the *Mercury,* and those on the sloop, were gathered together to be removed to Halifax under a guard sent by the governor. Montague ranted and raged on deck as one by one men descended the Jacob's ladder to waiting dories. Mr. Crawley stood calmly by, conscientiously ignoring the captain.

"General Cornwallis will hear of this, make no mistake!

The governor will rue this day! These men are in our charge!"

"Not anymore," said Crawley.

"I guess this is good-bye," said Ethan approaching the captain and extending his hand.

His face crimson, eyes blazing, Montague slapped it aside. "You did this! We don't know how you managed it, but you did. When we find the man who smuggled your communication to the governor he'll be disciplined! We'll see him cashiered! He'll rue the day he ever came under our command!"

"Captain, every man on board this tub rues the day he came under your command!"

"Insolent swine!"

"Arsehole!"

Montague lunged. Ethan sidestepped him and ran for the Jacob's ladder. Descending it, he ducked, narrowly avoiding the captain's saber.

Crawley came down after the last man, shaking his shaggy head and grinning impishly.

"Atrocious man. Atrocious man!"

51

JUNE 1776

★ **Over** the ensuing three days, much to Ethan's surprise and delight, no fewer than five of his men escaped. On the other side of the ledger three died. In the meantime thirteen, Ethan, Jacob Wall, Elisha Cummings, and Pierre Cariou among them, were confined to the Halifax jail. The remaining twelve were in the hospital suffering various stages of scurvy. Dr. Ffolkes hope was that all would recover. He seemed less than certain that they would.

Conditions in the jail were an improvement over those on

either the *Solebay* or the *Mercury*. The food was better and sympathetic townspeople brought baskets of fruit and vegetables. Ethan missed Pendennis Castle, also Boatwright, Heaslip, and Sheba. Despite recovering from scurvy, his health continued to worsen. He had always been robust and enviably healthy, but more than a year in confinement was leaving its mark. He was now thirty-eight, but looked fifty, according to Jacob. Assuming everyone's troubles, tirelessly boosting morale, squabbling with ships' captains for better food and better treatment had worn him out. The Halifax jail was an improvement over confinement at sea, but it was still confinement, and the building and facilities were over fifty years old.

They were held in one large common cell with twenty other prisoners, mostly local criminals. There were the inevitable excrement tubs, no bunks, not even cots, which forced everyone to sleep on the stone floor.

Having recovered from his scurvy, Ethan promptly fell ill of another ailment. He began suffering severely from nausea and quickly became badly dehydrated. By the end of his first week at the jail he became so weak and listless he was unable to get up from the floor. Pierre and Jacob helped him up to a sitting position against the wall.

"It will pass, *mon ami*," Pierre assured him.

"Who knows? Look at me, I bet I've lost sixty pounds since Montreal. It's been too long. A body can only stand so much. I feel weak as water."

Elisha Cummings came up and heard this last. "Ethan, Ethan, you're not giving up."

Ethan snorted. "Me? What do I look like, that simpleton who came to gawk at us that day at the castle? The one who couldn't take his hanky down from his nose? I may be weak in body, but the goddamned spirit is stronger than two horses! All I got to do is get rid of this sickly stomach so's I can keep something down, and get rid of this fever. I'm burning up."

That afternoon two nuns brought a laundry basket filled

with food and wine. To his elation Ethan was able to keep down everything he ate and drank.

"You see what decent food will do for you, Pierre? Feel my forehead, I do believe my fever's gone."

"It feels like it."

They could hear keys jangling. The door was opened, and another prisoner was ushered in. Ethan appraised him as did the others. He was tall, spare, and obviously a gentleman, his well-worn jacket and trousers and badly scuffed buckle shoes notwithstanding. He looked Ethan's way then strained his eyes for a second look. He came over smiling.

"You're Ethan Allen."

"I think. Excuse me for not getting up, I'm just getting over the galloping shits and a fever you wouldn't wish on King George. This is that kind of place."

"I'm James Lovell. With the Continental Congress of Massachusetts."

"Oh? What are you doing in Halifax?"

"I was kidnapped, shunted from pillar to post, ended up in Quebec and now here."

"What do they want with you?"

"Some snake, Lord knows who, evidently told General Clinton that I have influence with John Adams. Of course—aren't we both from Massachusetts? I had the pleasure of being interviewed by the general himself. I told him straight out that I don't know John Adams from Adam, apart from sharing the same commonwealth. He's with the Continental Congress and I'm with the Massachusetts Congress. But they think I'm lying."

"I don't follow you."

"Quite simply, they want me to get to Adams and turn him."

"You're a Loyalist?"

Lovell drew himself up indignantly. "Please. Although that was the general idea. I infect him with pro-Loyalist sympathies and he, in turn, will influence others in Congress."

"That's wild," said Jacob. "The bastards'll stoop to anything."

"My boy," said Lovell. "Has anyone told you there's a war on? All's fair. Anyway, I couldn't help them so I've been made to pay. You . . . all of you, were at Montreal." Ethan nodded. "In perhaps the most foolhardy, most downright simple-minded effort in the entire war."

"Easy, Monsieur," murmured Pierre. "Montreal was a . . . a *malentendu.*"

"Ha! Some misunderstanding."

Ethan cocked his head and eyed Lovell skeptically. "Are you a spy?"

Lovell jerked back his head and thumbed his chest. "Me?"

"You're who I'm talking to. Did the governor plant you here to listen in on our small talk? If so, guess what, you're going to show us how good a swimmer you are."

"I beg your pardon?"

"In that excrement tub there."

"Now see here, fellow . . . "

"Grab him, boys, it's ducking time."

Four men seized Lovell. He protested loudly.

"Okay," said Ethan. "You've got five seconds to start telling the truth."

"I am! I was abducted on Boylston Street in Boston. After dark. Blindfolded, whisked away, ended up in Quebec. Now here. What must I do to convince you?"

Ethan thought a moment. The disturbing impression arrived that he was letting his suspicion take over from his customary objectivity, perhaps because Lovell rubbed him uncomfortably almost from the moment he entered the cell. Ethan didn't like his smug look—the way he carried himself as if he was in charge. He was a snob, too glib, his tone syrupy, his story far-fetched. *Were* the British capturing civilians? What a waste of time and manpower. There weren't jails enough in all of North America to hold half the high-ranking Patriots, civilian and military.

"I still smell a fish." Ethan touched the side of his nose. "It's my instincts. They never let me down."

"I ask you again, what must I do to convince you I'm on your side?"

"You could pitch in and write a few letters. To Washington, Hancock . . . "

"Are you serious? Can't you think of a bigger waste of time?"

"What else can we do?"

"I'm sure you've written absolute bales of letters. And what have they gotten you?" He swept the cell with one hand. "Men like Washington and Hancock are too busy with the war to concern themselves with a handful of prisoners. As long as they know you're not in harm's way, why bother?"

"Because of who I am!"

"Oh, I forgot, the Hero of Ticonderoga."

"You got a real sarcastic tongue, you know?"

"You do all right yourself."

They stood staring each other down for fully a minute. By now nearly all the other prisoners had gathered round to enjoy the fencing.

Jacob spoke. "Don't quit yet, this is the most fun we've had in months."

"This is serious, Jacob," snapped Ethan, keeping his eyes fixed on Lovell.

"No it's not," said Lovell. "Not in the least. Look, we're stuck in here, let's at least pretend to get along. I shan't step on your toes, you keep off mine."

"I never step on anybody's," said Ethan. A chorus of hooting greeted this. "I don't! Don't listen to them, I'm the easiest man in the world to get along with."

Elisha came over. He had been standing at the door talking through the barred window with the guard. "Bad news, Ethan. Last night two more of the boys died in hospital."

"Who?"

"Little Ewan Dorsey."

"Oh God, he was just a kid. Oh damn!"

"And Thomas Coffin."

Jacob shook his head. "Where in hell was his guardian angel?"

Ethan slowly turned his way. "You know, Jacob, you can't make a joke about everything. Don't try. Anyway, that settles it. Between that butcher's shop they call a hospital and this lovely place we're all going to die, and be quietly buried in that cemetery behind that church we passed coming through town. There's only one thing for it. We get out. All of us, here and the hospital. Make a break for it. What do you say, Mr. Massachusetts? Are you game?"

"Keep talking. I'll decide."

He smiled gratuitously, touched the brim of his hat, and walked off.

"You do not trust him, do you, Ethan?" murmured Pierre.

"I don't know. That sure was a wild story he fed us . . . kidnapped on Boylston Street."

52

★ **On** the bright side, the Halifax jail was not Newgate Prison. Men had broken out before. Had even walked out, bribing guards, feigning illness necessitating their removal to the hospital and escaping en route, or in cleverer, more original ways. The guard on the door could be easily overcome and from there it would be down the corridor to the outside door, which was unguarded, out into the exercise yard, and over the fence. The darkest hour of the night would be the best time. A rainstorm would be convenient, though not mandatory. Getting through the sleeping town to the docks wouldn't be difficult, nor would stealing from the wide choice of boats. Then it would be off across Chebucto Bay, the harbor, and south to around Cape Sable to the coast of Maine. From Cape Sable a distance of well under two hundred miles.

On the dim side, the town was the most heavily fortified in all of Canada and infested with British troops. Every other vessel in the harbor was British. Getting out of the jail would be physically easy, but should they run into any wandering guards they could expect to be shot on sight. The thorniest problem would be the hospital patients. Ewan Dorsey's and Tom Coffin's deaths reduced their number to ten, but they were in varying stages of recovery, most almost completely cured, the rest continuing critical.

Ethan proposed a solution.

"We'll put off leaving for three days." Everybody groaned. "Will you let me finish? We've got to. That'll give the boys in the hospital time to recover enough so they can get out under their own power. And they'll be strong enough to survive what's to come."

"And those that are really bad off will probably have passed away by then," said Lovell.

Everyone stared at him.

"I hate to say it," said Ethan, "but he's right. So you're coming with us, Mr. Massachusetts?"

"I am, Mr. Grants."

"This is the plan," said Ethan, lowering his voice even further. "Whoever's on guard, we pull the old chestnut of one of us becoming deathly sick. He calls for a stretcher, two more guards bring it, all three come in here, we overpower 'em, and change into their uniforms.

"Our three guards lead the way out. Jacob, Elisha, Pierre, and I will take at least two of the guards' weapons and head for the hospital for the boys. By which time we'll all be on our own."

"Shouldn't we stick together?" Elisha asked.

"No. That'll only attract attention. It's best to break up into small groups. You can all figure out who you want to stick with before we set foot out the door. Now, Pierre?"

"Oui?"

"I'm putting you in charge of the key ring. As soon as the three of them come in with the stretcher you grab the ring, you lead the way out."

"Avec plaisir."

"Jacob, you're a born clown. Are you a born actor? Let's find out. You play sick; you know, roll on the floor grabbing your belly moaning and groaning."

"Appendicitis. Only I've had mine out." He smirked. "Pick somebody else."

"Just put on a great, good show. Boys, you'll be amazed this'll be so easy."

"One thing you're overlooking," said Lovell. "When we get out on the water. However many boats we steal we'll look like a fleet heading south. We'll have to run a blockade, at least until we're around Cape Sable and heading southeast."

Pierre spoke. "Ethan, maybe we should stick together and steal a sloop. Maybe the one they put the boys on out near McNab's Island."

"And who'll sail it? What do you know about sails, ropes, tides, and whatnot? No. Small boats. Nothing bigger than twenty-five feet. Any idiot can maneuver a small boat. And once we're out to sea we separate." He turned to Lovell. "That should solve your problem."

"I worry most about the hospital."

"Me too," said Jacob. "What if one or two of the boys is still too sick to travel? But *is* recovering. What do we do, just leave him?"

"Hardly! We use the stretcher they'll be bringing for you. And steal one or two more, whatever we need. Today's Tuesday. We'll set it for two a.m. Saturday morning."

"We'll have to wake up whoever's on guard to get him in here," said a man.

Everybody laughed, everybody's mood was suddenly up. Ethan himself felt lifted. The plan made sense. It would work here, though nowhere else. They'd never have broken out of jail in Montreal, never have escaped from any of the ships, never have gotten away from Pendennis Castle. Here they were next door to home. Once they landed in Maine they could walk home while the Canadians headed north.

"Abby, Abby," murmured Jacob. "Iron your wedding dress and pick some fresh flowers, I'm coming home."

"Coming home, Maw . . . " said Elisha, tears welling in his eyes.

Ethan grunted.

Home. Mary. The children. Freedom! Freedom! "Then back to the wars."

Pierre looked at him. "What, Ethan?"

"It's all over, *mon ami*. Before Saturday you'll be at sea and a free man."

Pierre crossed himself. "From your lips to Saint George, Martin of Tours', ear."

"Who?"

"The patron saint of soldiers," said Lovell. "I wonder, is there a patron saint of congressmen?"

Pierre snickered. "Try blessed Saint Jude."

"Who's he?" both asked.

"The patron saint of desperate situations."

53

★ **Ethan's** plan was fairly basic and, surprisingly, it went off smoothly. Outside the exercise yard the prisoners in his group scattered. He, Pierre, Elisha, and Jacob took off with the stretcher for the hospital.

The nurse on duty outside the ward sat at a small table reading by candlelight. She looked up sharply at the three Americans and one Canadian, Elisha carrying the stretcher. Ethan leveled the pistol he'd taken from one of the two guards who'd brought the stretcher into the cell for Jacob.

"Don't scream, Sister. Just relax. Go on with your reading." He handed the pistol to Pierre. "Keep her company, *mon ami.*"

Luck was with them. The delay in implementing the escape plan had given the two critically ill patients precious time to turn their respective corners. They were now well on the mend, capable of getting out under their own power. Everyone dressed and filed quietly out without waking any of the other patients. By this time Pierre had gagged the nurse and locked her in a broom closet. Outside the side entrance, a driveway led to Cogswell Street, which ran to the docks. The group broke into twos and threes. Good-byes were too hasty for Ethan. The end to the adventure came much too suddenly. He pumped Pierre's hand and embraced him. And did the same with the others, lastly Elisha and Jacob. Both looked suddenly misty-eyed. Ethan's throat lumped.

"See you in Bennington, boys. Today's Saturday, let's make it Saturday after next. Ten in the morning at Stephen Fay's Tavern. I'll be buying. Now, skedaddle!"

And they were gone. He looked after them running down Cogswell Street until they vanished into the night. He was preparing to follow when he heard horses behind him. Up came four redcoats brandishing muskets.

"Hold it right there. Raise your hands!"

Red. A red face, red ears, red hands, hair, beard. Governor Arbuthnot was an artist's mix of several shades of the color of the door sentry's tunic. He had gotten out of bed to come to his office and meet with Ethan. Dawn was just beginning to steal over Chebucto Bay, invade the town, and finger her way through the matching high windows on either side of King George's portrait behind the governor. Surprisingly, Arbuthnot was not in the least upset at being rousted out of bed at such an ungodly hour on his day off, although he did look a bit bleary-eyed, and there was still enough sleep in him to force an occasional yawn. Ethan sat opposite him. The sergeant in charge of the three men who'd apprehended him stood behind his chair. Ethan could hear him wheezing slightly.

"So, Governor, who spilled the beans. Lovell, right?"

"Congressman Lovell? You think he was placed among you to spy on you?"

"Wasn't he?"

"He fled with your men. They tried to."

"They got away . . . "

"Not a one. In your planning there's one thing you overlooked. They all do. Anybody escaping jail always runs to the docks. And we're always there waiting for them. They're all back in the cell. Even Lovell."

"Shit."

"Sorry."

"Just the thought of going back there roils my stomach, it stinks so."

"You won't be. You're leaving us. General Howe's orders."

"You mean by myself?" Arbuthnot nodded. "For where now?"

"New York City."

"Why New York?"

"General—"

"Howe's orders. I know. Hey, seriously, what about my boys? They've already paid six times over for my mistake, some with their lives, what with catching scurvy. How's about a blanket amnesty for 'em?"

"I wish I could grant one. I do. I suppose I could apply for one."

"Would you?"

"I can't promise anything."

"You can ship me off to New York City, you can ship me to Newgate, even Bedlam, just let those poor boys out so they can go home. God'll love you for it."

"I'll . . . try. As for you, you leave today. On board the *Lark,* Captain Smith commanding."

"Who's he? Another Montague? By the way, I do thank you from the bottom of my heart for delivering us from that sadistic son of a bitch's clutches. Of all the vicious cocksuckers . . . "

"Please, your language."

"It just occurred to me. If you plan to get an amnesty for the boys, how about me?"

"You, Colonel, are a different matter entirely. You've a certain value to the Crown."

"So I've been told. So what's happening in New York? Is your side in control?"

"Completely. The last rebel resistance is being mopped up. The jails are bursting with your so-called Patriots."

"So-called, I like that."

"Colonel, I know you've been through a great deal for your convictions. You've certainly shown the courage of them. I've no idea what it is that drives you, but don't you think it's time you gave it up? Renounced this, this foolishness and came round to reason and sanity?"

"Switch sides?"

"You're a brave man, highly respected in some quarters, capable, experienced. You could be a distinct asset to your sovereign and your country."

"Governor, I got no sovereign, and my country is America, not England. I was born and bred in Connecticut, this war'll end and I'll live out my life in Bennington on the Grants. And die there. In the meantime, if I can get away I intend to fight to my last breath for freedom and independence. And the devil take King George and Jack Bull. I, sir, refuse to."

Arbuthnot grinned. "Your feistiness is admirable even if your priorities are hopelessly askew. You asked about Captain Hosea Smith. It happens we both attend St. Paul's Church when he's in port. You'll find him a gentleman, he's considerate and without rancor or prejudice against Americans."

"That'll be a first. Although I have to say nobody's treated us fairer than you and Mr. Crawley. Dr. Ffolkes too."

"None of us sees any reason to take our disapproval of your politics out on you personally."

"You're a rarity."

Arbuthnot stood up. Ethan did also. They were the same height and a year or so before would have been the same build. Not now. The weight Ethan had lost in captivity made him much thinner than the governor.

"You'll remain here under guard until time for your departure. Captain Smith will be sending men to escort you to the docks. We probably won't see each other again." He extended his hand. Ethan shook it. "I wish you luck, Colonel. And a better future than your recent past."

54

★ **So** the boys had only gotten as far as the docks. What a disappointment. He pictured them filing back into the cell, rejoining the excrement tub. And for him it was on to New York, yet another filthy jail, prisoners overcrowded, underfed, and likely Loyalist ladies coming in with baskets or just to gawk at the animals. Meanwhile, a war was going on that he had no more part in than Sheba. Equally disheartening, it was beginning to seem that whatever years he had left to him would be spent behind bars, for he'd become something of a symbol of opposition to the Crown, a trophy of war to be held onto and jealously guarded.

The *Lark* was setting out for New York City with a cargo of salted cod and copper ore from the Gaspé Peninsula. Escorted aboard, Ethan stood waiting on the main deck, ordered to stand there by the mate in charge of his escort. He glanced about the *Lark*. It looked a clean and trim ship, unlike the *Mercury* and the *Adamant*, which were the filthiest ships he'd encountered on his travels. Crewmen went about their duties, paying no attention to him. He noticed that the mainmast was new. He deduced that the original main had likely toppled in a North Atlantic storm. He was speculating on this when a basso profundo called to him. Captain Smith approached, smiling broadly from behind a spectacularly full snow-white beard. He wore a patch over his left eye. His head was capless and the breeze played with his long, wavy hair.

"Welcome aboard, Colonel Allen."

His recent experiences with British sea captains prompted Ethan to hesitate before slipping his hand into Smith's. Was he setting him up, toying with him for his amusement? Within the hour would Smith come down on him as Montague had? A gentleman, considerate, unprejudiced toward Americans; Arbuthnot's brief description of Smith's character came back to him. The governor had treated him decently, fairly, why would he lie about Smith? And didn't they attend the same church?

"What do you think of her?" Smith's sweeping hand took in the whole ship.

"Fine. I have to be honest, Captain, the finest ship under sail doesn't really interest me. I've had enough of the sea to last a lifetime."

"I can't say I blame you. Let's get away from it. Come abaft to my cabin, we'll talk, have a bit of brandy. But before we go any further let me put your mind at ease. On board my ship you'll be treated as an officer and a gentleman."

Ethan swallowed lightly. It was so unexpected and so delightful to hear that tears came to his eyes.

"Thank you, Captain."

"You do drink, sir?"

"Only when it's within reach."

Smith laughed. Ethan liked him from his laugh. It was an

outstanding laugh. It came from well below his belt buckle and rolled and rumbled up to his throat, exploding out of it and lighting up his face as brightly as a beacon fire.

His cabin was smaller, the ceiling lower than Symonds's cabin on board the *Solebay,* and not nearly as luxuriously furnished. But the table, although similar to Symonds's, didn't have twelve knife nicks in it.

The brandy was superb. He was tempted to hurl it down like ale.

"Have you eaten anything today?" Smith asked.

"Not yet. I've been busy running around."

"Before they caught you."

Again that laugh, not as loud in respect to the limited dimensions of the cabin. Smith leaned out the door calling across the deck.

"Jessie, tell the cook to send somebody with some sandwiches from that glorious ham he cooked last night. On the good brown bread. And coffee."

"Aye, aye, Captain."

The food came presently, after the small talk had been dispensed with.

"Needless to say I've been out of touch, Captain."

"Hosea, please, Ethan."

"Hosea. How's the war going?"

"Good for us, not too good for General Washington. What's the last news you heard?"

"Colonel Benedict Arnold was trying to take Quebec."

"He failed to."

"I knew he would."

"You sound like you know him."

"Intimately. He got underfoot when my boys and I took Fort Ticonderoga."

"Well, since you Americans gave up on Canada, the home government has decided that inasmuch as half of the American population and their resources lie north of Chesapeake

Bay—New England alone having upwards of three-quarters of a million people—operations should be shifted from Boston to New York City, there to hold the line of the Hudson River while Carleton and Burgoyne lead an invasion force down from Canada."

"Cut New England off."

"Yes. So Howe, with heavy reinforcements from home, embarked on this campaign. Washington got wind of his coming and marched down from Boston and fortified New York City. Here, look." He stuck his index finger into his brandy snifter and drew on the table. "The way Washington deployed his troops, his left flank was thrown open here, across the East River beyond the village of Brooklyn. While his front, here, and on the harbor and the Hudson became open to a combined naval and military attack. He hadn't the manpower, you see, he had no choice.

"Howe drove him out of here, forcing him to abandon the whole of Manhattan Island. And there matters stand at the moment."

"Hell almighty."

"Would it be rude of me to ask you not to swear? I'm Church of England, you know, and . . . "

"Sorry. Force of old habit. Every now and then a curse word does slip out. Well . . . " Ethan poured himself more brandy, offering the decanter to Smith. "It appears the general could really use my services."

Smith winked good-naturedly. "Which may be why our generals are hanging onto you."

"It's comforting to know they hold me in such high regard. But that doesn't help George."

"General Washington?"

"Yes. We go way back. I've been writing to him, among others, asking them to arrange for my exchange. You can see what luck I've had."

"I daresay he's doing his level best for you."

"You think?"

"From what I hear he's a man of the highest integrity, loyal to a fault to his men. He doesn't have it easy."

"What do you mean?"

"He has no shortage of enemies in his own camp, those who are jealous of him and fault him for his mistakes. It's difficult to see how he survived the past year: the outspoken criticism of those who demand action, the party dissensions in Congress, the selfishness and stupidity on the part of so many of your countrymen, the exasperating shortages."

"And we're poor. Don't forget how poor we are."

"He shrugs all of it off. Would that we had such a man leading our army."

"I know some who are out to get him. John Hancock for one. He wants to be commander in chief. John Adams, Samuel Adams, Richard Henry Lee, Elbridge Gerry, they'd all like to see George replaced. On the other side, almost all of his generals are fiercely loyal to him."

"Is that a fact?"

"As I sit here living and breathing. You wouldn't have any cigars, would you?"

"Of course."

Smith lit both their cigars.

"As I say," Ethan went on, "plenty in the Congress would like to see him fall. Thomas Mifflin too, ex-quartermaster general. And Timothy Pickering. He doesn't dislike George, he'd just like to replace him. Pickering thinks he's God's gift to the military. Some people's heads are so big they can barely squeeze through the door."

"We've a few of those on our side."

"So what do you plan for me, Hosea?"

"Not my plan, I'm merely your Charon."

"My what?"

"Charon was the ferryman of Hades. He guided the ferry across the Acheron."

"I remember him."

Smith appeared astonished. "You do?"

"Sure. I had a year of college, you know. Charon rowed the dead across the Acheron. He charged a fare. He was gray and ugly, he wore filthy clothes. You don't look a bit like him. But I'm not dead."

"You're a well-read man, Ethan."

"Used to be. I haven't read a thing but the handwriting on the wall for over a year. And, oh yes, the *Dublin Intelligencer* in Funchal in the Madeiras. So what happens in New York? Have they picked out any particular jail yet?"

"I wouldn't know. In the meantime we'll make your voyage as pleasant as possible. Good food, decent brandy, and a cigar any time you want it."

Ethan puffed. "These are good. Not great. James Livingston over in Chambly on the Richelieu River, he had cigars that were amazing. I just kept smoking 'em one end to another until I ran out. That was just before Montreal."

"What happened there, Ethan?"

"We were planning the attack, somebody tipped the governor, we were surrounded, I surrendered. It was either that or be massacred. Since then it's been all downhill."

"How many men did you have?"

"By the time we were ready to move out, fewer than forty."

"What made you think you could take it with so few?"

"To tell you the truth, I didn't think too much about that, only about how close we were and how weak they were. And I had my friend Major John Brown coming at the other end of town. Only he just vanished into thin air. Hosea, you want to know what it really was? Conceit. Along about then, after taking Fort Ti, I thought I could do anything. No fort, no town, was too tough to turn over. Walking into Ti and taking it without a shot went straight to my head. My first and it looks like my last battle of the war. Can I have some more brandy?"

He didn't wait for an answer, he poured.

"Drink up, Hosea. Better days are coming. Or worse."

55

★ **By** late summer of 1776, General Sir William Howe, British commander in chief in America, had thirty-two thousand troops and vast quantities of supplies and equipment available to him. From the Duke of Braunschweig, from the Landgrave of Hesse-Cassel. From the Prince of Waldeck, England hired upwards of eighteen thousand Hessian mercenaries. General Howe's brother, Admiral Sir Richard Howe, was able to engage seventy-three warships manned by thirteen thousand seamen.

The Canadian army—which numbered fewer than seven hundred regulars when Ethan Allen ventured north with the invasion force, now totaled over thirteen thousand men. Against this formidable array of manpower and resources, General Washington was able to muster fewer than nineteen thousand largely untrained, undisciplined, poorly armed, meagerly equipped and supplied defenders. The Americans had not a single warship and no troop transports. Financing for the Revolution came mainly from a single printing press in Philadelphia frantically churning out paper dollars, worth only as much as the recipient was willing to give in goods or services and steadily shrinking in value as the summer of 1776 gave way to fall.

The Americans needed nothing additional to weaken and worsen their position. The British began to see a quick end to the fighting, and Howe pressed his many advantages. The vastly outnumbered American force was split between New York City and Long Island, with the East River between, and there was no way to keep open a line of communication should Admiral Howe send his warships into the arena.

By the time the *Lark* put in at New York harbor, General Howe was mopping up the remnants of Washington's troops scattered about the outlying areas. The British were now in firm control of New York and the square mile of lower Manhattan where virtually all of the colonial population was congregated.

At sight of the provost jail's forbidding brick exterior Ethan's morale slipped even lower. Inside, he and Captain Smith stood among people milling about. A large cell was packed with ragged, dirty, starved-looking civilians and soldiers in pieces of uniforms. A few women could be seen in the crowd. Thoughts of the cell on board the *Adamant* came back to Ethan. How did *these* people eat? Sleep? Get on? How did they relieve themselves? From what he'd seen of lower Manhattan while walking over from where the dory put in, the whole area looked like one great, sprawling cell, walled by water, perilously overcrowded, rife with disorder, strung with tension.

"Maybe they won't stick you in there," murmured Smith, nodding toward the holding cell.

"They'd need a boothorn. Hosea, before you go I have to say these past few days in your company have been a breath of fresh air." He pumped the captain's hand, clapping his free hand over the grip in friendly fashion. "I'll miss you, and I'll miss the food, the drink, and the cigars. The bed was the best I've had since home."

Smith's one visible eye twinkled gratefully. A line officer attired in dress scarlet with high fur cap and above-the-knee boots shouldered through the crowd toward them.

"Colonel Allen?"

"Yes."

"You'll come with me."

"Good-bye and good luck, Ethan," said Smith.

"Good-bye, Hosea, and thank you. I owe you. If we ever meet again I'll repay you handsomely."

"Nonsense, you'd have done the same for me. Just take care of yourself."

The captain gave him a look that spoke eloquently of the struggle over which neither had any control. Ethan followed the officer down a darkened, windowless corridor, threading through people who stood staring into space, to a door. To his surprise, the man held it for him to enter. He felt as if he'd turned a corner; respect, even consideration would be his lot from now on. Why? Inside was a rickety-looking table cluttered with papers, two chairs. That was all.

"Have a seat, Colonel. I'm Captain Given." He cleared a spot on the table and set down his hat. "I've papers here. Somewhere. Here . . . " He dipped a frazzled-looking quill into a stone inkwell. "Sign at the bottom. There . . . and there."

"What is this?"

"Your parole."

"Parole?"

"Yes. Didn't anyone tell you?"

"I just got off the ship. I haven't talked to a soul."

"You're to be paroled. On your own recognizance, of course."

"Mind if I read this?"

"It's the standard form. It simply states that you will not leave the immediate area, that is lower Manhattan. Under penalty of revocation."

"You mean I'm free to walk out of here?"

"Parole, Colonel. You're free with certain restrictions. This is no generous gesture on the part of the Crown, it's a matter of necessity. We've no room for you here. There's no room in any jail in the city. As an officer, and presumably a gentleman, henceforth you will be on your honor. You'll be allowed to move about during daylight hours providing, as I say, you stay in lower Manhattan."

"Where do I sleep?"

"I'm sure a man as resourceful as yourself will have no trouble finding a bed."

"Are you serious? Have you been outside lately? The streets are so crowded that anybody who passes out can't fall down. People must be sleeping on top of each other. And what do I do for money?"

"I'm afraid I can't help you there. Don't you have any friends here?"

"I don't know a soul. Can't the Crown lend me something? Enough to keep body and soul together? Pay for a bed in some rat-infested dump?"

"Colonel, this is not the Sisters of Mercy Charity. We don't dole out money."

"This is great. You put me on parole, make me fend for myself, with nothing to fend with. How about you? Could you lend me, say, twenty dollars?"

Mild shock slid down Given's fat face to his dimpled chin. "Me?"

"Ten?"

"I'm sorry."

"*You're* sorry? I can't do it."

"Do what?"

"Go out there and fend with empty pockets, a stranger, knowing not so much as a single fellow Christian."

"All right. Here. Here's five shillings. But you didn't get it from me, understand?"

"Can't you make it ten?"

"All right! Take it."

"Thank you, Captain, you'll get it back."

"I'm sure. Now sign your name."

"First let me read."

The parole listed specific do's and don't's. He wasn't to consort with fellow rebels, he was forbidden to carry firearms, he should not drink to excess, he must consider himself under the orders of any and all British officers and non-commissioned officers. One stipulation nearly caused him to burst out laughing. It warned against "fomenting sedition."

"Must I explain that?" Given asked.

"Who am I going to foment with? You mean I'm not to make friends with anybody on my side."

"You're not to conspire or assist in conspiring against the Crown. If you're caught doing so your parole will be summarily revoked and you'll be immediately remanded to solitary confinement."

"Where?"

"Probably here."

"You haven't got space enough to sit down, for Chrissakes!"

"Will you please sign and leave?"

He signed. He left, biting the coins the captain had given him. Then he added them one by one to the forty-two guineas in his pocket, what remained of the fifty guineas given him by the banker in Cork, the difference paid to Mr. Hines aboard the *Solebay,* for making him the handsome broadcloth suit he was wearing, and the second suit in his bag over his shoulder.

56

SEPTEMBER 1776

★ **It** was inevitable that Ethan would encounter other paroled officers while wandering about lower Manhattan. All had been captured in the recent local battles. A few made Fraunces Tavern their headquarters. As the senior member of the group, Ethan daily held court at a large corner table. He became particularly fond of a Lieutenant Walter Dunbar, who had been captured in the Battle of Long Island, where he had served under General William Stirling, who was in command of the Delaware and Maryland regulars. Ethan also befriended Captain Curtis Toombs who, to his everlasting regret, had served under the ineffectual General Israel Putnam. Four other paroled officers joined the group. Ethan, in the meantime, with Dunbar's help, had found a dormitory in a building on Broome Street. It was not as badly crowded as the provost jail. He rented a bed for five of Captain Given's shillings, in preference to sleeping on the floor for two shillings.

Prisoners on parole in the city were not without some resources. Sympathetic Patriots and even some good-hearted Loyalists provided them with food, money, and quarters. Freedom to roam, if only the lower end of Manhattan, was vastly preferable to being crammed into a cell.

Ale was served. Captain Toombs paid. He came from a wealthy Baltimore family and the others, less financially fortunate, were not reluctant to accept his generosity. Fraunces Tavern was oak-paneled throughout. It was considerably darker than Stephen Fay's Catamount Tavern in Bennington. However, the ceiling in Fraunces was not as intimidatingly low as Zadock Remington's ceiling. Fraunces was also absent the commingling of unpleasant odors that seemed a permanent part of the ambience at Remington's.

"Evil tidings this morning, chaps," said Dunbar. "Two of our merry band attempted to leave our island paradise. They got as far as the Bronx before they were apprehended. They tossed them into a jail somewhere up there, shackles, bread and water. What absolute dolts."

"You can't fault men for trying," said one of the others. "Sitting out the war on parole is even worse than being locked up."

"I disagree with that," said Ethan.

"We're all on our honor," Dunbar reminded him. "Attempting escape is tantamount to grinding one's honor under one's heel. It makes us look even more unprofessional to our enemies."

Ethan snorted. "Horseshit, Walter. You think they've as much respect for us as would fit into a gnat's arsehole? Besides, where's their honor? They come storming into our house uninvited, rearrange the furniture, bring in their own, and when we protest, start beating up on us. You call that honorable behavior?"

"Nevertheless, Ethan," said Dunbar. "Those of us who attempt to escape invariably fail, and all that does is make life more miserable for the honorable among us."

"I don't see anything so miserable about parole," said Ethan, raising his glass.

"Colonel," said Toombs, "tell us about Montreal. What actually happened?"

"The roof of the world fell in. Hell almighty, but I'm thirsty today . . ."

"I'll buy you another. I'll buy you two."

"I hate to sponge, but if you insist . . ."

"So tell us," said another man as all six at the table leaned closer.

"It was a foul night, raining pitchforks. We had a single eight-inch howitzer, a monster. We all risked hernias dragging it up to the Quebec Gate. We had ample powder but only one ball. My strategy was twofold: blow a hole in the gate clear to the hinges on both sides, throw the fear of God into the Montrealers, the redcoats especially."

"What happened?"

"Everything depended on the one shot. One crack at glory. The rain was coming down something fierce. We crowded around to shield the touchhole, keep her dry as possible. We set a lucifer, she blew. Into a thousand pieces."

"No!"

"You could have heard that explosion clear to Quebec. Killed fifteen men on the spot, wounded the rest, practically every man jack. I was one of the few lucky ones. I was thrown clear—thirty, perhaps forty feet through the air. Landed in a bush. Otherwise I'd have busted every bone in my body."

"Good Lord," murmured Toombs.

Every face around the table had assumed a stunned expression. Not a man moved as much as an eyelid. They sat, they stared.

"Of course, the explosion brought the Montrealers charging out. We, those of us still standing, were in shock. They surrounded us. That was it."

"But you did escape injury," said a man.

"Concussion, that's all. But I wasn't able to think clearly for two whole days. We didn't have a chance in hell, and for that I go down in history as the Hero of Ticonderoga who tried and failed to take Montreal."

"But weren't you vastly outnumbered as well?" asked Dunbar.

"At least five to one." Ethan touched the side of his nose and winked broadly. "But we had the gun. The monster. Dragged all the way up from Fort Chambly. To wind up doublecrossing us all. British made, you can bet. In Birmingham. Stamped right on it. Ironic, don't you think?"

"What's ironic," said a lieutenant to Ethan's left, "is that everybody thinks it was the height of rashness for you to try."

"Who can dissuade the king of beasts from attacking?" Dunbar asked sweeping an arm histrionically.

"Hear, hear!"

"You know, Colonel Allen," said Toombs. "If the average person took the trouble to learn the true facts about things they wouldn't be so quick to criticize."

"My sentiments entirely, Curtis. "Where's my second ale? Miss? Oh, Miss!"

Ethan met other young officers on parole, joining a group at Gaylord's tavern on Wall Street. Curiosity as to what actually happened on the night of his capture infected the gathering. His tankards filled for him—he had yet to spend a cent of his own money on drink—he regaled his listeners with the true facts.

"It was a foul night, raining pitchforks. We were down to

about forty souls, from well over two-fifty. But we knew that the town had no more than forty redcoats to defend her. All the same, my experience and my instincts warned me that trying to take her would not be easy. They were well-armed, they had artillery, they had the protection of the walls.

"I called my men around me, described the situation, and explained my reluctance. I told them that all we had on our side was the element of surprise and the dark and storm for cover. I advised that we bite the ball and back away, withdraw across the St. Lawrence and wait for reinforcements. To my amazement, they began shouting me down, so eager were they to go forward. Now you must understand, I'd had my glory at Fort Ticonderoga. They knew that I didn't need more. But they could taste theirs and refused to hold off. I begged and begged."

"But you were in command," said a man. "You don't disobey your commander."

"It wasn't that simple. They'd come a long way with me through thick and thin. In their eyes they'd earned this night. Even I had no right to deny them. I could see this in every face. So we went ahead, little dreaming that one of the scum who'd deserted us before we crossed the river didn't just leave. He decided to turn his coat."

"No!"

"He got inside and warned Prescott and Governor Carleton."

"They were waiting for you," said a captain.

"We didn't get within two hundred yards of the Quebec Gate before we found ourselves surrounded, outnumbered a good ten to one."

"I thought you said they only had about forty soldiers," said a man, his eyes narrowing suspiciously.

"The civilians armed themselves," said another.

"Of course," said Ethan. "Ten to one. Maybe twelve. We never had a chance."

"And all the while you were dead against even trying," said another man.

"Dead. But I was in command. I took full responsibility. Still do. I made a fatal tactical error that night. I looked into their eyes and listened to my heart instead of my common sense. And I've paid for it in hard coin since."

At Lagendorf's Tavern on Broadway, in the shadow of Trinity Church, which had suffered a devastating fire in September, a paroled captain asked about Montreal. Twenty parolees crowded around the little square table Ethan shared with Major Conrad Worthy of the First Pennsylvania Continental Regiment, who had offered to keep Ethan's glass from emptying.

"It was a foul night, raining pitchforks," Ethan began. "Men had been deserting me since the day before until by the time we came within sight of the Quebec Gate we were down to no more than forty. Counting British regulars inside and civilians we were probably outnumbered six or seven to one. But we had one thing in our favor."

"Surprise?" said the major.

He was clinging to Ethan's every word.

"That too, Conrad. I was referring to what we brought with us. Five hundred grenades from the armory at Fort Chambly, which we'd taken only days before. Five hundred grenades. Capable, if properly employed, of turning the tide in our favor. Think about it, we wouldn't have to breach the gate, wouldn't have to enter the town, just stand outside spread along the walls and toss in grenades."

"Man!" burst the major. "That would put the fear of the Almighty into the bravest heart."

"Exactly. I liked the idea. It might cause a few casualties, but it would be so demoralizing we likely wouldn't have to toss any more than forty or fifty. The gate would open, and out they'd rush straight into a line of upraised muskets.

Prescott would have no choice but to surrender the garrison and the town. I closed my eyes and envisioned Governor Guy Carleton handing over his saber."

"What happened?" asked one of the standing listeners.

"Catastrophe."

"What sort of catastrophe?"

"The worst sort imaginable. It almost defies imagining. There we were with five hundred grenades, British made of course, probably in Birmingham. I spread men the length of the river wall. I gave the prearranged signal, they counted one, two, three and hurled their grenades over in perfect unison."

"What happened?" asked the major.

"Nothing."

Men gasped and gawked and read one another's puzzled looks. Major Worthy's lantern jaw sagged to its limit.

"Nothing. They were faulty. Every last one. No doubt assembled in the factory by some good-hearted person or persons in sympathy with the cause of independence."

"You're saying it was intentional?" asked a man.

"How else do you account for such a thing? Not a single one blew."

"What did you do then?" asked the same man.

"I didn't panic. I gave a second signal and every man threw his spare grenade. Same result. By this time the people inside, the redcoats, realized what was up and moved to turn the tables on us. They came stampeding out the gate, caught us all spread out along the wall, a few shots were exchanged, but it was useless. We were forced to surrender to escape annihilation."

"Faulty grenades," said the major.

"Five hundred of 'em. Twenty minutes later we were all behind bars."

"What rotten, rotten luck," muttered a man. Others nodded, their eyes brimming with sympathy.

"Fortunes of war, boys, fortunes of war."

57

★ **In** December, General Howe declared the suspension of military operations until spring. General Charles Lee, formerly an officer in His Majesty's service now serving under Washington, was captured by the British. Howe's suspension of operations relieved Washington's exhausted forces from further immediate pressure. Lee's capture relieved him of the presence of one of his most overrated and uncooperative officers. Ethan thought Lee worse than that; he suspected that the Virginian was working behind the scene to divest Washington of command of the Continental Army.

Ethan was unable to fathom Howe's thinking. It was the British commander's responsibility to detroy the Continental Army. He had defeated it when and where he chose, but in deciding to go into winter quarters he deliberately and unaccountably threw away his advantage. Captain Dunbar offered his opinion. He and Ethan were walking down Broadway. It was snowing lightly, they had just come from breakfast and Ethan felt the need for fresh air. Since leaving Halifax his health had measurably improved. He'd put on much-needed weight, and his characteristic jauntiness had been restored to his step. He felt good despite his gnawing frustration at the interminable inactivity.

"Howe is no Clinton," announced Dunbar. "They're cut from different bolts entirely. Howe enjoys taking it easy. He evidently feels he's earned it."

"He's an idiot," said Ethan.

"Is he? It's getting colder every day, we're in for absolute tons of snow, ice storms in February. Our army's in no shape to put up even token resistance. Why not take it easy? Washington's not going anywhere, he's not going to get any stronger."

"Stopping fighting's just not done. Not by any commander worth his salt. War's not cricket, you don't take time out. Julius Caesar wouldn't do it. Alexander the Great wouldn't. I wouldn't. If I were Howe I'd mount twenty thousand men, march to south Jersey and catch Washington while he's still licking his wounds. I tell you, bad as things look, we're going to wind up winning this war!"

His sudden change in views caused Dunbar to laugh. "Sure."

"We are, O ye of little faith."

"Have you been eating opium?"

"Let me amend that. We're not going to win the war. They're going to lose it. With generals like Howe they will."

The winter was long, cold, and arduous for man and beast. Boredom assailed Ethan, and there was little to do to break the monotonous chain of dull and dreary days. A man could only write so many letters. He could only drink so much, only talk so much, only stand on an island controlled by his enemy and listen to so many bits and snatches of rumors about a war in which he no longer had any part. His frustration rooted. It flourished.

The social season of the winter of 1776–77 reached its apogee in March when General Howe was awarded the Order of Bath for his services in the battles of Long Island and White Plains and the capture of New York City.

Major Worthy and Ethan shared their usual table at Lagendorf's on a blowy March evening. Worthy sniffed disapprovingly.

"The Order of Bath. For services rendered. Some services. For evacuating Boston? For frittering away nearly two whole months on Staten Island? For letting our army, greatly outnumbered, get away on Long Island and again at White Plains? For not ending things last year when he had half a dozen chances to? For leaving his troops unprotected in New Jersey? For letting ten thousand experienced veterans under experienced generals be cooped up by half as many Patriots in Brunswick and Amboy for nearly six months?"

"So you agree he's even worse than Charles Lee."

"No. It's hard to compare them. Howe may be second-rate, but he's not insubordinate. Although, maybe on second thought, Howe is worse, because he has more power than Lee, greater responsibility."

All the parolees talked into the late hours about Howe, Washington, and other generals on both sides. They had all become detached observers of the history unfolding in the area, annoyed and disgusted with their lot. Ethan returned to the dormitory late that night, sneaking his way home from doorway to doorway, anxious not to be picked up for breaking parole curfew. Approaching his bed, he found an envelope on his pillow.

He read the message and whistled softly when he saw the signature.

" 'Sir William Howe, Commander in Chief British Army in North America.' What does he want with me? As if I didn't know."

58

★ **General** Howe's aide, Captain John Montresor, greeted Ethan in the anteroom.

"The general is waiting, sir."

"What's he going to ask me? To change sides, right? Does he know he's the latest in a line that's getting longer and longer?"

"I have no idea what this is about. But he's waiting. The coffee's hot."

Montresor's grin was so engaging, he was so polite, and the aroma of the coffee wafting through the partially open door was so enticing, Ethan dropped his defensive attitude and followed the captain's gesture inside. The general sat a Queen Anne chair at the coffee table. The furnishings were Queen Anne throughout. Howe gestured Ethan to sit opposite him. The commander in chief was forty-eight. His looks tended toward homely, his features uniformly thick, Teutonic-looking. He looked the result of an overfondness for rich food and drink. Tiny pink spots peppered his complexion. His hands, however, were as delicate as a woman's. He poured the coffee.

"Milk?"

"Black'll do me fine."

"Care for a scone?"

"I'm not much for scones."

Howe appeared to be trying but wasn't succeeding very well in making him feel comfortable. He stared as if sizing him up. His expression was not amiable. *Get this over with and get him out of here,* crossed Ethan's mind.

"Mind if I start?" Ethan said. Howe flung his hand lightly inviting him to do so. "Congratulations, General."

"Congratulations?"

"On being the highest-ranking officer yet to ask me to change sides. General Sims in England asked me but he was only a brigadier."

"Amusing."

"You think? I don't."

Howe sipped. "I'm curious. Ahem, how many actually have suggested to you that you join us?"

"To tell the truth, I've lost count. A dozen, maybe fifteen. Even some civilians."

"This will be different. Better. I've been authorized to put a particularly handsome offer on the table. Before I start, ahem, I advise you to keep one thing in mind. The situation has to have changed drastically from the last time you were asked. We're now here in force. Your tattered little army is on the run. Washington is at his wit's end. It'll be all over before summer. So before you respond, take a moment to consider. Wouldn't joining us now be infinitely more sensible than surrendering to us later?"

"I think you're overlooking something. I'm already your prisoner. I surrendered back in Montreal."

"Montreal, yes. Well, let's get on with it. You call yourself Colonel Allen."

"Colonel of the Green Mountain Boys."

"Yes, yes, colorful, colorful. Colonel, please listen closely. If there's anything you don't understand, feel free to interrupt. To begin with, I'm empowered to guarantee you in writing a colonelcy in His Majesty's forces. An appointment to command a regiment of Loyalists. You'd be sent to England, you'd consult with the colonial secretary, Lord Germain, you'd be accorded the finest treatment and the highest respect as a loyal subject."

"General, I wear England's finest treatment and highest respect on my back, and will for the rest of my days. No. I'm sorry."

"In addition, you could look forward to a royal audience in London. You'd be paid in guineas, given the customary uniform allowance and all perquisites due your rank. After a brief training period with your regiment you'd return here and join General John Burgoyne in the northern campaign."

"And retake Fort Ticonderoga."

"Possibly."

"Who better than the man who took it in the first place?"

"What do you say?"

"No."

"Most importantly, when the war ends—before this coming summer—in gratitude for your services you'll be given a vast tract of land in the New Hampshire Grants. Or in Connecticut. Your choice. There is my offer. Now what do you say?"

"I say I look at your offer of the land as similar to what the devil offered Jesus Christ."

"Wait . . . "

"I'll remind you of Matthew four, verse one. 'The Devil taketh him up into an exceeding high mountain, and sheweth him all the kingdoms of the world, and the glory of them. And saith unto him, All these things will I give thee, if thou wilt fall down and worship me.' "

Howe half-rose from his chair, his eyebrows rising, a scowl forming.

"Do I hear you correctly? Did you just call me the devil?"

"If the shoe fits . . . "

Howe sat. Ethan sipped his coffee and watched Howe regain control. "A simple *no* will suffice."

"I've been saying *no* all along."

"You actually reject this offer?"

"You didn't really think I'd consider it?"

Howe stood up frowning.

Ethan finished his coffee. "Delicious."

"You'll be escorted back to where you were picked up."

"I can get back by myself, thanks."

"You'll be escorted back."

"Are you mad at me?"

"You're making the biggest mistake of your life."

"I've made a lot. I'll make more. Good coffee. Really good."

He went out. Montresor came in, his eyes questioning.

"Vulgar, rude, a lout. That, John, was the face of our enemy. I feel as if I've demeaned myself even being in the same room. I'll fix him, damnable traitor. Get hold of Major Gilpin."

"Everett Gilpin, Intelligence?"

"I want to see him immediately. And tell him to bring along that American lieutenant who's been working for him."

VII

The Darkest Hours

59

★ **Ethan** was within sight of the burnt-out walls of Trinity Church when his escort decided to let him go the rest of the way by himself, turning off and vanishing into the crowd without a word. The long walk would have been invigorating had it not been so depressing. The scenes of human suffering on every side sickened and outraged him. A vengeful Crown seemed determined to starve the Patriot populace into submission. Beggars by the hundreds approached him. Women forced into prostitution by their plight pleaded for money. The area was mobbed with humanity, filthy, afflicted with myriad stenches. Disease and death were rampant, starvation the main cause.

A block from Broome Street he bumped into Curtis Toombs.

"Colonel!"

Sight of the captain's smiling face lifted Ethan's spirits. He accepted his invitation to late breakfast at Fraunces Tavern. Coming within sight of the place, they stopped abruptly. An emaciated throng, many in rags, women holding small children, was crowding the entrance. A riot appeared imminent as more people hurried up, swelling the crowd.

"Sam must have passed out his day-old bread," said Toombs. "Let's walk over to the Bull's Head."

The Bull's Head Tavern was on the Bowery between Bayard and Pump Streets. It was not yet midmorning, and tables were available. Ethan ordered kippers and wheat cakes, and told about his meeting with Howe.

Toombs set his coffee down, grimacing. "Sam Fraunces makes better coffee than this. It sounds like you left His Lordship with a taste just as bitter."

"He was disappointed."

"Watch out for him, he can be vindictive."

"He did act like he was taking it personally."

"I'm sure he did. As I say, be careful. You're a big fish. You have, how shall I put it, symbolic value. Don't be surprised if he has Gilpin assign somebody to shadow you to try and catch you misstepping."

Ethan smirked.

On his way back to Broome Street and the dormitory he turned Toombs's warning over in his mind. Howe *was* furious and showed it. Ethan came within sight of the building and was preparing to wedge through traffic to cross the street when a familiar figure hailed him. Mason Weeks, a corporal captured at White Plains, came up. He was no more than seventeen, and destitute. Ethan had given him money for food more than once. Weeks occupied a space on the floor near his cot.

He looked both ways and whispered. "Don't go upstairs."

"Why not?"

"There's a sergeant up there with two Germans."

"Hessians?"

"Waiting for you."

"What did they say?"

"They asked when you were expected back. They didn't say what they want, but nobody has to draw me pictures. They're fixing to take you in."

"What the hell for?"

"You must have done something."

Again Toombs's warning came back. "Mason, do me a favor. Big favor."

"If I can. If it doesn't get me arrested."

"It won't if you're careful. Go back upstairs and get my bag with all my stuff. Get . . . get five or six bags. Like you're collecting them. They'll have no way of knowing which one is mine, if you're clever about it."

"I get it. Give you yours, take the others back up."

"Right."

"They won't know what I'm up to."

"If you're clever. Casual. Talk a blue streak. You're a good talker. Tell 'em I'm probably at Fraunces Tavern, better yet over by the East River docks. Tell 'em I generally come back after lunch to check the mail. Lie in your teeth."

"Wait for me back across the street." Weeks pointed. "In that doorway, in the shadow."

"Go."

Just as the corporal vanished inside the building around the corner came Lieutenant Walter Dunbar. Ethan stepped out of the doorway he'd taken refuge in, waved and called. Dunbar crossed the street.

"Ethan, I was coming to see you. What are you doing hiding in a doorway?"

"Waiting for somebody to bring my bag. I'm leaving, Walter."

He explained hastily. Dunbar searched his pockets, found a pencil stub and a letter. Removing it from its envelope he scribbled on the envelope.

"This fellow keeps a stable on Wall Street. Play him like a violin and he'll give you a good steed at a fair price."

"I know how to horse trade."

Dunbar grinned. "I'm sure you do. Will you head for Bennington?"

"Straight."

"Not straight. Avoid the Boston Post Road. It's crawling with patrols looking for runaways. Head northeast parallel to it. Give Yonkers a wide berth. Port Chester too. But when you cross the line into Connecticut, into Greenwich, you should be reasonably safe from there on. Of course, you'd be a lot safer if you wait until dark."

"I've got a feeling if I wait I'll never make dark." He glanced warily about, then fixed on Dunbar, staring at him. "You surprise me."

"Oh? In what way?"

"You're always saying how stupid it is to try and escape."

"Not stupid, dangerous. But if you've no choice . . . "

"I don't. You should have seen Howe's face when I walked out of there. He's not sticking me in any jail."

"Brace yourself, old friend, they've started converting some of the hulks in the harbor into prison ships. The *Jersey,* for one. No, no question, you'd best get out while you can."

"Ethan! Ethan!"

It was Mason Weeks burdened with five sacks. Ethan relieved him of his own.

"What's this?" Dunbar asked.

The corporal explained. "Good luck, Ethan. It's been a real pleasure. If you ever get to Shrewsbury, Massachusetts, look me up. Say, I better get these other bags back upstairs before their owners show up."

"Good man, Mason. Good-bye, Walter." Ethan held up the envelope. "Thanks for the horse."

60

★ **Logic** had always been one of Ethan's stronger suits. So he told himself. On the one hand it seemed logical that Howe would avenge his rejection of his offer purely out of pique.

On the other hand it seemed illogical. With all he had to do, the responsibilities heaped on him, why bother with something so trivial? The only possible charge they could arrest him on would be for his "openly consorting with fellow rebel officers." Only he wasn't consorting, and the British knew it. He and the others fomented no sedition. They did nothing to invite punishment on the part of the military government.

He considered his chances. The majority of those attempting to flee were caught and either jailed or kept under house arrest, which failed to discourage others from trying. But the British went to great lengths to prevent escape and to track down those fortunate enough to make it out of the city.

They'd know where he'd be heading, but if he made it all the way to Bennington he could hide out in or near there until his pursuers lost interest. He checked Dunbar's directions. He was getting close to the stable. He stopped suddenly in front of a boarded-up bakery, slipping to one side out of the stream of pedestrians. Leaning against the door, he went over the situation. Buy a horse, with luck make it out of town, skirt the towns to the north and east keeping clear of the Post Road. A chilling thought struck. Had the patrols by now taken to shooting escapees on sight?

What about a boat? He'd had enough of the sea to last him a lifetime, but what about the river?

Too many enemy ships in the East River. In the harbor too, bringing in troops and supplies. But the Hudson . . . If he could get passage up to Albany, or four or five miles above it, and get off on the east bank, from there it would be less than thirty-five miles over the Taconic Mountains to Bennington. Hiding out aboard a boat could be risky, with no place to run if he was discovered. Were any of the captains to be trusted? And who could say how many redcoats were assigned to the towns along the way to watch out for escapees?

But through the onslaught of risks and concerns, the possibility of freedom at long last tugged his heart. Get out, get home, even if it meant hiding out for six months. Then back to the wars. Get home, see Mary and the children, friends, maybe Jacob Wall and Elisha Cummings. They could be back by now. Governor Arbuthnot in Halifax couldn't hold them forever. Too much trouble, too expensive.

He resumed walking. Ahead he could see the stable sign creaking in the breeze off the water. As he drew closer, suspicion snapped to mind like a whip cracking. Was it a trap? Would redcoats be waiting inside? *Had the British turned Walter Dunbar? Was that why he was so eager to help him get away?* He thought back. How had they first met? Dunbar approached him, introduced himself. Made friends within ten minutes. It wasn't the same with Curtis Toombs, Conrad Worthy, with none of the others, thinking about each one in turn.

Was he letting his imagination run away with him? He'd be stupid not to play it as safe as possible. He crumpled the envelope, tossed it away, and headed for the river. He would wait until dark before even inquiring about boats.

Few people frequented the riverside during the day other than stevedores handling cargoes. The hostilities seemed to have little effect on traffic. He found a boarded-up warehouse and sneaked under the loading dock to hide until nightfall. He could look out and see the river and all types of craft passing up and down.

He awoke to the sight of the sun setting over the Palisades. Shadows draped the river. A storm cloud threatened rain. Again he began analyzing the situation, trotting out the pros and cons of attempting to get away. By horse or by boat the risks were probably equal. He heard a boat whistle, heard seagulls scream petulantly, and abruptly it dawned on him.

"He wants me to go!"

Howe had set the stage with the sergeant and two Hessians waiting at the dormitory. Captain Montresor had probably sent them running down to Broome Street to get there before he did. Had Dunbar shown up to warn him a trifle late?

Mason Weeks beating him to it? Breakfast with Curtis Toombs had further delayed his return home.

Absolutely. *Howe wanted him to try and get away.* Then, when he was caught either give him one last chance to change sides or lock him up.

It had to be a trap. They had no intention of letting him mount a horse *or* board a boat. Attempted escape was tantamount to actually fleeing. In Howe's book it would be. He thought about the redcoats waiting in the dormitory. Weeks had said they'd told him outright who they were looking for. Then turned around and let him leave.

"They knew he'd warn me!"

He was right. He had to be. And wasn't it just like Howe? There was only one thing for it, turn around and go back, drop his bag off, check for mail and go looking for Lieutenant Walter Dunbar. And play the model prisoner from now on.

Mason Weeks was nowhere about when he got back. No one was in the dormitory. He found a letter on his pillow. He set his bag under the cot and sat down to read. It was from his brother Ira. Ethan had just passed through another flurry of letter writing himself: to Washington, Jonathan Trumbull, John Hancock, Mary, and others. At least six letters went to the Connecticut Committee of War complaining of his situation, asking that efforts be made to effect an exchange for him. The appeal was identical in every letter, but not one elicited any response, until now. It was his first letter in over a year. He tore open the envelope. Out dropped fifty dollars. He had to firm his hands to keep them steady as he read.

Dear Ethan,

We all know that your captivity must be boring you to death and is frustrating beyond comprehension, but we are doing everything humanly possible to get you released. By we I mean myself, Governor Trumbull, Hancock, and Washington. And, believe it or not, General Schuyler has maintained a deep interest in your case. Letters have been directed to the king, to Lord Germain, Lord North, to the Ministry, and members of both houses of Parliament, all to no avail thus far, but we'll keep at it. I wish I could say that any day now you may be pleasantly surprised, but it's been so long and up to now we've been unable to make a dent from any quarter, so I hesitate to be overly optimistic.

Ethan, I'm afraid that on top of everything else I must be the purveyor of heartrending news. Your beloved son Joseph has passed on.

Ethan caught himself. "No! No, no, no, no no . . . " He read on.

He contracted smallpox. It was, unfortunately, of the confluent variety, which Dr. Steele informs us is particularly severe, appearing in large patches instead of pockmarks, and producing shocking disfigurement. The mortality is distressingly high. I'll spare you further details but suffice to say the poor lad hadn't a chance.

Mary, however, has taken it remarkably well. She's been very strong. She's also fatalistic, her view being that it was God's will. Loraine and the other girls have been very supportive and troopers themselves. I hate having to be the one to impart these sorrowful tidings. It's a shocking blow, and for you to be apprised in this manner, in a letter, no doubt makes it even more painful. Your faith is in God, my dear brother. Please, please keep it there.

He crumpled the letter, dropping it between his feet. "My faith is in God. Shit too. Eleven years old. Joseph, Joseph, Joseph!"

Now he had to get away, get back to Mary, be with her,

comfort her in her grief. These bastards dare hold him? Shackle him here? He groaned. Howe held all the cards, and he sat at the table empty-handed.

Who was he trying to fool? What good would he be to them dead or locked up? There was still the chance that he'd be released. The wheels must be in motion. If he were to try and get away and be killed and the day after his release came through . . .

It was dark when he went looking for Dunbar. He went first to Fraunces Tavern. Before entering, he resolved that once inside, should Dunbar be seated at their table he'd get a look at him before the lieutenant looked his way. Important. *He must see his initial reaction at sight of him.* Would it be shock? Surprise? Disappointment? Whatever, it would tell him what he wanted to know.

He saw him first. He was sitting in profile regaling another young officer with his flowery vocabulary. Ethan watched him. *He* should run up and tell the whole table what they were sitting with, what he was. Dunbar turned when Ethan called his name. His jaw dropped. He swallowed, lightly, but definitely a swallow, confirming Ethan's suspicions.

"Ethan . . . !"

Ethan slipped between tables, making his way toward him. "Can we have a word outside?"

"Of course. Excuse me, boys. Save my seat. And somebody get one for Ethan."

They stood outside at the side of the entrance. The cloud seen earlier over the river had broken. It was raining lightly. The streets appeared less crowded. A dilapidated wagon drawn by a mule trundled past, threatening to fall apart before it got completely by. Dunbar put on his tricorn and stepped under the overhang.

"I thought you'd be halfway to the Grants by now. What happened, no decent horse available?"

"I never made it to the stable. I changed my mind. I'm not going."

"Oh?"

Temptation seized Ethan. He suddenly wanted to spit forth accusation. Brand him a turncoat to his face. Walk back into Fraunces and tell the whole table. The whole town! Expose him for the traitor he was! Except that it made more sense, and would no doubt be infinitely more gratifying to hold his peace. Keep it to himself and watch him from now on. Follow him around. Try and catch him talking to Major Gilpin or some other lackey of Howe's.

"Aren't you curious as to why I changed my mind?"

"Did you decide it was too risky?"

"Even better reason than that."

"What?"

"If I tell you you'll probably think the alcohol has finally gotten to my brain. Walter, I think Howe wants me to try and get away. So he'll have something on me. Enough to lock me up."

"That is crazy. Why go to all that trouble? He's in command, he can order any of us picked up anytime, for no reason at all."

"But wouldn't a reason be better? A good reason? Also, it could be he figures I'll knuckle under and accept his offer. Change sides."

"It sounds awfully far-fetched to me."

Ethan studied him. He was very good. The proverbial butter wouldn't melt in his mouth.

"Maybe you're right. Maybe I am stretching it," Ethan murmured.

"I think you are. Shall we go back in? I'll let you buy me a drink."

"You buy."

"You're on. Celebrate your not leaving us after all. Welcome back, Colonel Allen."

"I wish I could say it's nice to be back."

Ethan followed him inside, his eyes riveted on Walter's nape.

61

★ **Howe** proceeded to take his army by sea from New York to the head of the Chesapeake Bay. He marched up into Pennsylvania, where Washington had earlier withdrawn to watch him. On September 26 he entered the city of Philadelphia. The Americans had tried to check the British advance at the Brandywine River. On October 4, the Americans made a well-planned attack at Germantown on the outskirts of Philadelphia, but a dense fog caused it to fail.

Howe's victories in Pennsylvania were neutralized by defeats farther north. Burgoyne had marched from Canada in June to occupy Albany and make contact with Howe at the southern end of the Hudson. He finally drove the Americans out of Fort Ticonderoga and made his way through dense woods to Fort Edward below Lake George. General Schuyler, commanding the Americans in the area, retreated to Stillwater, thirty miles above Albany, barracading the roads and stopping Burgoyne. At this point the Congress, dissatisfied with Schuyler's efforts, replaced him with General Horatio Gates.

All of this came to the parolees in bits and pieces long after the fact. In January of 1777, Ethan and a number of other American officers, no longer including Lieutenant Walter Dunbar, were summarily removed from Manhattan to King's County on Long Island. On the day they arrived, Ethan received interesting news. The group had been assembled by the side of the road to await assignment of lodgings. It was nearing noon when Captain Curtis Toombs came up and sat on the bare and frozen ground beside him. It was bitter cold, the land flat, the wind blustering, bleak overhead, and threatening snow.

"I just heard something that might interest you, Colonel, concerning an old friend of yours."

"I don't have any old friends that aren't prisoners or dead."

"Benedict Arnold?"

"What about him?"

"It's now Brigadier General Arnold."

"Jesus Christ!"

"That is, it was. Year before last. Last February he started raising hell."

"Why? Does he want Washington's job?"

"Last February the Congress created five new major generals. He, Arnold, was the ranking brigadier. He was passed over."

"Good. Great!"

"They say the reason was because Connecticut already has two major generals. Anyway, Washington had to practically beg him on bended knee not to quit the service."

"Isn't that just like that son of a bitch? If he doesn't get what he wants he picks up his marbles and goes home."

"There's more. Two months later he attacked the British at Ridgefield, Connecticut."

"And . . . ?"

"He routed them. They barely made it back to their ships."

"He must have had some damned fine men under him. Experienced, brave, able to cover his mistakes."

"I don't think he made too many. In fact he did so well Congress made him a major general. They say he was brilliant. Congress issued a formal declaration of appreciation."

"That's nothing. They thank everybody. They thanked me for taking Ticonderoga. What's he up to now?"

"I don't know, but if I hear anything . . . "

"Don't go out of your way. I'm really not that interested."

Despite his frugality, Ethan's windfall of Cork guineas had long since been spent on food, drink, and other necessities, as had the fifty dollars Ira had sent him. But Ira, his other brothers, and friends sent more money, and on Long Island he was able to find board and lodging at the home of a Dutch farmer in New Lots. His standard of living improved markedly. For the first time since the trip down from Halifax aboard the *Lark* he was able to live comfortably. He ate well, slept until midmorning nearly every day in a feather bed, and walked about the little town grateful to be spared the grim and heart-rending sights, crowded conditions, and foul air of lower Manhattan. His old vitality returned. It brought back his optimism. Not even occasional reports of Benedict Arnold's continued successes in the field upset or depressed him.

But as winter approached its end and another spring beckoned, he began to grow restless. More than ever he yearned for action. As he saw it, depriving him of participation in the war was like denying him food. By late August, New Lots had become so boring, life so uneventful, so without challenge or excitement that he came to hate getting out of bed to face the day. On August 30 he addressed yet another letter to the Connecticut Committee of War.

Gentlemen,

I have now been in captivity for over two years. My situation has long since passed the point of tolerability. This is far more than flesh and blood can stand. If something isn't done soon, if I'm not liberated or exchanged, I shall surely go mad. In my absence my only son, the joy of my heart, has died horribly of the pox. My wife and daughters have not seen me in two years. Their absence from my life tortures me daily. Although I write to them regularly circumstances prevent my receiving any replies. In all these months I have received only eight letters, all from my brother Ira. His words of comfort and gifts of money, as well as money from friends that he encloses, are all that sustain me.

Need I remind you, gentlemen, I volunteered to fight for my country? I was the first man in Bennington to do so. It was I who organized the Bennington Mobb, which later became the Green Mountain Boys. I fought bravely with success and distinction. Had things turned out differently, had we taken Montreal, I'd have returned a hero and would be a major general by now. Like Benedict Arnold. But Fate dictated otherwise. Nevertheless, am I to rot in this barless prison of our enemies for the rest of the war? Am I fated to die of boredom? Or do I slit my throat or put a ball through my brain?

The decision is in your hands. You can save me if you so desire.

Yours faithfully and in fervent hope,
E. Allen
Colonel, Green Mountain Boys

62

★ **New** Lots was picturesque, indeed beautiful, certainly by comparison with New York City. It was tranquil, unhurried, people were friendly to the parolees. The only local tavern, the Horseshoe, was *the* gathering place for the locals and the prisoners. Few redcoats were about. The war was a million miles away in most minds.

Ethan became acquainted with many locals and maintained his close friendship with Curtis Toombs, Conrad Worthy, and other prisoners. But he became more and more dissatisfied with his lot. Unhappiness got a firm grip, his sense of humor deserted him, he no longer even smiled. He brooded constantly and complained without letup over the unfairness of his situation and the continuing lack of action by those in a position to help him. He complained in his letters to Ira and to others. In one letter to George Washington his frustration got the better of his common sense, moving him perilously close to insulting the commander in chief. He came to hate his life, and his loathing for the British fairly consumed him.

Nightly at the Horseshoe he declaimed bitterly to anyone who would listen. He got to be a peevish boor to his friends and all but those closest to him did their best to avoid him. His landlord, Jan Van Wolk, himself outspoken and far from easy to get along with, lost his temper one night when Ethan came rolling in at three o'clock singing at the top of his lungs and waking the household. Clad in nightshirt and cap, Van Wolk came striding in carrying an ax handle. Ethan had fallen on top of the bed with his clothes on and was snoring lustily.

"Wake up, Colonel Big Mouth! Up!" Ethan came awake bleary-eyed. "You stink to high heaven of drink, you bum!"

"Who you calling a bum? And what are you going to do with that ax handle?"

"I should beat you to a pulp! Maybe I just throw you out."

"What did I do?"

"Are you too drunk to understand if I tell you? You've become a pain in the arse, that's what. All you do is whine and complain and carry on like you're the only prisoner of war there is. You turn room into a pigsty and my Katrinka has to pick up after you. You vomit in chamber pot. You crack wall mirror. She sets place for you for dinner and you don't come. You rip perfectly good sheet because you're too lazy to clip your toenails. You wake us up almost every night reeling in from another drunk. You pick a fight with my neighbor, Jonas Brinker, my best friend. I could go on and on."

"I'm sorry."

"You're sorry. You hear that, Katrinka? He's sorry!"

"Not so loud, you're busting my head. So I had a little too much to drink . . . "

"Every night too much. I don't need your money, I don't need you. Find someplace else."

"No, no, no, Jan, Jan, my friend, have a heart . . . "

"I got one, why else would I take you in in the first place?"

"I'll tell you what I'll do."

"*Nej!* I tell you. You straighten out or you get out and stay out. I mean it, Ethan."

"All right, all right."

It was all the warning Ethan needed to pull himself up out of the doldrums and rein his rampant frustration. His attitude entered a new phase. Ignoring Toombs's and Worthy's warnings, he embarked on a new course that was bound to get him into trouble. He defiantly ventured out of New Lots in violation of his parole. Conrad Worthy warned him. They were having a midafternoon drink at the Horseshoe, the only parolees present. Worthy kept his voice down and got right to the point.

"You're begging for trouble, my friend."

"So I left town. I came back, didn't I? It's to relieve the boredom, Conrad. Don't you get bored with New Lots? Same faces, same houses, same everything day in, day out?"

"You're breaking your parole."

"Fuck it."

"Shhhh. Keep it down. They'll haul you back to the city and clap you in jail. Don't think Howe's forgotten you, forgotten how you turned him down flat when he proposed you change sides. In your customary gracious manner."

"That's water long over the dam. Are you going to lecture me or are we going to enjoy our drink?"

"I worry, that's all."

"Don't, I can take care of myself."

"They're watching you, Ethan."

"They don't know I'm alive. Drink up. I got money this morning, I'll buy the next round."

Two nights later, late in the evening, emboldened by some fine Scotch and scaling the heights of frustration with his lot, he left town walking west and crossed over the river into the city. He did it again the next evening. Deciding that Conrad Worthy's qualms were without foundation, that even if he were to be picked up outside the New Lots nothing would result other than a warning, he went into the city in broad daylight. He had a drink at Fraunces Tavern, walked down Broome Street for a look at his old building, even wandered over to the Hudson to see the boats and muse on what might have been.

Early in the afternoon of Monday, August 25, Ethan was sitting in the Horseshoe with Toombs, Worthy, and three other parolees enjoying a late lunch of turkey salad, feeling good about himself for the first time in ages.

"I've been getting out of this boring wide place in the road and going into the city."

"No!" gasped Worthy. "For God sakes, man, keep your voice down!"

"I've been in half a dozen times, the last two in broad daylight."

"That's very foolish," said Toombs, shaking his head and assuming a grim expression. Others did the same.

Ethan laughed. "Nobody cares, boys. I can't seem to make Conrad here understand that. They couldn't care less if I crossed town and swam over to New Jersey. Howe doesn't know, and he wouldn't care if he did."

"I think you're being very foolish," said Worthy. "Especially since it's so unnecessary."

"That's where you're wrong. It's necessary. I credit my newfound wanderlust with keeping my sanity. Do you know I have a drink at Fraunces every time I go in, just for old times' sake?"

"You're being stupid," said Toombs.

"Why, because none of you has the guts to do it? You're the ones being stupid. I recommend it highly."

There was a disturbance at the door. Four redcoats had come in, muskets and all. Ethan and his friends watched a brief argument with a local, whom Ethan recognized as Jonas Brinker, his landlord's friend. They watched the soldiers let him leave. They came marching over, straight to Ethan's table.

"Colonel Ethan Allen?" asked a corporal, a slender, ungainly boy displaying an overly large Adam's apple.

"What do you want with him?" Ethan asked.

"Are you him?"

"Why?"

"I must ask you to come with us, sir."

"What for?"

"You're under arrest."

The word quieted every table. All eyes were directed at Ethan. He stared.

"What for?"

"Violation of parole," said the man beside the corporal who'd questioned him.

"Come along quietly," said the corporal.

Worthy got up to let Ethan pass. He and the others watched as the four redcoats surrounded him, shouldered their weapons, and marched him out.

63

★ **Captain** Given had grown a scruffy beard. He looked straight at Ethan and slowly onto his face came recognition.

"You. What in hell are you doing here?"

"Misunderstanding," said Ethan.

"He violated his parole," said the soldier beside him who had taken custody of him from the New Lots redcoats and who barely came up to Ethan's shoulder.

"Bullshit!" snorted Ethan. "All I did was go for a walk. Couple walks. To get some air. And here I am being treated like a goddamn escapee!"

"He left New Lots," said the soldier. "Violation article four, paragraph two."

"Oh, shut up . . . "

"Calm down," said Given.

The three of them stood in the lobby of the provost jail building, with the large holding cell still crammed with prisoners in front of them, opposite the main entrance to the building. The area swarmed with visitors. The majority of them looked as ragged and deprived as the inmates. Some people stopped to stare at Ethan. The sun's rays through the fanlight above the double doors felt good on his forehead. Being jailed didn't upset him as it would have earlier; he was past caring. And parole was a farce, putting temptation in his way as it had.

Captain Given was scratching his head and eyeing the tips of his boots as he pondered. "Where do we put you?"

"Not in that menagerie there. I'll catch my death of never-get-over."

"Upstairs." He called over a guard. "Matthew, take this one upstairs."

"Come along," said the guard, an old man with no teeth and deep wrinkles netting his grizzled cheeks. "Don't forget your bag."

"Good luck," said Given.

"Mmmm."

They started for the stairs.

"Matthew, how long do I get for busting parole?"

"Depends on who fills out the arrest report. They set your sentence. Could be six months, could be a year."

"When they see the name they'll make it two. How's the food?"

"The same. Bad."

"Why do I ask?"

They climbed the stairs, Matthew favoring the sides of his feet.

"I got weak feet. I hate climbing stairs, and it's all I do all day long."

Men only occupied the cell, which was smaller than the holding cell downstairs. Ethan counted about a dozen prisoners.

"Colonel Allen . . . "

James Lovell came to the bars. He was still wearing the same suit, considerably the worse for wear since the last time Ethan had seen it. On came his waxen smile.

"Hello, Lovell, what are you doing here?"

"They brought me down last fall. Why, I've no idea. Disappointing, I fancied they might release me when they let your boys out."

"Arbuthnot let 'em go?"

"Not too long after you left."

"That's wonderful! And a load off my mind."

"Off theirs too, I shouldn't wonder."

"Sarcastic as ever, aren't you?"

"Are you listening, boys? The pot's calling the kettle black."

Ethan grinned. Lovell was not one of his favorite people, but it was good to see him, if only for the fact that it didn't make *him* the last one to be released. They swapped stories of their adventures since they'd last seen each other.

"You know, Lovell . . . "

"You can call me James, unless it's painful."

"Whatever. I confess, I had you pegged wrong. I thought you were shoved in with us to spy."

"Would you believe I gathered that? Although I still don't know what I said to create the impression."

"We don't have to go into that. Anyway, I was dead wrong and I'm sorry. But I'm curious, the night we broke out where did they catch you?"

"The others headed for the docks. I headed north for Bedford Basin. Needless to say, I never got near there. I got picked up on Windsor Street. I tried to brazen my way out of it, but of course my accent gave me away."

"What accent?"

"I don't sound British, I don't sound Canadian. What does that signify to you?"

"You don't have to get nasty."

"Sorry. Just thinking about it infuriates me so. I came so close."

"You didn't come close at all. You just got through saying you never got near the basin."

"May I have your full attention? I've some good news. For me. I received this letter . . . "

He got out a letter, handing it to Ethan. It was from the Massachusetts Committee of Safety.

"I know this bunch, they sent Benedict Arnold to Ticonderoga to get underfoot. I wouldn't trust 'em as far as I could throw him."

"Read on, they've been working to get me released. Free and clear. No exchange."

"Good."

"See the last paragraph? Thursday, that's day after tomorrow."

Ethan handed back the letter.

"So it's hello and good-bye. Well, I can't begrudge you getting out, even though you don't deserve it as much as I do."

"They can't hold you forever."

"Mmmmm."

Supper was pork—only partially cooked—and beans so hard he suspected they hadn't been cooked at all. He lay on the floor with his bag for his pillow, a far cry from Van Wolk's feather bed, a far cry from New Lots, its comforts and conveniences, not to mention privacy. What a precious commodity it was when you no longer had it.

He stared at the ceiling. How long would they keep him here? How much longer before his release? Lovell would be gone in two days, lucky dog. Of course his was a different case entirely. He hadn't fought, hadn't even put on a uniform.

He thought about Ticonderoga, about St. John's, Chambly, and the wild, abrupt, unexpected end to his career. It all seemed a century ago. Now here he was, like the last apple clinging to its twig, aging, rotting, ignored.

"Nobody cares. Nobody in the whole world."

64

★ **General** Gentleman Johnny Burgoyne was the focus of attention in every drawing room he entered, the delight of the royal family, the envy of his military peers and the master of many a boudoir other than his own. Handsome, dashing, and spirited, he eloped with the daughter of the Earl of Derby. He wrote flowery prose, poetry, and drama, delivered flamboyant speeches in the House of Commons where he represented Midhurst, intrigued at court, gamed and gambled to all hours, and also managed to make time for a military career. During the Seven Years' War he led the sixteenth "Light Horse" in Portugal in the capture of Valencia de Alcántara and of Villa Velha.

Like his fellow generals responsible for bringing the colonies to heel, he had not seen combat in more than ten years. He saw this as no impediment to success. He had one outstanding trait of character that transcended many others, a burning desire to triumph, but only gloriously. Before Howe was done reaping his victories in Pennsylvania, Burgoyne's campaign to conquer the northern colonies was already underway. It began on a lovely day in mid-June with the general's flotilla departing Canada to the accompaniment of four bands and a cheering citizenry. The vessels reached Lake Champlain and sailed grandly up between the lofty, rugged Adirondacks and the Green Mountains of the Grants. Five hundred colorfully painted and befeathered Indians led the way in slender birch-bark canoes. Six hundred fifty Canadians and Loyalists followed. Next came six thousand regulars, half of them Hessians led by Major General Baron von Riedesel, a superb soldier with a wealth of combat experience, despite being only thirty-eight, seventeen years younger than his commander.

With it, the flotilla brought a hundred thirty-eight artillery pieces, hundreds of two-wheeled baggage carts (more than thirty filled with Burgoyne's wardrobe, the handiwork of the finest tailors in Europe), and a thousand bottles of champagne. Women, children, sutlers, and dogs helped crowd the decks of every vessel.

The American Northern Department could not have been weaker or more faction-riddled. Chief among its difficulties was that Congress could not decide on command. General Philip Schuyler and General Horatio Gates had both been picked to lead the defense. Two more adversarial individuals could not have been selected. To add to the problem, their respective jurisdictions had not been properly designated. Despising one another as they did, they rarely conversed, and when they couldn't avoid doing so it usually ended in argument. Schuyler, long since recovered from the infirmities that had excused him from action on the Richelieu, was, for all his pomposity and overbearing nature, a selfless and dedicated Patriot. But he was wealthy, educated, and a snob, not accomplishments or a quality calculated to endear him to the New England farmers who made up most of the northern army. He was also a Yorker and Dutch, a patroon, not American as defined by New Englanders. Fed up with Gates, with the situation, with the enmity of his men, eager to resign, he was possibly the worst choice to rally the northern colonies against Burgoyne.

But pride and a praiseworthy sense of honor encouraged him to stick it out, as he had during the St. John's and Chambly campaign. He resolved to hold Fort Ticonderoga for its symbolic value as well as its worth as an obstacle to Burgoyne. The garrison of three thousand poorly armed Patriots had recently failed in an attempt to secure Mount Defiance, which commanded the route to the southwest, so Schuyler was left with more hope than faith in his men's ability to mount a successful defense against the approaching enemy.

Adding to the general's mental burdens was the death of Richard Montgomery in the failed attempt to capture Quebec. Had Schuyler himself been in good health at the time he would have led the assault. Whether he would have suffered the same fate as Montgomery or not was immaterial to him; not being present was all that mattered. He took Montgomery's death onto his conscience and kept it there.

His field commander at Ticonderoga was an able ex-British brigadier general, Arthur St. Clair. St. Clair hoped that Burgoyne would stage a frontal assault on the fort, emulating Howe's blunder at Bunker Hill. But on July 5, when Burgoyne arrived in the vicinity and ordered heavy ordnance placed at the summit of Mount Defiance, St. Clair's hope went up in his pipe smoke, leaving him no option but to evacuate. His troops had suffered through a harsh winter without sufficient supplies, clothing, or medicine, morale was desperately low and the prospect of facing six thousand seasoned redcoats haunted every man's thoughts.

The year before the Americans had blundered badly in their preparations, mainly in their engineering. They had fortified Mount Independence, a hill across the lake, and built a bridge connecting it to the fort. Then Schuyler and Gates, in rare agreement, decided that Sugar Hill, closer to the fort, was inaccessible, and did not bother to mount a single battery there. When Burgoyne's commander of engineers, preceding the invasion force, reconnoitered the hill he promptly ordered the mounting of batteries of twenty-four-pounders and eight-inch howitzers positioned to deliver fire into every angle of the fort.

On July 6, much to Schuyler's and Gates's consternation, St. Clair wisely evacuated Ticonderoga, loading his few boats with stores and sending them uplake to Skenesboro.

With Ticonderoga in hand, Burgoyne now controlled the passage to Lake George.

The Patriots fell back. A rear-guard action at Hubbardton, east of Ticonderoga in the Grants, resulted in an American defeat. Colonel Seth Warner's detachment was routed.

However, the British suffered heavy losses. Burgoyne assembled his army at Skenesboro and prepared to pursue the Americans, who were retreating through the dense woods of pine, spruce, and sycamore laced with innumerable streams and embracing great stretches of treacherous marshland. Burgoyne headed toward Fort Edward. Between Skenesboro and his objective were forty bridges, which the Americans systematically destroyed. They also felled trees across the narrow road and rolled up boulders to further impede their pursuers.

It was at this point that Burgoyne made a questionable decision. Things were going so well he decided there was no need to rush to Albany, some seventy miles away. But it was immediately after the skirmish between St. Clair's rear guard and a force of Hessians and redcoats at Hubbardton that Burgoyne made his biggest mistake. At Skenesboro, where he destroyed the supplies sent down from Ticonderoga earlier by St. Clair, he decided to press on overland rather than return to Ticonderoga to advance by way of Lake George, his original plan. His decision might have made sense had he sent a column ahead to capture Fort Edward. This would have been a telling blow to the already dispirited Americans and could well have opened the way to overrun the area all the way to Albany. Instead, he decided to keep his force intact.

Meanwhile the retreating Americans continued to destroy bridges in their wake, fell trees, roll up obstructing boulders, even filling Wood Creek with boulders, causing it to overflow onto the road the British were building to bring up their supplies and equipment. Schuyler's tactics, Burgoyne's lethargy, poor planning, and his vast burden of useless paraphernalia (including his wardrobe and champagne) combined to drastically slow the British advance from Skenesboro to Fort Edward. It took the invaders twenty-four days to travel the twenty-three miles separating the two sites. Burgoyne's scouts informed him that Schuyler had meanwhile retreated across the Hudson, moving southward to Stillwater, roughly parallel to Bennington, to the east.

Civilians fled before the British advance, deserting their farms, driving wagons bulging with belongings and bringing along their simmering hatred for the Mother Country. Disdaining officers' orders, Burgoyne's Indian allies scattered in advance of his army, falling upon the fleeing inhabitants, scalping and massacring them by the hundreds. Though informed of these atrocities, Burgoyne took no action for fear that the Indians would desert him.

His troubles increased. Engaging, even finding his enemy in the woods, was difficult enough, but Schuyler's evasive tactics and the obstructions he placed in Burgoyne's way gradually turned the glorious invasion force that had floated so grandly up Lake Champlain into a plodding, dispirited, and frustrated lot. Gentleman Johnny remained blissfully indifferent to the situation. He developed a fondness for snake meat, and he sang and drank and cavorted and amused himself nightly with his mistress, the wife of a commissary. Together, they consumed champagne by the gallon.

As Schuyler and St. Clair hoped and expected, Burgoyne's supply and transport problems finally bogged him down almost completely. He made a startling announcement to his officers. Wary of their surroundings and the difficulties in finding food and forage, he would not cross the Hudson and move down to Albany before collecting sufficient provisions for one month. He was also short of horses needed to bring up his artillery. He rejected Riedesel's suggestion that they abandon at least half the guns, to bring up later in the campaign when needed. Instead, Burgoyne ordered fifty-two cannons collected and sent out on a foraging expedition to round up food and horses.

It was a decision that astonished his officers, but no one saw fit to question it. He blithely sent off a report to Lord Germain, Minister of War, the same Lord Germain who had been court-martialed and dismissed from the army for cowardice at Minden, in Germany, in 1759 and was now in command of the overseas armies of the Empire. To Germain, Burgoyne crowed that he would lead his men into Albany before the end of August, as planned. Nothing rattled his confidence, no setback, no disaster, not Schuyler's tactics or elusiveness, not his own losses so far, not obstacles placed in his way, not even the fields burnt by fleeing colonials leaving not so much as a blade of grass for his horses.

But while he bragged and oozed optimism, the civilian population around him formed into a force of irregulars, the like of which no nation in Europe had ever seen take the field. Unlike Ethan Allen and his Green Mountain Boys, Patriots in general were hesitant to serve any great distance from their homes for the three years Congress required. But the men whom Burgoyne called "hoe wielders and manure shovelers" had no reluctance over protecting their farms and towns. Gentleman Johnny's turtle pace gave them ample time to organize and arm.

Burgoyne first became aware of what was going on around him when he assigned a Hessian lieutenant colonel to raid Bennington and capture sorely needed food and horses. He wanted to get rid of the slow, two-wheeled Canadian carts so that he could move faster. Under Lieutenant Colonel Friedrich Baum, who spoke no English, he sent Loyalists, Canadians, and Indians, along with a few grenadiers, light infantry, and a horseless dragoon regiment, eight hundred men, on the raid. General John Stark, who had seen service in the French and Indian War and had distinguished himself at Bunker Hill and Trenton, assembled the militia from Bennington and the surrounding farms and villages. Astutely, knowing the enemy was in the vicinity, days earlier he had sent out a call for assistance to Seth Warner, then at Manchester resting and recruiting troops who had fought at Hubbardton.

The populace girded for battle. Dishes, plates, and silverware were melted into musket balls. On August 16, Stark's militia surrounded the enemy. Baum's Hessians fought bravely after his Loyalists, Canadians, and Indians quit the field. The raider's ammunition ran out just before twilight. Baum was killed.

Victory theirs, the militia broke ranks to loot the dead and plunder the German baggage train. Stark was unprepared for action when Lieutenant Colonel Heinrich von Breymann appeared with nearly eight hundred fresh troops. In disarray, the Americans gave way. In the middle of the night Seth Warner arrived with his men. Von Breymann was driven off with heavy losses. The Americans pursued the Germans far into the night. Von Breymann managed to escape and inform Burgoyne of the bad news. Nine hundred of the invaders were lost at Bennington.

Burgoyne was as unaccustomed to defeat as he was to the alien environment in which he was being forced to do battle. The losses he'd incurred were serious since General Carleton, in Canada, failed, as promised, to provide him men to garrison Ticonderoga, permitting Burgoyne's own troops to rejoin the main force.

Major General Benjamin Lincoln of Massachusetts was sent by Washington and Congress to rally General Stark's victorious militia in Bennington, and within days they succeeded in severing Burgoyne's communications with Ticonderoga and Canada. Storm clouds were gathering over Gentleman Johnny's head. The Americans' ranks were swelling daily. Burgoyne still had little grasp of what he was up against. Fighting in dense woods was new to him, fighting an enemy that fought back from behind trees, walls, and rocks, who sneaked into his camp and burned or blew up his supplies, who used the terrain to its advantage, even used the weather and tactics found in no manual of war to harass him. In all, it was becoming more than he could deal with. Wherever he moved, militia numbering three and four thousand mysteriously materialized within hours, thwarting him and inflicting casualties at a steady rate.

He was an intelligent, capable, and courageous general, but not a great one. His vanity dimmed his objectivity and clouded his perception of reality. But victory was all to him. To Riedesel he confided that it was his reason for being. He'd enjoyed it many times before, he would enjoy it here in the wilds of North America: victory over the traitorous ragtag and bobtail farmers who brazenly called themselves Patriots.

After Bennington, he waited nearly a month while he assembled the necessary supplies for an advance on Albany. Meanwhile the Americans had come under the command of Colonel Thaddeus Kosciuszko, a Polish nobleman who had volunteered his services to the cause of Independence. Kosciuszko fortified Bemis Heights about five hundred yards from the Hudson. Dependent upon the river for his transport, Burgoyne had no choice but to neutralize the position before he could advance on Albany.

On September 13 he crossed the river to the west bank above Saratoga. This, he assured Riedesel and his other officers, would be the final phase of the long march to Albany. For six days it rained as his weary troops moved slowly southward. Burgoyne had no information as to where the Americans were or how strong they were.

On September 19 Burgoyne attacked Bemis Heights. Riedesel commanded his left column, Simon Fraser, his right column, and Burgoyne himself commanded the center. A deep, marshy ravine, rendered even more difficult to pass through by the steady rains, made attack on the Heights impossible. Burgoyne bypassed the head of the ravine and prepared to assault what he discovered to be an unoccupied position. Benedict Arnold, commanding the American left, had managed to persuade Gates to allow him to attack the British on the level ground. He sent Colonel Daniel Morgan with his Rangers against Fraser, soon following with his entire force. A bloody battle between Arnold and Burgoyne's and Fraser's columns ensued. Morgan's crack riflemen fought magnificently.

Arnold saw his chance to crush Burgoyne then and there and asked Gates for reinforcements. Fearing he would expose his camp, the general refused to send them. Losses mounted on both sides as the fighting went on. Late in the afternoon Riedesel approached Arnold's right flank and drove the Americans back. The following day Burgoyne established camp a mile north of the American position.

Thanks to Gates's timidity, the British could claim victory.

On September 15, two weeks after he planned to enter Albany in triumph, Burgoyne crossed the Hudson on a chain of hastily built rafts. In peaceful times, Burgoyne had gambled, winning and losing huge sums. Now he would gamble again. The stake, His Majesty's rebellious colonies in the north. He would win as Howe had won in New York and Pennsylvania. With St. Leger, coming from Oswego, they would close the trap and end the Revolution.

65

SEPTEMBER 1777

★ **Fresh** regiments poured in, adding to the ranks of defenders. Schuyler, despite his successful delaying tactics, had long since given over command to General Horatio Gates. The formal change was made three days after von Breymann escaped the Battle of Bennington. The Virginian was surprisingly popular in New England, and the aristocratic Schuyler, for all his successes, was still a despised Yorker and Dutch, and not to be altogether trusted in command of Yankee militia.

Gates, of medium height, ruddy complexion, with hooded eyes and scarce graying hair, looked nothing like a general. On the battlefield it could be said that his actions, rather lack of action, confirmed the first glance assumption. He was an able administrator, conscientious, ambitious, opportunistic. His faults aside he was a kindly, caring man and pleasant. Finding himself in command without competition, he sat down and carefully analyzed Burgoyne's progress and lack of it so far. Gentleman Johnny at the gaming table of war appeared to be succumbing to recklessness. Burgoyne now had fewer than half the troops he'd started out with, and yet he persisted in risking men in sporadic assaults rather than engaging in full-scale battle. None of his recent setbacks seemed to faze him. Morgan's Rangers and squads of Patriot marksmen sent his scouts fleeing and cowed his Indians so thoroughly that most of them deserted. Still, he blundered forward through the woods, his objective: Albany, the seat and source of victory.

On September 19, with no idea as to Gates's whereabouts, Burgoyne impulsively initiated battle. It started out a fiasco. While the capable Riedesel sat unutilized—guarding supplies and equipment on the river trail—Fraser, at the head of a second column, managed to get lost in the woods. Burgoyne, leading eleven hundred men, crossed a dry ravine with great difficulty toward Gates's center. He halted his men in a clearing where militia riflemen, reinforced by Benedict Arnold's regiments from the American right wing, promptly opened fire from the concealment of trees and underbrush. Each time the Americans pushed the enemy back, they themselves were pushed back by bayonet counterattacks. British officers fell by the score. It was only the onset of darkness and the arrival of Riedesel's troops that saved Burgoyne from annihilation. He counted six hundred casualties. The Americans lost slightly more than three hundred.

Two days of inactivity passed while both sides tended to their wounded and buried the dead. Burgoyne was preparing for a second try at Gates's militia when word arrived from General Henry Clinton, who had promised to deliver reinforcements to the invaders.

Clinton's message was to the point and most upsetting. He could provide no reinforcements. Undaunted, Burgoyne sent back word that Gates's troops outnumbered his two to one, that he was perilously low on supplies and ammunition, and that he awaited Clinton's orders.

His wording confirmed that he had begun seeking a way out of his dilemma. Failure to receive the promised reinforcements might not extricate him but, as one of his officers put it, "it was a step toward protecting his arse." Clinton's response was to send Major General John Vaughan north leading two thousand men. As Vaughan made his way up the Hudson, sight of American militia watching him from both banks so discouraged him he turned around and went back to New York.

Time was running out for Burgoyne, but he refused to believe it. For sixteen days he kept up his hopes and expectations for relief that was never to come. Gates waited. Militia continued to pour into his camp.

On October 5, Riedesel and Fraser approached Burgoyne, urging him to retreat. Burgoyne finished his last bottle of champagne, tossed it away, and refused. He would take Albany or die in the attempt. On October 7 he set out to place artillery on an elevation on the American left. In searching, he led fifteen hundred men into a wheat field. His scouting report was in error—the hill didn't exist. Gates attacked Burgoyne's flanks. Within minutes, Burgoyne's wings were decimated. But his center, led by Riedesel, held its ground until reinforcements arrived to cover his retreat.

The Americans attacked the British reserves. Arnold, who had been stripped of his command after a bitter argument with Gates, rode recklessly into the fight. Though wounded, he managed to take Burgoyne's far right redoubt and expose the enemy's entire line of defense.

The next day, with no options left for him, Burgoyne began to withdraw to the village of Saratoga. Gates hurried three columns forward to cover the British right and rear. At the same time, a large force of militia on the east bank prevented Burgoyne from crossing the Hudson.

His badly beaten force was surrounded. Day and night a relentless barrage from muskets and cannon poured in on him. As the Americans closed in, a flag of truce was raised. Burgoyne approached Gates to negotiate.

For nearly a week they haggled, but on October 17 Burgoyne signed Gates's agreement, permitting what remained of his army to sail to England on the proviso that neither he nor his men would serve further in North America.

For the Americans, Saratoga was a resounding victory, one that clearly signaled what was to come.

66

★ **James** Lovell was released from the provost jail. They came for him Thursday morning. He walked out beaming, his fellow prisoners looking on enviously. Ethan wasn't envious.

"Lucky you, James. Congratulations. Do me a favor, mail these six letters for me."

"Happy to. Good-bye, Ethan, and don't give up hope. It could happen for you. You could be out of this glorious place this afternoon. Tell you what, when I get back to Boston I'll check around, find out what they're doing for you."

"I don't know, James, I guess it's not all that hard to forget about somebody when they're stuck away this long. Out of sight, out of mind."

"Ira hasn't forgotten you, and you can bet he's keeping you fresh in other people's minds."

"Mmmmm. I just wonder how I'm doing in Washington's conscience. And Hancock's, and Trumbull's."

They shook hands. Lovell impulsively bear-hugged him. Then he waved and headed for the stairs with the two men who'd come for him. His step was jaunty, his chin high. Ethan half-expected that in the next moment he would break into a brief dance in celebration. The prisoners cheered him, wished him luck. All three disappeared around the corner.

Ethan went back to his six-month-old copy of the *New York Mercury,* rereading for the third time the lengthy article on Burgoyne's failure at Saratoga. Major General Benedict Arnold came out of it a hero, as usual. Still, the American victory was a great, good sign. With Washington's success at Trenton and other victories the tide now appeared to be turning. Other good signs were appearing. The Empire was beginning to show cracks. The rumor about the city was that Germain had taken to sharply criticizing both Howes. He signaled out the general for not cracking down hard enough on the rebellion. He also accused him of being too liberal in issuing pardons. And Admiral Howe appeared reluctant to attack rebel coastal installations and seemed willing to permit American ships to ply up and down the Atlantic with impunity. All of which infuriated Germain.

Ethan knew that both Howes were Whigs. Neither had favored the war at the outset, preferring to at least attempt to settle matters without bloodshed. But as loyal Englishmen, when war began they didn't hesitate to serve.

James Lovell's optimistic parting words, that Ethan could be out of there that afternoon, proved well off the mark.

Ethan remained in the provost jail from August, 1777, well into the following year. He continued to write letters, continued to receive money from Ira and others. He was reasonably well treated, particularly by Captain Given, though he couldn't escape the feeling that the prime of his life was running down the drain.

Meanwhile the British were beginning to falter. Rumors began circulating that France would come into the war on the Americans' side. It was known that Benjamin Franklin had been working feverishly to persuade Paris to ally with the colonies. Which meant that the war could end within weeks, and all prisoners would be liberated. The British were known to be weary of fighting and disheartened at the drain on their economy. The Royal treasury was badly depleted, the Crown was behind in its payments for Hessian mercenaries. The Landgrave of Hesse-Cassel alone had already received the equivalent of five million dollars. The House of Commons now included a majority voicing disapproval of continuing hostilities.

March 3 was a Tuesday. It had snowed all day Sunday. When the temperature rose early Monday morning, the streets of lower Manhattan turned into a sea of slush. That night the temperature plunged. By morning the entire island was armored in ice. The cell was frigid, the shivering prisoners even more dejected than usual, and grumbling without letup. Ethan was depressed.

Shortly after eleven a.m. a man in an ill-fitting wool overcoat and a scarf whose ends trailed to his knees approached the cell. He carried a briefcase. Matthew followed him, walking awkwardly on the sides of his aching feet, his key ring jangling against his britches' pocket.

"Ethan Allen?" asked the stranger: tall, heavy-set, in his twenties. Despite his looking like a clerk Ethan sensed he was a lawyer. "My name is Chapman. I'm here to inform you that you're to be released."

67

MARCH 1778

★ **Ethan** heard the words clearly, the last one leaping into his consciousness. It was like pebbles dropping, with the last one turning out to be a diamond. His face must have registered his shock because Chapman smiled toothily.

"Did you hear me?"

"You're kidding . . . "

"Guard?"

Matthew stepped gingerly forward, wincing as he came. "He give Captain Given the proper papers downstairs, Ethan." Other prisoners were suddenly crowding behind him. Matthew unlocked the door and held it. "Come on. Don't forget your bag."

The others cheered as he hoisted his bag over his shoulder, stepped out, turned, and grinned. "Do you boys believe this? Somebody pinch me!"

"It's all arranged," said Chapman. "You're to be exchanged for a Lieutenant Colonel Archibald Campbell. Come along."

"Gladly. Happily! Good-bye, one and all!"

He threw back his head roaring in triumph.

He'd won!

It had taken ten years crammed into three, but he'd finally won. Tears rolled down his cheeks. His heart sang lustily as he followed Chapman and Matthew down the stairs. Outside, he turned for one final look at his prison. Given was in his office window.

"That's a good soul," he said to Chapman. "Would you believe he was a vice president in a bank in Liverpool? Joined the army because his wife was crazy about uniforms? And he's crazy about her. You're looking at the most homesick man in America."

Given waved, Ethan returned it. He started off up the street.

"Wait, wait," said Chapman. "This way, we have to go down to the Battery. There's a procedure that has to be followed."

Chapman explained that he would be rowed out to a sloop in the harbor to remain on board until the formal exchange of prisoners. They walked south to the water. It was freezing out and treacherous underfoot. The wind whipping the panels of his coat, Chapman pointed out into the harbor. The sloop was the *Eloise,* a trim little craft in need of scraping. A rowboat waited. Minutes later Ethan followed Chapman up the Jacob's ladder and was warmly welcomed by the captain and his officers.

He bathed, shaved, and was given a new suit to replace his two well-worn broad-cloth suits. He ate lunch with the officers. Captain Bellows inquired about his confinement. Ethan swallowed a mouthful of beef salad and downed half a glass of wine and, ignoring his napkin in its ring, wiped his mouth with his sleeve.

"Which confinement? I've been confined on six ships, counting the trip down the St. Lawrence, and in three jails on dry land."

"How was it going over and coming back from England?" asked the first officer.

"Rotten. They were the two worst captains. The worst was Montague on the *Mercury*, that took us up to Halifax. Most sadistic bastard I've ever run into. As bad as General Prescott up in Montreal. Montague wanted to hang me then and there. Captain Symonds on the *Solebay* too. Willie Hales at Pendennis Castle flogged me. His cruelty I'll carry on my back till the grave. Captain Hosea Smith on the *Lark* was a prince. He brought me down from Halifax. I never got better treatment until here and now. Can I have some more wine?"

"Tell us about Montreal," said another officer. "Everyone's heard all sorts of versions, what really happened?"

Ethan cleared his throat dramatically. Bellows and the others leaned forward.

"It was a foul night, raining pitchforks. Men had been deserting me left and right since we crossed the St. Lawrence. I was left with about forty. We assembled a couple miles from the Quebec Gate and were preparing to march out when we suddenly found ourselves surrounded. All Prescott's regulars, every able-bodied man in town had turned out. Hundreds."

"Somebody betrayed you," said Bellows.

"Somebody? Everybody. I recognized at least a dozen, maybe twenty of the men who'd deserted us earlier. All French

Canadians. I developed a theory about that, that they only joined us *to* desert. We were doomed from the start."

"You don't think that attempting to take a town that size with only forty men wasn't . . . reckless?" asked the first officer.

"Nothing reckless about it. It was planned down to the minute we were to march out. If I'd enlisted honorable men, reliable men, we could have taken that place with a squad, probably without firing a shot. The same way I took Fort Ticonderoga. This wine is excellent. Is there any more?"

He ate too much lunch, too much dinner, and spent most of the night out in the bitter cold draped over the railing. But in the morning he felt fine and put on his new suit to greet Elias Boudinot, the American commissary of prisoners. It wasn't until just before Boudinot stepped on board with Lieutenant Colonel Campbell and two other men that Ethan learned from Captain Bellows who was responsible for his freedom. They stood by the Jacob's ladder watching Boudinot and Campbell's boat approach.

"I wonder who I'm supposed to thank for this," murmured Ethan.

"I understand that it came about after long negotiations between General Washington and the British North American Command."

"George. I knew it!"

"Your Continental Congress ordered the general to push for your release. A pity it took so long."

"Which wasn't his fault I'll bet."

"On the contrary, I've heard the reason was because George Washington was quite insolent in his dealings with General Howe."

"That's hard to believe. George is a gentleman. Howe's just thin-skinned, that's all. I should know, he was the one who had me thrown in jail."

Boudinot, Campbell, and the others ascended the ladder. Boudinot shook his hand warmly. Campbell eyed him disdainfully. Ethan returned the expression in kind. He was not about to get into a sniping match. Within the hour would come the end of it, of three years of detention, humiliation, dashed hopes, and cruelty. Why jeopardize the exchange? And why embarrass Captain Bellows, who'd treated him so hospitably?

"Colonel Allen, Lieutenant Colonel Campbell," said Boudinot.

They shook hands. Campbell's was moist, slightly sticky. Bellows let them use his cabin, hospitably offering a bottle of wine to toast the occasion. Papers were read and signed. The exchange took less than fifteen minutes. When they were done they returned to the deck. Bellows congratulated both men.

"Good luck, gentlemen. It's been a pleasure, Colonel Allen." Campbell sniffed and made the face he seemed to favor every time he looked Ethan's way. Bellows looked toward him. "Sir?"

"You keep calling him Colonel."

"His rank . . . "

"His rank, indeed."

Boudinot took a step forward. He was of average height and almost painfully thin. He exuded the energy of a terrier. He couldn't keep his hands still. "Gentlemen, gentlemen, we're all done here. Everything went off smoothly. Let's not say things we'll be sorry for."

Ethan grinned at Campbell. He had kept his eyes on him all through the interchange between him and the captain and during Boudinot's plea.

"I haven't said a word. Although I do have a question for the lieutenant colonel. I was captured at Montreal. Where were you?"

"Trenton."

"Trenton. Washington kicked Howe's arse there, didn't he?"

"Colonel, please . . . " said Boudinot.

"Just an observation."

Most satisfying, getting it off his chest. He and Campbell sat in opposite ends of the boat on the way to shore. Boudinot sat beside Ethan in the stern.

"If you don't mind my asking, Ethan, what really happened at Montreal?"

"Montreal. That night opened the sack and let out all these snakes. My life in captivity. I could write a book. Anyway, it was a foul night, raining pitchforks . . . "

68

DECEMBER 1778

★ **During** his time on parole in New Lots, Ethan had restored his lost weight and health with good food, fresh air, and exercise, including his long walks to the city. But in the provost jail his health declined, and he again lost weight, almost twenty-five pounds by the time he was released.

Deposited in the Battery a free man he first considered heading north to return home. Then changed his mind, deciding to journey in the opposite direction. He purchased a horse at the stable Lieutenant Walter Dunbar had recommended at the time of his escape attempt. He crossed over to New Jersey by boat and made his way through a snowstorm to Elizabethtown. From there, he rode out of the storm and turned south toward Pennsylvania.

An abandoned forge at the side of Valley Creek, which flowed north from the Schuylkill River gave the area its name. The land rose sharply from the creek to an uneven plateau about two miles long and slightly more than half that distance in width. Along the south edge of the elevation an irregular line of trenches had been dug in the frozen ground, as well as an abatis, which ran roughly north and south. Redans and redoubts had been constructed. Huts, each one housing twelve men, had been raised. They were crude affairs. The frigid wind whistled through cracks, and the fireplaces filled them with smoke at all hours. However, they did afford warmth and protection from snow and sleet.

The nine thousand men who had staggered the thirteen miles from Whitemarsh to Valley Forge were in pitiable condition. Half had no trousers or shoes. Many were without blankets. Nearly a quarter of them who had arrived on December 19 of the previous year, leaving bloodied footprints in the snow, were unfit for even the lightest duty. The commissariat was no longer functioning, nor was the quartermaster's department. Ironically, hogsheads of shoes, stockings, and other clothing lay about near the roads and in the woods in the area but could not be brought into camp due to a lack of horses and vehicles.

The shortage of clothing was calamitous, and the lack of food and the resulting gradual starvation became more than flesh and blood could tolerate as the harshest winter in years wore on. Men went without meat and bread for days.

Less than two weeks after arriving, Washington informed Congress that he had a mutiny on his hands. Not a single steer remained to be slaughtered. Only twenty-five barrels of flour were still available to make bread for nine thousand men. Salted pork and beef were so scarce men took to fighting over mere scraps.

Then, late in December, like manna falling from the sky, ninety barrels of salted herring arrived. Within ten minutes Washington found himself with a near-riot on his hands. The men had to be forcibly restrained from breaking open the barrels with their bayonets. Order was finally restored, they were lined up with their mess kits, and officers, themselves as famished as the men, began opening the barrels. The men cheered lustily as the top was pried from the first one. But out of the barrel rose a putrid stench. The herring had spoiled. Every barrel yielded the same results. One by one, opened and unopened barrels were rolled into a pile and set on fire. The stench was overpowering as officers and men stood watching their hope for their first decent meal since arriving go up in smoke.

Then, over the protests of the officers, the men slaughtered the horses that had brought in the two wagonloads. And ate the roasted flesh to the bone.

The next morning it was announced that henceforth the diet would be restricted to cakes made from flour-and-water paste baked on hot stones. Fire-cake and water became breakfast, dinner, and supper throughout camp.

There was even a shortage of water. It had to be carried in buckets from Valley Creek and the Schuylkill. Some of the men drank melted snow. Then typhus and smallpox struck. No medicine was available, there was no means of treating either affliction, and without adequate food the stricken found it impossible to fight off any illness.

Foraging parties searched endlessly for food in the area. The redoubtable General Anthony Wayne, leading a Pennsylvania brigade, captured cattle in nearby New Jersey. Major Light-Horse Harry Lee marched to Delaware and found cattle that were being fattened for the British. Captain Allen McLane cut off enemy expeditions and seized their cattle in areas around Philadelphia.

Despite their and others' efforts, as January gave way to February conditions worsened. Men and horses starved to death, five hundred of the latter. Impossible to bury in the frozen ground, their carcasses lay about rotting, further endangering the health of the men.

Luckily, before the entire army starved to death, Major General Nathanael Greene was appointed quartermaster general and with Commissary General Jeremiah Wadsworth set out to improve conditions. Between them they managed to find transportation to bring in foodstuffs, clothing, and even medicine.

Washington was in his headquarters, a large stone house at the western end of camp, when his orderly entered. The general returned his salute, the man stamping his feet and whipping himself with his arms.

"Sir, a civilian is coming in."

Holding the door against the wind, the commander in chief peered up the road. Astride a black-and-white stallion was a large-framed man in a long blue coat with a Patriot tricorn. As he drew closer, Washington could see that despite his imposing physique he looked haggard, his skin sallow, his eyes sunken with suffering. Up came a burly hand in a wave. Leather lungs projected loudly, "General!"

"Who . . . ?" began Washington.

"I don't recognize him, sir."

The stranger broke into a gallop and came swiftly up. He dismounted. He saluted.

"Colonel Ethan Allen reporting for duty!"

69

★ **Nathanael** Greene was becoming slightly jowly despite being only forty-six. Like his commander in chief he was clean-shaven. He was passably handsome; he was a superior general, having fought with distinction at Brandywine, Germantown, and elsewhere. Washington admired, respected, and liked him, and frequently used him as a sounding board in evaluating some of his less capable generals, an onerous but necessary task. The discussion at the moment, however, revolved around a certain colonel. Greene sat in Washington's chair while the general paced. The problem at hand carved deep lines in his forehead and brought worry into his penetrating blue-gray eyes. He ran a hand over his dark-brown hair back to his queue, as if to make sure it was still in place.

Greene chuckled. "You got him out, now here he is on your doorstep."

"I never dreamed he'd come down here. Why didn't he go home to his family?"

"He's been out of action a long time. He's hungry for shot and shell."

Washington shook his head. "What do I do with him?"

"He obviously expects you to take him in, give him a regiment. He *is* a colonel."

"Not really, he's never actually been commissioned. He's not a soldier, none of the Green Mountain Boys were."

"He's very grateful to you for getting him out."

"It took me long enough. I do admire him, Nat. He's quite original, there's a good deal to admire. He's been treated shamefully for three years, and he comes riding up all smiles, not a syllable of complaint, as enthusiastic as ever. And he must have some leadership qualities, how else would he have taken Ticonderoga? Now he wants a colonelcy and a saber."

"I don't see what the problem is, give them to him."

Again Washington shook his head and resumed pacing, his hands joined behind his back. "I don't know. Philip Schuyler insists he's a wild man. John Hancock agrees. Others too. He certainly went wild at Montreal. I've never seen such rashness. He has absolutely no sense of discipline. He'd probably go hog wild under fire. Oh, not that he's not brave, loyal, zealous . . ."

"Maybe he's changed since Montreal. Three years is a long time. And captivity does make a man reflect."

"But *has* he changed? Can we rely on him to behave responsibly in a command? Or do we turn him loose and watch him go out and try to beat the British all by himself?"

"Aren't you exaggerating?"

"I may be understating it . . ."

"So, you don't have to make him a colonel. What about a captaincy?"

"I couldn't do that. It'd be demoting him, a slap in the face.

After what he's done? After all he's been through? Why didn't he go home to Bennington?"

"So what will you do?"

Washington turned to pushing the center of his forehead with his index finger, as if to make a hole through which an idea might pass on into his brain. Slowly his serious expression began to dissolve. His eyes lit up.

"Must I be the one to decide? Go get him, Nat. He's probably with Anthony Wayne. They're cut from the same bolt, and Ethan's more or less gravitated to him. Hurry, I've an idea."

Greene brought Ethan back immediately. Washington set a chair for him.

"Ethan, now that you're a free man, what would you like to do?"

"I told you, General, join up. I've missed the whole war."

"Join up. Of course. Now then, your colonelcy was given you by your friends and neighbors, to lead the Green Mountain Boys."

"That's right, sir."

"Which you did superbly. What you want now is the same rank commissioned by Congress. The Congress commissioned me, General Greene, all of us. They'll commission you. But you'll have to make formal application. You must write to President Laurens."

"Hancock."

"Henry Laurens of South Carolina is president of Congress now. Tell him about yourself. Remind him of Ticonderoga, St. John's, Chambly. Request a commission. I myself will write in support of your application."

"Would you?"

"Gladly."

Ethan beamed. "I'd appreciate that!" He jumped up, seized Washington's hand, and pumped it vigorously, bringing a faint smile to the commander in chief's face. Greene lowered his face into his fist to hide his own smile.

"Together we'll do what we can to get you a full colonelcy. Pay, perquisites, all you're entitled to."

"How long will it take?"

"No more than a few days."

"Then I join you. Back into the war at last. Get back to licking Howe's arse!"

"Licking . . . ?" Greene asked. He grimaced and shuddered in amusement.

"General Howe's no longer British commander in chief," said Washington. "He resigned last month. Major General Sir Henry Clinton is now in charge. Ethan, I'll write that letter right away. I suggest you do the same. I've a courier leaving for Philadelphia at sundown. Let's get our letters into his pouch."

"Thank you, General, thank you, thank you!"

Ethan pulled himself up to his full height and executed a sharp salute. Washington returned it. Ethan spun about and made for the door. The general moved quickly and opened it for him. Out he marched. Washington leaned against the closed door. Greene smirked.

"Don't, Nat. Don't make fun of him. If we had a hundred more with his grit, his dedication, his resourcefulness, his . . . "

"Fanaticism?"

"Zeal. We'd all breathe easier. God bless him. And God forgive me for behaving so hypocritically."

"What?"

"For pushing this off on Philadelphia when I should be deciding myself. Hypocritical. I just didn't think I could find the words to explain my . . . reservations. And to overlook them would have been dishonest. Poor man, sometimes this job gets very difficult. Now, Nat, if you'll excuse me I've a letter to compose."

70

★ **A** prolonged thaw, unexpected but most welcome, found Valley Forge. Just as welcome was sight of a number of the ill, having recovered from the "putrid fever," as typhus was called, straggling back from the hospitals in the vicinity. A large hospital had been established at nearby Yellow Springs. Thirteen hundred cases of typhus and smallpox were under treatment. The Adventist Sisters at Ephrata had taken in as many men as they had room for, as had the Moravian Brothers at Bethlehem. The major problem was that every facility in the area was already crowded with the sick and wounded from the battlefields of Brandywine and Germantown.

Some patients had to be lodged in tents. Many straw beds were used by successive individuals without the straw being replaced. Typhus cases arrived in rags, swarming with vermin. The deadly fever became an epidemic. At Lititz two hundred fifty cases were cared for by only two doctors. Both contracted typhus. A third of the fifteen hundred patients being treated in one hospital died.

While Ethan waited impatiently for his commission to arrive he had little to do but wander about the camp. As a courtesy, Washington showed him the letter he'd written in support of his application to the Congress. He sympathized with Ethan but admitted to Nathanael Greene that at the same time he could not in conscience exactly plead for his services. Other than divulging them to Greene, he kept his reservations to himself, and Ethan optimistically considered the commander in chief's statements to be as encouraging as a man in his position might be expected to make them. They were not, after all, old comrades in arms.

As Greene mentioned to Washington shortly after Ethan arrived, it was to be expected that Ethan and Anthony Wayne would become friendly, so similar in so many respects were they. Wayne invited him to join one of his foraging expeditions. On a black night they rode their horses south toward Chadd's Ford, leading thirty well-armed Pennsylvanians. By this time the thaw had run its course, the temperature was dropping by the hour.

The two men had more in common than either could have imagined. Wayne was thirty-two, and though eight years younger than Ethan, far more experienced in battle. Both had suffered from the failings of fellow officers, although Wayne had never been captured. As John Brown had let Ethan down at Montreal, General William Smallwood and Colonel Mordecai Gist did the same to Wayne. Leading a force of Maryland militia, the two had been ordered to reinforce Wayne's post near Warren's Tavern in the defense of Philadelphia against Howe. They were late getting there, and drawing close and seeing British troops returning from the engagement, their men broke ranks and scattered. Wayne's defeat turned out extremely helpful to Howe, relieving him as it did of any concern over attack from the rear. He was able to go on to ultimate victory in the campaign.

"You mentioned John Brown at Montreal," said Wayne.

"John Brown who should have been at Montreal."

"He fought at Saratoga. I remember. Colonel John Brown."

"Colonel? Yes, I guess by this time he'd be a colonel. I didn't see anything in the newspaper reports about him. What did he do there?"

"His regiment was at Burgoyne's rear. He swooped down on Lake George and captured part of Burgoyne's flotilla. Burgoyne was counting on it to bring up badly needed supplies."

"Good for John. He's capable, as long as he's on his own."

Wayne grinned. "You mean as long as he doesn't have to rendezvous with somebody. Anyway, after he struck the flotilla, he advanced on your old stamping grounds. He held Ticonderoga in a state of siege for weeks."

"Mmmmm."

A mental image of the fort popped into Ethan's memory, only John Brown wasn't leading the attack, he was.

Having mentioned Ticonderoga, Wayne disclosed that he himself had been there, having earlier been placed in command of the fort by General Schuyler after an unsuccessful skirmish at Trois Rivières in Canada. It was during his brief time at Ticonderoga that he was awarded his star. They discussed the fort at length. Ethan rolled back the years to that fateful, rainy night, the good luck and bad, the strategy, the enemy's failure to post lookouts, the capture.

"When your colonelcy comes through, would you consider joining me?" Wayne asked as they rode into the teeth of the frigid wind, the horses picking their way carefully over the refrozen ruts in the narrow road.

"That's very kind of you, Anthony, but I'm hoping to raise men back in the Grants."

"Another contingent of Green Mountain Boys?"

"Only this time I'll call 'em the Ethan Allen Brigade."

They passed dimly lit farmhouses. The wind continued to blow furiously. Hamstrung by inactivity for so long, Ethan could hardly control his excitement. He began to envision a night raid on a farm as full-scale action, the gunfire, the smoke, the shouting, the danger.

A corporal, one of Wayne's point men, came galloping up, his horse snorting, sending up twin columns of vapor.

"General, there's a farm about a mile ahead. A barn as big as all outdoors. A couple of the boys sneaked up close and they say it stinks peculiar inside. Like sheep, Will Finn claims. He does know his sheep . . . "

"Sheep," said Wayne. "I was hoping to find cattle."

"Sir, if I may say so, nobody back at camp'll turn up their noses at lamb chops."

"Man's right," said Ethan. "I'm partial to 'em. And leg-o'-mutton."

"That barn's crammed with sheep," said the corporal.

"Anybody around?"

"The farmer's home and there's six horses tied to the hitch rack."

"Let's go have a look, Ethan. Maybe they'll be Loyalists, maybe we can snag us some two-legged sheep as well as four."

Wayne and Ethan crept up to a front window. Each peered in from a lower corner. Seated around a table were six redcoats and two civilians. They had finished eating and were drinking. The farmer was carrying on loudly. Everyone was enjoying themselves. In the faint light emanating from within Ethan saw Wayne's eyes light up.

"A colonel, a major, and four non-coms."

They ducked clear and stood with their backs against the house on either side of the window. Ethan chuckled.

"They're here for the same reason we are, Anthony."

"Let's get the boys. We'll assign two squads to round up the sheep and drive them north. The other six men, you and I, will take us a few prisoners."

The last word was barely out of his mouth when the door swung wide and out stepped a sergeant brandishing a pistol. Snapping his head right, he fired wildly at Wayne. The bullet missed his head, lodging in the side of the house. Ethan jerked out his saber, rushed the man, and ran him through, crumpling him. The shot galvanized the others to action. Men began shouting and firing wildly through the front window from inside. Wayne's men came racing up, leveling their muskets through the windows. Seeing that they were outnumbered, the redcoats dropped their weapons.

"Come out with your hands high," called Wayne.

The colonel was the first to emerge. Red-faced and portly, he was furious, trembling with indignation.

"Damnable rebel trash!"

He still had his napkin tucked in his collar. Ethan jerked it out.

"Save the insults," he growled, covering him with his pistol. With his other hand he undid his belt and flung it away, saber and all.

The redcoats and the two farmers were herded into a group. Rope was found in the barn and they were tied in tandem.

"What do you intend doing with us?" the colonel demanded.

"We're taking you to the garden spot of Pennsylvania," rejoined Ethan. "Valley Forge."

"You're not forcing us to walk!" burst the major. "We have horses."

"Not anymore," said Wayne. "They're now the property of the Continental Army. You'll walk. The exercise'll do you good. You especially, Colonel."

Inside, men were taking turns emptying two bottles of ale and the redcoats' tankards. The barn doors had been opened and the sheep were being brought out, men on horseback keeping them bunched.

"You dare steal my sheep!" exclaimed the farmer. His son looked like his twin. Both had prominent noses that bent in the same direction, tiny eyes, and uneven teeth.

"Hell almighty," rasped Ethan. "Are you slow or what? What do you think we're doing here?"

Wayne was writing on a piece of notepaper. "How many sheep have you?"

"Almost five hundred."

"It looks closer to three. I'll split the difference with you. Let's say four hundred counting the lambs. Hang onto this receipt."

The younger man sneered. "A damned lot of good that is. We'll never see a red cent and you know it, you filthy traitor!"

"This is good to know," said Ethan to Wayne. "That these bastards are Tories. It'd trouble my conscience more than a little bit if they were on our side."

"Their sheep sure are," said the corporal who'd informed Wayne of the discovery.

Wayne handed the farmer's son the receipt. "For four hundred, and you're getting the best of it."

"A Continental dollar and a half a head?" burst the man. "They're worth at least four!"

"They're worth what they fetch. And tonight they fetch a dollar and a half. Or would you prefer one dollar even?"

"Shut up, Elrod," growled his father.

Prisoners and sheep were moved out. So slowly did the sheep move, despite the urging of Wayne's men, that by the time the foragers got back the sun was whitening the ice clamping the banks of the Schuylkill. Ethan fell asleep in his hut pleased with the night's success, gratified that the men would awaken to the heartiest breakfast they'd enjoyed since arriving at Valley Forge.

He himself was in for a surprise. In his absence shortly after midnight four officers rode into camp. One he knew. Well.

71

★ **Into** Ethan's hut around noon the next day strode John Brown. Everyone else occupying the hut was up and outside. Through bleary eyes set stinging by the fireplace smoke as soon as he opened them, Ethan recognized his old friend. He took stock of him as his brain cleared. Other than the change of insignia on his shoulders he looked the same as the last time they'd seen each other before parting company on the south bank of the St. Lawrence. Ethan's second impression was an assumption, that Brown had come looking for him before he learned of his arrival in camp and sought him out.

"Sorry to wake you, Ethan."

Ethan yawned. "You didn't. How are you, Colonel? And congratulations on the promotion."

"John, please." Brown looked uncharacteristically nervous, self-conscious. "Mind if I sit? You're looking well, Ethan. Considering."

"Considering . . . "

"I heard you were here. I expect it sounds addle-pated after all this time, but I feel I still owe you an explanation. I lost all my men, Ethan, that is most of them. I ended up on the Montreal side of the river with fewer than fifty."

"I had fewer than that."

"The problem was, as I'm sure you figured out long ago, I had no way of getting word to you."

"That you'd changed your mind. You were calling it off and going back across the river."

"Yes."

"I was in the same boat: no way of contacting you. But you know what I figured? I figured I'd better stick it out. Rather than risk letting you down."

"I deserve that."

"I guess we both found out that night how different we are." He had gotten up and was sitting on the side of the bed in his long underwear. "Would you mind kicking over my boots there?"

Brown picked them up, setting them within reach.

"Would that have made sense to you?"

Ethan stared and blocked a yawn with his fist. "Would what?"

"That both of us, all of us be taken prisoner?"

"Not a bit."

Relief passed over Brown in a wave, leaving a smile. "There you are."

"No," said Ethan, "that wouldn't make sense. Except sometimes a man has to stop and consider the situation and because somebody else is involved—like a good friend, like a dear friend—he has to take chances that he wouldn't ordinarily take because they don't make much sense. How would you describe that, John? Is that what they call sticking your neck out?"

"Aren't you overlooking something? We were four miles apart. What possibly could either one of us do for the other?"

"Not a thing."

"Not a thing." Now it was Brown's turn to stare at Ethan. "I know, only I left and you stayed. What we should have done was arrange a signal for calling it off the same as we did for starting out: you remember, the crow call. Neither of us thought of that, the possibility we might have to call it off."

"Do you think after all these years I'm bitter about it, John?"

"I have no idea. Are you?"

"No. Never was. Just surprised you pulled out. You might even say flabbergasted. What's the matter? Why are you looking so down for all of a sudden?"

Brown got up, turned his back, and addressed the door. "To tell the truth . . . " He turned. "This isn't what I expected. You should be hopping mad at me. Still. Madder even than that night."

"Who says I was mad? I told you what I was . . . "

"For three years it's been chewing my conscience. Early on it was so bad I had to force myself to look in the mirror to shave. I think back, we had the canoes, I could have sent two men downriver to tell you we were getting out. Of course they would have had to find you, you weren't near the bank. I figured you weren't . . . "

"Forget it, John."

"Goddamn it all I can't! Don't you understand? You don't know what it's like living with it. You've no idea! What in hell's the matter with you? You sit there calmly not even raising your voice. Why don't you explode? Why don't you hit me? Like Ira."

"Ira hit you?"

"He was livid. He nearly broke my jaw."

"That's news to me."

"Be honest, wouldn't you like to hit me?"

"What for?"

"Oh for Christ's sakes!"

"Don't get upset. You know what the Bible says—'To err is human, to forgive divine.' "

"That's not the Bible, it's Alexander Pope. From the 'Temple of Fame,' or 'An Essay on Criticism.' I don't know. Who cares! Ethan, don't you understand? I don't want to be forgiven."

"But it's not up to you."

"No it's not."

"On second thought I don't see that it calls for forgiveness. It wasn't a mistake, it was a judgment you made."

"That you wouldn't have made. That you didn't. That's what you're saying."

"But we're different."

"I . . . never realized how different till now."

"What are you doing here at Valley Forge, John?"

"Can we please not change the subject? Was it . . . awful?"

"Being a guest of the Crown? It had its moments. What I hated most about it, though, was missing out on the war. On Quebec, on Saratoga, here around Philadelphia. I understand you've been busy."

"Goddamn it!"

"What's the matter now?"

"I despise this! When I found out you were here I thought we could finally have it out. Clear the air between us once and for all. I tell you what happened, you tell me."

"But don't we both know already?"

"I'd better just go. I hear you're waiting for your commission. So you'll be getting back into it."

"Finally."

"Good luck, Ethan."

"Good luck to you, John."

"Can I ask, I mean would you mind . . . shaking my hand?"

"Of course."

They shook hands. Brown was at the door, opening it, when Ethan called to him.

"I do have one question." Brown turned. "Have you ever told anybody, anybody at all, that Montreal was your idea?"

Brown thought a moment. "Not that I recall. Why, is that important?"

"Important to you, so it seems."

VIII

Home the Hero

72

★ **Late** that afternoon George Washington sent his orderly out after Ethan, who minutes later stood before the commander in chief and saluted.

"Have a chair, Ethan. The courier came in a little while ago. He brought this for you."

Washington smiled and held up an envelope. He then passed it to him. Ethan tore it open and hurriedly read it.

"They've commissioned me a colonel!" He paused, corrugating his brow.

"What is it?"

"There must be some mistake."

He handed the single page to Washington who perused it. "It's a brevet commission."

"In the reserves. What is this shit? I mean . . . "

"They've made you a full colonel. With pay of seventy-five dollars a month."

"In the reserves? Not active duty? What the hell is the reserves?"

"Please calm yourself. Many, many good men, able men, are

put on reserve status. It's regulation, it's until you're called up for active duty."

"And when'll that be? Next year? The year after? When Clinton and the rest of 'em are all aboard ships heading back?"

"Ethan . . . "

"General, I was in a bottle for three years. I come back, I offer my services. What do they give me? Me, the Hero of Ticonderoga? Colonel in the reserves. On a shelf. It's pure bullshit! They file me away until needed, which'll likely be never."

"You could be called up sooner than you think."

Ethan paused, mulled this over. "Is that possible?"

"Of course. In the meantime don't you think you deserve a rest? The Congress thinks so, and I'm inclined to agree. Listen to me, go home to Bennington. Back to your family, your friends, secure in the knowledge that you're a full colonel earning seventy-five dollars a month, that the Congress appreciates your talents, your accomplishments, your experience, and is only waiting until you're needed to call you up."

"Maybe you're right."

"Do you know who showed up this morning and will be heading north? General Horatio Gates, the hero of Saratoga. You two can ride together, keep each other company until you turn off for Bennington. You should find a great deal in common."

"Me? With a general?"

"Ticonderoga, Bennington, that whole arena."

"General Horatio Gates and me, traveling companions?"

Washington consulted his pocket watch. "General Greene's due here in a couple minutes. When he and I are done I'll introduce you to Horatio."

"Would you?"

"Come back in say fifteen minutes."

"Gladly, gladly!"

"I'll see you then, Colonel. And congratulations." He handed back Ethan's commission. "Keep this in a safe place."

"I will. Colonel. That's what I am. Finally."

"That's what you are."

Ethan saluted and left. Two minutes later Nathanael Greene came in.

"I just saw Ethan leave here, heading for Anthony Wayne's hut."

Washington told him the news.

"In the reserves, you say? He must have been disappointed."

"He was."

"Will he be called up?"

"For his sake I hope so, Nat."

"Only you doubt he will."

"I'm afraid I do. If they wanted him active they would have made him active. Not doing so right away is a sure sign they don't. I felt ashamed lavishing optimism on him, encouraging him. It felt . . . hypocritical."

"It's not your fault, you're just caught in between. Too bad. Anthony Wayne told me he'd love to have Ethan join his brigade. After all he's been through, this is the thanks he gets."

"He's a strange man, Nat. At first he was disappointed, then when he thought about it his spirits revived. I've never seen anybody so optimistic about everything. He's incapable of seeing the dark side. He'll be leaving for home tomorrow. I confess I'll miss him. He's a breath of fresh air. He told me about Howe calling him in and offering him the moon to change sides. Ethan claims he put him in his place with a vengeance." He snickered. "Come to think of it, if I have my dates right, it was shortly thereafter that Lord George Germain began criticizing both Howes in earnest. Which finally led to their resignations."

Washington introduced Ethan to General Horatio Gates. The Virginian wasn't quite what Ethan expected or hoped he'd be. He found him a bit too English. Gates, being the son of an upper servant in the family of the Duke of Leeds, was not the aristocrat Ethan assumed he was. His abilities, however, in administration and elsewhere, more than offset his relatively low position on the social ladder.

Ethan, despite his backwoods upbringing, his rustic ways, his rough edges, was a snob. Had anyone accused him of being one he would have denied it with blasphemy, but his attitude toward his friends and neighbors in the Grants could be patronizing. He felt that he was better educated, that better-bred people had a greater appreciation for his talents and intelligence, and that his neighbors took his for granted. He was a gentleman, and none of them were. He was literate and most of them, even his wife, were not. Through no fault of his own, other than a desire to better himself, if such could be considered a fault, he was superior. Their reason for not appreciating him was because they didn't understand him.

He said good-bye to Washington and Greene, also to John Brown and Anthony Wayne.

"I'm sorry to see you go, Ethan," said Wayne, while at the same time John Brown, standing to one side, looked to Ethan to be relieved at the prospect.

"I'm sorry I couldn't get to serve under you, Anthony. But even if they didn't stick me on the shelf, as I told you I would have raised my own brigade up in Bennington. I bet I could have talked at least ninety percent of the old Green Mountain Boys who went home after Canada to join up again. This is really a crying shame. The Congress and the army end up losing out on account of just plain dumbness."

"This war's going to last a while," said Wayne. "I'm sure our paths'll cross again. And you and Colonel Brown here are bound to see each other."

"I'd like that, Ethan," said Brown quietly.

"Me too, John."

Wayne gave him a saber. Gates was on his horse waiting. Washington's orderly held Ethan's horse for him. He mounted. They started northeast in the direction of Trenton.

Well up into New Jersey they would pick up the Post Road. They rode out of a different camp from the one Ethan had rode into less than a week earlier. The weather was getting warmer, for the first time in months there was sufficient food and clothing, the men's spirits were reviving, and patients in the area hospitals, having recovered, were returning in increasing numbers. Horses, transport, supplies, and other necessities were coming in from all directions.

But during the terrible winter Valley Forge saw a severe reduction in troops by death and by desertion. Whole companies deserted, most of the men fleeing to Philadelphia where they sold their weapons for food or joined the British. So while the Americans lost men, the British gained them. By winter's end Washington's force of nine thousand had been reduced to under six thousand, with no more than half fit for duty.

Gates's curiosity regarding Ethan's captivity was boundless. He fired question after question. There was no need for Ethan to exaggerate his experiences as he did recounting the night at Montreal to his fellow parolees in Manhattan and the officers on board the *Eloise* in the harbor while waiting to be exchanged. He related incident after incident, from his jail cell in Montreal to his most recent stay in the provost jail.

"Some of the lads captured around Philadelphia ended up on prison ships in the East River in New York," said Gates.

"Like the *Jersey*, I know."

"I can't say you were lucky in your confinement, but those on board ships like the *Jersey* had a foul time of it. The food was swill, the Hessian guards were extremely brutal. They'd deliberately leave the dead in with the living in the stifling holds, until they got around to burying the corpses."

"I never had it that bad."

"You were never tortured?"

"Only flogged."

"My word . . . "

"Only once. In Pendennis Castle in England. That was the

low point of the three years. We all thought we were heading for Tyburn Hill."

"You were, until cooler heads prevailed and brought the king to his senses."

"Not to change the subject but I hear you took General Arnold's command away from him at Saratoga."

"I did. Is he a friend of yours?"

"Mine? I couldn't stand the sight of him."

"Difficult man."

"I think shithead is more apt."

"I had my problems with him. There was an engagement on September nineteenth, a place called Freeman's Farm. Afterward, friends of Schuyler whom, incidentally, I also had a hard time seeing eye-to-eye with . . . "

"Me too. I can't stand snobs."

"Friends of Schuyler gave credit for the victory to Arnold. I wrote a letter to Congress clearing up the matter. He came to my headquarters, one word led to another . . . "

"Which is what always happens with that son of a bitch."

"Ahem, yes. At any rate, we quarreled. Later he wrote to me. I responded. A pointless correspondence ensued. I finally put an end to it by relieving him of all command and excluding him from headquarters. The man's ungovernably shallow, unprincipled, unstable in character, but, curiously, a good commander. I might even say a great one."

"You would?"

"Oh yes. A sound strategic instinct, quick insight into a given situation, audacious, resourceful. None braver." Ethan put on a sour expression. "You disagree?"

"I wouldn't know, I only worked with him the one time. And then we really didn't work. I was in command, he was just underfoot."

"I have to give the devil his due."

"Whatever you say, General."

"Outstanding field commander. Superb. But as haughty,

opinionated, and uncooperative as they come. I considered myself well rid of him."

"But he was . . . ?"

"What?"

"That good."

"Most definitely. I daresay I would have had a difficult time winning the Battle of Saratoga without him.* So what are your plans when you get back to Bennington? Of course you'll be reunited with Mrs. Allen. You must be bubbling over with anticipation. I mean, it's been three years. I confess I miss my dear wife and family. So what will you do when you get home besides sleep late and eat six meals a day?"

"Start rounding up men for when they call me to active duty."

"As a colonel."

Ethan tapped the envelope in his inside jacket pocket. "In the Continental Army. No more militia for me!"

Four days later the general and the colonel parted company, Gates stopping at his headquarters on the Hudson, Ethan continuing on and eventually turning east over the mountains to Bennington. By the time he dismounted in front of Stephen Fay's Tavern he was on the verge of collapse. His months in the provost jail had worn him back down to the near-wraithlike figure he had become before recovering his health in New Lots. The journey to Valley Forge, his short stay there, and the long trip north had badly depleted what remained of his energy.

He stood outside the tavern looking up at the stuffed catamount high atop its pole. It looked ready to fall apart. People passed him as he stood holding his reins. Men looked and looked again, as if to make doubly sure it was him before they welcomed him, patted him on the back, and shook his hand.

The sun was setting over the Green Mountains. His Green

---

* *Historians are in almost unanimous agreement that it was Philip Schuyler and Benedict Arnold who "won" the Battle of Saratoga, the acknowledged turning point in the War of Independence, not General Horatio Gates.*

Mountains, his boys, his war. Who else could be said to have started it, at least in the Grants? In that instant in his mind's eye Ticonderoga wasn't a fort, it was Buckingham Palace, that the king had bought for the queen seventeen years before. He blinked and could see the royal standard flying, the ceremonial changing of the guard. Buckingham Palace, and he had taken it with Their Majesties asleep inside. A voice jolted him out of his daydream.

"Ethan!" It was Jacob Wall, all smiles, bursting with vigor and good health. He came running up. He threw his huge arms around him, squeezing, flattening Ethan's lungs. "Ethan, Ethan, Ethan . . . !"

"Hello, blacksmith. You made it."

"*You* did. Elisha, all of us, were despairing we'd ever see you again in this world. Come inside, let me buy your first one!"

"Calm down, Jacob, you'll have a heart attack."

They commandeered a corner table. Others Ethan knew came up to welcome him and wish him well. There was no sign of Elisha or Wilkie O'Doul.

"Did Wilkie get away when he jumped overboard down off Cape Fear?" Ethan asked.

"You bet. He swam about six miles up the coast and got away easy. He was the first one home."

Dr. Jonas Fay came over. He was heavyset, with most of his weight collected above his belt buckle. He had taken over running the tavern from his father, Stephen, who had been a captain in the Green Mountain Boys. Ethan had always been fond of the younger Fay, and his interest and affection were returned in kind. Jonas sat with them as the waiter brought up their whiskies. Jacob reached for his money but Jonas stopped his hand.

"This round's mine. They all are. It isn't every day the Hero of Ticonderoga comes home!" He looked around then got to his feet. "Boys, this gentleman is the redoubtable and famous Colonel Ethan Allen, come home at last after three years a prisoner of the British. Let's give three rousing cheers to the Hero of Ticonderoga!"

The cheering threatened to lift the roof. Ethan felt his cheeks glow as he burrowed into his drink to hide his embarrassment. Jonas got carried away, announcing that drinks were on the house. Within three minutes the place was mobbed.

"A lot's been going on while you were away living off the Crown," said Jacob.

Jonas nodded. "We are now the free and independent Republic of Vermont."

"Ver . . . "

"Mont," said Jacob. "Dr. Tom Young suggested it. We started out with New Connecticut but nobody figured we owed anything to the old one, so . . . "

"We've drawn up our own constitution," said Jonas. "Unusually liberal. It guarantees every man the vote. Slavery's abolished. We're on our own, Ethan. We recognize no outside political authority. Meaning the Yorkers . . . "

"We've even held elections," added Jacob.

Ethan felt bewildered. "Ira never said a word in any of his letters. Maybe he was saving it all for a surprise. Independent. It's a dream come true. Even before Ticonderoga I was hoping in my heart that one way or another we'd get the Yorkers out of our hair, keep 'em from swallowing us up and get our chance to go it on our own."

Jonas assumed a serious expression. "We haven't exactly gotten rid of the Yorkers. Governor Clinton threatened to send troops in, only lucky for us, the Northern Department of the Continental Command couldn't spare them. Clinton's been shooting off his mouth and sending bales of dispatches, but nobody pays any attention."

Ethan raised his glass. "Let's drink to the Republic of Vermont. I mean I would if I had anything in my glass."

Jonas laughed. Another round made it to the table.

"Everything isn't exactly rosy," said Jacob in between Ethan's friends and neighbors pushing up to the table to shake his hand. "Gates doesn't want to offend Clinton. He can't undo what we've accomplished here, but he can block recognition by Congress."

"Not forever he can't," said Ethan. "How's the war doing around here?"

"Things are getting better," said Jacob. "The British are getting out of Ticonderoga and Crown Point. They're heading back to Canada."

"Where's Ira now?"

"In the house in Arlington. Mary's keeping house for him. She's there with your daughters." Jacob leaned closer. "They couldn't run the farm alone, not and turn any profit."

"Arlington. Not far. Whatever happened to Seth Warner?"

"He took his regiment to General Gates's headquarters on the Hudson, south of here," said Jonas. "Getting back to our problem. It's not really military, not just political, Ethan. It's economic. Everybody around Bennington is like everybody in the Republic: poor as church mice and satisfied to be. Very little cash in circulation. Them that has it are hiding it. Almost everything's bartered these days."

"It always was," said Ethan.

Jonas shook his head. "I have to be honest, the situation's getting close to desperate. Another thing that hurts us is that we're so new there's a sizable number of people who are dissatisfied with the way things are going and refuse to pitch in. Refuse even to vote."

"There are still a lot of Tories around," said Jacob. "I suggested at the last meeting we set traps for 'em. Bait 'em with money. The idea was turned down. Nobody's got any imagination."

Jonas clapped Ethan on the back. "But now you're back you can help us find solutions to our problems. After you've settled in, seen your wife and family."

"I don't know, Jonas. Politics may just have to wait. Boys,

you are looking at a full-fledged colonel in the Continental Army Reserves. I'm back for only as long as it takes for Congress to call me up. I have to line up volunteers. Jacob, you've had yourself a nice long furlough, what do you say? How about getting back into harness?"

"Ohhhhh, Ethan. I don't know about that. It'd be just my luck to sign up, go into battle, and get captured again. And do the whole round from Montreal to England to Halifax all over." He showed his wedding ring. "Abby and I got hitched. She waited, kept picking those flowers, ironing that dress, what could I do? She wouldn't exactly jump up and down and clap her hands if I was to tell her I'm going back to war."

"Then I'll tell her," said Ethan. "My pleasure."

Jonas laughed. "Same old Ethan. Drop everything and follow me, boys, we're going out and knock Jack Bull off his horse!"

Ethan finished his drink. "Don't go making up your mind right away, Jacob. Give it some thought. Meanwhile spread the word. I want Wilkie O'Doul, Elisha Cummings, all the old faces. We need experience. It'll be like a reunion, the boys who took Ticonderoga and nearly took Montreal getting back together to give it another go! Isn't that something to think about? Isn't that tempting?"

Jacob grunted and drank. Jonas laughed.

73

June 1779

★ **Ethan** stopped by the house to visit his son Joseph's grave. He searched about and finally found it under an apple tree. An appropriate site, Joseph had spent half his brief life climbing the apple trees and sitting high in one or another for hours. Ethan spoke briefly to him, but when tears reached his eyes, dimming sight of the mound, he remounted his horse and set out for Arlington. Near his home his brother had built a sawmill and gristmill. Ira was not at home. Loraine, Lucy, Mary Ann, and Caroline were with their mother. Removing his hat, Ethan stood in the doorway waiting to be invited in. The children did not run to him, although Mary Ann came up and shook his hand. Ethan studied her, she'd grown six inches, and looked exactly like her mother. After she shook his hand she shyly withdrew to the farthest corner of the room.

"Outside, girls," said Mary. "Your father and I have to talk."

They filed out obediently. She closed the door. He could hear their happy shouts outside, as if they were pleased to get away from him.

"Mr. Allen . . . "

"Mary. It's been a long time. Did you get my letters?"

"Yes."

"I got yours. I thank you."

"Praise God from whom all blessings flow."

"Where's Ira?"

"Gone to Shaftsbury for the day on business."

"Oh. I passed through there coming up from Bennington."

"The road does pass through."

"How have you been, my dear?"

"The same. Whatever changes with me? You look thin. Have you been eating properly?"

"Trying to."

"Vegetables? Vegetables are very good for you."

"I know. May I sit?"

She gestured the five empty chairs. "Wherever you please." He sat. "Are you home for long?"

"I'm now a full-fledged colonel in the Continental Army Reserves. I'm home for as long as it takes Congress to call me up to active duty. I don't know when that will be, but it should be soon."

"Then you'll leave again."

"Yes. It's my duty, Mary."

The pause that followed was so long and so awkward for want of something to occupy his hands he began clapping them to his knees, rubbing circulation into the joints, and taking away his hands. This he did repeatedly.

"What are you doing?"

"Touch of rheumatism. They get sore."

"I shouldn't wonder, the life you lead."

"I didn't choose to be a prisoner, Mary. Is there anything to drink?"

"Sit down at the table and I'll bring you sweet cider."

"No ale?"

She brought ale and sat at the other end of the table, her chin in her hands and staring at him. She wasn't pleased at his return, wasn't displeased, he could see no reaction whatsoever. She had not made him feel welcome, now she was making him feel uncomfortable.

"Do you plan to stay here?" she asked at last.

"If there's room."

"There's room. As you know. You know this house."

"When will Ira be back?"

"I told you, he went for the day. So tonight."

He drank. The ale could have been cooler, but it did chase the dust. "I missed you, Mary. I did write . . . "

"Loraine read me your letters. She wrote one for me to the queen."

"Ira told me, I appreciated that."

"It musn't have done any good, since they didn't let you go till now."

"The week before last. I planned to come right home but I had to stop first at Valley Forge."

"Where is that?"

"Ah . . . Pennsylvania."

"Only a little out of your way."

"Valley Forge is General Washington's winter quarters. I re-

ceived word of my commission while there. Then rode back
to Bennington."

"To Jonas Fay's Catamount Tavern."

"I stopped there, yes. That's where I learned that you'd left
the farm and were living here." He smiled hopefully. "So here
I am."

"Praise God from whom all blessings flow."

"Will you be mad at me for the rest of your life?"

"I'm not mad."

"You seem . . . "

"Am I any different from the last time you came home?
Have I changed any?"

"No, but . . . "

"I'm not mad. You're not the only one who went off to war.
Of course, some men stay home and care for their wives and
children. It's a choice, and you made yours."

"Yes."

Had the ale turned or was her bitterness causing this sudden sour taste? Wasn't she curious about his imprisonment?
His experiences? How close he'd come to hanging? His treatment? The ups, the downs? Evidently not.

"You look weary," she said.

"I could sleep a week."

"Do you want to go to bed when you've finished your
ale?"

Was she inviting him to bed? He seized the horns.

"If you'll come."

"I can't. I promised Lucy I'd make cookies. The dough's
all ready."

"Couldn't you start baking a bit later?"

"The oven's heating."

"Oh."

"You can go to bed. But fold the quilt neatly when you take
it off. Set it on the chair."

"I will."

She stood up. The signal for him to leave the room? She looked even skinnier than the last time he'd seen her. She ate next to nothing. She was the only woman he'd ever known who cooked and baked and while doing so never even tasted her handiwork.

"Welcome back, Mr. Allen."

"It's nice to be back, Mary."

"It is?"

"Yes, my dear."

"That's odd. One would think you'd come back more often. The room's two doors down on the left from the top of the stairs. And remember, careful of the quilt. Oh, you may want to bathe before you get into bed."

The way she crinkled her nose seemed to insist that he bathe. He did so. She brought him a towel.

He fell asleep almost immediately. When he awoke the sun had lowered and was sending bright orange rays through the trees on the far side of the cornfield, across the short green shoots, and over the sill. He smelled cookies. It was home he was smelling, even though the house was his brother's. He propped himself up on one elbow and kneaded his eyes with his fists. It wasn't until he looked down the length of the bed that he noticed her, standing straight as a rake, her arms folded, her chin defiant, in her face the expression of indifference she seemed to favor above all other looks. She had on her nightgown.

74

★ **The** children were in bed. Mary sat darning. Ira had come back from Shaftsbury. At the sight of Ethan he was elated, clasping his upper arms, pumping his hand.

"How are you, big brother?"

"Okay. Just on pins and needles waiting for word from the Congress."

"It'll come. Mary, if you'll excuse us, we have a lot of catching up. We'll go into the sitting room."

"It's your house."

Ira set a chair for Ethan and drew them ale.

"Tell me everything, Ethan. From the beginning."

"I'd really rather not, little brother. The short of it was shackles and poor food, insults and bullying, crossing and re-crossing the ocean, back to Canada, down to New York, to Valley Forge, and here. What's more important is what I hear has been going on here."

"What hasn't? It's like that old tune, 'The World Turned Upside Down.' There's a meeting of the Assembly in Bennington day after tomorrow. You must come. By now everybody in the area knows you're home. They'll all be turning out. You're still their hero, Ethan, about the only one we've got. They'll all want to see you and shake the hand that shook the world under King George."

They talked until late: politics, the war, Vermont, the fragile present, the shaky-looking future, the hopes, and the dreams. The next morning a messenger arrived with Ethan's first month's colonel's pay, and $400 described in the accompanying letter as back pay for his three years of captivity. At seventy-five dollars a month he calculated his back pay at $2,550, figuring it to be two months shy of three years. But as thick as they appeared he wasn't about to split hairs. The money meant nothing, active service was all.

That night he gave half the money to Mary.

"What will I do with it?"

"What you please, my dear."

They were getting ready for bed. Ethan had taken a second bath. He had on his nightshirt; Mary, her nightgown. She set the money and the candle on the night table and slipped under the covers.

"I've never seen so much money."

"When I get back in I'll be sending you forty or fifty every month. You can depend on it."

"I don't need it. I don't want it. Money frightens me. It changes people. Makes them greedy, miserly, it brings out the bad."

"It also pays the bills."

"I don't have bills. I keep house for Ira, he keeps the roof over all our heads."

"But you'll be going back to Bennington?"

"I don't think so. I like it here. It's pleasant, it's a nicer house than ours. Bigger. We've everything we need. Praise God from whom all blessings flow. Are you going to stand there staring or are you getting into bed? I can't blow out the candle till you do."

"Blow it out, my dear."

They lay in silence, both with their hands under their heads staring at the darkened rafters. He sensed that they were breathing in unison. For a time they continued to. He saw it as one of the few things they'd ever done together, ever had in common. Then she broke the rhythm and he was unable to reestablish it.

"Mary . . . ?"

"Yes?"

"I'm . . . I'm hard. And please don't say, 'Praise God from whom—' "

"Don't be blasphemous, Mr. Allen."

His finger found her and began to gently probe. His heart beat faster. It had been so long, far too long. She lay like a fallen log, no response, no evidence that she felt anything, her expression unchanging in the moonlight. She had yet to move a fraction of an inch from the position she'd assumed upon lying down.

"Are you awake, my dear?"

"Can't you see my eyes are open?"

"But are you awake?"

"Yes. Also tired."

"Then should I mount you? Get this over with?"

"It's your doing, Mr. Allen. It's not up to me."

"Just asking."

He sighed, mounted her, and began inserting his penis. Still she did not move, other than to spread her legs slightly farther apart to accommodate his entry.

"Are you enjoying yourself, Mr. Allen?"

Her question surprised him. She'd never asked such a thing before. *Did* she want to know or was she being sarcastic?

"Are you?" she repeated.

"Immensely."

"Immensely?"

A long pause. He went on. The bed jiggled. He was beginning to perspire.

"Are you nearly done?" she asked.

"Nearly." Another pause, then: "There."

He got off her. She gestured for the piece of toweling and cleansed herself. Then, turning on her side, she fell immediately to sleep. He propped his head on his elbow, staring at her shoulder barely moving up and down.

"Mary, Mary. Praise God from whom all blessings flow."

75

★ **Word** from the Congress did not come, and continued to not come. Ira continued to be optimistic, but Ethan was fast losing his optimism. They sat in Jonas Fay's Tavern downing flip, killing time until the assembly meeting.

"It may not come for another month, big brother, but it will. I'll bet my life on it."

Ethan was about to respond when somebody called his name. It was Elisha Cummings. Ethan shot to his feet. They bear-hugged and shook hands. He invited Elisha to join them.

"How's your mother?"

"I met a girl, Ethan. A week after we got home from Halifax. Susannah Moultrie."

"Name's familiar," said Ira. "Isn't her father the tanner?"

"And does your mother approve?" Ethan asked.

"She can cook and sew, do everything. And she's great fun to be with. She keeps me in stitches. And she loves me. Would you believe it? We're going to be married. I already asked her and she said yes, yes!"

"Shhhh. You're in a public place, Elisha. I asked you, does your mother approve of her?"

"She's not like other girls. She can even ride a horse! And she's strong. We arm wrestle. And beautiful. She looks like her mother. Her father's homelier than a mud fence."

"So when's the wedding?"

"We haven't set the date yet. But soon. And you're coming. You and Mrs. Allen. You too, Ira." Elisha stood up. He seemed to Ethan to glow all over. His eyes sparkled. "I've got to go meet Susannah."

"There's an assembly meeting," said Ira.

"I'll make the next one, I promise. Right now I've got to meet her and go for a walk down by the Walloonsac. She loves walking by the river. I'm getting to love it." He rolled his eyes. "I'll see you, boys. Next assembly meeting, Ira, promise. It's great you made it home, Ethan. I want to hear all about what happened to you after Halifax. I really do. Only I can't now."

"Susannah . . . "

"Susannah." Again he rolled his eyes. "My Susannah."

"And I take it your mother really likes her."

"My mother? Oh, she's not around anymore."

"She died?"

"No, she went to live with her sister over to Woodford. We see each other once in a while. That reminds me, I've got to make sure she comes to the wedding. See you, boys."

"Amazing." Ira's eyes questioned. "How easily people

transfer their affections from one person to another. Susannah Moultrie. I must meet that little girl, Ira. She turned the head of a man I could never imagine any woman could turn. She must have something."

The wily farmer and close friend of the Allens, old, one-eyed Tom Chittenden had been elected president of the Republic. He chaired the assembly meeting that night, held in the Bennington Meeting House at the foot of the hill that led up to Fay's Tavern. Not the brightest man in Vermont or the most successful, Chittenden nevertheless had the respect and confidence of the people.

But with Ethan's return it was inevitable that Vermonters turned to him for leadership. He may have been guilty of mistakes in military strategy, he may have been undisciplined, impulsive, and lacking in self-control under General Montgomery, but now the battlefield was behind him, he was home, he was fearless and dynamic, none of his friends and neighbors could forget that it was he who had kept New York from swallowing up the Grants for the six years prior to Ticonderoga and the outbreak of war. Even his most hostile critics, including the majority of the clergy from St. Albans to Bennington, could scarcely deny that he was the most powerful figure in the new Republic.

Chittenden rapped his gavel and called upon Ethan to address the gathering. The tumultuous applause lasted four minutes by Ira's pocket watch.

"Friends, neighbors, fellow Vermonters, it's good to be home."

For three minutes more the cheering and applause thundered. He finally quieted the crowd.

"My brother Ira has filled me in on all that's been going on in my absence, and I must say I'm impressed, deeply impressed, with all that you've accomplished. I understand, however, that . . . well, to put it bluntly, the Republic is broke.

Now sitting up the hill in the Catamount I got an idea as to how we can raise money."

"We already tried to, Ethan," said Chittenden. "There's just no way."

"We tried taxation," said Jonas Fay. "But what good is taxing people when nobody's got any money to pay?"

Ira took the floor. "Last winter we set up a public loan office here in Bennington. We advertised for money in newspapers in Maine and Connecticut, even New York. We guaranteed repayment at six per cent within a year's time. But the response was woefully weak."

"It was pitiful," Chittenden corrected him. "We have to find a better way. Only like I say, Ethan, there is none."

"There may be one." Ethan paused for dramatic effect and let his glance circle the room. "We confiscate Tory property and auction it off."

"We already tried that," said Ira.

Ethan stared. Ira explained. He'd suggested that the provisional Committee of Safety which, back then, governed the Republic, confiscate and auction off Loyalist estates around Bennington and all the way up the west side.

"We did fine at first," said Chittenden. "But now all the land left by those who ran off to join the British has been sold. A hundred and fifty-eight lots in all."

"Where's the money?" Ethan asked.

"Spent," said Ira. "Supporting a government without taxes is expensive. The cupboard's bare, Ethan."

"Maybe you gave up too easily. Maybe you're letting the Tories off too easily. You confiscated property around Bennington and up the west side, what about the east side? And not all have run off. Jacob Wall tells me there are many still living over there. They intend to stay. They're disloyal, they're dangerous, they're in contact with the British. Why else would they stay but to help the enemy? They're a viper in the womb of the newborn Republic, damned if they aren't. With the help of the British they could run roughshod over us. Is that a risk we want to take?"

"Nooooo!"

"I say we go to work and ferret out every Tory in Vermont. Pass a law. We'll call it the . . . the Banishment Act. We'll establish confiscation boards in every county to hear and decide on all charges of disloyalty. There are acres and acres of Tory property out there that should rightfully be government property. Property of the Republic of Vermont."

Ethan's suggestion was voted on. The vote in favor was unanimous. The Banishment Act was proposed and passed three days later. As Ethan observed to Ira. "If you're going to do a job, do it right."

By this time word had reached every corner of Vermont. Ethan Allen was home.

76

★ **Two** more weeks passed. There was still no word from the Congress summoning Ethan to duty. He stayed over in Bennington to help Tom Chittenden, Ira, and others tend to the complicated machinery of the new government. While he continued to wait for his call up, he made a decision. He would not return to Mary in Arlington. She was content keeping house for Ira. The children appeared happy, but his "homecoming" after so long an absence persuaded him that he wasn't welcome, wasn't needed, and wasn't wanted. The last was open to question. Mary had not seemed disappointed that he'd come home, but she did not act pleased. She had no way of knowing when he'd show up, or even that he'd been freed; he'd planned to surprise her. It frustrated him when she greeted him with her old coldness, with not the slightest indication that she was glad, or even relieved. It was as if he'd come back from an hour's visit to town. He talked about it with Ira in Fay's Tavern. It was early afternoon. There were few patrons. Jonas was nowhere about—he was Bennington's only doctor and was rarely around during the day.

Ira was leaving for Arlington and took it for granted that Ethan would be going with him. Ethan slowly turned his half-filled tankard, keeping his attention on it, his eyes from his brother's.

"I think I'll stay here, Ira."

"Not permanently."

"Until I'm called up."

"But why? Don't you want to be with your wife, your family? Is it the house, Ethan? Is it because it's my house? You mustn't feel that way. You know you're welcome. And don't we always share everything? You're the giver in the family, how about giving me a chance to reciprocate?"

"It's not the house, it's Mary and me. We don't fit together. We're married, but for us that's just a word. There's no bond, no relationship."

Ira scoffed. "In case you haven't noticed you have five children."

"Four. But raising a family doesn't strengthen a marriage, doesn't make one when neither party's really interested."

"I don't believe this. You've been together sixteen years."

"Hardly together. Who else do you know who can leave home for three years and his wife doesn't turn a hair? Couldn't care less? Mary prefers it. Is that a marriage? If you had a wife and a relationship like that would you call it normal?"

"I'll concede she's not a very warm person."

"Please, I'm not putting it all on her. Not any. I'm the absentee. Ira, she is what she is, I'm me. And looking back over the years we were never right for each other. Don't tell me you don't see that."

"Can I say something without you losing your famous temper? Something personal?" Ethan grunted. "Ethan, you're the liveliest man I've ever known. You explode with energy, with enthusiasm. You take the bit in your teeth quicker than anybody. Everything about you is extreme. Your laugh is the loudest laugh. You cuss, you cuss worse than any three men. You eat to excess, drink to excess, live to excess. But Mary . . . Forgive me, Ethan, Mary's dead."

"That's not fair."

"She is. And celebrates it. In not smiling—forget laughing—in burying her emotions so deep you wonder if she's got any, in never showing interest or enthusiasm over anything, in casting a pall over everything. She has dozens of good points, but oh, Lord, is she a rain cloud!"

Ethan shook his head. "All of which only proves you don't know her at all."

"You don't agree?"

"Completely. Just because she's . . . different."

"Her unhappiness is what makes her happy."

"Leave her alone. My point is there's *no* point in our trying to pick up the reins. She's just not interested."

"She said that?"

"Does anybody have to *tell* someone they're not interested? Doesn't it shout without words?"

"So you want to split up. You stay here in Bennington."

"It's better."

"You'll have to break it to her. You can't just drop your marriage in the nearest trash barrel without at least explaining."

"I guess . . . "

"So what will you do, move back into your house here?"

"No, there's an empty place I've my eye on about halfway down the hill."

"That's Everett Newcomber's house. It's been vacant for years."

"Maybe he'll rent. It won't be for long."

"Just till you're called up."

"Good location, practically the center of town."

Ira grinned. "And only a few steps from a nice cold ale. I

have to get back to Arlington before the rain. Coming?"

"Mmmmmm."

The rain held off. The area needed it badly. The roads had become troughs of dust, the young corn and other vegetables were withering, the rivers and streams were showing their banks. They arrived at Ira's house. Ethan followed his brother in. Mary sat at the table with her apron on, peeling potatoes. Her raptorlike hands held the potato so firmly Ethan wondered what kept it from squashing. Her grip had always been iron. A stew simmered on the stove. Ethan watched a solitary fly cruise about and land in silence on the windowsill.

"Mary . . . " said Ira.

"Ira. Mr. Allen."

"My dear . . . " Ethan looked about. "Where are the girls?"

"Out playing by the gristmill."

Ira stood between them looking uncomfortable, eyeing first one, then the other.

"Mary," said Ethan, "could you leave that for a few minutes?"

She placed a peeled potato in the bowl of water. "What for?"

"I'd like to go outside for a walk."

"A walk? What's gotten into you?" She looked toward Ira. "He's never asked me to walk in all the years we've been married." She snickered without smiling. "Must be a touch of the sun."

"Just a short one."

"What for?"

"We have to talk."

She took pains to make it appear a sacrifice almost beyond her capacity to endure. She sighed getting up, shook her head at the unpeeled potatoes remaining, and cast a worried eye toward the pot on the stove. They went outside walking toward the sawmill. He could hear the children playing off in the other direction.

"Mary, if you've no objection I'd like to stay in Bennington. Until I'm called up."

"That may never be."

"I'm sure they'll call me."

"Well, you know and I don't. But if you're not, will you
stay in Bennington?"

"Yes. If that's all right with you."

"It's for you to decide. But won't you rattle around in the
house all by yourself?"

"I'm thinking about a smaller place. I may sell the farm, if
you're sure you want to stay here in Arlington."

"Very sure. I much prefer it to Bennington. And Ira needs
me. It's . . . nice to be needed."

He sighed without showing it. He faced her. "It'll be better this way, don't you think?"

"Yes. Definitely."

She was reacting with more enthusiasm than he thought it
called for. Suddenly she seemed very pleased. He even imagined he could see her eyes light up. Or could that be the setting sun?

"Then I guess it's settled," he said. "Now all I have to do
is tell the girls."

"*I'll* tell them, Mr. Allen."

"But I'm their fa—"

"I'll tell them."

"It probably won't be for long. I should be hearing from
the Congress any day now."

"If that's all, I should go back. My stew must be boiling
over."

Ethan moved into Everett Newcomber's house and continued to wait for word from Philadelphia while battling his
growing pessimism. Impulsively, he dashed off a letter to President Henry Laurens asking for active duty. He stressed the
urgency of his situation, using phrases like "champing at the
bit," "eager to get back into harness." Nothing strikingly

original, but he felt they underscored his dilemma. His hope was that in the mass of work confronting the delegates his reserve status had been overlooked, and he told himself that he was only reminding Laurens of his situation.

No sooner was the letter on its way then he regretted posting it. However cleverly it was worded he was begging, and the Hero of Ticonderoga should not lower himself to begging. But he could ill resist pointing out that in his three-year absence from the war, others had been given their chance to fight, and many did so with distinction, rising in rank.

While waiting he threw himself into work on the Bennington Board of Confiscation. He considered confiscation of Loyalist property as eminently fair. It was a game of cards between them and the Patriots. At the outset, many Patriots had lost everything to the Loyalists and the British. It was no more than fair that the Loyalists should now be the ones to suffer.

While sitting on the Board of Confiscation, Ethan helped convict eight Loyalists in less than two weeks. He was paid about a hundred dollars. The landowners convicted by the board were directed to leave the Republic immediately with no property except what they could carry. The last Loyalist of the eight was a Josiah Parmelee who owned a huge tract of land between Bennington and Woodford to the east. Parmelee had a near-notorious reputation among his neighbors. He was a religious fanatic, an acid-tongued loudmouth, and a skinflint. He held mortgages on a number of smaller farms and did not hesitate to foreclose when the leasers failed to make the necessary payment. He refused anything except cash and little cash was in circulation in the area. Even Jonas Fay accepted payment in barter for drinks.

Parmelee stood scowling before the group of seven board members, with Ethan in the center charged with the responsibility of explaining the situation to the accused. He had known Josiah Parmelee long before organizing the Bennington Mobb, which later was to become the Green Mountain

Boys. He had once approached Parmelee asking for a contri-
bution to the group, money desperately needed for arms and
ammunition. Not only did Parmelee turn him down but he
took the opportunity to lecture him on disloyalty; not toward
the Crown but toward the neighboring Yorkers. Why any
man in the Grants should show partiality toward New York at
the expense of his neighbors mystified Ethan. He came away
telling himself that Parmelee's views were the spawn of sheer
orneriness and a cover for his miserliness.

"Mr. Parmelee, it has been decided by unanimous vote of
the board that your properties be confiscated forthwith to be
sold at auction."

"You can't do this, Allen."

The seats occupied by the audience represented about four-
fifths of the space. The people looking on were orderly and
attentive, but the prospect of Josiah Parmelee and Ethan Allen
locking horns triggered interest. People sat up straight,
stopped whispering among themselves, and looked on ex-
pectantly.

"It's not _I_ doing anything, Mr. Parmelee, it's the situation
that prevails. You chose sides, and in any choice of this nature
there's a winner and a loser."

"We haven't lost anything, this war is far from over!"

"As far as you're concerned, sir, it ended two minutes ago
with the vote."

"You have no power, no standing, no reason to exist."

"We represent the government of the Republic of Vermont."

Parmelee snorted, spat on the floor, and dismissed this and
Ethan with both hands. "You're a pack of thieves. What you
decide, what you do is meaningless to me. I'm leaving here,
going home, and staying there. And if any man dares set one
rebel foot on my property, I'll blow his head off!"

"If you're so foolish as to leave this room I'll be the first to
set foot on your property. And when you shoot and miss, I'll
blow you to kingdom come!"

"Here now," said Tom Chittenden. "Let's not get all worked up over nothing."

"Over principle, Tom," Ethan corrected him. "This one's typical of the Loyalist vermin in our midst, working to undermine the Revolution and bring down the Republic, cooperating with the enemy in every way they can. Mr. Parmelee, do you deny you sold corn to General Burgoyne last year when he couldn't get his supplies up Lake George? That you and others like you came to his rescue? You fed the enemy, Mr. Parmelee. That's treason, and that's why we want you out of here! Jacob, Elisha . . . seize that man!"

Jacob Wall and Elisha Cummings came running forward, each one grabbing an arm. Three other men, almost as big and strong as they, rushed forward and began grappling with them. Tom Chittenden threw up his hands.

"His sons, Ethan. My God, didn't anybody think to bar them from entering?"

The confrontation quickly degenerated into a melee. The audience, composed entirely of Patriots, watched fascinated as the combatants wrestled and punched one another. The older Parmelee, caught in the middle, yelled and threatened and cursed. The Parmelees, father and sons, were finally subdued with the help of three members of the Board of Confiscation. Jacob Wall emerged from the fray with a swollen eye.

The board authorized Ethan to fulfill the provisions of the Banishment Act. The eight Loyalists were to leave the Republic first thing in the morning for Albany. Ethan would lead the escort. The group set out in the rain. The plan was to meet General John Stark, the hero of the Battle of Bennington, to whom Ethan would turn over the prisoners.

But some unknown individual sympathetic to the Loyalists' situation managed to send word on to Governor George Clinton. Parmelee and the others insisted that they were not Loyalists but simply loyal Yorkers who, lacking sympathy with the "so-called Republic of Vermont," had been singled out and summarily stripped of their property, an illegal act, and so characterized "in any court in the land."

Ethan and the escort reached Albany, less than forty miles away, in bright sunshine. General John Stark was waiting. They met in a tavern while the escort stood outside with the prisoners. Ethan was unaccountably thirsty; he downed tankard after tankard.

"General, as a member of the Board of Confiscation and a representative in good standing with the Republic of Vermont I hereby request that these prisoners be sent where they belong, through enemy lines."

"Request duly noted and granted."

"Thank you, sir. My compliments on your good work in the Battle of Bennington."

"Thank you, Colonel. But I'm curious, I thought by now you'd be back in action."

"I thought so too. Still waiting."

A disturbance erupted outside. The tavern was located two miles out of Albany on the Menanus Road. Both men hurried outside to see what was going on. A squad of soldiers had arrived, clad in the familiar Yorker uniforms of blue and buff facing that Ethan had last seen on the Ile-aux-Noix. In command was a Lieutenant Cox. He was little, wiry, and very much in charge. Dismounting, he strode up to General Stark ignoring Ethan and presenting the general with an envelope.

"From Governor Clinton." Stark made no move to open the envelope. Ethan knew that he knew its contents. "Sir, would you mind reading it?"

"Why don't you tell me what it says, Lieutenant?"

"In short that these men are not Loyalists, they are neutrals, they should not be deprived of their property and should be given over to my custody."

Stark opened the envelope and read. "That's what it says."

Ethan, looking on, needed no explanation. What upset Clinton was the action of the Board of Confiscation. He obviously considered it a brazen affront to his authority. The governor of New York did not recognize the Republic of Vermont. Nothing had changed, the Grants were still a part of New York and subject to New York law, not the specious laws of an upstart government of self-styled Vermonters, whose authority nobody beyond their boundaries recognized. To sanction the proceedings against the eight would be tantamount to recognizing the Republic as legitimate while in fact it was still a part of New York.

"These men will be turned over to me," said Cox. "To be turned over to His Excellency. If they are to be tried it will be under New York jurisdiction."

"Go pound sand," said Ethan.

A look from Stark quieted him. The general spoke. His tone was mild, but it carried authority.

"Lieutenant, you may tell Governor Clinton that I, General John Stark, cannot in conscience turn these men over to you. I intend to carry out the directive of the Board of Confiscation and the Banishment Act."

"By what authority?"

"If you'll take the trouble to look behind you, you will see my authority."

Lined up behind the lieutenant and his men, materializing as if by magic during the conversation, was a full company. Every man armed, every man wearing a broad smile.

"This is an outrage!" exclaimed Cox.

"*This* is not your business, not the governor's. It is Vermont business. Colonel Allen has brought these men to me and I intend to remand them to the custody of General Gates."

Gates had recently removed his headquarters from the banks of the Hudson to White Plains. Stark went on to explain that the prisoners would be taken to White Plains and from there sent to the British lines.

"The governor finds this totally unacceptable," said Cox.

"He probably will. But he hasn't yet. Why don't you and

your men turn around, go back, and inform him?"

Cox looked behind him a second time. Stark's men were still smiling. The lieutenant grumbled something unintelligible and mounted his horse. An hour later Ethan was on his way back to Bennington with the escort, relieved of the situation and grateful that of all the generals to whom he could have given custody of the eight, John Stark had been Tom Chittenden's choice. Stark was all Yankee, he had no affection for Yorkers, he was as stubborn as a new stump; the opposition's rank, even that of governor, impressed him not at all.

77

JULY 1779

★ **Butter-and-eggs** flourished in pasture and field. In the woodlands around Bennington, yellow lady slippers and orchids sprang up to tint the darkness. Violets abounded. Sticktights clung to Ethan's britches as he walked by himself along the side of the road to Searsburg just to kill time and ponder his situation.

He came back to his rented house to find Ira waiting along with Mary and the girls. It was a Saturday afternoon. Ira had scheduled a picnic. Ethan thought as his brother explained that it was a long way for them to come, upwards of twenty-five miles, for a blanket on the grass and combat with ants. But then, Ira's motive was all-too obvious.

After the picnic, which, although not unpleasant, was not particularly enjoyable for Ethan, he took Ira aside while Mary played with the girls. To the west was the farmhouse, now abandoned, up for sale but yet to attract a buyer.

"Why did you do this, Ira? And why pick this spot of all places?"

"It's nice. Trees. Cool out of the sun. The lemonade was ice cold, and you ate like a horse."

"It's the best thing I know to keep from talking."

"Mary didn't seem to want to talk."

"What did you expect for God's sakes? We decided."

"*You* decided."

"Why must you stick your nose in?"

"You're my brother."

"You're mine, but not my father-confessor. You don't pilot my conscience. We live apart because it's right for us both. She accepts that, why can't you?"

"I'm sorry, Ethan. I don't have a wife and family. Maybe because I don't, I see them as more . . . precious, more valuable."

"I value them!"

"Shhhh, she'll hear you."

"Don't ever do this again, Ira, promise me."

"I won't."

"I'll go say good-bye and head for home. And don't you ever pull this on me again!"

"I said I won't."

"I know you mean well, but . . . "

"It was a mistake. I presumed too much. It's not my business. I'm sorry."

"Stay here, give me a minute."

Ethan went over to where Mary was playing ring-around-the-rosy.

"Go," she said to the girls. "See who can run the fastest to that old barn and back."

Off they ran.

Mary tried a smile. It failed to materialize. "Mr. Allen . . . "

"I'm sorry about this, Mary."

"Sorry about a picnic?"

"It's awkward."

"We enjoyed it. Ethan . . . ?" He looked up sharply. She almost never called him by his Christian name. It signaled seriousness. "Can you come back to Arlington with us?"

"You mean now?"

"There's room in the carriage. Or you could bring your horse."

"I can't, Mary."

"You don't want to."

"I mean I can't. I'm leaving within the hour for White Plains for General Gates's headquarters."

"Oh? Have you been called up?"

"I'm hoping the general can arrange it. He probably can. If so, I'll be away some time."

"Three more years?"

"I can't put a number on it. But if all goes well I will be back to enlist men."

"The Green Mountain Boys?"

"The Ethan Allen Brigade." His daughters came running back all out of breath. "Good-bye, my loves. Good-bye, my dear, wish me luck."

"I wish you don't get a musket ball in your back or your horse doesn't throw you into a thorn bush."

With this, she and Loraine picked up and folded the picnic blanket, retrieved what remained of the food, and walked off toward the carriage where Ira stood waiting. Loraine came skipping back, and one by one his daughters said good-bye, matter-of-factly and with not a flicker of emotion on any of their faces. It wasn't until they were climbing into the carriage, carrying on animatedly, that it occurred to him that Mary had said the identical words in parting when he and Seth Warner were preparing to leave for Philadelphia three years before.

Everyone waved as Ira drove off. He, alone, smiled. Ethan watched the girls' faces until they were lost in the distance. He grunted.

"As ye sow, Colonel, so shall ye reap."

78

★ **Jonas** Fay bid Ethan good-bye the next morning. They stood by the stuffed catamount pole in front of the tavern. It was not yet nine a.m., but already sweltering out with not so much as a whisper of breeze. Ethan, nevertheless, wore his best suit, the woolen suit given him by Captain Bellows on the *Eloise,* and his tricorn, and sweated accordingly. He also wore the saber given him by Anthony Wayne and a fine, almost brand-new pair of heavy Hessian riding boots with big spurs, part of the plunder taken by John Stark's men in the Battle of Bennington.

"I wasn't able to interest as many fellows in joining the Ethan Allen Brigade as I'd hoped, Jonas. Fewer than fifty, and half of them are wavering."

Jonas shrugged. "Them that wanted to go to war are long gone."

"It's bottom-of-the-barrel scraping time. Of course, some have come home, like Jacob Wall and Elisha Cummings. I talked to both like a Dutch uncle, but now that Jacob's married and Elisha as good as . . . " He shook his head. "Fewer than fifty. I need ten times that."

"Can I ask you something, Ethan? Why do you keep calling it the Ethan Allen Brigade? You're a colonel. A colonel commands a regiment, doesn't he?"

Ethan gave in to sly smile, winked, and touched the side of his nose. "But when I raise a brigade they'll have to promote me, make it all proper. One regiment, a colonel; two regiments equal a brigade and a general in command."

"You deserve it."

"One step at a time."

"What if your active duty notice comes through while you're away?"

"It makes no difference. Gates will have heard, everybody in the Northern Department will have. If the papers do arrive, send your brother Joseph down to White Plains."

"That's got to be over a hundred miles."

"Closer to one-thirty. It's okay, Joseph enjoys riding."

Jonas shook his head. "Mister, you sure do live life loose."

Ethan clapped a hand on his shoulder. "Which helps make it interesting, Jonas. Good-bye, old friend. Wish me luck."

"I do, I just hope it doesn't turn out a wild goose chase."

"It won't. General Gates and I rode together for nearly a week. We got close as skin. I tell him I'm fed up waiting. I want active duty, he'll get it for me. Maybe not there in White Plains, but in the Northern Department. Oh, Jonas, Jonas, this feels so good, it's so right, so gratifying. I should have left here three weeks ago."

"You've been busy with the Confiscation Board."

"That's my problem, I always try to wear too many hats. Oh, I can feel the old fire starting up in my belly. The Ticonderoga fire. I'll be back for the men, back a full colonel with a general's star just around the corner. That's what the boys need to drum up their interest, the old war horse returned to active duty and prepared to lead them into the fray!"

"I suppose."

"Your enthusiasm overwhelms me."

"I just hope you won't be disappointed."

"Jonas, I've talked my way into everything I've gotten in life. I'll talk Horatio into this. If need be, if he's unwilling to help me, although I can't imagine such a thing, I'll just stop there overnight and continue on to Philadelphia in the morning. Beard Henry Laurens in his den. I promise you, the next time you see me you'll see a colonel. Good-bye, and don't forget to tell Joseph."

Off he galloped, kicking up dust, causing Jonas to sneeze.

He shook his head. "Ethan, Ethan, if only this stupid war appreciated you as much as you do it."

He turned to reenter the tavern. Jacob Wall was walking toward him arm-in-arm with his bride, Abby. They looked a handsome couple, she in a housedress of light blue luting and with a muslin cap.

"Wasn't that Ethan?" Jacob asked Jonas.

"Off to White Plains after his active duty."

Jacob's grin faded. "He's chasing a will-o'-the-wisp. If they wanted him they would have called him two days after he got back."

Abby frowned. "Why would General Washington do such a thing? Why would the Congress? It's just plain malicious to dangle a commission in front of him just out of his reach."

"Well said," said Jonas. "Awkward situation. But maybe whoever lost him in the shuffle, meaning President Laurens, will change his mind and call him up. It's a slap in the face he doesn't deserve. It's time *somebody* recognized it. Maybe they will."

He shifted his glance from Ethan's dust back to the Walls. And saw nothing like hope in the eyes of either.

Ethan had long since persuaded himself that he didn't need hope or even optimism. His thoughts raced ahead of the horse. He saw himself meeting with Gates at his headquarters. Gates already knew the situation, they'd discussed it coming up from Valley Forge. The general was sympathetic. He could order him called up, he had the authority. Washington wouldn't question it, and if *he* didn't, Laurens wouldn't. Common sense said that all the delegates would be content to leave it to Gates.

He was three years behind everybody. Everybody had risen in rank: Arnold, Brown, Seth Warner, he could think of twenty-five. Even Gates, who'd started out an adjutant three years before was now a major general. But Montreal and all that followed had left him in the dust. They'd snatched his war from his grasp and were keeping it from him.

He slept that night in Spencertown, just over the Massachusetts border from New York. He had ridden nearly seventy miles, pushing his horse all but into the ground in his eagerness to reach his destination. By his calculations he would arrive in White Plains sometime the next day.

79

★ **General** Horatio Gates's headquarters in White Plains was located at an encampment called Chatterton's Hill. During the Battle of White Plains, possession of the hill had been important to the Americans, to protect the right flank of the army, whose lines ran from northeast to southwest across the town. Essentially, Chatterton's Hill was all that stood in the way of Howe launching a full-scale attack against Washington's retreating forces. Greatly outnumbered—thirteen full British regiments against only twelve hundred Americans—the Patriots obstinately contested every foot of ground but were finally compelled to give way.

The action impressed Howe to the extent that he decided an attack against Washington's main force would be too hazardous, and he ordered reinforcements from Mamaroneck and New York. There was a subsequent skirmish near neighboring Horton's Pond, which was indecisive, but from then on the British made no attempt on the Americans while they remained at White Plains.

The town itself was situated in the midst of lovely rolling tree-covered hills and picturesque stretches of meadowlands in the valley of the Bronx and Mamaroneck rivers. General Gates met with Colonel Seth Warner in the shade of a towering maple. The two sat on a picnic blanket and shared a pot of tea while two finches serenaded them from overhead. Concern lined Warner's handsome face. The general refilled his cup and stirred the milk and sugar in his own.

"What seems to be the problem, Seth?" Gates asked.

"My conscience, sir. Sitting around between actions, nothing to do, inclines one to fall back on memory. I've been thinking about Ticonderoga and the Canadian campaign, and Ethan."

Gates sobered. "We rode up from Valley Forge together last spring."

"I know."

"When did you last see him?"

"Just before the debacle at Montreal. Up in the Richelieu River country. I hear from Colonel John Brown that General Washington contacted Congress for Ethan and he got back word that he's been made a colonel in the reserves."

"Yes. And?"

"I assume he's still waiting in Bennington to be called up. Will he be, General?"

"That's difficult to say."

"Forgive me, but that, sir, says it all. Knowing Ethan he's got to be going stir crazy. He's been out of it for three years."

"I know, I know, damned shame."

"General, we both know his reputation. No point in raking him over the coals. He has his flaws—who doesn't? But all things considered, don't you think he deserves active duty?"

"Schuyler gave him his chance."

"I know, I was there. Actually, Schuyler declined to put him on active duty."

"All the same, he got it, as a scout, which, I understand, satisfied him at the time."

"He accepted what was given him, sir. I don't know as he was particularly satisfied."

"Look how even that turned out."

"Sir, nobody's suffered more, nobody's paid more heavily for Montreal than Ethan."

"I know, and I sympathize with him. I'm being sincere, Seth. I got to know him quite well riding up from Valley Forge. Charming fellow."

Warner started, his eyes rounding. "Charming? Ethan?"

"Winning, then. Uniquely colorful. More colorful than Anthony Wayne and Burgoyne rolled into one."

"The most dedicated Patriot we have."

"And the most undisciplined? I don't hold with Philip Schuyler's opinion on much, but he and others—"

"General, Ethan's been on the sidelines for three years. Three years a prisoner; the suffering, the deprivation, the humiliation has to have had a sobering effect on him. Has to have tamed his willfulness, his wildness, and given him ample time to take stock of himself."

"Are you saying you think he's changed from Montreal?"

"Absolutely."

Seth's heart sank. Gates appeared to be trying his utmost to be gracious, even playing devil's advocate, but he was showing no enthusiasm for bringing back Ethan.

Seth suspected the reason. Gates was inordinately ambitious. In helping organize the Continental Army he had rendered exemplary service. He knew administration as did few other officers, and had proved tireless in performing his duties. He was also a capable field general. But it was no secret that he preferred intrigue to combat, and rarely took risks in the political arena of the military. Putting Ethan on active duty would be doing exactly that.

"Ticonderoga aside," Seth went on, "the Green Mountains Boys was his idea. He assembled us, raised the money to arm us, whipped us into shape, kept up morale. He didn't lead the attack as much as inspired it.

"He's had a rough life. He has a terrible marriage. He fought for six years for the people of the Grants against the

Yorkers, and after all he did they denied him command of the Green Mountain Regiment. He had his brief burst of glory, now it's all behind him, and nobody gives a damn. Nobody sees what shunting aside a man like Ethan can do to his spirit. Still he's never soured on the fight for independence, he never complains, never blames others for his mistakes, not even John Brown.

"And he never gave up all those years in prison. Howe tried to get him to change sides. Lots of men in the same situation didn't hesitate to. Not Ethan. Never. Most men would be feeling sorry for themselves and drinking out of the bottle by this time, but not him. He keeps his smile on, even when he's turned down for active duty. He's ready, General, goddamnit—"

"All right! All right! I promise I'll think about it. Just remember it was the Congress that stuck him on the shelf, not me."

"Of course not, sir, but only you can take him off it."

Warner's stare asked for agreement. Instead, Gates scoffed, lightly shaking his head. "I knew it would come down to this. Riding up from Valley Forge with him I said to myself this is going to wind up in your lap. But I do give him credit, he never begged."

"He's too proud, sir. Besides, I think he was convinced his active duty would come through any day."

"It'll never *come* through, Seth. Somebody has to push it."

"Sir, you can write his name on the active duty roster right now. I'll get word to him in Bennington. He can be down here in two days."

"Slow down. Let me think about it." Warner groaned just loud enough to bring a mild frown to Gates's face. "Patience. I promise I won't drag it out all week."

"You'll never regret pulling him aboard."

"Never say never, Seth. None of us controls his destiny to that extent, that he can afford *that* luxury."

*   *   *

Seth was among the first to see Ethan ride into camp late that afternoon. For a full twenty seconds the two stared at each other, Ethan on his weary horse, his old friend and fellow Green Mountain Boy looking up at him, grinning.

"Speak of the devil himself," murmured Seth.

"You talking about me, Mr. Warner? Excuse me—Colonel Warner."

"I was. With General Gates no more than an hour ago."

Men who recognized Ethan gathered around his horse, attracting others who knew him only by reputation. Basking in their attention, Ethan dismounted. One man obligingly took his horse for him.

"You know why I'm here, Seth. I'm itchy. I can't stand any more of this fidgeting on the sidelines." Seth walked him away from the crowd to the relative privacy of a large woodpile behind the quartermaster's tent. "What's the matter, you don't look exactly overjoyed to see me."

"I'm delighted to see you, it's just that you're a bit early."

"For what?"

"Ethan, I've been working on Gates. I think he's at a point where he just might call you up."

"Great! Now that I'm here I'll help him decide."

"Please . . . You musn't push him. He *is* on your side. He sympathizes with you."

Ethan spat and scowled. "Sympathizes? What in hell do I need with his sympathy? Does he think he'll be doing me some kind of favor? In case it hasn't dawned on him, I can contribute. He won't be taking on dead weight!"

"Shhhh."

"Ethan? Is that you?"

"Oh damn . . . " muttered Seth.

Benedict Arnold came limping toward them, pulling himself forward with a cane. His smile temporarily covered his pain.

"Well, well, well."

"Colonel," said Ethan.

"General," Seth corrected him.

"It's been ages," said Arnold. "You're looking fit. A bit thin . . . "

"You look fine yourself, General. Congratulations, I hear big things about you. Heard you caught another bullet in your bad leg at Saratoga. It looks painful as hell."

"Not as bad as Quebec. Say, word just came that the commander in chief will be arriving."

Ethan gasped and beamed. "Washington here?"

"Not White Plains. I understand he'll be staying at the Miller House in North Castle."

Ethan seized Warner's arm. "Get directions for me, Seth, would you? I'll ride over and see him."

"I . . . think he'll be quite busy," said Arnold. "At least for the first few days. Ahem, I take it you're here hoping to be put on active duty."

"That's right." Ethan looked at Seth. A cloud was passing over his friend's face.

"So talk to General Gates," Arnold went on.

"I intend to. *And* General Washington. We got to know each other very well down in Valley Forge."

"Mmmmm. Well, it's good to see you again, Ethan. Looking so fit. It was a relief to hear that you got through your ordeal. I must say, I commend you."

"What for?"

"I understand that General Howe offered you the moon to turn traitor. And you turned him down cold."

"What would you expect?"

"Knowing you, exactly that."

"Thank you, Col—General." Arnold limped off, Ethan looking after him. "Hell almighty, he sure became cock-o'-the-walk, game leg and all."

"Mmmmm. Ethan, despite the treacle, you know he's not exactly a big supporter of yours."

"What's the matter, you think he'll put in a bad word for me with the general? I wouldn't worry about that, anything

bad he says about me to Gates, Gates'll think just the opposite. They can't stand each other."

"Well, if you're not worried, I guess there's no reason for
me to be. But I have to say this, it's been a long time since
Ticonderoga."

"That it has, my friend. What are you getting at?"

"You shouldn't carry a chip on your shoulder against
Arnold. Let me be candid: You shouldn't be jealous of him."

"Me, jealous of that conniving little snob?"

"You know you are."

"How far is North Castle from here?"

Seth narrowed his eyes. "Why?"

"I think I'll run over there and have a word with Washington."

"Go over Gates's head?"

Ethan studied him. "No, eh?"

"Bad politics. The worst. The general's on your side, at least
leaning that way. Don't alienate him at this stage."

"You know this is pure shit, this politics."

"You loved politicking against the Yorkers."

"That's different, that *is* politics. This is war. There should
only be room for fighting. Now if you'll excuse me, I'd like
to go say hello to Horatio."

"Ethan . . . "

"Just to let him know I've arrived. Wish me luck."

He waved and walked off. Warner threw up his hands.

80

★ **Major** General Benedict Arnold came to Colonel Seth
Warner's tent so promptly, Warner imagined that when Arnold
left him and Ethan still standing by the woodpile he only

withdrew to where he could watch them without being seen to wait for him to become available.

"Some surprise, Colonel, Ethan showing up. Can we talk outside? It's sweltering in here."

"Yes, sir."

They found a hillock in a small grove of trees and sat on the grass. Arnold displayed his friendly smile.

"I expect I should get right to the point. I know how close you and Ethan are. I also know how scrupulously honest you are. I pose a question, you'll give me a straight answer. In confidence of course."

"What is it, General?"

"Do you think Horatio wants to put Ethan on active duty?" Warner stared silently. Arnold chuckled, with, Warner noted, slight embarrassment. "You think I should ask him? You're quite right."

"Do *you* think General Gates should?" asked Warner.

Arnold waggled a reproving finger and grinned. "It could be risky. You're the last person I'd have to remind about Ticonderoga. Far be it from me to criticize Ethan, but he wasn't exactly the gracious victor. I thought at the time he handled things rather . . . Of course, he conducted himself quite admirably during the attack."

"He did."

"A pity he's been inactive for so long, and even before had such relatively little experience in the field."

"Isn't he entitled to his chance? Wouldn't you say he's earned it?"

Again Arnold chuckled. "Do you know, I thought you were going to say 'his chance to fall on his face.' I'm sorry, that's not funny."

"He hasn't yet. He wasn't responsible for what happened at Montreal, John Brown was."

"John did share the responsibility. Don't misunderstand, I hold no grudge against Ethan for the way he behaved after we occupied the fort. Water over the dam and all that. It's just . . . "

"What, sir?"

"You have instincts about men, don't you know? You get enough experience under your belt and you can *feel* whether or not somebody's up to the challenge."

"You don't feel Ethan is."

"That's just it. That's what makes this so hard. I don't know what I feel."

"I think he is. I think General Gates does. Up to the challenge, as you put it."

"You both could be right."

"General, I have to go look in on the quartermaster. We've a huge problem, he and I. If there's nothing more . . . "

"Nothing, nothing, no, no."

Warner got to his feet and saluted. Leaning on one elbow, Arnold returned it.

"Come in, Ethan, this is a pleasant surprise. Welcome. Is it too hot in here for you? I confess I like the heat. One gets used to it living in Virginia. So, you're down from Bennington to ask about your status. By the way, are you getting your monthly pay?"

"Yes, sir."

"Good. And you want to go on active duty." Gates nodded and nodded.

"I do."

"Your friend Seth Warner—and a good friend he is—has been beating the drum for you. Earlier today, matter of fact. I've thought it over. I've decided to put you on active duty, Colonel."

"You have? You will! That's great! That's wonderful!"

"For now, until we can work out our manpower assignments—everything's up in the air at the moment—I'm assigning you to join Colonel Warner and his regiment. Only temporary. We'll know by the end of the week what the permanent assignments will be. General Washington's come up. We'll be holding high-level meetings the rest of the week. At any rate, congratulations and welcome aboard."

"Thank you again, sir." Ethan snapped off a salute. Gates returned it.

"I'll see that the necessary paperwork is put through at once. You'll be set in no time. So that's about it. Dismissed, *Colonel* Allen."

Ethan rushed to Warner's tent to relay the good news.

In July of 1778 when Ethan arrived in White Plains, the Americans could boast nearly seventeen thousand rank and file fit for duty. Valley Forge was an unpleasant memory, as were the defeats around Philadelphia and New York. Two months earlier, the British had withdrawn from Philadelphia, out of fear of a large French fleet reported near Chesapeake Bay. Washington planned to take back New York City. Between eleven and twelve thousand men were now in the White Plains area. With the commander in chief's arrival at New Castle, the army would prepare to reorganize. Generals Horatio Gates and Alexander McDougall would be dispatched to Danbury, Connecticut; General Israel Putnam would take his troops north to West Point; Baron DeKalb would relocate in Fredericksburg, New York, and General William Stirling would take up a position between Fredericksburg and West Point.

One of these generals paid a call on Gates shortly after Ethan left to tell Warner the good news. Gates and his visitor held a brief meeting, the general left, and Gates came out of his tent seconds later looking disconcerted. His orderly trailed him.

Gates stood with his chin propped on his palm, fingers supporting his cheek, brow rumpled, eyes dark in thought. "Go find Colonel Allen and bring him to me."

"Yes, sir."

Ethan walked with Gates in the beginning twilight. He could still scarcely contain his excitement at this sudden good turn in his fortunes. It was the sort of thing one has to tell every-body, stopping perfect strangers on the street. Along with cov-eted active duty it put a permanent end to what he'd come to call his "existence in limbo," floating about between the past and a future that promised to restore the glory that Ticon-deroga had brought him and Montreal had taken away.

The sun was preparing to settle behind the Appalachians, the insects and birds were resting, although a thousand star-lings continued chirping raucously, tirelessly.

Gates appeared to be looking for something on the ground. "It distresses me to have to say this, Ethan, but I'm afraid I'm going to have to hold off putting you on active duty."

Ethan stopped and gaped. "What?"

"For the time being you'll still be reserved." Ethan con-tinued stunned. "Just the time being."

"Time being, my arse!"

"Easy . . . "

"What happened? Somebody been shoveling manure on me to you?"

"Try and control your temper."

"I'm sorry. What did happen?"

"To be honest, you showed up a bit too soon. You didn't give me time to consider all the aspects of the thing."

"What aspects? What is this, second thoughts? Are you going to throw things up to me now like Schuyler did at Fort Ti?"

"Will you please let me explain? There's going to be all sorts of reshuffling. That's why the commander in chief is here. The fact is, I simply do not have a command for you. Not at the moment."

"We covered that. You said I'd be with Seth Warner till you did."

"I know. I was . . . premature."

"Premature, my arse. Spit it out, Horatio, somebody's got his knife out for me, isn't that really it? I don't need three guesses who. And you're knuckling under."

"I didn't hear that, Ethan."

"I said it loud enough!"

"Please. I thought I could help you. I can't. Not at this time. But, as I say, it's only temporary."

"Shit too!"

"You're still in the reserves, available to be called up at a moment's notice. Still drawing down your seventy-five dollars a month."

"Fuck the money. You and Arnold and Laurens and the whole Continental Congress can put your arseholes together and shove it up far as it can go!"

With this, he turned and strode off cursing.

"Ethan . . . Ethan!"

Ethan ignored him. It was getting dark. The starlings had quieted. If he got out of here, if he pushed his horse, he could make it to Pawling before midnight. Lay over, and get home sometime around noon tomorrow.

Or maybe the opposite direction? Philadelphia? Laurens had made him a colonel in the reserves; why couldn't he sign the paperwork, put him on active duty? He had the authority.

He wished Hancock was still president. Him he could talk to like a friend. As a fellow New Englander and fellow Yankee, he'd surely be sympathetic. But Henry Laurens? Of South Carolina?

"No."

Pawling by midnight. On home to Bennington tomorrow.

"Fuck this war, horse, and everybody in it!"

81

★ **Ethan** spent much of his time en route home rationalizing, telling himself that a man could only push so hard, that others had to meet him at least a quarter of the way, if not a fair half. Nobody, not the Congress, not Washington, not Horatio Gates, really wanted him in the army. Gates's good heart had temporarily dominated his judgment, but only until someone, probably Arnold, got to him and reminded him of the risks he'd be assuming in putting the wild man of Bennington back in the field.

Ethan reached Bennington early the next afternoon, his pace slowed by a driving rain. He dismounted in front of the Catamount Tavern and hurried inside. He found Jonas about to leave to visit a patient.

"Hello, Jonas," said Ethan, plumping down wearily and beating water out of his hat against his knee. "Just stand there and let me look at you a second. It sure is good to see a friendly face, a man I can trust."

"That bad, eh? Tell me about it. Only before you start I'm afraid no mail came for you. From Philadelphia or anywhere else."

"No surprise there. I won't be going on active duty after all. They're overloaded with officers." He chuckled grimly. "You notice once the war started going our way all those who switched their allegiance to Loyalist are starting to come back. Where were the bastards in the dark hours? When we really needed them?"

"The woods are full of fair-weather Patriots, Ethan."

Ethan related in brief what had happened at White Plains. "He gave me active duty, Jonas. It was mine. I had it in my hand, in my heart. The long wait was finally over, I was back. And believe me, I would have done great things for us on the battlefield."

"You would."

"I took Ticonderoga. Me, Ethan Allen."

"You."

"I took it to the British. The first time, Jonas. Gave 'em a taste of what they'd be up against."

"You did. You're shivering, you need a drink."

"I need a bottle. Weren't you on your way out?"

"Alton Sawyer's bowels are kicking up again. They can wait."

They sat drinking hot rum to chase the dampness and the shadows menacing Ethan's spirit.

"What will you do now?" Jonas asked.

"Stay home. Work on the Confiscation Board, work for Vermont. If you think about it, that's a lot more important than the war. Hell almighty, the war is about over and Vermont is just getting started. Question of priorities. The war ends, Vermont goes on. And on and on."

"We sure can use you."

"I'm glad somebody can." Ethan paused, his drink halfway to his mouth. He glanced about. The tavern was about a third full of patrons. "Yes sir, Jonas, I'm home to stay."

"Oh, oh, oh . . . "

"What?"

"I forgot. You've a visitor at Newcomber's house. Mary came down from Arlington today. I saw her go in just before the rain hit. She had a mop and bucket and broom."

"*My* Mary?"

"Who else? You *are* still married, aren't you?"

"What in hell is she doing here?"

"It could be she misses you."

"Jonas, I've been away three years."

"You've been home a few weeks. You leave now and she expects you'll be back."

"Maybe I shouldn't be surprised. The last time she and I talked, at that picnic Ira organized down here, she came right out and asked me after we picked up the blanket if I'd come back to Arlington. I told her I was leaving for White Plains. She seemed . . . "

"What?"

"Disappointed. I recall her very words, probably because they surprised me so. Can you beat it, she actually invited me back to Arlington."

"Now she's come to you. Only how did she know you'd come back?"

"I told her I would, to raise troops after they put me on active duty. Mary . . . "

"I imagine she's still at the house."

"I should go on home, anyway, get my poor horse into the barn and rub him down. He must be hungry."

"And I have to get on over to Alton's. Ethan, I don't know if it's right for me to say this. Don't know if it's what you want to hear, but I'm glad you're not going on active duty. Glad you're back. We need you more than Gates does."

Ethan grinned. "That's not saying much for the Hero of Ticonderoga."

"You know what I mean. See you later."

Mary answered the door. "Mr. Allen . . . "

"My dear. I'm back to stay."

"Mind you use the scraper there, don't go tracking that mud in. I just finished the floor."

Ethan studied her. "Why did you come back to Bennington?"

"This house is a rat's nest. I swan, men can't live by themselves, they just let the keeping slide. I don't much like this house, too dark. Smells musty too. I miss the farm, don't you?"

"Yes."

"Lately I've been thinking I should move back there." She started. "You haven't sold it, have you?"

"No. Haven't really tried."

"Yes, I would like to go back. So would the girls. It is home."

"What about Ira?"

"Oh, he'll have no trouble finding a cook-housekeeper. With all the men off to war." She eyed him. "Would you really want to?"

"Move back? Sure."

"I mean with us."

"I'd like that, my dear."

"Wait, wait, you've still mud on your left boot there. Scrape it properly."

"Yes." She watched him. The rain was letting up, the sun struggling to emerge. "Only I'll just have to do it all over again by the back door. Got to take my horse around to the barn. I'll only be a few minutes."

"I'll put on water for tea. You do have tea?"

"Somewhere around the kitchen."

"I'll find it while you're out back. I'm glad, Mr. Allen, and relieved that you're not going back to war. You aren't, are you?" She looked suddenly worried.

"I'm not. I guess I'm glad too."

"Go around back and do what you have to. I'll put the kettle on and look for the tea."

He had one foot on the sill preparing to enter. He got his foot back just in time as she closed the door. Retrieving his horse, he went around to the barn.

"Mary . . . Mary . . . "

"Vitam regit fortuna non sapientia."

Epilogue

★ **Ethan** Allen never did go on active duty with the Continental Army. During the years that followed his rejection by General Horatio Gates, the Republic of Vermont sought repeatedly to win recognition from Congress and gain admission as a state in the Union. But it wasn't until March 4, 1791, two years after Ethan's death, that Vermont was accepted.

Mary Brownson Allen died of consumption in 1783. A year after Mary's death, Ethan married Fanny Montresor Buchanan. He was forty-seven; she was twenty-four. Ethan died at the age of fifty-two.

The War of Independence ended with Cornwallis's surrender at Yorktown on October 19, 1781, although technically the war dragged on until 1783.

On September 22, 1780, Major General Benedict Arnold, whose extravagance had put him heavily in debt, joined the enemy after sixteen months of secret negotiations with British Commander in Chief Sir Henry Clinton. Arnold was the only high-ranking American officer to commit treason. In exchange for a commission in the Royal Army and six thousand pounds, he arranged to turn West Point over to the British.

The plot to deliver West Point was thwarted when Major John André, whom Clinton sent to make final arrangements, was captured. André was executed as a spy. Arnold escaped to England. He returned to America to fight for the British.

Following the failure to capture Quebec, Benedict Arnold performed outstanding service for his adopted country on the battlefield. He was far superior to other generals whom the British approached: Philip Schuyler, John Sullivan, Israel Putnam. And colonels Daniel Morgan and Ethan Allen.

Unlike Arnold, all were honorable men.

Author's Note

★ **This** book might best be defined as a novelized biography, rather than a historical novel. The chronology of Ethan Allen's life during the period of the story is accurate. Many incidents are factual, others fictional, as are all the conversations. Many factual incidents contain speculative elements. This is done to ensure pacing, suspense, and drama, necessary developments in any work of this nature. And which, because of the vagaristic nature of every person's life, are unattainable in a realistic biography.

Liberties are taken with incidents and events and the individuals involved. Remember Baker and Noah Phelps were real Green Mountain Boys; Jacob Wall and Elisha Cummings are fictional Green Mountain Boys.

Many historians agree that ninety barrels of salted herring arrived at Valley Forge and turned out to be putrid. Dramatizing the incident, culminating it with the Americans roasting and consuming the horses that brought the fish underscores their plight.

James Lovell, the Massachusetts congressman Ethan meets in the Halifax jail, was a real person. He was, however, never abducted by the British; but to fictionally link him with Ethan in Halifax and later in the provost jail in New York, with Lovell being released while Ethan is forced to continue his sentence, adds another facet to the hero's dilemma.

In real life the two never met.

EARL FAINE
Stamford, Connecticut